A true voluptuary will never abandon his mind to the grossness of reality. It is by exalting the earthly, the material, the physique of our pleasures, by veiling these ideas, by forgetting them altogether, or, at least, never naming them hardly to one's self, that we alone can prevent them from disgusting.

—LORD BYRON

W9-AWG-152

Antæus

EDITED BY

DANIEL HALPERN

NO. 70, SPRING, 1993

Founding Publisher
DRUE HEINZ

Founding Editor
PAUL BOWLES

Managing Editor
JOHN FULLER

Associate Editor
STEVE HILL

Promotion Manager
WILLIAM CRAGER

Assistant Editors
LAUREN K. BAIER
THOMAS W. THOMPSON

Editorial Assistant
JISOOK LEE

Contributing Editors

ANDREAS BROWN   JOHN HAWKES
JOHN FOWLES   STANLEY KUNITZ
DONALD HALL   W.S. MERWIN
MARK STRAND

ANTÆUS *is published semiannually by The Ecco Press, 100 West Broad Street, Hopewell, NJ 08525.
Distributed by W. W. Norton & Company, Inc., 500 Fifth Avenue, New York, NY 10110, Ingram
Periodicals, 347 Reedwood Drive, Nashville, TN 37217, and B. DeBoer, Inc., 113 East Centre St.,
Nutley, NJ 07110. Distributed in England & Europe by W. W. Norton & Company, Inc.*

Contributions and Communications: ANTÆUS
100 West Broad Street, Hopewell, NJ 08525.
Four-issue Subscriptions: $30.00. Back issues available—write for a complete listing.

ISSN 0003-5319
Printed by Haddon Craftsmen, Inc.
ISBN 0-88001-326-5
Library of Congress Card Number: 70-612646
Copyright © 1993 by ANTÆUS, *Hopewell, NJ*
Cover art:
Girl In Red Dress with Cat and Dog *by Ammi Phillips, 1834–1836.*
Collection of The Museum of American Folk Art, New York.
Cover design by Jeanne Ensor
*Publication of this magazine has been made possible in part by a grant
from the National Endowment for the Arts.*
Logo: Ahmed Yacoubi

Books from The Ecco Press are available to *Antæus* subscribers at a 10% discount. Please write
for a catalogue: The Ecco Press, 100 West Broad Street, Hopewell, NJ 08525.

CONTENTS

R. K. NARAYAN

Grandmother's Tale

The borderline between fact and fiction, between biography and tale wears thin and ultimately vanishes in the following chronicle. Readers are bound to question how much of it is history and how much is fiction. I do not know the answer myself. The composition grew as I wrote it from my grandmother's narration, in daily instalments, of her mother's search for her errant husband, who left no address after uttering a laconic good-bye, "I am going away." That it might not all be imaginary could be concluded from the fact that the descendants of the couple in the story are present in our midst in different walks of life, scattered here and there, with this author being one of them.

I was brought up by my grandmother in Madras from my third year while my mother lived in Bangalore with a fourth child on hand after me. My grandmother took me away to Madras in order to give relief to an over-burdened daughter.

My grandmother Ammani was a busy person. She performed a variety of tasks all through the day, cooking and running the house for her two sons, gardening, counseling neighbors and the tenants living in the rear portion of the vast house stretching away in several segments, settling disputes, studying horoscopes and arranging matrimonial alliances. At the end of the day she settled down on a swing—a broad plank suspended by chains from the ceiling; lightly propelling it with her feet back and forth, chewing betel, she was completely relaxed at that hour. She held me at her side and taught me songs, prayers, numbers, and the alphabet till suppertime.

I mention "suppertime," but there was no fixed suppertime. My uncles returned home late in the evening. The senior uncle conducted a night school for slum children. (Some of them, later in life, attained eminence as *pundits* in Tamil language and literature.) The junior uncle worked in the harbor as a stevedore's assistant and came home at uncertain hours. Suppertime could be based not on their homecoming but on my performance. My grandmother fed me only when I completed my lessons to her satisfaction.

I had to repeat the multiplication table up to twenty but I always fumbled and stuttered after twelve and needed prodding and goading to attain the peak; I had to recite Sanskrit verse and *slokas* in praise of Goddess Saraswathi and a couple of other gods, and hymns in Tamil; identify six *ragas* when Granny hummed the tunes or, conversely, mention the songs when she named the *ragas;* and then solve arithmetic problems such as, "If a boy wants four mangoes costing one *anna* per mango, how much money will he have to take?" I wanted to blurt out, "Boys don't have to buy, they can obtain a fruit with a well-aimed stone at a mango tree." I brooded and blinked without a word, afraid I might offend her if I mentioned the stone technique for obtaining a fruit. She watched me and then tapping my skull gently remarked, "Never seen a bigger dunce . . ." It was all very taxing, I felt hungry and sleepy. To keep me awake, she kept handy a bowl of cold water and sprinkled it on my eyelids from time to time.

I could not understand why she bothered so much to make me learned. She also taught me some folk songs which now, I realize, were irrelevant, such as the one about a drunkard sleeping indifferently while his child in the crib was crying and the mother was boiling the milk. The most unnecessary lesson however, in my memory as I realize it now, was a Sanskrit lyric, not in praise of God, but defining the perfect woman — it said the perfect woman must work like a slave, advise like a *Mantri* (Minister), look like Goddess Lakshmi, be patient like Mother Earth and courtesan-like in the bed chamber — this I had to recite on certain days of the week. After the lessons she released me and served food. When I was six years old I was ceremoniously escorted to the Lutheran Mission School nearby and admitted in the "Infant Standard."

Later I grew up in Mysore, with my parents visiting my grandmother in Madras once a year during the holidays. After completing my college course, I frequently visited Madras to try my luck as a freelance writer.

My junior uncle, no longer a stevedore's assistant but an automobile salesman for a German make, set out every morning to contact his "prospects" and demonstrate the special virtues of his car. He took me out with him, saying "If you want to be a writer, don't mope at home listening to Grandmother's tales. You must be up and doing; your B.A. degree will lead you nowhere if you do not contact 'prospects.' Come out with me and watch . . ." He drove me about, stopped here and there, met all sorts of persons and delivered his sales talk, making sure that I followed his performance intelligently. I avoided his company in the evenings, since he wined and dined with his "prospects" to clinch a sale. During his morning rounds, however, I went out with him to be introduced to men who, he thought, were in the writing line. He left me in their company to discuss my literary aspirations. Most of them were printers, established in the highways and byways of the city, or publishers of almanacs, diaries, lottery tickets and race-cards, who were looking for proofreaders on a daily wage of ten rupees.

My uncle urged me to accept any offer that came: "You must make a start and go up. Do you know what I was earning when I worked at the harbor? Less than twenty-five a month, in addition to occasional tips from clearing agents. That is how I learnt my job. Then I moved on to a job at a bookshop on Mount Road, cycling up in the morning, with a lunch packet in hand, and selling books till seven in the evening. It was hard work, but I was learning a job. Today, do you know what I get? One thousand for every car I sell, in addition to expenses for entertaining the prospects. You will have to learn your job while earning whatever the wages might be. That is how you should proceed."

After brooding over these suggestions, I began to ignore his advice and stayed at home much to his annoyance: "Well, if you do not want to prosper, I will just say G.T.H. (go to hell), I have better things to do . . ." (However, he relented subsequently after the publication of my novels, the first three, in England.) In 1940, when I started a quarterly journal, *Indian Thought,* in Mysore, he took it upon himself to help its circulation, applying his sales talk at high pressure. Carrying a sample copy of *Indian Thought* from door to door, he booked one thousand subscribers in Madras city alone in the first year. Unfortunately, *Indian Thought* ceased publication in the second year since I could not continue it single-handed.

Although aging, my grandmother was still active and concerned herself with other people's affairs, her domestic drudgery now mitigated by the presence of two daughters-in-law in the house. She sat as usual on the swing in the evenings, invited me to sit beside her, and narrated stories of her early days — rather of her mother's early life and adventures, as heard from her mother when Ammani was about ten years old.

Day after day, I sat up with her listening to the account, and at night developed it as a cogent narrative. As far as possible, I have tried to retain the flavor of her speech, though the manner of her narrative could not be reproduced as it proceeded in several directions back and forth and got mixed up with asides and irrelevancies. I have managed to keep her own words here and there, but this is mainly a story-writer's version of a hearsay biography of a great-grandmother.

She was seven when she was married, her husband being just ten years old. Those were days of child marriages, generally speaking. Only widowers re-married late in life. It is not possible for me to fix the historical background by any clue or internal evidence. My grandmother could not be specific about the time since she was unborn at the beginning of her mother's story. One has to assume an arbitrary period—that is, the later period of the East India Company, before the Sepoy Mutiny.

My grandmother could not specify the location of their beginnings. It might be anywhere in the Southern Peninsula. She just mentioned it as "that village," which conjures up a familiar pattern: a hundred houses scattered in four or five narrow streets, with pillared *verandas* and *pyols*, massive front doors, inner courtyards, situated at the bend of a river or its tributary, mounds of garbage here and there, cattle everywhere, a temple tower looming over it all, the temple hall and corridor serving as a meeting ground for the entire population, and an annual festival attracting a big crowd from nearby hamlets—an occasion when a golden replica of the deity in the inner shrine was carried in a procession with pipes and drums around the village. "What God was He?" I could not resist my curiosity; my grandmother knew as much as I did, but ventured a guess, "Could be Ranganatha, the aspect of Vishnu in repose in a state of *yoga* lying on the coils of the thousand-headed Adisesha. The God was in a trance and watched and protected our village. They were married in the temple—my father and mother. Don't interrupt me with questions, as I have also only heard about these events. My mother told me that she was playing in the street with her friends one evening when her father came up and said, 'You are going to be married today next week.' "

"Why?" she asked and did not get an answer. Her father ignored her questions and went away. Her playmates stopped their game, surrounded and teased her, "Hey bride! Hey bride!"

"Wait! You will also be brides soon!" she retorted and rushed back home to her mother, crying, "Whatever happens, I am not going to marry. My friends are making fun of me!" Her mother soothed her and explained patiently that she was old enough to marry, something that could not be avoided by any human being, an occasion when she would be showered with gifts and new clothes and gold ornaments. The girl, however, was not impressed. She sulked and wept in a corner of their home. After fixing the date of the wedding, they kept her strictly indoors and did not allow her to go out and play. Her playmates visited her and whispered their sympathies.

On an auspicious day she was clad in a sari, decked in jewelery and taken to the pillared hall of the temple where had gathered guests and relations and priests, a piper and drummer creating enough noise to drown the uproar of the priests chanting *mantras* and the babble of the guests. She was garlanded and made to sit beside a boy whom she had often noticed tossing a rubber ball in an adjoining street whenever she went out to buy a pencil, ribbon or sweets in a little shop. She felt shy to look at him now, sitting too close to him on a plank. The smoke from the holy fire smarted her eyes and also created a smokescreen blurring her vision whenever she stole a glance in his direction.

At the auspicious hour the piper, drummer and the chanting priests combined to create the maximum din as Viswa approached the girl, seated on her father's lap, and tied the yellow thread around her neck — and they became man and wife from that moment.

In a week all celebration, feasting and exchange of ceremonial visits between the bride and bridegroom parties ceased. Viswanath the bridegroom went back to his school run by a pedagogue on a brick platform under a banyan tree on the riverside. He was ragged by his class-fellows for getting married. He denied it and became violent till the pedagogue intervened and brought his cane down the back of a teasing member. The boy said between sobs, "He is lying. I was at the temple with my father and ate, along with the others, a big feast with four kinds of sweets. Viswanath wore new clothes, a gold chain and a big garland around his neck. If I am lying, let him take off his shirt and show us the sacred thread . . ." He bared his chest and held up his sacred thread to demonstrate that he had only a bachelor's three-strand thread.

The teacher was old, suffered from sore throat, and could not control his class of twenty-five children when a babble broke out on the subject of Viswa's marriage. A few cried, "Shame, shame," which was the usual form of greeting in their society. The teacher tapped his cane on the floor and cried out over the tumult, "Why shame? I was married when I was like Viswa. I have four sons and two daughters and grandchildren. My wife looks after those at home still, and runs the family; and they will all marry soon. There is no shame in marriage. It's all arranged by the God in that temple. Who are we to say anything against His will? My wife was also small when we married . . ."

The girl's life changed after her marriage. She could not go out freely, or join her friends playing in the street. She could not meet her husband, except on special occasions such as the New Year and other festival days when Viswa was invited to visit his wife's home with his parents. On those occasions, the girl was kept aloof in a separate room and would be escorted to his presence by young women who would giggle and urge the young couple to say something to each other and then leave them alone for a little time.

The couple felt embarrassed and shy and tongue-tied but took that opportunity to study each other's features. When they got a chance, the very first sentence the girl uttered was, "There is a black patch under your ear." She made bold to touch his face with her forefinger. Apart from holding each other's right hand before the holy fire during their wedding ceremony, this was their first touch. He found that her finger was soft and she found the skin under his left ear rough but pleasant. When she removed her finger she asked, "What is this patch?" She thrust her finger again to trace that black patch under his left ear. "Oh, that!" he said pressing down her finger on the black patch. "It's a lucky sign, my mother says."

"Does it hurt?" she asked solicitously.

"No. They say it's lucky to have that mark," he said.

"How much luck?" she asked and continued, "Will you become a king?"

"Yes, that's what they say." And before they could develop this subject, others opened the door and came in, not wanting to leave the couple alone too long.

After that they discovered an interest in each other's company. But it was not easy to meet. It was impossible for the girl to go out, unless chaperoned by an elder of the family. Even such outings were limited to a visit to the temple on a Friday evening or to a relation on ceremonial occasions. Viswa wished he could be told when and where he could see her. Occasionally he found an excuse to visit her home on the pretext of wanting to meet his father-in-law but it did not always work as that man would be away in his coconut grove far away.

Viswa did not possess the hardihood to step into the house to catch a glimpse of his young wife. She kept herself in the deepest recess of the house for fear of being considered too forward and he would turn back disappointed. But he soon found a way. He spied and discovered that she was more accessible at their backyard, where she washed clothes at the well. There was only a short wall separating their backyard from a lane, which proved a more convenient approach since he could avoid a neighbor always lounging on the *pyol* and asking, "Ay! Visiting your wife! Insist upon a good tiffin . . ." It made him self-conscious. He would simper and murmur and hasten his steps only to be met by his mother-in-law at the door. Now the backyard could be approached without anyone accosting him, but the lane was dirty and garbage-ridden; he did not mind it. On his way back from school if he took a diversion, he could approach the lane and the short wall. He placed a couple of bricks close to the wall, stood on the pile with his head showing up a few inches above it. It was a sound strategy though her back was turned to him, while she drew water from the well and filled a bucket and soaked her clothes. He watched her for a few moments and cried, "Hey!" When she did not hear his call, he clapped his hands, and she turned and stared at him. He said, "Hey! I am here."

Looking back watchfully into their house she asked, "Why?"

"To see you," he said.

"Come by the front door," she said.

And he said promptly, "I can't. It's no good. How are you? I came to ask," he said rather timidly.

"Why should you ask?" she questioned. He had no immediate answer. He just blinked. She laughed at him and said, "You are tall today."

"Yes," he said. "Is your name Balambal? It's too long."

"Call me Bala," she said, picked up her bucket and suddenly retreated into the house. He waited, hoping she would come back. But the back door shut with a bang, and he jumped off muttering, "She is funny. I should not have married her. But what could I do? I was never asked whether I wanted to marry or not . . . ." He ran down the lane and sought the company of his friend Ramu, who lived in a house next to the temple and knew when the *pujas* at the temple were performed and when they would distribute the offerings, sweet rice and coconut pieces. If one stuck to Ramu, one need not starve for snacks. He could take Viswa to see the God at the appropriate moment when the evening service was in progress and wait. After the waving of camphor flames and the sounding of cymbals and bells, the offerings would be distributed. Piously standing on the threshold of the sanctum, Ramu would whisper, "Viswa, shut your eyes and pray, otherwise they will not give you anything to eat!"

At the next session he was more successful. Standing on the pile of bricks, he told her: "On Tuesday evening I went to the temple."

"Did you pray? What for?" she asked. Seeing his silence, she said, "Why go to temple if you don't pray?"

"I don't know any prayer."

"What did you learn at home?"

He realized she was a heckler and tried to ward off the attack. "I know some prayers, not all."

"Recite some," she said.

"No, I won't," he said resolutely.

"You will be sent to hell if you don't say your prayers."

"How do you know?" he asked.

"My mother has told me. She makes us all pray in the evenings in the *puja* room."

"Bah!" he said. "What do you get to eat after the prayers? At the temple if you shut your eyes and prostrate before the God, they give you wonderful things to eat. For that you must come with me and Ramu . . ."

"Who is Ramu?"

"My friend," Viswa said and jumped off the pile of bricks as there were portents of the girl's mother appearing on the scene. He was now satisfied that he had been able to establish a line of communication with Bala although the surroundings were filthy and he had to tread warily lest he should put his foot on excreta, since the lane served as the public convenience.

They could not meet normally as husband and wife. Bala, being only ten years old, must attain puberty and then go through an elaborate nuptial ceremony before she could join her husband.

Viswa had other plans. One afternoon he stood on the brick pile and beckoned her. She looked up and frantically signaled to him to go away. "I have to talk to you," he said desperately and ducked and crouched while her mother appeared at the door for a moment. After she had gone in, he heard a soft voice calling, "Hey, speak."

His head bobbed up again over the wall and he just said: "I am going away. Keep it a secret . . ."

"Where are you going?"

"I don't know. Far away."

"Why?"

He had no answer. He merely said, "Even Ramu doesn't know."

"Who are you going with?"

"I don't know but I am joining some pilgrims beyond the river."

"Won't you tell me why you are going away?"

"No. I can't . . . I have to go away—that is all."

"Can't you mention a place where you are going?"

"I don't know . . ."

She began to laugh. "Oh! Oh! you are going to 'I don't know' place. Is that it?"

He felt irked by her levity and said, "I don't know really. They were a group of pilgrims singing a *bhajan* about Pandaripura or some such place . . . over and over again."

"Are you sure?"

"You won't see me for a long time . . ."

"But when will you come back?"

"Later," he said and vanished as he noticed her mother coming again and that was the last the girl saw of him for a long time to come.

She remained indifferent for a week or ten days and then began secretly to worry. She thought at first Viswa was playing a joke and would reappear over the wall sooner or later. She wanted to tell her mother, but was afraid she might begin to investigate how she came to know Viswa had disappeared, and then proceed to raise the wall to keep him off. She suffered silently, toyed with the idea of seeking Ramu's help but she had never seen him. Others at home did not bother. Her father was, as ever, interested only in his coconut grove, the price of coconut, coconut pests and so on. He left home at dawn after breakfasting on rice soaked over-night in cold water, packed a lunch and returned home at night tired, leaving domestic matters to his wife's care.

Bala's mother noticed her brooding silence and gloom and asked one day, "What is ailing you?"

Bala burst into tears. "He . . . He . . . is gone," she said.

"Who?"

Bala replied, "He . . . He . . ." since a wife could not utter her husband's name. When Bala's father returned home from the garden, the lady told him "Viswa has disappeared." He took it lightly and said, "Must be playing with his friends somewhere, where could he go? How do you know he has disappeared?"

"I have not seen him for a long time. He used to come up to see you, but as you were always away, he would turn back from the door."

"Poor boy! You should have called him in. . . . Young people are shy!"

"Bala also shut herself in whenever he came . . ."

"She is also young and shy . . . I must take him with me to the grove some time." The lady persuaded the man to stay away from the coconut grove the next morning and they went over to Viswa's house. "After all they are our *sambandis* (relations through a matrimonial alliance) and we must pay them courtesy visits at least once in a while."

Viswa's parents lived in what was named Chariot Nook (where the temple chariot was stationed in a shed).

After a formal welcome and the courtesy of unrolling a mat for the visitors, Viswa's father and Bala's father asked simultaneously, "Where is Viswa?" When they realized no one knew the answer, Viswa's parents said, "We thought he was in your house. We were planning to come and see him."

Next they visited the schoolmaster, who said he had not seen Viswa for more than ten days.

It became a sensation in the village. Well-wishers of the family and others crowded in, speculating, sympathizing, and suggesting the next step, vociferous and excited and talking simultaneously. A little fellow in the crowd said, "I saw him with a group crossing the river . . ."

"When?"

"I don't remember."

"Didn't you talk to him?"

"Yes, he said he was going to Delhi." There was ironic laughter at this. "Delhi is thousands of miles away . . ."

"More."

"I hear sepoys are killing white officers."

"Who told you?"

"Someone from the town . . ."

"Who cares who kills whom while we are bothered about Viswa?"

Someone suddenly questioned Viswa's father, "Are you in the habit of beating him?"

"Sometimes you can't help it."

Viswa's mother said, "Whenever his teacher came and reported something, you lost your head . . ." and burst into tears. "Teachers are an awful lot, you must pay no attention to what they say."

"But unless the teacher is strict young fellows can never be tamed."

Viswa's mother said, sobbing, "You thrashed him when that awful man came and said something."

"He had thrown cowdung on the master when he was not looking."

"You slapped," said the mother.

"I only patted his cheek." Everyone nursed a secret fear that Viswa had drowned in the river. Then the whole company trooped out, stood before the God in the temple hall, prayed and promised offerings if Viswa came back alive. If Bala had announced what she knew, it would have been a relief to everyone but she remained dumb.

As time passed Bala found existence a sore trial. She was no longer the little girl in a pigtail, dressed in a cotton skirt and jacket. Now she had reached maturity—rather stocky with no pretensions to any special beauty except the natural charm of full-blown womanhood, she could not pass down the *agraharam* street without people staring at her and whispering comments behind her back. Sometimes some friend of the family would stop her on her way to the temple and ask, "Any news? Do you hope he will come back?" She found it a strain to be inventing answers. She snapped at her questioners sometimes but it made things worse. "Where is he?" people persisted in demanding. She said one day, "In Kashmir, making a lot of money, has sent a message to say he will be back soon."

"Who brought the message?" She invented a name. Next time when they questioned her again, she just said, "He has gone there as a priest in some temple." She soon tired of it all and showed herself outside home as little as possible, except for a visit to the temple on Tuesday and Friday evenings. She would gaze on the image in the sanctum when the camphor flame was waved to the ringing of the bells and prayed, "Oh, Lord. I don't even know whether my husband is alive. If he is alive, help me reach him. If he is dead, please let me die of cholera quickly." Other women looked at her strangely and asked among themselves, "Why is her mother not coming with her? There must be some reason. They are not on talking terms. She must be hiding something. He is no more but they are keeping it a secret. Instead of shaving her head and wearing white, she oils and combs her hair and decks it with flowers! And comes to the temple with *kumkum* on her brow, pretending to be a *sumangali*. A widow who pretends to be otherwise pollutes the temple precinct and its holiness is lost. She should be prohibited from entering the temple unless she shaves her head and observes the rules. Her mother must be a brazen woman to allow her out like this. We should talk to the priest."

The priest of the temple visited them one afternoon. Bala's mother was all excitement at the honor, unrolled a mat, seated him, offered him fruits and milk and made a lot of fuss. The priest accepted it all and looked around cautiously and asked in a hushed voice, "Where is your daughter?" Bala generally retired to a back room when there was a visitor but listened to their talk. The priest was saying: "I remember Bala as a child, in fact I remember her wedding." He paused and asked, "Where is her husband, that boy who married her? I notice Bala at the temple some evenings." Her mother was upset and was not able to maintain the conversation. The priest said: "You know the old proverb: 'You may seal the mouth of a furnace, but not the mouth of gossip.' Till you get some proof to say he is living, it is better that you don't send Bala to the temple. Its sanctity must be preserved, which is my duty; otherwise as a priest of the temple, my family will face God's wrath." At this point of their talk Bala rushed out like a storm, her face flushed, "You people think I am a widow? I am not. He is alive like you. I'll not rest until I come back with him some day and shame you all." She threw a word of cheer to her mother and flounced out of the house.

Bala's mother tried to follow her down the street but Bala was too fast for her. People stood and stared at the mother-daughter chase. Bala halted. When her mother came up she whispered, "Go back home. People are watching us. Keep well, I will come back. Remember that the priest is waiting in our house." Mother was in a dilemma. She halted as Bala raced forward, dashed in and out of the temple before anyone should notice her. She rushed past all the gaping men and women, past all rows of houses to Chariot Nook to Viswa's house and knocked. Her mother-in-law opened the door and was aghast, "Bala! You look like *Kali* . . . what is the matter? Come in first. You should stay with us."

"Yes, when I come with my husband." She took a pinch of vermilion from a little bowl on a stand and pressed it on her brow, fell prostrate at her mother-in-law's feet, touched them reverentially, sprang back and was off even as the lady was saying, "Your father-in-law will come back soon, wait . . ." Before her sentence was completed, Bala was gone.

Up to this point, my grandmother remembered her mother's narration. Beyond this, her information was hazy. She just said, "Bala must have gone to the village cart-stand in the field beyond the last street, where travelers and bullock carts assembled. Bala must have paid for a seat in a carriage, traveled all night and reached a nearby town. Even in her hurry, before leaving home she did not forget to pack a small bag with a change of clothes, some money she had saved out of her birthday and other gifts, a few gold ornaments, and above all a knife in case she had to protect her honor and end her life. At the town she stayed in a *choultry* where an assortment of travelers and pilgrims was lodged. Her mind harped on a single word: Pandaripur. She made constant inquiries of everyone she came across and set forth in that direction. After many false starts, she got on the right track and joined travelers going on foot or by some mode of transport and reached Poona about a year later."

My grandmother's account had many gaps from this point onward. How Bala survived, what happened to her mother and where was her father all the while? What happened to Viswa's parents? Above all, why did she go to Poona to search for her husband? What led her steps to Poona? These questions never got an answer. My grandmother only snapped: "Why do you ask me? Am I a wizard to see the past? If you interrupt me like this, I'll never be able to complete the story. I can only tell you what I have heard from my mother. I just listened, without interrupting her as you do now. If you don't shut your mouth and keep only your ears open, I'll never tell you anything more. You can't expect me to know everything. If you want all sorts of useless information about the past, I cannot help you. Not my business. Whenever my mother felt like it, she would gather us around and tell her story — so that we might realize how strong and bold she was at one time. She would boast, 'You only see me as a cook at home, feeding you and pampering your father's whims and moods but at one time I could do other things which you petted and spoilt children could never even imagine.' "

By the time Bala reached Poona, she had exhausted all her gold and cash and was left with nothing. She felt terrified and lonely. People looked strangely different and spoke a language she did not understand. She reached a public rest house, a charity institution where *roti* was distributed, and held out her hand along with the others and swallowed whatever she got in order to survive. She made the rest house the central point and wandered about studying the faces of passersby, hoping to spot out Viswa. She feared that if he had grown a beard, she would not be able to recognize him. All that she could remember was the head peeping over the wall and the black patch under his left ear, which he boasted would make him king — perhaps he was now the king of this town. She thought in her desperation of stopping some kindly soul to ask: "Who is the king here?" But they might take her to be a madcap and stone her.

The bazaars were attractive and she passed her time looking at the display of goods. She was afraid to move about after dusk for fear of being mistaken for a loose woman soliciting custom. She returned to the rest house and stayed there.

One day she was noticed by an elderly lady who asked in Marathi, "Who are you? I see you here every day. Where are you from? What is the matter?" Of course Bala could not understand her language, but felt it was all sympathy from a stranger and was moved to tears. The old woman took her hand and led her out of the rest house to her home nearby where men, women and children surrounded her, joked and laughed. To their questions, all that she could answer was to point to the *thali* around her neck. They understood she was a married woman. When they questioned her further, she burst involuntarily into tears and uncontrollably into Tamil. She made up in gesticulation whatever she felt to be lacking in her Tamil explanation. She said, "My fate . . ." She etched with her forefinger on her brow: "It's written here that I must struggle and suffer. How I have survived these months which I have lost count of, God alone knows. Here I have come to this strange city and I have to behave like a deaf-mute, neither understanding what you say nor making myself understood." They listened to her lamentation sympathetically without understanding a word, only realizing that it was a deeply felt utterance. Someone in the crowd recognizing the sound of the language asked, *"Madarasi?"*

"Must be so, she doesn't cover her head," said another. Bala could guess the nature of the query and nodded affirmatively. "I can take you to a man who came here many years ago. He may understand you." He beckoned her to follow him. She indicated that she wanted a drink of water, feeling her throat parched after her harangue.

A boy was deputed to guide her. She followed him blindly, not knowing or caring where she was going. The boy took her through the main street past the bazaars and crowds but proved too fast, running ahead. It was difficult to keep pace with him. She was panting with the effort. "Where are you taking me?" she asked again and again, but he only grinned and indicated some destination. Finally she found herself under an archway with a path leading to a big house. Leaving her there, the boy turned round and ran off before she could question him, perhaps feeling too shy to be seen with a woman. She was puzzled since there was no one in sight.

Beyond the archway and gate there was a garden. Presently a gardener appeared above a cluster of plants. He looked at her for a moment and stooped down again to resume his digging. Not knowing what to do next, she sat down on a sentry platform beside the arch, felt drowsy and shut her eyes. She woke up when she heard the sound of a horse trotting. She saw the rider pass under the arch and dismount in front of the house, helped by an attendant. He had thrown a brief glance at her in passing. He was dressed in breeches and embroidered vest and crowned with a turban—very much a man of these parts. Rather lean and of medium height. Could this be the man from the Tamil Land? Seemed unlikely. She did not know what should be her next step. She continued to sit there. A little later, she noticed him again coming out on his horse. She was all attention now, staring at him when he passed under the arch. She noticed his moustache curving up to his ears. He threw at her another brief glance and passed. She decided to sit through and wait indefinitely, hoping to find some identification mark next time. She invoked the God in their village temple and prayed: "Guide me, O Lord! I don't know what to do . . ."

A couple of hours later the horse and the rider appeared and once again he threw at her the briefest glance and passed.

An attendant in livery approached her from the house. He asked, "Who are you? Master has seen you sitting here. Go away, don't sit here. Otherwise he will be angry and call the *kotwal*. Go away." She shook her head and sat immobile.

"Go away . . ." He gestured her to go. He kept saying, *"Kotwal, kotwal,* he will come and take you to prison." She would not move. The servant looked intimidated by her manner and backed away. Ten minutes later he reappeared and asked her to follow him. She felt nervous wondering what sort of a male she was going to encounter. The front steps seemed endless and she felt weak at the knees and crossed the threshold expecting the worst. The man lounging in a couch watched her enter. She could not understand whether this was the beginning or the end of her troubles. She tried to study his face. There was not even a remote resemblance between the head she last saw over the wall and this man. He had no turban on and he was bald on top though his whiskers reached up to his earlobes. Gazing at his face she wondered what would happen if she made a dash for his whisker and lifted it to look for the black patch below his left ear; this might prove conclusive and the end of her quest. While she toyed with the idea, he thundered in Marathi, "Who are you? Why do you sit at my gate?"

She said, "They said that you speak Tamil." He shook his head. Took out his purse and held out some money and tried to wave her off. She refused the money. He summoned a servant to show her out. She sat down on the floor and refused to move. "They said you are from the South. Keep me here. I have nowhere to go. I am an orphan. I will be your servant, cook for you and serve you. Only grant me a shelter." He gave an order to the servant, suddenly got up, went upstairs and shut himself in a room. She began to doubt her wisdom in depending upon the urchin who guided her. So far this man had shown no sign of understanding Tamil, in which she was addressing him. He had no identifiable feature except the greenish color of his eyes, something that did not alter with years. She felt it might be wiser to sneak away quietly.

The servant fetched two *kotwals* who stood over and commanded her to get up. She felt she was making a hideous mistake in accosting a stranger and they were likely to think she was a characterless blackmailer. As the *kotwals* were trying to move her physically, she screamed in Tamil, "Don't touch me, I will reduce you to ashes. *(Thoddade, unnai posikiduven.)*" She looked fierce and the *kotwals,* though fiercer in grotesque uniforms and headgear, shrank back. While this was going on entered a woman nearing middle age and authoritative. She scowled at the men and cried, "What are you doing? Leave her alone." They tried to explain but she dismissed them instantly. She helped Bala to rise to her feet, seated her in a chair and asked: "Who are you? I heard you speak. Do you not understand our language?" Bala shook her head.

The other woman asked in Tamil: "Who are you?"

At this point, Bala had the shrewdness to conceal her purpose and just said: "I came with some pilgrims to fulfill a vow at Pandaripur, got stranded and separated from a group." And spun a story which fell on sympathetic ears. "You are fortunate to live in a home like this, so comfortable and beautiful with its garden," said Bala.

"Yes, we love plants." She pointed upstairs, "He is a keen gardener himself. When my father lived, he had no time left. All his hours he spent in his shop and came home late at night. After my husband joined us, my father got some relief." Bala refrained from asking any question for fear of betraying her purpose but allowed the other to ramble on, gathering much information. She was on the point of asking his name but checked herself as the woman referred to him only as "He" or "Bhatji." Suddenly Surma cried, "Oh, how thoughtless of me to be sitting and talking like this without even asking if you are hungry! Come in with me." She got up and led Bala to the kitchen, lifted the lid off some vessels, bustled about, picked up a plate, set it on a little platform and put up a sitting plank and said, "Sit down and eat. I have something still left. We are both poor eaters. He is so busy at the shop, he seldom eats at home—only at night. I make something for myself. Don't like to spend too much time cooking. I also sit in the shop part of the day, especially when he has to go on his rounds. He is an expert in judging diamonds and all gems. His advice and appraisal is sought by everyone in this city. We have a large collection of precious stones . . . apart from getting our supply from the mines in this country, we also import . . . he has to go to Bombay sometimes when ships arrive at the port."

She fed Bala, which revived her since she had had nothing to eat after a couple of free *rotis* and a tumbler of water in the morning. She became loquacious and spirited. She washed the dishes at the backyard well and restored them to the kitchen shelf. The lady took her round the house and the garden. "My father built this in those days when we could engage many servants who kept the house clean, but now we have only ten. He always rests upstairs. Shall we go up and see the rooms there?"

Bala said, "Later, let us not disturb him now."

"Come, I'll show you your room. You should stay with us. Have you left your box in the rest house? Let us go and fetch it."

Bala said, "I came only with a small bag, but that was stolen on the way. Robbers set upon us and took away everything."

"My first glimpse of Bhatji was when he came into our shop one morning long ago," said Surma: "My father, with his eyeglass stuck on one eye, was selecting diamonds for a party. I was minding something else, bent over a desk. He was standing at the entrance — how long I could not say. When I looked up he was there. There were people passing in and out of the shop, he was unnoticed. When the shop was clear of the crowd, he was still there at the doorway. I asked, 'What do you want? Who are you?' There was something about his person that touched my heart. He was lanky and looked famished. My first impulse was to rush to his help in some way, but I held myself back. I was a young woman of over eighteen years, he might be older. Somehow I felt attracted to this lean boy with hair falling on his nape untended, covering his forehead and unshaven face. It must have been months and years since a barber came near him. 'Father!' I called suddenly, 'Here is a boy waiting since the morning.' It was a propitious moment since Father, instead of losing his temper, as was his habit whenever anyone stepped into the shop without any business (he was suspicious of youngsters particularly), took off the eyeglass, and asked mildly, 'What do you want?' He answered promptly, 'I want to work' in Marathi and then gave an account of himself. How he had started from a southern village, travelled up and about, visiting other parts of the country, working his way . . .

" 'How did you learn our language?'

" 'I was in Bombay and learnt it.' Father took to him kindly. He asked him to step in and questioned him in detail. Father enjoyed the narration of the boy's adventures in other cities and his descriptions fascinated him. That a village boy from far off south should have had the courage to go out as far as Delhi (which was beyond Father's dreams) and survive seemed to my father a great achievement. He engaged him immediately as a handyman, gave him a room above our shop and arranged for his food and other comforts.

"Very soon he became my father's righthand man, doing a variety of jobs in and out of the office and shop. He relieved Father of a lot of strain and understood not only the nature of the trade but a lot about gems, their qualities and value. Father was impressed with the boy's intelligence and the ease with which he could be trained. Within six months he left a lot of responsibilities to him, trusting him absolutely. At the earliest opportunity my father set a barber on him and made him presentable with his head shaved in the front, leaving an elegant little tuft on top. Later, after we married, I induced him to grow whiskers so that he might have a weighty appearance. My father did not approve of our proposal to marry at first. He threatened to throw him out not only from our shop but from this country itself and ordered me not to talk to him and confined me at home. I had a miserable time. We eloped to Nasik and were married in the temple of Triambaka — a sort of marriage, quiet and private. Eventually, Father reconciled himself to the situation. When he died the gem business and the house fell to my share."

Surma constantly expressed her admiration and love for Viswanath: "When I saw him first, he was so young and timid; now he manages our business and is often called to the court and high places for consultations and supply of gems . . ."

The story-writer asked at this point: "Were they the only ones in that house?"

"Yes, must be so," said my grandmother.

"What happened to the rest of the family — there must surely have been other members of the family!"

"Why do you ask me? How do I know?" said my grandmother. "I can only tell the story as I heard it. I was not there as you know. This is about my father and mother who were still apart though living under the same roof."

I asked the next question, which bothered me as a story-writer: "Did Surma Bai have no children?"

"I don't care if she had or had not or where they were, how is it our concern?"

"But you say they were living together for fifteen years!"

"What a question! How can I answer it? You must ask them. Anyway it is none of our business. My mother mentioned Surma and only Surma and not a word about anyone else. If you want me to go on with the story, you must not interrupt me. I forget where I was . . . I am only telling you what I know." She stopped her narration at this point and left in a huff to supervise her daughters-in-law in the kitchen.

Bala's opportune moment came when Surma said one evening, "I am joining some friends who perform *bhajans* (group singing) at the Krishna temple on Fridays. I will come back after it is over. You won't mind being alone?"

"Not at all," said Bala, "I'll look after the house and take care of everything."

"He is in his room, may come down if he wants anything . . ."

"I'll take care of him, do not worry about him," said Bala reassuringly and saw her off in her *tonga* at the gate. The moment the *tonga* was out of sight she ran back into the house, shutting the front door, ran upstairs and entered Viswa's room. He was reclining on a comfortable couch reading a book. She shut the door behind her softly. He did not look up. He pretended to be absorbed in the book. She stood silently before him for a few moments, and then said, "What is the book that grips you so completely that you do not notice anyone entering your room?"

"What are you blabbering? Get out! You have no business to come up here."

"Oh, stop that tone. Don't pretend. Not good for you."

"Are you threatening me? I'll call the guard and throw you out."

"By all means. I know the guards. I am not what I was on the first day. I can speak to them myself. In fact, I am closer to them than you are. Call them and see what happens."

"Oh!" Viswa groaned. "Go away, don't bother me . . ."

She said, "We must end this drama and how we are going to do it, I can't say now. But leave it at that." He pretended not to understand her language. But she said, "Your whiskers do not hide your face. If you lift the left one slightly, as you did the other day while washing your face, the black is still there, which had proved correct my guess and also what you said years ago when you peeped over the wall, that it was lucky and would make you a king. You are lucky, rich and favored at the court . . . I have waited long enough." She fingered her *thali* and said, "This can't lie. You knotted it in the presence of God." He protested again, "No, no, I don't know what you are saying," but she was hammering her point relentlessly.

Ultimately he was overwhelmed. "Be patient for some more time. Be as you are, Surma is a rare creature. We must not upset her."

"I will wait, but not forever." By the time Surma came back from the *bhajan,* she found nothing unusual. Bala was at her post in the kitchen. Viswa was in the garden trimming a jasmine plant. Once again Viswa and Bala took care to move in separate orbits in the house. Bala was in no hurry. Now that she had established her stand, she just left him alone until the next *bhajan* day when Surma was away. She said: "This can't go on much longer. We must go back."

"Go back where?" he asked in consternation.

"To our village, of course," she said calmly.

"Impossible!" he cried. "After all these years! I can't. I can't give up my trade."

"You may take your share and continue the business anywhere," she said calmly. She knew his weak point now and could exploit it fully. Any excitement or anger would spoil her plan. She was very clear in her mind about how she should carry out her scheme. She had worked out the details of the campaign with care, timing it in minute detail.

He knew it was going to be useless to oppose her. He pleaded, "I'll tell her the truth and you may continue here as my wife, and not as a domestic."

"I want to get back to our own place and live there. I have set a time limit; beyond that I won't stay, I'll go back."

"Certainly, I will make any arrangement you may want and send an escort to take you back home safely."

"You will be the escort, I'll not go with anyone else."

"Then stay here," he said. At this stage they had to stop their discussion, since they heard Surma return home. He felt nervous to remain alone with Bala and was terrified of her tactics.

"I can't live without Surma," he kept wailing.

"You will have to learn to live with your wife."

"Surma is also my wife."

"I know she is not. I know in this country it is not so easy. You have kept her, or rather she has kept you."

He realized in due course that there was no escape. He said, "Give me time. I'll see how we can manage it."

"I've given you all the time . . . years and years. The trouble and the risk I have undergone to search you out, God alone is our witness! I am not going to allow it to go to waste. I am taking you back even if you kill me. I have set the date of our departure—not later than the next Full Moon."

At their next meeting he said, "I can't survive without Surma, she must also come with us. I don't know how to tell her."

"Try to persuade her to stay back. We will have to tell her the facts. After all, you are going back to our legitimate home to your real wife."

"No, I can't. You don't know her nature. She will commit suicide."

"I will commit suicide if you do not come away. Which of us shall it be?"

He felt desperate and said, "I can't live without her. Let her also come with us. We shall go away. Show some consideration for my feelings also."

"Very well, if she doesn't agree to go with us?"

"Please don't drive me mad. Who asked you to come all the way to torment me like this?" At this point she lost her patience and left him.

When Surma asked him later: "You look rather tired and pale, shall I call the physician?" he demurred. But she lost no time in calling a physician who said, "He is disturbed. He must take medicine and rest. Something is troubling his mind."

Surma too became agitated: "I have never seen him so sick at any time. What could it be? He was all right." She put him to bed and stayed by his side, leaving all household work to Bala. Viswa tossed and groaned in bed. Bala carried food to his bedside upstairs. She made it unnecessary for Surma to come down except for her bath, food and *puja;* Surma then went up and sat by his side silently. The physician had given him some potion which acted as a sedative and put him to sleep.

Bala assumed an air of extreme gloom to match Surma's mood in sympathy. A week later she said, "Bhatji looks better. You should not fall sick moping at home. We will leave a guard at his side and go out for a little fresh air. Let us visit the temple and offer *puja* to Vitobha and stroll along the lake. You will feel refreshed."

"No. I can't leave him alone."

Four days later Bala repeated her suggestion and added, "Ask him, he may like you to go out for your own good. I am sure he will have as much concern for your welfare."

Surma eventually agreed. Bala said, "You must think of the shop too."

"Guru looks after the shop, he is a good man," Surma said. "He brings the accounts and reports every day, very dependable . . ."

"Even then," Bala said, "you must go there or Bhatji can go as soon as possible. It'll also refresh him."

"True, he is worrying about the shop silently. I do not know what to do . . . I have never been in this predicament before."

When Guru came the next evening they went out in the *tonga,* leaving him in charge of Viswa. They visited the temple first and then went on to the lake. Strolling round the lake, which reflected the setting sun, Bala cried, "Oh, see how beautiful! See those birds diving in."

"I wish I could enjoy the scene and the breeze but my mind is troubled. How I wish Bhatji were well . . . his normal self, riding his horse, sitting in the shop with his diamonds and customers; then I could sit here and watch the lake with a free mind."

"He must travel and go out for a change . . . We could plan for a three or four months' absence. Guru and his son could look after the shop. That will make a new man of Bhatji."

"Where can we go?"

"We may go south, so many temples we could visit — I have especially in mind Gunasekaram where mental sickness is cured miraculously through offerings and *puja* to that God."

"We can't, so far away and so long it'll take!"

Bala did not continue, but left the subject at that. But she repeated the suggestion whenever she found a chance. Surma thought it over and discussed the matter with Viswa and worked out the details and settled on a date for the journey after consulting their astrologer and physician.

"I remember," said Ammani, "my mother mentioned that they were carried in two palanquins and had a retinue of bearers who took over in relays at different stages, and many torch bearers and lance men to protect them from robbers and wild animals when they crossed jungles in the mountain ghats. Arrangements for the journey were made by Surma and Viswa, who had influence at the court and got the *Peshwa's* support. I am sure the *Peshwa* sent word to his vassals and subordinates along the route to protect and help the party. On the day fixed, Bala and party began their journey, arrived about a month later in Bangalore and camped in the rest house on a tank bund. I think from the description it is the same tank known as the Sampangi* today."

They camped for three days. All the three were very happy; Bala because she was on the way home, Viswa because they had succeeded in persuading Surma to undertake the tour, and Surma because Viswa already looked better and eagerly anticipated the visit to the temples. He did not wish to think of the future beyond.

On the fourth day they wound up the camp, all packed and ready to start onward. Bala however had made up her mind differently. From the rest house one set of steps led up to the highway where the palanquins were waiting. All other members of the party, the bearers and guards, Surma and Viswa went up the steps. Bala however lagged behind, suddenly turned right about and went down the steps leading to the water's edge. At first they did not notice her. When they reached the road Surma asked, while climbing into their palanquin, "Where is Bala?"

Viswa said: "She seems to be taking her own time. Probably a last-minute wash. Let us start. We should reach the next stage before

Actually at present, it is Nehru Stadium, the tank having been drained many years ago.

nightfall. She will follow." The bearers had lifted the palanquin containing Surma and Viswa.

Viswa hesitated and said, "Stop! I see that she is going down the steps. Why?"

Surma said, "It looks to me strange. Oh, God, she has stepped into the water. Oh, stop!" she said in alarm when she heard Bala's scream: "I'm drowning . . . Viswa come for a moment." Viswa jumped off the palanquin and reached the water's edge. By that time Bala stood neck-deep in water. Viswa shrieked in alarm: "What are you doing?"

She replied with the water lapping her chin, "I am not coming with you."

"Are you mad? Why this scene?" He made a move to go down and pull her up.

She said, "If you take another step, I'll go down. Stay where you are and listen. No, don't come near, you can hear me where you are."

"All right, I won't come forward. Don't stand in the water, come up and speak."

"I won't come up until you turn Surma back to Poona."

Surma had meanwhile come down and was standing behind Viswa: "What! What have I done to you that you should say this?"

"You have been like a goddess to me, but I can't go home with you. Our village will not accept you. I am Viswa's wife. You see this *thali* was knotted by him. He is my husband, I can't share him with you."

Surma was shocked. "We were such good friends! Let me also drown with you."

At this Viswa held her back firmly. Bala said, "Viswa, take her with you and leave me alone. I am already shivering and will die of cold — if you don't make up your mind quickly whether you want me or Surma. Send her back honorably home. Let the palanquins be turned around with her, if you want to save me."

They pleaded, appealed and shed tears but the palanquins and the entourage had to run around and head for Poona before Bala would come out. She did not want any of Surma's entourage to stay back.

"Ammani," I (this writer) said, "I can't find any excuse for the way your mother maneuvered to get rid of the other woman. Your mother was too deep and devious for the poor lady, who had shown so much trust in her, whom she had sheltered and nourished when she was in desperate straits, not to mention the years she cared for and protected Viswa who had after all strayed his way to Poona and was literally a tramp at the start . . ."

"Don't talk ill of your ancestors. Not right. He was not a tramp but a respected merchant and official at the *Peshwa's* court," Ammani retorted.

"He had only been a lowly clerk in her father's shop, remember?"

"What of it? Whatever it is, he rose high because of his mettle."

"And mainly through Surma's support — he should have remembered it at the time he yielded to your mother's coercive tactics."

"What else could a poor woman like her do to recover her husband? Only a woman can understand it. To a woman, her husband is everything. She can't lose him. Remember in what condition Bala had left home and what trials she must have gone through to reach Poona and how much misery she faced before she could reach him! Everything is justified, all means are justified in her case. Did not Savitri conquer Yama himself, and trap him into promising her a boon? And the boon she asked for was to beget children and he had to give her his blessing that she should have children. After accepting the boon, she asked how it would be possible when he as the God of Death was carrying away her husband's life, leaving his inert body in the forest — and then Yama had to yield back Satyavan's life. You could not imagine a greater woman than Savitri for austerity and purity of mind."

"Still I am unable to accept your mother's tactics — she could have adopted some other method."

"Such as?" she said suppressing her irritation.

"She could have revealed that she was his wife on the first day itself."

"Surma would have bundled her off or got rid of her in some manner."

"Would not Viswa have protected her?"

"No, he was completely under her spell at that time."

"Was it necessary to drag the poor woman with false promises up to Bangalore? Could they not have managed it in some other way?"

"Such as?" she asked again.

"I don't know. I'd have thought of more honorable ways."

"You cannot manipulate people in real life as you do in a story," she said.

As my remarks incensed her, she refused to continue her story and abruptly got up with the excuse, "I have better things to do at this time than talk to a fellow like you . . ." For nearly a week she ignored me while I followed her about with my notebook. She ignored me until I pleaded, "You must please complete the story. I want to hear it fully. You know why?"

"Why?"

"Otherwise I will be born a donkey in my next *janma.*"

"How do you know?"

"The other day I attended a Ramayana discourse. A man got up in the middle of the narrative and tried to go out of the assembly but the *pundit* interrupted himself to announce, 'It's said in the *Shastras* that anyone who walks out in the middle of a discourse will be a donkey in his next birth,' and the man who was preparing to leave dropped plump back in his seat when he heard it. And so please . . ."

"Tomorrow evening. I'm going to be busy today." Next evening after she had pottered around her garden and had her evening cold bath and said her prayers, she summoned me to the hall, took her seat on the swing and continued her story.

At Bangalore the parting of ways was harrowing. Surma, always so assured, positive and a leader, broke down and humbled herself to the extent of saying, "Let me only go with you. I have surrendered Viswa to you, only let me be near you. I have loved you as a friend. I'll come with you and promise to return to Poona after visiting the temples. Please show me this consideration. I accept with all my heart that he is your husband. I'll never talk to him again or look at him even. But let me be with you . . . Viswa, talk to her please."

Viswa turned to Bala and said, "Let her come with us. She will visit the temples and go back. I promise."

Bala stood thinking for a while, wept a little, controlled herself and said firmly to Surma, "No, it won't be possible. In our place we will be hounded out. I'll advise Viswa to go with you, anywhere, back to Poona or forward. Only leave me alone. You have got to choose."

It was pathetic and humiliating with their retinue and palanquin bearers watching the scene. Bala put her arms around Surma, rested her head on her shoulder and then sobbing, bowed down and prostrated at her feet, got up and moved away from her towards the tank again, whereupon Surma cried desperately, "Don't! don't! I am leaving. May God bless you both." She hurried up her retinue and got into her palanquin and left while Bala stood on the last step of the tank and watched. Viswa stood dumbstruck, not knowing what to do. That was the last they saw of Surma. She was not heard of again: whether she went back home to Poona or ended her misery by walking into the next available tank on the way, no one in my family knew.

Viswa would have frantically raced behind the palanquins but for the check of Bala's stare in silence. They stayed in the same rest house for three more days, waiting to join other travelers going south. Meanwhile Bala summoned a barber and persuaded Viswa to shave off his whiskers, saying, "In our part of the country you will be taken for a ghoul and children will run away screaming at the sight of you." She stood away from him after the shave and observed, "Now I can recognize you better. The patch under the ear is intact. I am doubly assured now — the same features which I used to see over the backyard wall, only filled up with age. Whatever made you hide such a fine face behind a wilderness of hair!"

"At the *Peshwa's* court it was customary and considered necessary."

At this point Ammani interrupted herself to warn me: "Don't ask how long they took to reach their village. All I can say is ultimately they did reach it." Only the river was there and the temple stood solidly as ever, but the old priest whose remarks had driven Bala out of her home and to whom she vowed to prove that her husband was alive was not there. The temple had a new priest who did not remember the old families. All the same, the very first thing Bala did was to enter the temple and stand before the God with her husband, praying for continued grace. She ordered an elaborate ritual of prayers and offerings and distributed food and fruits and cash to a little gathering of men, women and children. Viswa had left the place thirty years, and Bala about twenty years, before. Most of the landmarks were gone, also the people. Bala went back to her old house in the 4th street and found some strangers living in it, who said, "We bought this house from an old woman who went to live her last days in Kasi after her husband's death. Their only daughter had run away from home and was not heard of again."

Viswa searched for his old house but could not locate it. That neighborhood had been demolished and he could not find anyone to answer his questions, except a man grazing his cow, who just said, "Ask someone else. I know nothing." Viswa tried here and there, but could get no news of his parents or his relatives. The village seemed to have been deserted by all the old families. Bala's main purpose to visit the temple and offer *puja* to Ranganatha accomplished, she saw no reason for staying in the village. They decided to move to a nearby town where Viswa could establish himself as a gem merchant and start a new life.

*   *   *

At this point I could not get my grandmother to specify which town it was. If I pried further, she said, "I was not born then, remember that fact."

"What was that town? Could it be Trichy?"

"Maybe," she said.

"Or Kumbakonam?"

"Maybe," she said again.

"Or Tanjore?"

"Why not?" she said mischievously.

"Or Nagapattinam?"

"I was not born. How could I know? I tell you again and again — but you question me as if I could see the past."

"From your village, the nearby town must have been within fifty or a hundred miles. Have you not heard your mother mention any special landmark like a river or a temple?"

"She only mentioned that the river Kaveri was flowing and it was a place with several temples; she mentioned that every evening she could visit a temple, a different one each day of the week."

"Let us take it as Kumbakonam. Where did your marriage take place?"

"On a hill temple, not far from where we lived."

"It must be Swami Malai in Kumbakonam. Were you so ignorant as not to notice where you were being married?"

"I was eleven and followed my parents."

"Extraordinary!" I said, which offended her and she threatened to stop her narration. But I pleaded with her to continue. I realized that she knew it was Kumbakonam but was only teasing me.

Viswanath established himself as a gem expert in Kumbakonam. He acquired a house not far from the river. He sat in a small room in the front portion of his house and kept his wares in a small bureau, four feet high, half glazed.

(The heirloom is still with the family. When I was young I was given that little bureau for keeping my school books and odds and ends. I had inscribed in chalk on the narrow top panel of this bureau, "R. K. Narayanaswami B. A., B. L. Engine Driver." My full name with all the honors I aspired for, I wonder if one can detect any trace of that announcement now. I have not seen the heirloom for many years.)

Viswa's reputation spread as an expert appraiser of gems. People brought him diamonds for evaluation and to check for flaws. Through an eyeglass he examined the stones and gave his verdict before they were handed over to the goldsmith for setting.

Bala turned out to be a model wife in the orthodox sense, all trace of her adventurous spirit or independence completely suppressed. One could hardly connect her with the young woman who had tramped all alone across hundreds of miles in search of her husband and succeeded in bringing him back home — dominating, devious and aggressive, till she attained her object. Now she was docile and never spoke to her husband in the presence of others. Her tone was gentle and subdued. It was a transformation.

She wore an eighteen-cubit length of silk sari in the orthodox style, instead of the twelve-cubit cotton wrap favoured in Poona. She wore diamond earrings, decked herself in a heavy gold necklace and bangles and applied turmeric on her cheeks and a large vermilion mark on her forehead. She rose at five in the morning, walked to the river, bathed and washed her saris, took them home for drying, filled a pitcher and carried it home, also drew several pails of water from the well in their backyard to fill a cauldron for domestic purposes.

She circumambulated the sacred *tulasi* plant in the backyard and then sat down in the *puja* room with lamps lit and chanted *mantras* and by the time Viswa woke up at six, lit the kitchen fire and prepared his morning porridge or anything else he needed for breakfast. She cooked for him twice a day, buying vegetables from a woman who brought them to their door in a basket. She went to the temples in the evening with offerings and oil for the lamps in the shrines.

Their firstborn came two years later — a daughter, and another daughter, and then another daughter — "that is myself," said my grandmother. The fourth was a son.

The next twenty years, roughly, were years of prosperity. Viswa's business flourished. In proper time, he found bridegrooms for his daughters and sent his son Swaminathan to study in Madras at the Medical College; he was among the first batch of Indians qualified for the medical profession.

Viswa was past sixty when he found himself isolated. His daughters were married and gone. "I was the youngest and last to leave home," said Ammani. "My husband (your grandfather) was a sub-magistrate and posted to work in different villages of our district—here, there and everywhere, until we came to rest in Madras after his retirement. We bought this house in which we find ourselves now, he also acquired a number of other houses in this street, and bungalows in the western area on Kelly's Road, agricultural lands somewhere, and a garden. (The garden was known as *Walker Thottam* and supplied vegetables to the wholesale market at Kotawal Chavadi in George Town.) And all his time was taken up in managing his estates."

"You said he was started on less than fifty rupees. How did you manage to buy so many houses and lands?" I asked.

"We did not actually have to depend upon his pay."

"Oh, I understand. I will not question you further."

"Even if you asked, I wouldn't be able to explain how a magistrate earned—money just poured in, I think. We had a brougham and horse, a coachman and so much of everything. My own family consisted of three daughters and two sons. The eldest daughter was married and died in Madurai and my family was reduced to four. Your mother was my second daughter . . . I always felt that the kind of wealth your grandfather amassed was illusory, because within six months of your grandfather's death, by a court decree all his property was lost through a foolish business venture of his in steel. His trusted partner declared insolvency and fled to Pondicherry and your grandfather's properties were attached and auctioned to make good a bank loan—something to do with the notorious Arbuthnot Bank crash.

"Even this house was nearly gone but for the help of a neighbor, who loaned us five thousand rupees to redeem it at the last moment. Our creditors had already stuck notices of auction on our door, and by beat of tom-tom and loud announcements were inviting bidders. Crowds gathered at our door. You were due to be delivered in a couple of weeks, but the bustle, crowd and tom-tom beats were nerve-racking and affected your mother, who had come for her confinement and was in a delicate state of pregnancy. She became panic-stricken and got labor pains in that excitement. Your birth was rather premature. Only this house was saved of all your grandfather's properties—thanks, as I mentioned, to the last-minute help of our neighbor Mr. Pillai who lived in Number Two Vellala Street."

(One morning, two years ago, I had a desire to revisit Number One Vellala Street in Purasawalkam, where all of us were born in one particular room. We habitually considered the house as the focal point of the entire family scattered in other districts, visiting it from time to time. My friend Ram of *The Hindu* was also curious to see the house and the environs mentioned in *My Days*. One morning we drove down to Vellala Street in Purasawalkam, but found no trace of the old house. It was totally demolished, cleared and converted into a vacant plot on which the idea was to build an air-conditioned multi-storied hotel. Among the debris we found the old massive main door lying with "One" still etched on it. Ram made an offer on the spot and immediately transported it to his house, where it is mounted as a showpiece.)

To go back to the main theme. Changes were coming in Viswa's life. His son Dr. Swaminathan was appointed District Medical Officer at Kolar in Mysore State.

When Dr. Swaminathan left for Kolar, Viswa and Bala missed their children and found life dull. Viswa, now nearing seventy, worked less, finding it tedious to continue his gem business. He felt irritated when customers came for advice and discouraged them. Gradually he stopped all business, although his little bureau had a stock of precious stones.

Bala too had become rather tired and engaged a cook, a woman, who brought along with her a twelve-year-old daughter. Bala found their company diverting. The woman, who had been a destitute, now felt she had found a home and worked hard, relieving Bala of a lot of drudgery. Gradually, Bala preferred to lounge in bed, hardly stirring out, leaving the management of the house to the woman and her daughter.

Viswa too stationed himself all day in an easy chair on the veranda overlooking the street. Bala often implored him to go out and meet his cronies in the neighborhood who used to gather in the temple corridor, sit around and chat after a *darshan* of the God. But now he never went out, secretly worried about Bala's declining health. He sent for the *vaid*, who came every other day, studied her pulse and prescribed a medicine, a concoction of rare herbs, he claimed. Viswa wrote a letter to his son expressing anxiety, but official work kept Dr. Swaminathan busy. He could come only four weeks later. When he found his mother's condition serious, he struggled hard to retrieve her but with all the medicines and needles in his bag, he could not save her.

"When the obsequies were over, my brother and sisters returned to their respective places. My husband was a magistrate in Tindivanam. I had two daughters at that time and we also left."

Viswanath was persuaded to go to Kolar with his son. The house was practically locked up, with one or two rooms left open for the woman, with her daughter, to live there as a caretaker on a monthly salary.

Viswanath's life entered yet another phase: he had to live in Kolar with his son, whose family consisted of his wife, a daughter and a son, both under ten. At first Viswa had protested and resisted, but the doctor persuaded him to wind up his establishment in Kumbakonam.

At Kolar Dr. Swaminathan lived in a bungalow set in a spacious compound. Viswa enjoyed an early morning walk in the compound and then inspected the kitchen garden in the backyard, and from the veranda watched the birds and trees, watched his two grandchildren going off to a nearby mission school, and his son leaving for the hospital in the morning. He turned in at noon for his bath and then said his prayers in the *puja* room. His daughter-in-law, although reserved and formal, looked after his comforts and needs hour-to-hour. He had a room and he enjoyed his siesta after lunch. In spite of all the comfort and security, he missed Bala and felt a vacuity at times. "No one can take her place," he often told himself. Sometimes he thought of Surma too but the intensity of feeling was gone; it was just a faded memory revived with effort, without any pangs of recollection. His son, the doctor, was a busy man having to attend the Government Hospital as well as administer medical services in the whole district and he had to be away on "circuits" frequently.

Viswa felt proud of his son, especially at the beginning when he brought his salary home and handed over the cash, about four hundred rupees, in a net bag. Viswa carried it in after counting the amount, and called his daughter-in-law, "Lakshmi, come and take charge of this cash. Count it properly and spend it wisely. You must also build up savings. I want nothing of this. I have no use for this cash. I have my own. This is all yours, keep it safely." This was a routine statement every month. He awaited the salary day month after month and the routine continued.

He was happy as long as it continued, but when the practice was gradually given up for practical reasons and Swami began to hand his monthly salary directly to his wife, Viswa became resentful secretly. He tried to overcome it, hoping that next time or the next time, Swami would resume the courtesy of recognizing his presence when he brought home the salary. This was probably a temporary aberration or an absent-minded lapse. Viswa bore it for three months. At the end of it, he said to himself: "I'll intercept him tomorrow evening when he comes in with the salary. I will not leave the veranda until he arrives, test whether he'll hand me the bag or still give it to his wife." Brooding over it, he had magnified the situation and imparted an undue significance to it.

Next day Dr. Swaminathan did not come in the evening but at noon suddenly, and was in a great hurry. He did not enter the house but called from outside, "Lakshmi." When she emerged from the kitchen, he held out the salary bag from the veranda. "I can't come in now. People are waiting. We are off to a nearby village where ratfalls are reported." He rushed back to the medical team waiting at the gate in a horse carriage. They were to go out and investigate a possible outbreak of bubonic plague and inoculate the population.

Viswa, who had been gathering coriander leaves in the kitchen garden, came in with a sprig for seasoning the lunch items. Lakshmi presented to him the money bag. "What is this?"

"Salary. He brought it now."

Viswa glared at her, and asked, "Why at this hour? Why did he not call me?"

"He was in a hurry, people waiting at the gate."

"Oh!" he said, "He is a big man, is he?" and ignored the bag, dropped the coriander on the floor, marched off to his room and bolted the door, came out at lunchtime, ate in grim silence, retired to his room again, sat on his bed and brooded: "He is becoming really indifferent. This morning he left without a word to me. All of them are behaving callously. Children get out and come in as they please. They don't notice me at all. Lakshmi thinks her duty is done after feeding me as she would feed a dog without a word. The last three days Swami never spoke to me more than three sentences. They think I am an orphan depending on their favors. This is the curse of old age. I will teach them a lesson!"

He briskly made up a bundle of clothes, stuffed them in a small jute bag, put on his long grey shirt, seized his staff and started out. "Lakshmi," he called. She came out and was taken aback at the sight of him. He just said, "I am off . . ." as he had said to Bala over the wall before absconding years before. That tendency seemed to be ingrained in his blood. "Where?" she asked timidly.

"Never mind where — did your husband tell me where he was going? That is all." He briskly got down the steps and was out, leaving the lady staring after him speechlessly. The children had gone out to school. He found his way to the railway station, waited for a train, got into it, changed trains and ultimately reached Kumbakonam and was back in his home in Salai Street — surprising the caretaker and her daughter.

My grandmother's actual words: "That was a disastrous step he took.

What mad rage drove him to that extent no one could say. The caretaker and her daughter were not the kind he should have associated with. They were evil-minded, coming from a nearby village notorious for its evil practices such as fostering family intrigues, creating mischief and practicing black magic. When my father knocked, they were rather surprised but welcomed him with a great show of joy. They fussed over him. They consulted him on what he liked to eat and cooked and fried things and bought choice vegetables and fruits to feed him. They washed his feet whenever he came in after a short visit outside. They treated him like a prince till he must have begun to think, 'My son and wife treated me like a tramp and hanger-on, not a day did anyone ask what I liked. They always restricted my eating with the excuse, "You should not eat this or that at your age." My son thought that as a doctor, he was *Brihaspathi* himself! They denied me all delicacies, whereas this woman and her daughter know what I want.' The house was filled all the time with the smell of frying—chips, *bondas, pakodas* and sweets. Viswa was a very contented man now. He had a sturdy constitution which withstood all the gluttony he was indulging in.

"One fine day we got information that he had married the caretaker's daughter in a quiet, simple ceremony conducted by the woman who managed to get a priest from her village. It was a culmination of his rage against his son. He could think of no better way to assert his independence. He was seventy-five and the girl was seventeen. He married her convinced that it would be the best way to shock and spite his family, all of whom seemed hostile to him."

Now the woman had him under her control, in course of time she took further steps to consolidate her position. She began to suggest that they were no longer mere caretakers of the house but his family, and that the young wife and her mother should be made the owners of the house through a deed of transfer. She found a pleader who prepared a document and presented it to Viswa for his signature. At this point he still had some sense left. He hesitated and delayed while his mother-in-law kept up her pressure—through persuasion, bullying and even starving him. He dodged the issue with some excuse or other, and began to wonder if he should not have continued in Kolar. He was losing his cheer and his young wife nagged him to sign the document.

They had their eyes on his stock of precious stones, which he always kept with him although he did no business now; he also had enough cash left but took care to keep it with a banking friend, drawing just the amount he needed at a time. This irked his mother-in-law who had aimed high:

she now goaded her daughter to sulk and nag him at night. He dodged her by taking his bedroll to the *pyol* on the excuse that he found the room too stuffy, thus evading his wife's pillow talk. He avoided her all through the day too while the mother-in-law murmured asides and remarks. He was beginning to brood and plan a return to Kolar. The thought of his son was exhilarating and Kolar seemed a paradise and a haven of peace.

The woman was shrewd and began to guess from his mood that he might slip away. She told her daughter, "I have to go to our village on some important work and will be back tomorrow. Keep a watch on your husband. Keep him in and shut the front door."

At their village the woman consulted the local wiseacre, explaining the difficulties her son-in-law was creating. The wiseacre's income was through his claims to magic, black or white, the exorcising of spirits and the making of potions and amulets. He said, "You must tell me frankly what you want. Don't hide anything." She explained that while she wanted her son-in-law to be friendly and amenable, he was becoming tough and hostile. She said tearfully, "Out of compassion for the fellow in dotage, I agreed to give him my daughter so tender and young. But he is becoming indifferent and ill-treats her. You must help me."

The wiseacre pretended to note down points and said, "Come next week and bring two sovereigns. I'll have to acquire some ingredients and herbs, which will cost you something. I won't charge you for my service, that's my guru's command." She went home thinking, "Only a week more."

When she came back to the village a week later, the wiseacre gave her a packet. "There are two pills in it. Give them both to him with his food. They are tasteless and will dissolve and when the pills get into his system, he'll follow his wife like a lamb and treat you as his guru."

The woman went back home gloating over the possibilities ahead, with the packet tucked in a sari at her waist. On the following Friday she prepared a special feast explaining that this Friday was particularly sacred for some reason. She was secretive about the pills and did not mention it even to her daughter, but planned to get him to sign the document next day after the pill was completely assimilated in his system, with the document ready at hand. Viswa, a confirmed glutton these days, was pleased and seemed relaxed, bantered with his wife and mother-in-law in anticipation of the feast saying, "This indeed is a pleasant surprise for me. What a lot of trouble you take!" The fragrance of delicacies emanating from the kitchen was overpowering. When the time came for lunch, the woman spread two long banana leaves side by side saying that the couple must dine together today, and heaped the leaves with item after item — the high point of the feast being almond and milk *payasam* in a silver bowl for him and in a brass cup for his wife. Before serving it, the woman managed to dissolve the two pills in the silver bowl.

My grandmother concluded, "That was the end. My husband was a sub-magistrate at Nagapattinam when we got information that Viswa's end had come suddenly. I have nothing more to add. Don't ask questions."

(My — this writer's — mother, Ammani's second daughter, who was ninety-three at the time of her death in 1974, used to maintain that she had a hazy recollection of being carried on the arms of her mother at Kumbakonam and witnessing a lot of hustle and bustle following a funeral, people passing in and out of the house and some boxes being locked and sealed by the police and a motley crowd milling around.)

I asked my grandmother, "What happened to that woman and your young stepmother?"

"I don't know. I have no idea."

"No inquest, no investigation, no questioning of that woman?"

"I don't know. We could not stay away from Nagapattinam too long since the Collector, an Englishman, was coming for inspection and the magistrate was required to be present. We had to leave. My brother, Dr. Swaminathan, came down from Kolar and took charge of the situation and my father's assets. I can't tell you anything more about it. All I know is what I could gather from my brother later. He spoke to our neighbors who mentioned to him the woman's schemes; the pleader had a lot to say about that woman's ambition and maneuvers to grab the wealth and property. My brother could not stay on for long either but before going back to Kolar he made some arrangement for the disposal of that house . . . that's all we know."

EVAN S. CONNELL

Au Lapin Gros

Being unspeakably tired of—no, no, dissatisfied with myself—yes, that's it. Being unspeakably dissatisfied with myself, I happened upon the simplest possible solution. And what was that? Nothing could be more obvious. I would re-create myself.

Why had I failed to think of this sooner? I don't know. I can't imagine. It's mysterious. In any case, I resolved that no longer would I tell the truth about myself provided I could think of a plausible lie. Well, how does one prepare to substitute fiction for truth? After much thought I grew a little beard which I trimmed to a point like a Russian anarchist and I began to wear tinted glasses. I bought a shabby overcoat which I wore all the time. I obtained a job as menial factotum to a druggist and I rented a musty room in the shadow of St. Sulpice.

What attracted me to this terrible room? A pot of starving geraniums on the window ledge and one disconsolate ray of sunshine that hesitantly approached the moth-eaten rug each afternoon between four and five o'clock. It seemed to me that the person I had decided to become would live in just such a room. The bed, I concluded, would be suitable for a dying leper. As to the armoire, leaning for support against a mildewed wall, it appeared to have been constructed during the reign of Charlemagne. There was, I admit, a handsome oval wash basin embellished with painted roses and a decorative brass faucet. This excellent basin, owing to an ancient fracture, was capable of holding water up to a certain level but no higher. If the handle could be persuaded to turn, which on certain days proved inexplicably difficult, there came an agonized shriek followed by guttural music from below, followed at last by a spitting noise, then a blast of water that a thirsty horse would view with suspicion. Of the indomitable cockroaches who for countless generations had patrolled the baseboards, I say nothing. In short, a *clochard* accustomed to life under the Pont Neuf would turn up his nose at such quarters. Consequently, having rented this room, I asked myself what I had done, a question to which there was no reasonable answer. Nevertheless, I reflected, even if I could get my money back, which I could not, the next place I rented might be worse. Life is, after all, the study of contradictions.

Because I have no instinct for cooking I took all my meals at a restaurant from the Dark Ages that smelled of cabbage and mice and also of disinfectant. Among its distinguished patrons this establishment boasted five or six gentlemen with hairy arms who seemed to be playing chess with their knives and forks and whom I had observed at work on a sewer, various picturesque ladies who did not appear until after sunset, and a tribe of students less notable for brains than for bawling voices and the lack of civility one would expect in a railroad station. What a detestable place. Three times a day I went there, shuddering as I entered and clutching my stomach in pain as I departed because the meals filled me with gas. Then, after strolling along the quai belching and fouling the air like a policeman's horse at every intersection, I proceeded to the Lapin Gros in search of adventure. There I would select a table with a nice view of whatever might happen and I would sip coffee while pretending to read *Le Figaro*. That is how I became acquainted with Meretricia Istanapoulos, whom I shall never forget.

She strode into the café one rainy night like a murderess, water dripping from her long black trenchcoat. She walked toward me with gigantic strides and sat down at the next table. Already I felt myself enslaved. I observed that her sandals were huge, which did not surprise me because she was tall as a flagpole. Around the pages of *Le Figaro* I smiled in the most ingratiating manner, but she did not notice. She was muttering to herself in Greek, a language of which I understand scarcely more than five words.

All at once she turned her passionate gaze upon me. Monsieur, she demanded with a voice like a cello, if you please, a match?

I was astounded. Certainly, I replied, and like the most obsequious servant I scuttled to the counter. When I returned with a packet of matches she seemed to have forgotten me. In one hand she held a cigarillo black as the devil's own, which I hastened to light. Four bony fingers of the other hand, bristling with imitation gems, tapped the marble surface of the table as though despatching a message.

Permit me to introduce myself, I ventured. My name is Arturo Sanchez de La Coruña. But having said this I trembled. I am not adept at lying. When I was a child my parents could tell immediately if I was lying; they would look at my feet, which I found myself unable to control. My tiny feet would begin to creep in circles as though ashamed of my behavior. Now I felt them growing restless and was thankful that if she glanced down she would not know what had aroused them.

For some reason she ignored my overture. Possibly she had not heard me. Whatever the explanation, I determined to press forward. And as she continued muttering to herself I took advantage of the situation to study those black Greek eyebrows, the nose, the lips, the chin. I imagined her profile on a vase. I saw her wearing a peaked gold helmet and carrying a long spear as she advanced upon her enemies, who fled in terror. This woman, said I to myself, is a goddess, the daughter of Athena. I risked another peek at her sandals. Again she failed to notice. How was I to proceed? Audacity is not part of my temperament, nevertheless it seemed imperative to act.

Mademoiselle, I began, and made an effort to fortify the voice which was dying in my throat. Mademoiselle, I repeated, forgive me but you appear somehow vexed. On the chance that I might be of service I throw myself at your feet.

Ah! cried this extraordinary creature. It's nothing, monsieur. I have just now come from a meeting of the Opposition. Tell me your name.

I braced myself for the lie. Arturo Sanchez de La Coruña, I said. But to my amazement I felt almost no discomfort.

You do not sound like a Spaniard, she said, puffing on her cigarillo. In fact, you do not look like a Spaniard.

I am — as perhaps you deduce from my surname — a *gallego*, I continued boldly. I was brought to France while a mere infant, which is why you discern no accent. My parents, God rest them, were obliged to flee the war.

Your father, then, he was a Loyalist?

I hesitated. I had not expected her to know anything about that struggle which concluded long before she was born. Indeed, I myself knew next to nothing about it. Caution seemed advisable. I screwed up my eyes as though deliberating. Through a cloud of purplish smoke I could see her staring at me like a basilisk. I had no idea what to say. I wanted to hide behind the newspaper. My heart thumped against my ribs. I'm no good at fakery, I said to myself, I have no panache. Then, to my alarm, this Amazon hitched her chair a few inches closer and it became obvious that she was unaccustomed to bathing, but whether the somewhat agricultural fragrance was intoxicating or repugnant, or both, I was at a loss to decide.

Have you not failed to introduce yourself? I inquired with mock reproach. And from the confidence of my voice one might have assumed that somebody else was speaking.

She sucked in her breath. Ah! Meretricia Istanapoulos.

Meretricia! whispered I to myself. It was a name one could not forget. Meretricia! Meretricia! I felt an urge to embrace her. I wanted to stroke and squeeze those colossal feet. After so many solitary evenings at the Lapin Gros perhaps I was on the verge of a conquest.

Your profession, monsieur?

Please, I said, not 'monsieur.' Arturo.

Arturo, she repeated thoughtfully. Arturo.

What did she mean by that? Twice she had pronounced the name. I felt encouraged.

Your profession?

Correspondent, said I. After all, if she knew what I did for a living the affair would end in a moment.

She glanced at *Le Figaro* and the significance of this did not escape me. I reflected that it would be unwise to claim a position on *Le Figaro*. If, by chance, she was acquainted with somebody at the paper and inquired about me — well, I would be finished. Nor could I say, for example, *Paris Soir*. On the other hand, having represented myself as a journalist, something further was expected. I had no idea what to do. I decided to take refuge in evasion.

Figaro? I remarked as though the subject merited no discussion. Oh, it can be entertaining enough, but hardly sufficient to engage one with serious concerns. It lacks — what should one say? — a certain depth? And I made a disparaging gesture.

Then you do not, monsieur, write for this — as you express it — 'entertaining' journal?

I smiled politely, indicating that I had no wish to condemn *Le Figaro*. As to the publication which employs me, I said, let it remain anonymous. No doubt you agree, mademoiselle, that under certain circumstances one may wish to avoid scrutiny by a repressive and stupid government.

But of course, she murmured, leaning toward me as though we were conspirators.

At this moment, I confess, I found myself hypnotized. Always I had championed the cause of free will, but if just then Meretricia had commanded me to annihilate myself I would have rushed to do so. At the same time it occurred to me that she was less than intelligent. Her admirably bright eye — like that of a seagull — was vacant.

I would love a Campari, she said, so naturally there's no waiter. How are they able to vanish? She looked around the café, squinting. I realized that she was nearsighted.

Allow me, I said and was about to rise when five red talons sank into my arm.

Don't move! she hissed. We are being watched. Behind you is a fat man with the Legion of Honor who has been ignoring us while drinking chocolate.

Could you be mistaken? I asked.

Monsieur, I am not mistaken.

You say he ignores us?

Ah, you fail to understand! The fact that he pays no attention is absolute proof. Furthermore, they work in pairs, although just now I don't see the accomplice.

Meretricia, I said as calmly as possible. Meretricia, luxuriant flower of Ionia, be kind enough to listen. Were it not for a single consideration I would beseech you to clasp my arm throughout eternity.

Monsieur, what is that consideration?

Your fingernails are draining my life blood.

Presumably she understood. In any case, she withdrew her claws while I gave thanks to a God whose supervision of the universe appears at times incomprehensible. I then had the impression, although I do not know why, that she was about to serenade the café with an exuberant Greek folk song. This, I suspected, might not be well received by Madame Ponge behind the cash register so I asked if she would care for a sweet — an ice cream, a pastry of some sort.

Ah, oui! The millefeuille! she sang with that melodious voice. Ah, I adore the millefeuille!

Scarcely a minute had elapsed since she was dying for Campari. Well, I thought, women are capable of jumping like mountain sheep from here to there. How they do it is impossible to learn.

A millefeuille, said I. Of course.

By the time I returned after ordering a pastry the fat man with the Legion of Honor had vanished. I asked where he had gone.

That one! she exclaimed. Who knows, monsieur? And then her resolute face grew pensive. I have been thinking about you. Yes, she went on while stroking my sleeve with her talons, it is true.

Meretricia, zephyr of the Aegean, said I with my heart in my throat, will you call me 'Arturo'? Say that you will.

If you wish it. Naturally, monsieur.

You were thinking about me? I asked before she could forget.

I have come to a decision, she said. I believe you are one of us. I'm prepared to risk everything.

This disturbed me. If she chose to be a revolutionary, which I suspected might be the case, well and good, but it was no concern of mine. I am not one to mount the barricades. Let others give heroic speeches and get shot, that's how I view the matter. Frankly, what attracted me more than all the political manifestoes in Europe were those two indescribably long feet underneath her table. It was with the greatest difficulty that I prevented myself from staring at them.

Monsieur, she said, would it be correct to assume that you have been outraged by the unjust trial and false imprisonment of Jacques Chatelet?

Who, I wondered, is Jacques Chatelet? I had never heard this name. I was on the point of asking, but the manner in which Meretricia pronounced it — as though he were a saint — warned me against such a question.

For reasons I cannot disclose, I said, I have been prevented from following the progress of this shameful affair.

Just then, by good luck, the millefeuille arrived. Meretricia did not hesitate. I observed with fascination the tiny silver fork traveling rapidly between the plate and her voluptuous mouth — back and forth, back and forth — as though it had developed a life of its own. Her eyes half closed with pleasure. What provocative noises she made while munching! How I envied those crisp little flakes of pastry! I intend to begin writing epic poetry, I said to myself, which I shall dedicate to this imposing and excitable foreigner.

Suddenly the fork came to a stop in midair while Meretricia gazed frantically at the plate. I could not imagine what was wrong. Her bosom heaved. You must pardon me, monsieur, she said. You must pardon me. You must — I am about to sneeze.

Neither of us moved. Well, I said after a moment, how goes it?

She lifted the fork. Next, a cataclysm.

Listen to that! she exclaimed. And having rubbed her nose like a child she turned once more to the task of devouring pastry.

You are prepared to risk everything . . . ?

Ah! You made me forget. What a little goose I am! Then with the majestic dignity of enormous women she leaned toward me. I reflected that every patron of the Lapin Gros, to say nothing of Madame Ponge, must be watching.

The trial, she whispered. A disgrace! The government will do anything to discredit the Opposition.

Why did she choose to whisper? Possibly she was an actress. I would be honored to make the acquaintance of Jacques Chatelet, I remarked while staring at a flake of millefeuille which clung like a moth to that monumental bosom.

If you wish to wait nine years and three months, she said.

Having considered her statement I began to view these *sans-culottes* differently. My passionate conspirator evidently belonged to an organization devoted to more than the deliverance of furious speeches. What Monsieur Chatelet had done, or to whom, I had not the faintest idea, but I believe he had not merely disobeyed a traffic signal. I recalled that on some festive day of the previous year a bomb had exploded in front of the stock exchange. All right, I said to myself, I've been hoping for adventure, let's see what happens next. But it then occurred to me that my companion may have been correct about the fat man drinking chocolate. Well, to be identified as the associate of a bona fide anarchist wasn't what I had in mind. One shouldn't antagonize the authorities, that's how I look at it. Life under any circumstances is problematic, so it's best to remain invisible. Nothing would give me greater satisfaction than to be informed that the government had absolutely no record of my existence. In short, I felt torn between my desire for this Mt. Everest of a woman and a quite sensible desire for anonymity.

How do you know, said I, that you are not discussing this business with an agent of the national security? How do you know I am not an accomplice of the fat man with the Legion of Honor? It was you yourself who assured me that he was not alone.

You are not an agent of the national security, she said. If that were the case you would behave more cleverly. For one thing, you wouldn't exercise yourself by peeking at me while you think I am unaware.

But that is unavoidable, I said.

For what reason is that unavoidable?

Because I am bewitched.

Ah, monsieur, she said, you are very wicked.

But how could I fail to admire you? I replied while stroking my beard. Where you are concerned, I admit to being without shame. I think of you as a mermaid swimming through the maelstrom that Paris has become.

No, my complexion is too dark, she said. I am unattractive, as you see. And she touched her hair.

Allow me one liberty, I said.

What is that liberty, monsieur?

Permit me to devour you. Permit me to feast upon you like a millefeuille.

I will consider it, she said. In the meantime, I permit you to accompany me to the métro.

What about the rain? I asked because I felt that my position was not yet established. Look, there's a waterfall outside and you didn't bring an umbrella.

That's true, she said. But you have one.

I hadn't expected such a logical remark. Perhaps, I suggested, I may accompany you beyond the métro?

As to that, it will depend. We shall see.

All right, let's be off, I said, putting on my beret. And with the umbrella under my arm I stood up. The situation was progressing. I had extracted no promise, nevertheless a certain something in her attitude gave me hope. Besides, the rain might prove useful. I would remind her that upon emerging from the métro she would again appreciate the value of an umbrella. And whose umbrella was it?

Meretricia stood up.

I had known, of course, from the moment she strode into the café that she was almost a giant, and when it became obvious that she had her eye on the adjoining table I had said to myself, very good, she's marching this way, I look forward to the challenge. Now, as the saying goes, it was a different story.

Sit down, she said, and she pulled me down. We are being watched.

This, in fact, was so. A theatrical audience could not have been more attentive than the patrons of the Lapin Gros. Madame Ponge herself had turned a crocodile gaze in our direction.

Pretend you do not know me, Meretricia commanded. I have located the accomplice.

Does he wear the Legion of Honor? I asked.

He's Algerian, she whispered while pretending to search for something in the pockets of her trenchcoat. I know the type. Be careful. Don't look at me.

Obediently I stared at a poster for the Comédie Française. Why do you think he is the accomplice? I asked.

There's no mistake, she whispered. This is dangerous, monsieur. You have been observed with me.

Our lives are entwined, I said while inspecting the handle of my umbrella. Authors a century from now will write of us as another Héloïse and Abélard.

He's getting up, Meretricia said between her teeth. He's approaching. Pay no attention.

I am prepared to sacrifice myself a thousand times, I replied in a menacing voice. I will bite his hand.

He has turned around, she murmured. I believe he is going to the lavatory for a conference with the other one. Let's get out of here.

This I thought was a splendid idea. Because of a shy disposition I feel uncomfortable on stage. Also, I did not care to have a strange Algerian walk up behind me, especially after I had been talking with this remarkable woman about whom I knew nothing. I recalled my first impression of her — a murderess — and it occurred to me that I was planning to accompany this formidable creature to an unknown destination. Always, throughout my life, I have taken discreet pride in my judgment, but now I began to wonder if it had evaporated. Still, I reflected, had I not come to the Lapin Gros in hopes of some such adventure? Very well, Arturo, said I bravely to myself, proceed. The truth, however, was a little different. After considering various possibilities my natural cowardice reasserted itself and I wished that I had been less anxious to escort her as far as the métro, or perhaps beyond.

Meretricia, you shall teach me Greek, I announced when we emerged on the rue St. André des Arts. I will become your favorite pupil. Every lesson will be a joy. And having spread the umbrella I held it high in the air.

Ah, but you are droll, she replied. Wait! There's another! And she squinted toward somebody getting out of a cab.

It's a conspiracy, I said. We are surrounded.

We must go back. There's no time to lose.

What do you mean? I asked. What are you talking about? Are you suggesting that we go back into the café?

We'll go out the other side. Hurry! she exclaimed, giving me such a push that I staggered.

Inside the Lapin I dared not look toward Madame Ponge who, I felt certain, must be eyeing us with displeasure. All the same, since Meretricia was leading the way I had no choice but to follow. I could see nothing except her broad shoulders.

Well, what do you think? I asked when we once again stood outside, having entertained everybody by marching like comedians in one door and out the other.

Soon enough they'll catch on to our trick, she said. It would be wise to take the Odéon métro. Then like a goddess she contemplated me with an expression that was possibly amorous and said, Monsieur, no matter what happens I won't betray you.

I could not imagine what she meant.

I understand why you must keep quiet, she said. You are an assassin.

These words astonished me so much that I was unable to speak. My thoughts, which until that instant had leapt and circled with the grace of ice skaters, now bumped clumsily against each other. Having no idea what to do, I tugged my beard and glanced shrewdly all around. I was then still more astonished when Meretricia bent down and kissed my forehead. Naturally I attempted to fling myself upon her but she muttered something in Greek and brushed me aside. I am not a large man.

With stupendous strides she set off toward Odéon while I trotted alongside throbbing with desire. Her monstrous feet splashing through puddles reminded me of salmon. I could hardly control myself. Villains! Pigs! I cried, doubling up my fist to show how much I believed in the cause. Leeches! Termites! We will crush them! I imagined us marching side by side against enemies of the Opposition.

She did not respond. As we approached the rue Danton she murmured in a sorrowful voice: Nine years. They will stop at nothing, monsieur, nothing.

I wondered why he had been imprisoned although I was reluctant to ask because I had hinted that I knew about the government's infamous behavior. As a matter of fact, I had no idea which government was responsible.

Brunetti! she exclaimed in a tone of scorn. Who could believe that Jacques Chatelet would be represented by Eugenio Brunetti? I tell you it's unbelievable!

Brunetti, I thought. Chatelet. Istanapoulos. This sounds like the Internationale. What next? A Bulgarian? A Portuguese? I began to regret that I had neglected to follow the trial in the newspaper. I could recall absolutely nothing about it. Not a word. Also, I was afraid to ask what we were opposing. Sooner or later it will come out, I said to myself. What's important at the moment is to demonstrate solidarity.

The world is a bottomless cesspool, I heard Meretricia saying in the words of, I am positive, Jacques Chatelet. Regard the deputies, she went on. Serpents! Regard the advocates. Behold how they mortgage their souls for a sou! Can anyone deny this?

I replied that I was too overcome with disgust to speak.

Ah! There you have it! The police walk around hoping for an excuse to crack the heads of workers. Innocent people find themselves detained. It makes one sick!

The masses are content to sleep, I said. To wake up the common people would require an earthquake.

Or a volcano, said Meretricia. Beyond doubt you've put your finger on it. Then she gazed over my head with a feminine expression. In the café, surely, you didn't find me attractive?

Meretricia, I said, I am overwhelmed by the need to abduct you. To run away with you. To hold you captive. I am engorged! Yes, exactly, that's the word. If instead of being a journalist I were a poet you would comprehend my passion.

I don't think I believe you, she said. I'm not at my best. I didn't sleep comfortably last night. You should see me when things are going well.

Tell me about yourself, I said. From the first day, from the first instant of your existence. How do you come to be in Paris? Why have we not met before? Tell me everything. Withhold nothing. Exclude only the men you have loved because they no longer have meaning.

Ah! she gasped with that suggestive intake of breath which drew me to the brink of madness. You wish to know about my life? I summarize my life in three words. Resistance. Purity. Rebellion.

The second word appalled me. As a matter of fact, I cared for none of it. I had a feeling she was altogether under the thumb of that imprisoned Svengali. This disposition to subordinate themselves is something about women I have never understood. In any case, Meretricia's politics interested me less than her exceptional stride—like that of an American basketball player. The flapping of those immense sandals on wet pavement reduced my brain to pudding. I found myself out of breath while attempting to keep up with her.

Don't allow yourself to become excited, she said. It's not the most important thing in the world. What's important, monsieur, is to lift the yoke of capitalism from the necks of our brothers and sisters everywhere. That is our mission.

She kept talking while I shook my fist and nodded enthusiastically, although I confess that political rhetoric makes me yawn. Justice! she exclaimed with great bitterness. Tell me, monsieur, what chance has the worker? None! And she went on about government abdicating its responsibility abetted by lackeys of God in lace collars who would drink a poor man's blood if it would please the rich, and so on and so forth. Well, I said to myself, that's all true enough and I wish things were different, but they aren't, and so far as I can see they won't be much better tomorrow. In my opinion it wasn't going to make the least difference whether Monsieur Chatelet spent the rest of his days in the Bastille or whether he was appointed Minister of Finance.

Why did they do away with him? she asked. Because they feared him, that's why. Because he, alone, understands the truth. Don't authorities always fear the truth?

Exactly! I cried. You've got it just right! And I wondered what sort of impression I made by shouting. With my little beard and tinted glasses, wearing a beret worth less than a centime and a discouraged overcoat, it seemed to me that I might easily be mistaken for a disenfranchised radical, possibly a bolshevik. I noticed Meretricia squinting along the boulevard. We were very close to the Odéon métro.

What's your opinion? I asked while trying to slip an arm around her waist. Are we out of danger?

It looks all right, she admitted, but of course that's what they want us to believe. In any event, you'll allow me to borrow the umbrella, will you not? It's a long walk to my apartment from Gare du Nord.

Now wait a minute, I said. In the first place, I don't live right around the corner and this is a torrent. What about me?

A few drops won't hurt you, she said with a playful expression and before I knew what was happening she had seized the umbrella.

Now don't be hasty, I said without letting go. Look at it this way. We've been observed together. The fat man was watching us and also the Algerian. You yourself said it was dangerous. I'd better come along to protect you.

I assure you I'll be fine, she said while twisting the umbrella away from me. I'll meet you next Wednesday at the Lapin. Don't worry, monsieur, I know how to take care of myself.

Well, it was an awkward situation. What was I to do? I'm not good at taking the initiative. Wednesday? I called while she descended the steps. You'll be there?

She waved and said something in Greek before disappearing.

I should have been forceful, I thought. I should have asserted myself. But everything happened so fast. She was too quick for me.

I returned to my room shivering and wet as a cod, already counting the days until I would see her again. I remembered that when she entered the café she had seemed distraught. Why? She had just come from a meeting of the Opposition, therefore something disagreeable must have occurred. What? I tried to imagine the meeting. Fifteen or twenty malcontents packed into a squalid closet reeking of wine and department store cheese. There would be a Scandinavian because there are Scandinavians everywhere — perhaps a sallow boy with a bad complexion who carried a guitar and cleaned the wax out of his ears with a little finger. I had seen such a boy at the café. An American Negro with a booming voice and huge white teeth and hands that could strangle a horse. I imagined him playing the bongo drum. Several of my countrymen would be there, stingy and quarrelsome and dissatisfied as always. Another Greek. Russians, naturally. Germans. Yes, anything political attracts Germans. They would attempt to dominate the meeting. And what would be the purpose of this stupid affair? Would they pass a resolution to hurl a bomb at the Palais Nationale? Or, since I did not know which government was to be opposed, they might resolve to attack the embassy of Greece. Or that of the Netherlands. What difference did it make? I wondered if the Opposition had an official song.

However, I spent most of every day thinking about Meretricia. I planned to be at the café well ahead of time. I imagined her pushing through the door with my umbrella, squinting in the direction of our tables, marching toward me like a basketball player. I would put aside the newspaper, rise, press my lips to one of those baguettes on her fingers. No doubt she would ask for another millefeuille. And this time our conversation would make more sense because I had prepared a list of interesting topics to discuss.

Wednesday. A day I thought would never arrive. When it did, I grew convinced that it would never end, but at last the supper hour approached.

After a hasty meal of putrid lamb flavored with venomous herbs accompanied by a poultice of exhausted spinach and wine that would corrode a shovel, followed by a dish of scabrous chocolate — doubtful that I could survive many more such meals without submerging my stomach in lactates and sulphates and mineral water — I all but trotted along the rue St. André des Arts.

Finding our tables unoccupied, I seated myself with an air of nonchalance and pretended to read *Le Figaro* while sipping coffee, although in fact I comprehended nothing. Each time the door opened I held my breath.

Not until past midnight did I give up hope and no sooner had I returned to my room than I felt convinced she had been delayed and even now must be hurrying to meet me. Next I told myself that I had failed to pay attention — that she had said we should meet not this Wednesday but the week following.

Night after night I waited at the Lapin Gros.

It was only much later that I learned she had run off with a Turk. A wrestler. I knew I would never see her again.

STUART DYBEK

We Didn't

We did it in front of the mirror
And in the light. We did it in darkness,
In water, and in the high grass.

—"We Did It," YEHUDA AMICHAI

We didn't in the light; we didn't in darkness. We didn't in the fresh cut summer grass or in the mounds of autumn leaves or on the snow where moonlight threw down our shadows. We didn't in your room on the canopy bed you slept in, the bed you'd slept in as a child, or in the backseat of my father's rusted Rambler which smelled of the smoked chubs and kielbasa that he delivered on weekends from my Uncle Vincent's meat market. We didn't in your mother's Buick Eight where a rosary twined the rearview mirror like a beaded, black snake with silver, cruciform fangs.

At the dead end of our lovers' lane—a side street of abandoned factories—where I perfected the pinch that springs open a bra; behind the lilac bushes in Marquette Park where you first touched me through my jeans and your nipples, swollen against transparent cotton, seemed the shade of lilacs; in the balcony of the now-defunct Clark Theater where I wiped popcorn salt from my palms and slid them up your thighs and you whispered, "I feel like Doris Day is watching us," we didn't.

How adept we were at fumbling, how perfectly mistimed our timing, how utterly we confused energy with ecstasy.

Remember that night becalmed by heat, and the two of us, fused by sweat, trembling as if a wind from outer space that only we could feel was gusting across Oak Street Beach? Wound in your faded Navajo blanket, we lay soul-kissing until you wept with wanting.

We'd been kissing all day—all summer—kisses tasting of different shades of lip gloss and too many Cokes. The lake had turned hot pink, rose rapture, pearl amethyst with dusk, then washed in night black with a ruff of silver foam. Beyond a momentary horizon, silent bolts of heat lightning throbbed, perhaps setting barns on fire somewhere in Indiana. The beach that had been so crowded was deserted as if there was a curfew. Only the bodies of lovers remained behind, visible in lightning flashes, scattered like the fallen on a battlefield, a few of them moaning, waiting for the gulls to pick them clean.

On my fingers your slick scent mixed with the coconut musk of the suntan lotion we'd repeatedly smeared over one another's bodies. When your bikini top fell away, my hands caught your breasts, memorizing their delicate weight, my palms cupped as if bringing water to parched lips.

Along the Gold Coast, high rises began to glow, window added to window, against the dark. In every lighted bedroom, couples home from work were stripping off their business suits, falling to the bed, and doing it. They did it before mirrors and pressed against the glass in streaming shower stalls, they did it against walls and on the furniture in ways that required previously unimagined gymnastics which they invented on the spot. They did it in honor of man and woman, in honor of beast, in honor of God. They did it because they'd been released, because they were home free, alive, and private, because they couldn't wait any longer, couldn't wait for the appointed hour, for the right time or temperature, couldn't wait for the future, for Messiahs, for peace on earth and justice for all. They did it because of the Bomb, because of pollution, because of the Four Horsemen of the Apocalypse, because extinction might be just a blink away. They did it because it was Friday night. It was Friday night and somewhere delirious music was playing—flutter-tongued flutes, muted trumpets meowing like tomcats in heat, feverish plucking and twanging, tom-toms, congas, and gongs all pounding the same pulsebeat.

I stripped your bikini bottom down the skinny rails of your legs and you tugged my swimsuit past my tan. Swimsuits at our ankles, we kicked like swimmers to free our legs, almost expecting a tide to wash over us the way the tide rushes in on Burt Lancaster and Deborah Kerr in their famous love scene on the beach in *From Here to Eternity*—a scene so famous that although neither of us had seen the movie our bodies assumed the exact position of movie stars on the sand and you whispered to me softly, "I'm afraid of getting pregnant," and I whispered back, "Don't worry, I have protection," then, still kissing you, felt for my discarded cutoffs and the wallet in which for the last several months I had carried a Trojan as if it was a talisman. Still kissing, I tore its flattened, dried-out wrapper and it sprang through my fingers like a spring from a clock and dropped to the sand between our legs. My hands were shaking. In a panic, I groped for it, found it, tried to dust it off, tried, as Burt Lancaster never had to, to slip it on without breaking the mood, felt the grains of sand inside it, a throb of lightning, and the Great Lake behind us became, for all practical purposes, the Pacific and your skin tasted of salt and to the insistent question that my hips were asking, your body answered yes, your thighs opened like wings from my waist as we surfaced panting from a kiss that left you pleading *oh Christ yes,* a yes gasped sharply as a cry of pain so that for a moment I thought that we *were* already doing it and that somehow I had missed the instant when I entered you, entered you in the bloodless way in which a young man discards his own virginity, entered you as if passing through a gateway into the rest of my life, into a life as I wanted it to be lived *yes* but O then I realized that we were still floundering unconnected in the slick between us and there was sand in the Trojan as we slammed together still feeling for that perfect fit, still in the *Here* groping for an *Eternity* that was only a fine adjustment away, just a millimeter to the left or a fraction of an inch further south though with all the adjusting the sandy Trojan was slipping off and then it was gone but yes you kept repeating although your head was shaking no-not-quite-almost and our hearts were going like mad and you said yes Yes wait . . . Stop!

"What?" I asked, still futilely thrusting as if I hadn't quite heard you.

"Oh, God!" you gasped, pushing yourself up. "What's coming?"

"Julie, what's the matter?" I asked, confused, and then the beam of a spotlight swept over us and I glanced into its blinding eye.

All around us lights were coming, speeding across the sand. Blinking blindness away, I rolled from your body to my knees, feeling utterly defenseless in the way that only nakedness can leave one feeling. Head-lights bounded towards us, spotlights crisscrossing, blue dome lights revolving as squad cars converged. I could see other lovers, caught in the beams, fleeing bare-assed through the litter of garbage that daytime hordes had left behind and that night had deceptively concealed. You were crying, clutching the Navajo blanket to your breasts with one hand and clawing for your bikini with the other, and I was trying to calm your terror with reassuring phrases such as, "Holy shit! I don't fucking believe this!"

Swerving and fishtailing in the sand, police calls pouring from their radios, the squad cars were on us, and then they were by us while we sat struggling on our clothes.

They braked at the water's edge, and cops slammed out brandishing huge flashlights, their beams deflecting over the dark water. Beyond the darting of those beams, the far-off throbs of lightning seemed faint by comparison.

"Over there, goddamn it!" one of them hollered, and two cops sloshed out into the shallow water without even pausing to kick off their shoes, huffing aloud for breath, their leather cartridge belts creaking against their bellies.

"Grab the sonofabitch! It ain't gonna bite!" one of them yelled, then they came sloshing back to shore with a body slung between them.

It was a woman — young, naked, her body limp and bluish beneath the play of flashlight beams. They set her on the sand just past the ring of drying, washed-up alewives. Her face was almost totally concealed by her hair. Her hair was brown and tangled in a way that even wind or sleep can't tangle hair, tangled as if it had absorbed the ripples of water — thick strands, slimy-looking like dead seaweed.

"She's been in there a while, that's for sure," a cop with a beer belly said to a younger, crew-cut cop who had knelt beside the body and removed his hat as if he might be considering the kiss of life.

The crew-cut officer brushed the hair away from her face and the flashlight beams settled there. Her eyes were closed. A bruise or a birthmark stained the side of one eye. Her features appeared swollen — her lower lip protruding as if she was pouting.

An ambulance siren echoed across the sand, its revolving red light rapidly approaching.

"Might as well take their sweet-ass time," the beer-bellied cop said.

We had joined the circle of police surrounding the drowned woman almost without realizing that we had. You were back in your bikini, robed in the Navajo blanket, and I had slipped on my cutoffs, my underwear still dangling out of a back pocket.

Their flashlight beams explored her body causing its whiteness to gleam. Her breasts were floppy; her nipples looked shriveled. Her belly appeared inflated by gallons of water. For a moment, a beam focused on her mound of pubic hair which was overlapped by the swell of her belly, and then moved almost shyly away down her legs, and the cops all glanced at us — at you, especially — above their lights, and you hugged your blanket closer as if they might confiscate it as evidence or to use as a shroud.

When the ambulance pulled up, one of the black attendants immediately put a stethoscope to the drowned woman's swollen belly and announced, "Drowned the baby, too."

Without saying anything, we turned from the group, as unconsciously as we'd joined them, and walked off across the sand, stopping only long enough at the spot where we had lain together like lovers, in order to stuff the rest of our gear into a beach bag, to gather our shoes, and for me to find my wallet and kick sand over the forlorn, deflated-looking Trojan that you pretended not to notice. I was grateful for that.

Behind us, the police were snapping photos, flashbulbs throbbing like lightning flashes, and the lightning itself still distant but moving in closer, rumbling audibly now, driving a lake wind before it so that gusts of sand tingled against the metal sides of the ambulance.

Squinting, we walked towards the lighted windows of the Gold Coast, while the shadows of gapers attracted by the whirling emergency lights hurried past up toward the shore.

"What happened? What's going on?" they asked us as they passed without waiting for an answer, and we didn't offer one, just continued walking silently in the dark.

It was only later that we talked about it, and once we began talking about the drowned woman it seemed we couldn't stop.

"She was pregnant," you said, "I mean I don't want to sound morbid, but I can't help thinking how the whole time we were, we almost — you know — there was this poor, dead woman and her unborn child washing in and out behind us."

"It's not like we could have done anything for her even if we had known she was there."

"But what if we *had* found her? What if after we had — you know," you said, your eyes glancing away from mine and your voice tailing into a whisper, "what if after we did it, we went for a night swim and found her in the water?"

"But, Jules, we didn't," I tried to reason, though it was no more a matter of reason than anything else between us had ever been.

It began to seem as if each time we went somewhere to make out — on the back porch of your half-deaf, whiskery Italian grandmother who sat in the front of the apartment cackling before "I Love Lucy" reruns; or in your girlfriend Ginny's basement rec room when her parents were away on bowling league nights and Ginny was upstairs with her current crush, Brad; or way off in the burbs, at the Giant Twin Drive-In during the weekend they called Elvis Fest — the drowned woman was with us.

We would kiss, your mouth would open, and when your tongue flicked repeatedly after mine, I would unbutton the first button of your blouse revealing the beauty spot at the base of your throat which matched a smaller spot I loved above a corner of your lips, and then the second button that opened on a delicate gold cross — that I had always tried to regard as merely a fashion statement — dangling above the cleft of your breasts. The third button exposed the lacy swell of your bra, and I would slide my hand over the patterned mesh, feeling for the firmness of your nipple rising to my fingertip, but you would pull slightly away, and behind your rapid breath your kiss would grow distant, and I would kiss harder trying to lure you back from wherever you had gone, and finally, holding you as if only consoling a friend, I'd ask, "What are you thinking?" although, of course, I knew.

"I don't want to think about her but I can't help it. I mean it seems like some kind of weird omen or something, you know?"

"No, I don't know," I said. "It was just a coincidence."

"Maybe if she'd been further away down the beach, but she was so close to us. A good wave could have washed her up right beside us."

"Great, then we could have had a *menage à trois.*"

"Gross! I don't believe you just said that! Just because you said it in French doesn't make it less disgusting."

"You're driving me to it. Come on, Jules, I'm sorry," I said, "I was just making a dumb joke to get a little different perspective on things."

"What's so goddamn funny about a woman who drowned herself and her baby?"

"We don't even know for sure she did."

"Yeah, right, it was just an accident. Like she just happened to be going for a walk pregnant and naked, and she fell in."

"She could have been on a sailboat or something. Accidents happen; so do murders."

"Oh, like murder makes it less horrible? Don't think that hasn't occurred to me. Maybe the bastard who knocked her up killed her, huh?"

"How should I know? You're the one who says you don't want to talk about it and then gets obsessed with all kinds of theories and scenarios. Why are we arguing about a woman we don't even know, who doesn't have the slightest thing to do with us?"

"I *do* know about her," you said. "I dream about her."

"You dream about her?" I repeated, surprised. "Dreams you remember?"

"Sometimes they wake me up. Like I dreamed I was at my *nonna's* cottage in Michigan. Off her beach they've got a raft for swimming and in my dream I'm swimming out to it, but it keeps drifting further away until it's way out on the water and I'm so tired that if I don't get to it I'm going to drown. Then, I notice there's a naked person sunning on it and I start yelling, 'Help!' and she looks up, brushes her hair out of her face, and offers me a hand, but I'm too afraid to take it even though I'm drowning because it's her."

"God! Jules, that's creepy."

"I dreamed you and I were at the beach and you bring us a couple hot dogs but forget the mustard, so you have to go all the way back to the stand for it."

"Hot dogs, no mustard—a little too Freudian, isn't it?"

"Honest to God, I dreamed it. You go off for mustard and I'm wondering why you're gone so long, then a woman screams a kid has drowned and immediately the entire crowd stampedes for the water and sweeps me along with it. It's like one time when I was little and got lost at the beach, wandering in a panic through this forest of hairy legs and pouchy crotches, crying for my mother. Anyway, I'm carried into the water by the mob and forced under, and I think, this is it, I'm going to drown, but I'm able to hold my breath longer than could ever be possible. It feels like a flying dream—flying underwater—and then I see this baby down there flying, too, and realize it's the kid everyone thinks has drowned, but he's no more drowned than I am. He looks like Cupid or one of those baby angels that cluster around the face of God."

"Pretty weird. What do you think it means? Something to do with drowning maybe, or panic?"

"It means the baby who drowned inside her that night was a love child—a boy—and his soul was released there to wander through the water."

"You really believe that?"

We argued about the interpretation of dreams, about whether dreams were symbolic or psychic, prophetic or just plain nonsense until you said, "Look, you can believe what you want about your dreams, but keep your nose out of mine, okay?"

We argued about the drowned woman, about whether her death was a suicide or a murder, about whether her appearance that night was an omen or a coincidence, which, you argued, is what an omen is anyway: a coincidence that means something. By the end of summer, even if we were no longer arguing about the woman, we had acquired the habit of arguing about everything else. What was better: dogs or cats, rock or jazz, Cubs or Sox, tacos or egg rolls, right or left, night or day—we could argue about anything.

It no longer required arguing or necking to summon the drowned woman; everywhere we went she surfaced by her own volition: at Rocky's

Italian Beef, at Lindo Mexico, at the House of Dong, our favorite Chinese restaurant, a place we still frequented because they had let us sit and talk until late over tiny cups of jasmine tea and broken fortune cookies earlier in the year when it was winter and we had first started going together. We would always kid about going there. "Are you in the mood for Dong, tonight?" I'd ask. It was a dopey joke, and you'd break up at its repeated dopiness. Back then, in winter, if one of us ordered the garlic shrimp, we would both be sure to eat them so that later our mouths tasted the same when we kissed.

Even when she wasn't mentioned, she was there with her drowned body — so dumpy next to yours — and her sad breasts with their wrinkled nipples and sour milk — so saggy beside yours which were still budding — with her swollen belly and her pubic bush colorless in the glare of electric light, with her tangled, slimy hair and her pouting, placid face — so lifeless beside yours — and her skin a pallid white, lightning-flash white, flashbulb white, a whiteness that couldn't be duplicated in daylight — how I'd come to hate that pallor, so cold beside the flush of your skin.

There wasn't a particular night when we finally broke up, just as there wasn't a particular night when we began going together, but I do remember a night in fall when I guessed that it was over. We were parked in the Rambler at the dead end of the street of factories that had been our lover's lane, listening to a drizzle of rain and dry leaves sprinkle the hood. As always, rain revitalized the smells of the smoked fish and kielbasa in the upholstery. The radio was on too low to hear, the windshield wipers swished at intervals as if we were driving, and the windows were steamed as if we'd been making out. But we'd been arguing as usual, this time about a woman poet who had committed suicide, whose work you were reading. We were sitting, no longer talking or touching, and I remember thinking that I didn't want to argue with you anymore. I didn't want to sit like this in silence; I wanted to talk excitedly all night as we once had, I wanted to find some way that wasn't corny-sounding to tell you how much fun I'd had in your company, how much knowing you had meant to me, and how I had suddenly realized that I'd been so intent on becoming lovers that I'd overlooked how close we'd been as friends. I wanted you to know that. I wanted you to like me again.

"It's sad," I started to say, meaning that I was sorry we had reached a point of sitting silently together, but before I could continue, you challenged the statement.

"What makes you so sure it's sad?"

"What do you mean, what makes me so sure?" I asked, confused by your question, and surprised there could be anything to argue over no matter what you thought I was talking about.

You looked at me as if what was sad was that I would never understand. "For all either one of us know," you said, "she could have been triumphant!"

Maybe when it really ended was that night when I felt we had just reached the beginning, that one time on the beach in the summer between high school and college, when our bodies rammed together so desperately that for a moment I thought we did it, and maybe in our hearts we had, although for me, then, doing it in one's heart didn't quite count. If it did, I supposed we'd all be Casanovas.

I remember riding home together on the El that night, feeling sick and defeated in a way I was embarrassed to mention. Our mute reflections emerged like negative exposures on the dark, greasy window of the train. Lightning branched over the city and when the train entered the subway tunnel, the lights inside flickered as if the power was disrupted although the train continued rocketing beneath the Loop.

When the train emerged again we were on the South Side and it was pouring, a deluge as if the sky had opened to drown the innocent and guilty alike. We hurried from the El station to your house, holding the Navajo blanket over our heads until, soaked, it collapsed. In the dripping doorway of your apartment building, we said goodnight. You were shivering. Your bra showed through the thin blouse plastered to your skin. I swept the wet hair away from your face and kissed you lightly on the lips, then you turned and went inside. I stepped into the rain and you came back out calling after me.

"What?" I asked, feeling a surge of gladness to be summoned back into the doorway with you.

"Want an umbrella?"

I didn't. The downpour was letting up. It felt better to walk back to the El feeling the rain rinse the sand out of my hair, off my legs, until the only places where I could still feel its grit was the crotch of my cutoffs and in each squish of my shoes. A block down the street, I passed a pair of jockey shorts lying in a puddle and realized they were mine, dropped from my back pocket as we ran to your house. I left them behind, wondering if you'd see them and recognize them the next day.

By the time I had climbed the stairs back to the El platform, the rain had stopped. Your scent still hadn't washed from my fingers. The station—the entire city, it seemed—dripped and steamed. The summer sound of crickets and nighthawks echoed from the drenched neighborhood. Alone, I could admit how sick I felt. For you, it was a night that would haunt your dreams. For me, it was another night when I waited, swollen and aching, for what I had secretly nicknamed the Blue Ball Express.

Literally lovesick, groaning inwardly with each lurch of the train and worried that I was damaged for good, I peered out at the passing yellow-lit stations where lonely men stood posted before giant advertisements, pictures of glamorous models defaced by graffiti—the same old scrawled insults and pleas: FUCK YOU, EAT ME. At this late hour the world seemed given over to men without women, men waiting in abject patience for something indeterminate, the way I waited for our next times. I avoided their eyes so that they wouldn't see the pity in mine, pity for them because I'd just been with you, your scent was still on my hands, and there seemed to be so much future ahead.

For me it was another night like that, and by the time I reached my stop I knew I would be feeling better, recovered enough to walk the dark street home making up poems of longing that I never wrote down. I was the D. H. Lawrence of not doing it, the voice of all the would-be lovers who ached and squirmed but still hadn't. From our contortions in doorways, on stairwells, and in the bucket seats of cars we could have composed a *Kama Sutra* of interrupted bliss. It must have been that night when I recalled all the other times of walking home after seeing you so that it seemed as if I was falling into step behind a parade of my former selves—myself walking home on the night we first kissed, myself on the night when I unbuttoned your blouse and kissed your breasts, myself on the night that I lifted your skirt above your thighs and dropped to my knees—each succeeding self another step closer to that irrevocable moment for which our lives seemed poised.

But we didn't, not in the moonlight, or by the phosphorescent lanterns of lightning bugs in your backyard, not beneath the constellations that we couldn't see, let alone decipher, nor in the dark glow that had replaced the real darkness of night, a darkness already stolen from us; not with the skyline rising behind us while the city gradually decayed, not in the heat of summer while a Cold War raged; despite the freedom of youth and the license of first love—because of fate, karma, luck, what does it matter?—we made not doing it a wonder, and yet we didn't, we didn't, we never did.

ROBERT COHEN

Adult Education

Sylvia I say very frankly this will not do.

Sylvia nodding pats her stomach.

Sylvia I say this will not do. I am not ready. I have an idea in my head I say and this idea is not so much an idea but a kind of vision, a vision concerning readiness. I have this idea that concerns and surrounds readiness like a glove but the problem Sylvia as I see it is that without the hard defining hand of readiness inside it the idea is limp and of no use whatever when it comes to carrying things.

Sylvia smiles dreamily, munches a cracker.

The thing is Sylvia that the world is equipped in a certain way, or rather people are equipped in a certain way, that is people have different kinds of equipment that ready them for different kinds of work, and these differences of equipment account for certain differences in schedules and timing when it comes to the actualizing of certain inchoate needs, if you will, and these needs as such are —

Sweetie, Sylvia says, I'm going to lie down now.

— neither good nor bad in any valuative way, but simply exist, like rocks and trees, like . . . like rocks and trees. Let's keep things plain, let's keep things solid, because Plato notwithstanding we live in a world of solid objects Sylvia after all, and against these solid objects our various whims and yearnings are really not very substantial when you examine them closely, not very —

Whims says Sylvia. Ha. This is not whims.

I know Sylvia I know I say but see that's my point that's exactly my . . . it's so good and typical of you to discover it. You are right that this is not whims. This is a solid object with some fluids in it that will eventually become more and more solid despite having more and more fluids in it, and pretty soon according to what I have heard from other people all these solids and fluids are going to drive us right out of this life of ours that's been going so well without them.

It hasn't been going so well says Sylvia. If you knew anything you'd know it hasn't been going so well. What makes you think it's been going so well?

You have done it again Sylvia I say. You have put the finger of meaning right on the very throbbing pulse of the problem. Because it hasn't been going so well has it? We have issues among us and between us, and these issues are lingering and penetrant, like most issues, and cannot be ignored, and therefore clearly the last thing we need, the last thing that would be advisory under the circumstances, that is given the expanding network of pressures we operate under and the frail not to say delicate state of our emotional health—

Expanding says Sylvia. I'll show you expanding.

— or at least *my* emotional health, such as it is Sylvia such as it is. This emotional health of mine, how do I say this? This emotional health of mine is an extremely small and unseaworthy metaphoric boat that is presently getting pounded by a very strong metaphoric wind, and right now, before it sails off into the black distance or capsizes forever, I would like offer a few words just for the record by way of eulogy. Ladies and gentlemen, we were close once, my emotional health and I. Frequently we went out together back in our youth, drank at bars together and so forth, long nights studded like stars with possibilities, we were allies the two of us in the hectic bloody wars of existence and as happens in combat we grew close. The melancholy fact is that I miss my emotional health. It was never very sturdy but it deserved a longer life. It may be sentimental of me, but the thought of it out there now, pale, bloated, pecked by circling fowl, losing the last of its shape to the blind currents, this makes me want to cry out loud. This makes me want to *act*.

Good says Sylvia. Would you mind very much acting your way over to the popcorn?

Fine I say. But it was your friend too Sylvia once, I know it was. I beg you search your heart for a sign of it, some small flicker of this thing you once prized but apparently prize no longer. I beg—

Let's watch the news says Sylvia. She plumps a pillow and sticks it behind her back. Reaches for the popcorn.

— you, please before it's too late, search inside yourself. What do you see when you search inside yourself Sylvia.

You saw it too says Sylvia. At the doctor's.

That wasn't me Sylvia I say. That wasn't me. That was only this construction that wears my name. That was only this puppet of cartilage and bone that attends to the world while the real me cowers in dark rooms, wondering when the movie is going to start. I have no idea at all Sylvia what doctor you're talking about. What doctor? I haven't been to a doctor, oh, in a long, a long —

Don't be silly she says. We looked at it together. You squeezed my hand.

No. That was not me. That was only the puppet and his puppet reflex. It had nothing *intentional* in it. For intention to register Sylvia there must be a seedling of conscious forethought involved, there must be —

You cried she says.

Same thing. The exact same phenomenon I say. I rest my case.

Look she says and points to the frenzied screen. Famine. War. She puts the popcorn down and holds her stomach as if someone very big has entered the room and threatened to hurt her. Volcanic lava she says.

Volcanic lava?

Red and flowing she says.

Red and flowing?

Red and flowing.

Sylvia I fail to understand —

Quite all right she says. Failure is forgivable.

It is?

Understanding comes later she says after the fact. As in art. One regards the object and one is simultaneously seized by something blind and thirsty inside oneself and then very slowly this seizure yields an oblique recognition of connection between the object and oneself and in this way is the ineffable sublime approached.

Sylvia I say where did you learn to talk like this all of a sudden?

Adult education she says.

Sylvia I say come to bed now and make this planet spin. Bring all the attendant blindness and thirst you can muster.

Not now she says. I'm a little nauseous. You're going to have to carry me.

Okay. I am going to have to carry you.

Just a few steps she says.

Nothing. Hardly measurable.

You're sweating she says.

Not me.

Beads of sweat. Your brow is full of them.

A natural process.

Look she says. I can play connect the dots on your head.

A small irritation, Sylvia, under the circumstances.

Are we almost there?

Almost I say.
And when we arrive? What then?
I don't know.
Will you carry me back?
I don't know if I'll have the strength.
I know you don't know she says. Just say you will.
I don't see the point of saying I will I say when I don't know if I will.
I know you don't know she says.
Well if you know I don't know then it stands to reason—
Stands shmands she says. Say you will.
Of course I'll say it.
You will she says.
I will.

AMY BLOOM

Semper Fidelis

I shop at night. Thursday nights I wave good-bye to the nurse and drive off, feigning reluctance. The new mall has three department stores, a movie theater and hundreds of little shops and I have been in all but the Compleat Sportsman. It makes no sense to me but I cannot sit through a movie knowing I'm supposed to be shopping. I eat warm peanut butter cookies and wander around for almost two hours, browsing through the very slim jazz sections of the mall record stores, skimming bestsellers. At nine-thirty, when the mall is closing and it's just me and the vagrant elderly and the young security guards, I go grocery shopping.

All-night grocery stores seem to be the personal savior and favorite haunt of dazed young women of all colors, who haul their crumpled, sleeping babies like extra groceries in the cart; single middle-aged men and women too healthy and too lonely to fall asleep at ten o'clock and people like me, who are scared to go home. It is my belief and sometimes my wish that my husband will die while I am out on one of my Thursday night sprees.

Max and I have been together for almost ten years, since I was eighteen and he was fifty. We are no longer a scandal or a tragedy. His wife's friends and the other witnesses have moved away or fallen silent or become friends, the limited choices of a small town. Max and I are close to ordinary, made interesting only by our past and its casualties. Women who would have, may have, spit in my soup at painfully quiet dinner parties ten years ago now bring pureed vegetables for Max and articles on the apricot-pit clinics of Mexico. I have become a wife, soon to be a widow, and I feel more helpless and unknowing after ten years of marriage than I was at eighteen, moving into Max's apartment with two T-shirts, a box of records and no shoes. On our first outing Max introduced me to the chairman of his department and bought me sneakers.

He has not been out of bed for three weeks and he has not spoken since the morning. I always pictured myself as an Audrey Hepburn-type widow, long-necked and pale in a narrow black linen dress. Instead, I am nearly drowning in a river of sugar and covering myself in old sweatpants and Max's flannel shirts. I only dress up on Thursday nights, to go out in a big sweatshirt, as long as a short dress, and black tights, playing up my legs with high-heeled black ankle boots. I have never dressed like this in my life and I am glad to put my sneakers and my jeans back on before I go into the house.

Ray, at the Deli Counter, is the one I've been looking for. He first admired my boots and then my whole outfit and after three Thursdays in a row, I felt obliged to buy another top for him to look at, and he leaned over the counter to tell me how much he liked it and winked as he went back to work. Ray can't be more than twenty-two and I assume he is a recovering addict of some kind, since he is presently the picture of good health and says things like, "Easy does it," and "One day at a time," which are the kinds of things my brother, a not-recovering alcoholic, says whenever he calls to wish me well or borrow money. I think Ray is a good choice. I think we would not discuss poetry or symbolism or chemotherapy or the past and I think I would have a beer and he would not and I would lay my hand on one thick thigh until I felt the cloth tighten under my fingers and when we were done I would climb out of his van, or his room in his mother's house and thank him from the bottom of my heart and go home to Max.

I come home to see the nurse leaning over Max, smoothing his covers as her big, white nylon breasts swing slightly and shadow his face. He smiles and I see that he is unaware of my presence and the nurse is not.

"The pearls," she says, continuing their conversation, "were extremely valuable and irregardless of the will, my sister and I both think the pearls should have come to us. Our mother's pearls should have come to us, because they were already ours."

I cannot even begin to understand what she's talking about but it feels ominously metaphorical. Maybe the pearls represent Max's health, or his first marriage or our vow to cleave unto each other; things irretrievably gone and valued more in their absence than in their presence. I want to shut her up, to keep her from tormenting us both, but Max smiles again, a quick softening of his bony, grey face and even I can see that he is not tormented. I knock against the door frame knowing that Max as he is now is too innocent and the nurse too self-absorbed to appreciate the irony of my knocking. I am performing without an audience, which is how it has been for some time; if you feel sorry for yourself, can it still be a tragedy? Or are you reduced to a rather unattractive second lead, a foil for the heroes, blind and beautiful, courageously polishing the brass as the icy waters lap at their ankles? It seems to me—and I would not be sorry to find out—that I have disappeared.

"Sweetheart," he says and the nurse frowns.

"He's been asking for you," she says and I forgive her bitchiness because she seems to care about him, to feel that it matters that he misses me. The other nurses are solicitous of his health, of his illness, but his feelings are nothing more than symptoms to them. For one minute, I love her for loving him; he has made me love people I would dislike if he were going to live.

"Dawn's mother passed away recently, she was telling me." Shaken by love, touched by his effort to keep us together and to keep us his, I smile at Dawn.

"I'm so sorry," I say, trying to be good. "I lost my mother just last year. And I've got a sister, too." That's it. I cannot think of any more astonishing coincidences which will bind us together.

"My sister's my best friend," Dawn says, sitting in the armchair near the bed, as though she'd dropped in on Max for a visit.

"Mine, too." Amazing. My sister, Irene, is my best friend and while my father wept and my mother murmured congratulations from the far side of a scotch-and-soda, my sister took me upstairs, to what had been her room, to discuss my marrying Max.

"You can have anyone, you know. Even after all this. You can transfer to a school in California and know one will ever know. You don't have to marry him."

"I love him, Reen. I want to marry him."

"Okay. Okay, I'll be there. At least he won't leave you for a younger woman. Not without being arrested. Is this justice of the peace or train-and-veil?"

"Justice of the peace. Wednesday."

"All right. How about a suit? Silk suit, roses in your hair? It won't kill you to go to a beauty parlor."

And my sister got my legs waxed, my pores cleaned and my eyebrows shaped in less than forty-eight hours. In the photographs, I look radiant and only a little too young for the ivory silk suit, which Irene found, unpinned from a mannequin, and paid for in less than forty-five minutes. I have ivory roses in my upswept black hair and Max is laughing at the camera, held by his oldest friend, who is astonished, amiable and drunk for the whole afternoon. My sister looks like the mother of the bride, exhausted, vigilant, more pleased than not. My own parents weren't there because I didn't invite them, despite Max's pleas.

Dawn turns to go and I can see that she doesn't love Max; he is just a better than average case, less trouble than some of the others. I am free to hate her and I walk her to the door and open it for her, without speaking, a form of civilized rudeness I've picked up from my mother.

"Lie down here," Max says, but I cannot lie in that bed.

"I'll lie on the cot." When we left the hospital, a smart, angry woman in the support group told me to get a cot and she didn't even pretend to listen when I said that we would continue to share a bed.

"Undress slowly, sweetheart. I can still look." In the books I keep hidden, the guides to grief, the how-to books of widowhood and the period that comes before, the authors mention, delicately, that the surviving spouse usually suffers hurt feelings and frustration due to the dying person's lack of sexual interest. This doesn't seem to be the case with Max.

I throw off my clothes and lie on the cot, like a Girl Scout, still in my T-shirt, panties and socks. I hear a wet, bubbling noise, which is how he laughs now.

Max rests one cool, brittle hand on my stomach.

"How was the supermarket?"

"It was okay. I got some groceries."

"And the mall?"

"It was fine. I got some socks."

He strokes my stomach with two dry fingertips and I feel the flesh at the end of each finger, dragging slightly after the bone. I want to throw up and I want to weep.

"Do you ever meet anybody?"

"Like who?" I ask. Despite everything, I don't think of Max as a jealous man; we have simply misunderstood each other, most of the time. He would remind me, as we drove home from parties, that he had made a point of not admiring the younger women, so people wouldn't think that I was part of his youth fetish, that I was less than unique. He said I owed him the same consideration, and should conceal my impulsive sexuality, lest people think that my marriage to him was just adolescent, hormonally driven mindlessness. We agreed, many times, that he was not jealous, not insecure, not possessive and we must have had that conversation about flirting a hundred times in our ten years together.

Max pokes me lightly. "I don't know, like anybody. Some nice young man?"

"No. No one." I roll over on my side, out of reach of his fingers.

"All right, don't get huffy. Dawn gave me my meds already. Good night, sweetheart."

"Good night." You sadistic old shit.

I lie on the cot, listening to his chalky, irregular breath until he falls asleep and go downstairs to pay bills. His room, our room, fills up at night with a thick wet mist of dark fluids and invisibly leaking sores. This is something else I don't say.

The next Thursday, I smile encouragingly at Ray, who is very busy with the second-shift shopping crowd and I find myself taking a number behind a dark, dark boy, so dark the outline of his whole brown body seems drawn in charcoal. He is all roundness, high, full Island cheeks, round black eyes, rounded arms and shoulders, his pants rounded front and back. My own fullness has begun to shrink and loosen, the muscle sliding down from the bone a little more each year. I want to cut this boy open like a melon and eat him, slice by slice. Cut him and taste him and have him and hurt him. I could tell Max that I understand him better now than I did ten years ago but he would be horrified that I think this mixture of lust and resentment is anything like his love for me. I am only horrified by myself; what I want to do to this boy Max would never do to me.

Ray and I exchange several devoted, affectionate glances; as aspiring lovers we are so tenderly playful and wistful it seems odd that all we really want is to fuck each other senseless and get home before we're caught. My attitude is not good.

I go home to Max and Dawn. She is in my kitchen sipping tea out of my mermaid mug, a gift from Max after a terrible rainy week on Block Island. Her iridescent blue tail is the handle and Dawn's smooth fingers cling to it.

After she leaves, Max questions me again.

"I don't meet anyone, for Christ's sake. Who would I meet? I'm not a girl. I'm twenty-eight and I probably look ninety. Who would I meet?"

"You might meet anyone. Look at me, I'm sixty, I'm a dying man riddled with cancer and I met Dawn."

"Great. I hope you'll be very happy together." I turn out the light so he cannot see me change and I wonder if he gets Dawn to strip for him on Thursdays.

"Really," he says, surrounded by pillows so he can't lie down and be engulfed by his own lungs. "Tell me. Why shouldn't you meet someone?"

I try to see him in the dark as he is, everything that was broad and hard-boned now transparent at the edge, softly dimpled and concave at the center.

"Who would I meet?"

"Some good-looking young man at the mall. Not a salesman, you never like salesmen. They try too hard, don't they?"

"Yes." I want to tell him to rest but I don't think I would be saying it for him.

"Big and dark. Sweet-natured, not terribly bright. Not stupid, of course, but not intellectual. Not an academic. I want to spare you a long, pedantic lecture when you've only got a few hours."

"Good idea. How long do I have?"

"Well, you know your schedule better than I. Two hours at the mall, an hour and a half at the supermarket. We can skip aerobics, I think. I cannot picture you with a man who goes to aerobics class."

He's right. I like them big and burly or lean and lithe but I cannot bear the compulsively athletic, the ones who measure their pulses and their biceps and their cholesterol levels.

"Tell me, sweetheart. Tell me about the man you met in the super-market."

"Not the mall?"

"Don't play games with me. Tell me what happened."

"He's dark-haired but fair. Black Irish and big. Not tall, but wide. Built like a wall." I realize that I am describing the Max I have seen only in photographs, a big, wild boy with one cocky foot on his Army Jeep; ramming his way through Harvard a few years later, grinning like a pirate as the wind blows both ends of his scarf behind him.

"Go on," Max says, as if I am talking about someone else.

"I do see him at the supermarket. I change my clothes to go there." And I tell Max the truth about my clothes and he says "Ya-hoo" when I came to the black ankle boots. We are having some kind of fun in this terrible room.

"That'll get him. Do you wear a bra?"

"Come on, Max, of course I wear a bra."

"Just slows you down. All right, at least it's one of your pretty ones, I hope, not those Ace bandage things. How about the purple and black one with the little cut-outs?" Max likes silky peek-a-boo lingerie and I buy it but I do not wear seventy-dollar hand-finished bras and garter belts for every day. Most of the time I wear cheap cotton tubes which he hates.

"I do wear the black and purple one."

"And the panties?"

"No panties."

"Wonderful. The first time I put my hand on your bare ass I thought I had died and gone to heaven. And then I was afraid that it wasn't for me, that you just never wore them."

"Max, you asked me not to wear them, remember? I always wore underpants." I'd had some, more than enough, sex with boys and by myself when I met Max, but I had never had a lover. Everything important that I know, about literature, about people, about my own body, I have learned from this man and he is leaving me the way we both expected I would leave him, loving, regretful, irretrievable.

"Tell me about this big guy."

"Big guy" is what I used to call Max who, having been married to a woman who called him "my dear" and pursued by highly educated young women who called him Professor Boyle and thought he was God, found terms like "Big Guy" and "Butch" to be refreshing endearments.

"He's the night manager." I have given Ray a promotion; I'm sure in time someone with his good looks and pleasant manner would be made manager and a sexual encounter with Ray, the Head Roast-Beef Slicer, seems to demean us all.

"Fine. Where did you do it?"

"Jesus, Max, what is wrong with you?"

"Need you ask? Come on, come on, don't get skittish now. Where did you do it?" That angry pushing voice used to scare me to death and I cannot bear that it doesn't scare me anymore.

"We went to Wadsworth Park." Where Max and I used to go when I was still living with my parents and he was still living with his then-wife. Just recently, while sorting out his pills or shaving his distorted face, I find myself thinking, this is what a wife is. Now that we cannot see ourselves in the curious excited eyes of other people, the differences which defined us are fading away. We are just a man who is dying and a woman who is not.

"A little buggy?"

"Not too bad." I stall to avoid making a mistake, afraid that I am not telling the right story.

"But you had a blanket and you didn't notice the bugs."

"Max, what do you want from me?"

"I want you to tell me what happened when you got into the woods. You led him to those big rocks, by the stream?"

The woods are thick on both sides of the water, sheltering twin slabs of granite. When we were there Max would press me so far backwards to the ends of my hair trailed in the cold water, collecting small leaves as I lay under him.

"All right. We went to the rocks and we made love. Then I changed my clothes and came home."

"Don't tell me like that," he says and begins to cough, loosely, his whole body bouncing on the plastic mattress. He falls asleep still coughing and I go downstairs and do nothing.

For the rest of the week, he floats in and out of conversations and medicated dreams. On Thursday I put on my shopping costume while Max watches and smiles, alertly. Dawn is reading magazines, waiting for me to leave.

"Tonight?" he asks, barely pushing the words out of his lips.

I don't answer, just tie up my boots and sit down to brush my hair.

"You know who Dawn reminds me of? Not coloring, but the build? Eren Goknar. Remember?"

I remember and I keep brushing my hair.

"I wonder where she is."

"I don't know," I say. "Maybe she went back to Turkey."

"Don't think so. She wrote to me from California, teaching at Berkeley. Marvelous girl," he says, struggling with each consonant. I walk out of the room.

I put up some hot water for me and Dawn and go back to check on Max, afraid that he will die while I'm angry with him.

"Ready?"

"Yeah. I'll be back in a couple of hours."

"I slept with Eren," he says and sighs.

"I know," I say, although I hadn't known until then. And I know that he is pushing me away, furiously, as though I will miss him less because he had sex with Eren Goknar. He can no more lose me than I can lose myself, we are like those housekeys that beep in response to your voice; they practically find you. I kiss the air near Max's face and return to Dawn, who has made tea. We chat for two hours, in between her runs upstairs, and she doesn't ask me why I don't go out. I send her home at eleven.

Max barely opens his eyes when I turn on the night-light to undress. He lifts one hand slightly and I go to him, still in my underwear.

"Off," he whispers. He turns his head and coughs, the harsh, rude sound of a straw in an almost empty glass.

I take everything off and climb into the bed, trying not to press against him, now that even the sheets seem to hurt him.

"Did you?"

I slide closer to him until we are face-to-face and I kiss his dry lips and feel the small bumps and cracks around his mouth.

"Yes, I found him, the one I told you about. The big one. He was getting off work early, just as I got there. I didn't even have to wait."

Max closes his eyes and I put his hand on top of my leg.

"It was so dark we didn't go to the park. We went to a motel. There was very tacky red wallpaper and the bed was a huge heart with a red velvet bedspread."

"Route 68," he says.

"That one. Remember that big bed? And the headboard with the little posts, the handholds?"

I move his hand up and down my leg, very gently.

"He undressed me, Max. He knelt down and took off my shoes and then he laid me on the bed and undressed me. He was still in his suit."

"Suit?" Max whispered.

"His work clothes, I mean. Not a suit. He left the light on and he began to kiss me all over but every time I tried to touch him he'd put my hands down. He wouldn't let me touch him until later."

Max moves his head a little to nod and I prop his pillows up.

"He kissed the insides of my thighs and the backs of my legs and then he kissed my back for a very long time and when he turned me over he was undressed. And he pulled me up to him, about two feet in the air and then he threw us both down on the bed and he came inside me and he just kept coming and coming at me until I started to cry and then we got under the covers and we both cried, until we fell asleep."

I lay my wet face next to Max's and listen for his breathing.

"It was the best, Max. Nothing in my life was ever like that. Do you hear me? Nothing in my life was ever like that."

JOYCE CAROL OATES

The Radio Astronomer

There was this old professor emeritus from the college, in his late eighties, who'd had a stroke and needed a live-in nurse so I was hired, had a nice tidy little room down the hall from the old man's bedroom in one of those big brick houses near the college and the days were routine mostly but sometimes at night he'd wake up not knowing where he was and get excited and want to go home so I'd say gently, You *are* home, Professor Ewald, I am Lilian here to care for you, let me help you back to bed? — and he'd stare at me half blind with his sad runny eyes like egg yolks, his lips quivering, not remembering me exactly but knowing why I was there and he should cooperate if he didn't want things to get worse. Usually they cooperate, a stroke victim has a memory like a dream I suppose of how things were at the time of the collapse and at the hospital, anything is better than that so they cooperate. Professor Ewald should have been in a nursing home by then but that was between him and his children (grown-up children older than me, one of them a professor himself in Chicago), none of my business for sure. I hate those places, hospitals yet more where it's forms and procedure and people bossing you around and spying on you, I didn't blame the Professor for trying to live in his house as long as he could, he'd lived here he said for fifty years! — and that's all elderly people want, to live at home as long as possible, as long as there's money for it, who can blame them?

Even the smart ones like Professor Ewald who'd been chair of the Astronomy Department at the college and director of the Fine Observatory (as I was told many times, to impress me I suppose, yes I *was* impressed) have this idea their condition is only temporary, they'll be back to their old selves if they hang on, do the therapy and take the medication and have faith. And you tell them that's so, you assure them. That's your job. An old man or woman in a diaper, bars up on their bed like a crib but if they can talk you'll hear they're planning how when they go back home, when they're on their feet again, it's maybe a pet cat out of the kennel, or a golf game with somebody's probably been dead ten years. You never contradict them or scare them, that's your job.

And sometimes they reward you, with nobody else to know. Jewelry, a fancy black-and-gold Parker pen, outright cash. That's just between you and them.

Professor Ewald had his good days and his rough days but all in all he wasn't bad. Except for people not visiting him much he rarely complained. He had old papers he'd sift through, computer printouts with weird signs and equations but I don't believe he could see them that well even with his magnified glasses. He'd work on these papers, he'd talk and fuss to himself, but also for me to overhear, I believe, so I'd know he was *working*. The kind of man he was, even at eighty-six or -seven, it was important for him to be *working*.

He'd tell me how he'd been a radio astronomer for more than sixty years, did I know what a radio astronomer was, I said I knew what an astronomer was, a man looking at stars through a big telescope, so he explained he hadn't just looked but listened too, radio waves meaning radiation not radio stations as on earth and some of them coming from billions of light-years away . . . but I have to admit I wasn't listening to every word, and the words I did hear like *light-year* I did not comprehend, because you can't, no point in trying, it's like you're the dead wife or husband to them, the children who never stay long when they visit, or don't visit at all, they aren't really talking to *you*. Professor Ewald had a way of talking, too, like he was lecturing, in a large room, when his voice lifted in a certain way I knew he was making a joke, yes and he *was* funny sometimes, I could see he'd been a popular lecturer so all I needed to do was laugh, nod and laugh and say, Is that so! or, My goodness! while I helped him dress or undress, onto the toilet or up from it, in or out of the tub (where we had a wooden stool he could sit on and I'd operate the shower and lather him up real good). On sunny days he'd be so eager to sit in the sun porch he'd walk there himself just using his walker, he'd sit in his chair dozing and listening to the classical music station on the radio, wake up thinking he'd heard some other kind of noise, static, or interference, or maybe a telephone ringing, but no it was nothing most of the time, No Professor: nothing, don't be upset.

Lilian, I am not upset, he said, enunciating each syllable as if I was the one hard of hearing and not him, but smiling to show he wasn't angry,—I am *hopeful*.

I'd been in the hire of Professor Emeritus Ewald for maybe seven weeks when one day, a cold November day but the sun was wonderful and warm streaming through the windows in the sun porch, he opened his eyes from what I'd thought was a nap, and said, When did you come here, and what is your name? so I told him, I kept on with my knitting unperturbed, for there was nothing hostile in his voice, only questioning. And when will you leave? he asked.

Now I did falter a bit with the needles, then picked up the stitch again and continued. My hands are the kind of hands that must keep busy at all times, even in my sleep I will be dreaming of doing something useful though I am not a nervous woman, and never have been. I said, Professor Ewald, I don't know: I guess I'll be here as long as I'm needed.

That seemed to satisfy him so nothing more was said on the subject.

He got to talking about the sun, now you'd think there wasn't much to be said about such a thing, but he was always one to come out with the darndest things, D'you know, Lilian, the sun we see isn't the actual sun, it takes eight minutes for the sun's rays to get to earth, the sun could be dead and gone and we wouldn't know for eight minutes, and I gave one of my shivery little laughs not glancing up from my knitting, Is that so! — and where would the sun go if it was gone, Professor? but he didn't hear, asking did I know what *lookback time* is, and I said, Well I guess you told me, Professor, but I kinda forgot, so he lectures me on *lookback time* for many minutes, asking did I realize the stars I saw in the night sky were all in *lookback time* meaning they weren't really there, long dead and gone, so I laughed and said, Whew! that's one on me I guess, *I* never knew any better! though he'd told me all this before, or things like it. His voice went sharp asking what was so funny, why did I think that was funny, and I saw how he was looking at me with those runny yellow eyes that had a kind of light in them, and I remembered how I'd been told the old man had been pretty well known at one time, what you'd call famous in his line of work, a long time ago, and I felt my face burn, yes I was embarrassed, mumbling, Oh it's so hard to think about things like that, it almost hurts a person's brain to think about things like that, and I thought this would let me off the hook but Professor Emeritus just stares at me and says, Yes but can't you for God's sake *try*.

Like all his life he'd been dealing with the ignorant like me, and he was weary of it.

Yet: his left hand was all stiff and bent like a bird's talons, his left leg dragged and the left side of his face fell away like collapsed putty from the right side, what of *that*, I wanted to ask him, Professor Emeritus you're so damned smart.

But always when they try to boss you, or turn mean and sarcastic, you can hear the pleading beneath, the voice quavering. No purpose then in getting angry.

Yes and you know you'll outlive them, too. No purpose in getting the least little-bit angry.

So things changed then, like a day that starts out warm then the temperature drops. That afternoon he was excitable and wouldn't take his medication, and refused to lie down for his nap, and the evening meal was all sulking and childish-nasty behavior (like spitting out a mouthful of mushy food) but I didn't let any of it bother me, I never do, it's my job. Then around seven-thirty there was a telephone call that was a wrong number, just my luck damn it, that set him raving saying it had been his daughter but I'd kept him from her, and so on and so forth, you know how they get. I reasoned with him suggesting why didn't he just call his daughter back, I'd make the call for him, but he just fumed and fussed talking to himself, then at bedtime he said, Nurse I'm sorry, I could see he'd forgotten my name and I smiled assuring him it was all right but after we got him undressed and about to climb into bed he started crying, he took hold of my wrist and started crying, I should say here that I do not like to be touched by anybody, no I do not, but I tried not to show it listening to the old man rave how they made him retire at the peak of his powers, they promised him time on the telescope, all the time he wanted, they lied to him refusing him time, this was the very radio telescope he'd been the one to design and helped raise funds to make, his enemies were jealous of his reputation and fearful that his new research would refute theirs . . . he'd spent eleven years after his retirement until he'd gotten sick listening for signals, unnatural patterns that might mean radio communication from another galaxy, did I know what that meant? and I said yes, I was kind of impatient wanting to get him to bed, I didn't like the way he was squeezing my wrist in his skinny, strong fingers like claws, I said yes maybe, and he said, spittle showing on his lips, There is no more important work for science than the search for other intelligence in the universe, time is running out for us, we must know we are not alone, and I said, Yes Professor, oh yes trying to humor the old man, helping him into bed, except he kept on saying how many years he'd wasted sifting through other men's data, now he had a direct approach using his own powers with no gadgets interfering, one night last year he'd picked up a clear and orderly signal *dot dash dot dot dash dot dot dot dash dot dot dot dot dash dot dot dot dot dot dash dot* from somewhere in the Hyades, in the constellation Taurus, billions of light-years away, an unmistakable radio communication not noise but before he could record it static interfered, and on other occasions when he'd heard signals from distant galaxies they were interrupted by static, a terrible buzzing and ringing in his head. I said, Yes Professor it sure is a shame, but maybe you should take your medication? try to sleep? and he said, Nurse you could go to the newspapers with the story, it would be the story of the century, you could help all of mankind if you just would, and I finally pried his fingers off my wrist, I do not appreciate being touched saying, as if the old fool had been joking with me and not bawling like a baby, Yes Professor but if there's life on other planets like in the movies how d'you know they might not be evil, maybe they'd come to earth and eat us all up? and he just looked at me, blinking, and said, stammering, But — if there was intelligent life elsewhere it would confirm our hope, and I said, helping him in bed and settling him back on his pillows, Hope of what? and he said, Mankind's hope of — not being alone, and I said, with a little snort, Some of us, we're not alone enough.

And switched off the light.

And that would have been the end of it for one night I thought, except I was in my bed later and on the edge of falling asleep, like slipping over a ravine, that feeling you have more precious than any even sex, even love, for you can live without sex and love, as I have done for half my life, but you sure can't live without sleep, and there's a crashing noise in the Professor's bedroom down the hall and I get out of bed and grab my bathrobe and run in hoping he hasn't had another attack, I switched on the light and the weirdest thing — there's Professor Ewald in his pajamas crouching in a corner of the room beyond his bed, he'd knocked over his aluminum bedside stand, he was shielding his head from me screaming, You're death aren't you! You're death! go away! I want to go home! and I stood there pretending not to see him, out of breath myself and excited but maintaining calm as you must do, tying my bathrobe snug around me, you learn to do with them like they are children, like it's a game, hide-and-seek and the old man is peeping at me through his fingers whimpering and begging, No! no! you're death! no! I want to go home! so I pretended to be surprised seeing him back there in the corner, and smoothed his pillows for him, and said, Professor, you *are* home.

STEVEN MILLHAUSER

The Princess, the Dwarf, and the Dungeon

The *dungeon.* The dungeon is said to be located so far beneath the lowest subterranean chambers of the castle that a question naturally arises: is the dungeon part of the castle itself? Other underground chambers, such as the storage cellars, the torture chamber, and the prison cells used for detention during trial, are merely the lowest in an orderly progression of descending chambers, and maintain a clear and so to speak reasonable relation to the upper levels of the castle. But the dungeon lies so far beneath the others that it seems part of the dark world below, like the place under the mountain where ogres breed from the blood of murdered children.

The castle. The castle lies on a steep cliff on the far side of the river, three hundred feet above the water. In bright sunlight the castle seems to shine out from the darker rock of the cliff and to thrust its towers gaily into the blue sky, but when the air darkens with clouds the castle draws the darkness into itself and becomes nearly black against the stormy heavens. From our side of the river we can see the Princess's tower, the battlements of the outer wall, including the vertical stone spikes on the merlons, and two arched gates of darker stone. Beneath the Princess's tower lies her walled garden. We cannot see the garden walls or the garden itself, with its paths of checkered stone, its turf-covered benches, and its shady bower of trelliswork sheltering two couches covered in crimson silk. We cannot see the courtiers walking in the Court of the Three Fountains. We cannot see the Prince's oriel overlooking the slate roof of the chapel, we cannot see the row of marble pillars three of which are said to come from the palace of Charlemagne at Ingelheim, we can only imagine the hall, the brewhouse, the bakehouse, the stables, the orchard, the park with its great alleys of shade trees, the dark forest stretching back and back and back.

* * *

Tales of the Princess. There was once a beautiful Princess, whose skin was whiter than alabaster, whose hair was brighter than beaten gold, and whose virtue was celebrated throughout the land. One day she married a Prince, who was as handsome as she was beautiful; they loved each other entirely; and yet within a year their happiness turned to despair. Some held the Prince to blame, saying he was proud and jealous by nature, but others accused the Princess of a secret weakness. By this they meant nothing less than her virtue itself. For her virtue, which no one questioned, made her secure against the attentions of admirers, and prevented her from imagining even the possibility of unfaithfulness. Because of her deep love for the Prince and her knowledge of her own steadfastness, she failed to fortify herself with haughtiness, reserve, and a sense of formidable propriety. Instead, while acting always within the strict constraints of court etiquette, she was unaffected in manner, generous in spirit, and open to friendship with members of her husband's intimate circle. Moreover, her love for the Prince led her to follow closely all matters at court, in order that she might understand all that concerned him and advise him sagely. It was therefore in no way unusual that she should take an interest in the stranger who arrived one night on a richly caparisoned horse, and who quickly won the friendship of the Prince by virtue of his nobility of bearing, his boldness of spirit, his thirst for knowledge, and his gift of ardent speech, but who nevertheless, saying only that he was a margrave, and that he came from a distant land, bore on his escutcheon the word *Infelix:* the Wretched One.

The two stairways. The stairways are circular and are composed of heavy blocks of stone that wind about a stone newel. Both stairways spiral to the right, in order to give the advantage to the defender, who with his right hand can wield his sword easily in the concavity of the round wall, while the attacker on the lower step is cramped by the newel's outward curve. One stairway winds up past slit-like openings that give higher and higher glimpses of the little river, the little town with its double wall, the little mills along the riverbank, until at last it reaches the chamber of the Princess at the top of the tower. The other stairway begins in a subterranean corridor beneath the torture chamber and winds down and immeasurably down, in a darkness so thick that it feels palpable as cloth or stone. After a time the steps begin to crumble, sprouting black vegetation; gradually the outlines of the steps become blurred, as if the reason for steps has been forgotten. This stairway, which some imagine to narrow slowly until there is space only for the rats, descends to the dungeon.

The window recess. The Prince, who was often closeted for long hours with his councilors in order to discuss a pressing matter of territorial jurisdiction, was grateful to the Princess for attending to his new friend. The Princess, accompanied by two ladies-in-waiting, walked with the margrave in the walled garden beneath her tower, or sat with him in a small receiving chamber attached to her private rooms in the great hall. The small chamber had a pair of tall lancet windows set in a wide recess with stone window seats along the sides. The many-paned windows looked down upon wooded hills and a distant twist of river. One day as the Princess stood at the window, looking out at the far river, while the margrave with his sharp brown beard and amethyst-studded mantle sat back against the angle formed by the stone seat and the windowed wall, the Princess was startled from her revery by the sound of suddenly advancing footsteps. She turned quickly, raising a hand to her throat, and saw the Prince standing in the arched doorway. "You startled me, my lord," she said, as the margrave remained motionless in shadow. The dark stranger in the corner of the window seat, the startled, flushed wife, the stillness of the sky through the clear panes of glass, all this caused a suspicion to cross the Prince's mind. He banished the thought instantly and advanced laughing toward the pair at the window.

The riverside. Directly to the west of the town, on the bank of the river between the copper mill and a grist mill, lies the broadest of our town meadows. To reach it we must first cross the dry moat on a bridge made of oak planks, which is let down every morning by chains from within the gate-opening in the outer wall, and is raised every night so that it fits back into the opening and seals the space shut. The meadow is supplied with shade trees, mostly lime and oak; a path runs along the river, and there are fountains carved with the heads of devils and monkeys. Here on holidays and summer Sundays the townsfolk play bowls, wrestle, dance, eat sausages, stroll along the river, or lie on the bank. Here wealthy merchants and their wives mingle with pork butchers, bricklayers, rope makers, laundresses, apprentice blacksmiths, journeyman carpet weavers, servants, day laborers. Here at any moment, throwing back our heads to laugh, or shifting our eyes slightly, we can see, through the sun-shot branches of the shade trees, the shimmering river, the sheer cliff, the high castle shining in the sun.

Thoughts in sun and shade. As the Prince walked in the shady park, stepping through circles and lozenges of sunlight that made his dark velvet shoes, embroidered with gold quatrefoils, seem to glow, in his thoughts he kept seeing the Princess turn suddenly from the window with her hand on her throat and a flush on her cheek. The persistence of the image disturbed and shamed him. He felt that by seeing the image he was committing a great wrong against his wife, whose virtue he had never doubted, and against himself, who admired forthrightness and disdained all things secretive, sly, and hidden away. The Prince knew that if anyone had so much as hinted at unfaithfulness in the Princess, he would without hesitation have cut out the false accuser's tongue; in the violence of the thought he recognized his inner disorder. He was proud of the frankness between him and the Princess, to whom he revealed his most intimate thoughts; in concealing this thought, of which he was ashamed, he seemed to himself to have fallen from a height. Walking alone along the avenue of the park, through lozenges of sunlight and stretches of shade, the Prince reproached himself bitterly for betraying his high idea of himself. It seemed to him suddenly that his brown-bearded friend with the amethyst-studded mantle was far worthier than he of his wife's affection. Thus it came about that in the very act of self-reproach the Prince nourished his secret jealousy.

The tower. From dawn to dusk she sits in her tower. We catch glimpses of what appears to be her face in the tower window, but isn't it likely that we are seeing only flashes of sunlight or shadows of passing birds on the high windowpanes? In all other ways she is invisible, for our solemn poets fix her in words of high, formal praise: her hair is more radiant than the sun, her breasts are whiter than swansdown or new-fallen snow. We saw her once, riding through the market square on a festival day, sitting on her white horse with black ostrich plumes, and we were shocked by the gleam of raven-black hair under the azure hood. But in the long days of midsummer, when the rooftops shimmer in the light of the sun as if they are about to dissolve, her raven hair is gradually replaced by the yellow hair of the poets, until the sight of her astride the white horse seems only a midday dream. High in her tower, from dawn to dark she paces in her grief, and who can say whether even her sorrow is her own?

Legends of the river. The river breeds its own stories, which we hear as children and never forget: the fisherman and the mermaid, the king in the hill, the maid of the rock. As adults we recall these legends fondly, even wistfully, for we no longer believe in them as we once did, but not every tale of the river passes into the realm of cherished, harmless things. Such is the tale of the escape of the prisoner: the splash, the waiting boat, the voyage, and there, already visible in the distance, the flames consuming the town and the castle, the blackness of the sky, the redness of the river.

Infelix. The Princess, who had been startled by the Prince as she gazed out the window in the recess of her private chamber, gave the incident no further thought. Instead she continued to think of the margrave's story, which he had revealed to her one day while they were walking in the garden, and about which she had been brooding when the Prince interrupted her revery. The margrave had told how his younger brother, secretly lusting after the margrave's bride, had stolen the girl and locked her in a tower guarded by forty knights. Upon learning that the margrave was raising an army to free his bride, the brother sent him a jeweled casket; when the margrave opened the casket he saw the severed head of his bride. Half crazed with grief and fury, the margrave led his knights against his brother, at last slaying him with his sword, cutting off his head, and razing the castle. But the margrave could not rest. Haunted by his bride, unable to bear his empty life, he fled from that accursed country, seeking adventure and death — death, which disdained him — and coming at last to the castle of the Prince. The Princess, pained by the margrave's tale, did not try to console him; and now each day, when the Princess dismissed her ladies, the margrave spoke to her of his slain bride, whom he had loved ardently; for though he had vowed never to speak of her, yet speaking eased his heart a little.

The town. Our town lies on the lower slope of a hill that goes down to the river. The town extends from the bank of the river to a point partway up the hill where the slope becomes steeper and the vineyards begin. Above the vineyards is a thick wood, which lies within our territorial domain and harbors in its darkness a scattering of sandstone quarries, charcoal kilns, clearings yellow with rye, and ovens for manufacturing glass. Except for the grist mills, the saw mills, the copper mill, and the bathhouse, which stand on the bank of the river, our town is entirely enclosed by two meandering walls: an outer wall, which is twenty feet high and eight feet thick, with towers that rise ten feet higher than the battlements, and a vast inner wall, which is forty feet high and twelve feet thick, with towers that rise fifteen feet higher than the battlements. Between the two walls lies a broad trench covered with grass, where deer graze and where we hold crossbow matches and running contests. Should an enemy penetrate the defenses of the outer wall, he must face the defenses of the towering inner wall, while standing in the trench as at the bottom of a trap, where we rain upon him arrows and gunshot, rocks large enough to crush a horse, rivers of molten lead. Flush against the outer wall stands a dry moat, broad and very deep, which an enemy must cross in order to reach our outermost defenses. Although we have enjoyed peace for many years, guards patrol both walls ceaselessly. Inside the walls, steep-gabled houses with roofs of red tile line the winding stone-paved streets, carts rumble in the market square, fruit sellers cry from their stalls, from the shops of the iron workers and the coppersmiths comes a continual din of hammers, servants hurry back and forth in the courtyards of the patricians' houses, in the shade of the buttresses of the Church of St. Margaret a beggar watches a pig lie down in the sun.

The pear tree. The Princess was quick to sense a change in the Prince, who looked at her strangely, often seemed on the verge of saying something, and lay restlessly beside her at night. She waited for him to unburden himself, but when he continued to keep his mind in shadow, she determined to speak. One morning when she and the Prince were walking in the walled garden, where she had lately walked with the margrave, the Prince stopped beside a pear tree to pick a piece of fruit. With a melancholy smile he handed the yellow pear to his wife. The Princess took the pear and thanked him, but said that she would like to share it with her lord, reminding him that she was not only his wife, but his dearest friend, who asked no higher pleasure than to share his joys and sorrows, and to ease the burdens of his heart. The Prince, who wished only to conceal the ignoble secret of his suspicion, felt a motion of irritation toward his wife, who by her words had put him in the position of having to deceive her, and he replied coldly that he had picked the pear not for himself, but for her alone; and turning his face away he added that he had cause to believe that his new friend, who was also her friend, had dishonest intentions toward him. The Princess, though hurt by his cold refusal of the pear, was nonetheless pleased that he had unburdened himself at last. She replied that she knew not who had been trying to divide the Prince from his friend, but for her part, she could assure her lord that the margrave was as trustworthy as he was honest, and as loyal as he was trustworthy, and that he was entirely devoted to the Prince and to all that concerned him. The Prince, ashamed of his suspicion, convinced of his wife's honor, yet hearing in her words a disturbing ardor, repeated sternly that he had cause to doubt the stranger, and wished to request of the Princess a small service. Though stung by his tone, the Princess put herself instantly at his disposal. Plucking a second pear roughly from the tree, the Prince asked the Princess to test the admirable devotion of his friend by offering to him what was most dear to the Prince in all the world. To put matters plainly, he desired the Princess to go to the margrave in his bedchamber that night, to lie down beside him, and to report the outcome to the Prince the next morning. In that way, and in that way alone, he hoped to be able to dispel the doubt that had arisen in his mind. The Princess, who all this while had been holding the first pear in her hand, looked at the Prince as if she had been struck in the face. The Prince watched the yellow pear fall from her long fingers and strike the ground, where it rolled over and revealed its split skin. Her look, like that of someone frightened in the dark, made the Prince taste the full horror of his moral fall, even as it sharpened the sting of his suspicion.

Patricians. The patricians of our town are powerful men with broad shoulders, keen eyes, and a touch of disdain about the lips. In their steep-gabled houses with arcaded ground floors and three upper stories, furnished well but without ostentation, one sees handsome door panels, table centerpieces of chased silver, and heavy paintings of themselves and their wives: the patricians in their broad berets and their dark robes trimmed with fur, the wives in plain bodices with velvet-trimmed sleeves. From their paintings the patricians stare out fearless as princes. Indeed, in times of danger they leave their counting houses and their seats in the Council Chamber, put on sturdy armor forged by our master armorers, mount their proud horses, and lead well-armed citizens in maneuver and battle. The patricians are wealthier and more powerful than the nobles of the castle, against whom they have relentlessly asserted their rights as free citizens, thereby further weakening the always declining power of the Prince. And yet these keen-eyed merchants, in the pauses of their day, will raise their heads for a moment, as if lost in thought; or striding along the slope of an upper street, suddenly they will stare out between the walls of two houses at the river below, the sunny cliff, the high castle. Some of our patricians purchase for their wives cloaks modeled after the cloaks of court ladies, and hang on their walls ceremonial swords with jeweled hilts. We who are neither nobles nor patricians, we who are of the town but watchful, observe these manifestations without surprise.

The keeper of the dungeon. The keeper of the dungeon, whom no one has ever seen, is said to dwell in a dark cave or cell beside the winding lower stair, twenty-two steps above the dungeon. The keeper is said to have thick, matted hair so stiff that it is brittle as straw, a flat nose, and a single tooth, shaped like the head of a crossbow arrow; he is so stooped that his face is pressed against his knees. In one hand he clutches, even when asleep, the heavy key to the dungeon, which over the years has impressed its shape in the flesh of his palm like a brand burned into the flesh of a criminal. His sole duty is to open the iron door of the dungeon and to push in the iron bowl of gruel and the iron cup of brackish water delivered from above. The keeper, whom some describe as an ogre, a one-eyed giant, or a three-headed beast, is said to have a single weakness: he is fond of small, bright objects, like glass beads, gold buttons, and pieces of colored foil bound between disks of clear glass, all of which he places in an iron box concealed behind a loose stone in the wall beside his bed of straw. It is by manipulating this weakness that the dwarf is able to work his will upon the keeper, who in all other respects is ruthless and inflexible.

The margrave's bedchamber. The Princess, who not only loved the Prince deeply but had been raised in the habit of unquestioning obedience to a husband's slightest wish, did not for a moment think of disobeying him. Instead she thought only of persuading him to take back a request that had been born of some unpleasant rumor in the court, and could lead only to unhappiness for her, for his friend, and for himself. When the Prince proved adamant, the Princess lowered her eyes, rose naked from the bed, and sorrowfully, in the chill night air, drew on her long chemise ornamented with gold, her close-fitting underrobe, and her high-waisted tunic with wide sleeves, all the while hoping to be commanded to stop; and over her tight-bound hair she drew her thick-jeweled net of gold wire, so that not a single hair was visible. Then with a beseeching look at her lord, who would not meet her eyes, she betook herself to the margrave's bedchamber, where by the trembling light of her candle she crept fearfully to the curtained bed, parted the curtains no more than a finger's breadth, and looked in. The margrave lay fast asleep on his back with his head turned to one side. The Princess extinguished the candle and, offering up a silent prayer, slipped into the bed between the margrave and the curtain. Anxiously she lay awake, with wide-open eyes, starting whenever the margrave stirred in his sleep, yet hoping that he might not wake and find her there. But as she lay thinking of the change in the Prince, and his cold words beside the pear tree, her heart misgave her and she fell to weeping. The margrave, wakened by the noise, was startled to find a woman in his bed; and feeling sharp desire, he asked who it was that so honored him in his bedchamber, meanwhile reaching out his hand to touch her. But when he heard the voice of the Princess, he drew back his hand, which had grazed her shoulder, as if he had felt the blade of a sword. She said in a strained voice that she had come to offer him companionship in the night; she hoped she had not disturbed his sleep by her visit. Now the margrave loved the Prince, and revered the noble Princess above all women; and a sorrow came over him, even as he felt desire in the dark. He replied that he was more honored by her visit than by a gift of gold; and because he honored her above all women, he would remember this night until his dying day. Yet he thought it most fitting that she should return to the Prince, her lord and husband, and not trouble herself about one who longed only to serve the Prince and do her honor. The Princess was well pleased with this speech; but mindful of the Prince's cruel command, that she test the margrave in the night, she said that she hoped he did not find her so foul that he would wish to banish her from his bed. The margrave replied that far from finding her foul, he found her of all women the most fair; and so far was he from wishing to banish her from his bed, that he would abandon the bed to her, and lie down on the floor of his chamber, in order to keep watch over her rest. The Princess thanked him for his thoughtfulness, but said she could not dispossess him of his bed, and urged him to remain; whereupon the margrave graciously agreed, saying only that he revered her rest as much as he revered the Princess herself; and drawing forth the sharp sword that he kept always beside him, he placed it between them on the bed, pledging to protect her from all harm in the night. With that he wished her a good night, and drew himself down under the coverlet, and feigned sleep. The Princess, well pleased with his answer, tested him no more, but lay anxiously beside him until the first graying of the dark, when she returned to the Prince, who lay restlessly awaiting her. She reported all that had passed in the night, praising the delicacy of the margrave, who had not wished to injure her feelings even as he revealed his devotion to the Prince, and assuring her lord that his friend had been slandered by evil tongues. The Prince, although soothed by her account, was troubled that his wife had lain all night by the side of the margrave, even at the Prince's own bidding; and whereas before this he had been haunted by the image of his wife in the window recess, now he was tormented by the image of his wife in the bed of the margrave, offering her breasts to his greedy fingers, rubbing her legs against him, and crying out in pleasure. For the Prince so desired his wife that he could not believe any man capable of resisting her, if she offered herself in the night. Wherefore he thought she was deceiving him in either of two ways: for either she had lain with the margrave, and pleasured him in the dark, or else she had not gone to him, as she had said. Therefore the Prince replied harshly that though the margrave had not betrayed him, yet he could not be certain whether it was from loyalty or sheer surprise, to find the wife of his friend beside him in the dark; and now that the Princess had shown a willingness to deceive her husband, it was necessary for her to pay a second visit to the margrave, and test him in his full knowledge. To this the Princess replied coldly that she would do all that her lord demanded; only, she would sooner plunge a dagger into her heart, than return to the bed of the margrave.

The reflection. During three days a year, at the height of summer, the position of the sun and the position of the cliff combine to permit the castle to be reflected in the river. It is said that by staring at the reflection one can see inside the castle, which reveals the precise disposition of its arched doorways, high halls, and secret chambers, the pattern of hidden stairways, the shadows cast by flagons and bunches of grapes on abandoned banquet tables, and there, high in the tower, the Princess pacing wearily, while far below, in the depths of the immaculate reflection, so deep that it is beneath the river itself, a shadow stirs in the corner of the dungeon.

Town and castle. Long ago, in the darkness of an uncertain and perhaps legendary past, a Prince dwelt within our walls, in a fortress where the merchants' hall now stands. One day he decided to build a great castle on the cliff on the far side of the river. The decision of the Prince to move outside our walls has sometimes been interpreted as the desire of an ambitious lord to build an impregnable fortress in an unstable world, but a respected school of historians has argued that the change of residence occurred precisely when the power of the patricians was growing at the expense of the Prince, who after his move was expressly forbidden by the Council to build a fortified home within the town walls, although he continued to receive an increasingly ritual homage as lord of the town. A second school, while accepting the historical explanation, sees in the move a deeper stratagem. The Prince, so the argument goes, sensing the loss of his power, removed himself from the town and placed himself above it in order to exercise over our people the power of imagination and dream: remote but visible, no longer subject to patrician pressure, the Prince and his castle would enter into the deepest recesses of the people's spirit and become ineradicable, immortal. A minor branch of this school accepts the dream explanation but attributes it to a different cause. They argue that our ancestors first settled on the far side of the river, in the shadow of the castle, and only gradually withdrew to our side, in order to be able to look across the river and dream continually of nobler, more passionate lives.

The Prince's doubts increase. Now nightly the Prince drove his wife to the margrave's chamber, and restlessly awaited her return; and every morning the Princess returned to say that the margrave had remained steadfast. The Prince, tormented by the growing certainty that he was being deceived, and exasperated by the hope born of her daily assurances, longed for proof of her faithlessness, in order to ease his heart of uncertainty. One night, sorrowing alone, he remembered suddenly a time before his life had taken a crooked turn. He and the Princess were walking in the park, in the avenue of acacias, and something he had said made her laugh aloud; and the sound of that laughter, and the sunlight pouring down through the acacia leaves onto the graveled path, and the Princess's throat, half in sun and half in trembling shade, seemed as remote and irrecoverable as his own childhood. At that moment he saw with terrible clarity what he had done. He vowed to beg forgiveness on his knees and not to rise until he was permitted to return to his lost paradise. But even as he imagined the Princess laughing in the sun and shade of the acacia path, he saw her hand rise to her throat as she turned from the window, where a devil with a sharp beard and amethyst jewels in his mantle leaned motionless against the shadowed stone.

Scarbo. Among the many devoted servants of the Prince was a dwarf, whose name was Scarbo. He was a proud little man, with stern features and a small pointed beard; he dressed in the latest fashion, was a master of court etiquette and of all questions concerning precedence, and was noted for his disdainful glance, his penetrating intelligence, and his unswerving devotion to the Prince. Once, after a courtier had humiliated the little man by picking him up and tossing him lightly in the air, while others had watched with smiles and laughter, Scarbo lay on his bed in silent fury for two nights and two days. On the third night he crept into the bedchamber of the offending courtier and plunged his little sharp sword into the sleeper's throat. After that he cut off both of the dead man's hands and laid them with interlocked fingers on the coverlet. The Prince forgave his dwarf, but sentenced him to a month in prison; some say he was confined in the dungeon itself, and absorbed its darkness into his soul. But if his proud and disdainful nature was immediately apparent, earning him an uneasy respect never far from ridicule, Scarbo's most remarkable feature was his delicacy of feeling—for he possessed a highly developed and almost feminine sensitivity to the faintest motions of another person's mood. This unusual development in the realm of feeling, born perhaps of an outsider's habit of extreme watchfulness, increased his danger as an enemy and his value as a trusted servant and councilor. Combing his beard in his private chamber, handing the Prince a goblet of ruby wine, listening at night to the footsteps of the Princess moving past his door toward the margrave's chamber, the dwarf knew that it was only a matter of time before the Prince would summon him.

Stories. Our town takes pride in the practical and useful arts. We are well known for our door panels and brass hinges, our stove tiles and weathervanes, our tomb effigies and stone crucifixes, whereas our literature rarely rises above the level of doggerel verses, carnival plays, and dull philosophical poems in monotonous meters and rigid rhymes. Our imagination is far better expressed in the famous work of our metal masters, above all in the brilliant productions of our church bell casters, our bladesmiths, our makers of spice mills, astrolabes, and articulated figures for clocks. And yet it would be a mistake to think of us as entirely deficient in the art of the word. Although we are practical citizens, who keep our accounts strictly and go to bed early, we have all listened to tales in the nursery, tales that are never written down but may appear suddenly in distorted or fragmentary form in a song heard in a tavern or at a carnival play; and foremost among these stories of our childhood are tales of the castle. The same tales are told by minstrels in the courtyards of inns, and sung by peasants in the fields and villages of our territorial domain. In another form the tales show themselves in the early parts of our chronicles, where legend and fact are interwoven, and many episodes have been joined together by unknown hands and written down on sheets of parchment, which are bound in ivory and metal on wood, purchased by wealthy merchants, and read by their wives. Such stories, reaching far down into the deepest past of our town, attach themselves likewise to the castle of the present day, so that the actual dwellers in the castle come to seem nothing but passing actors asked to perform the changeless gestures of an eternal play. Thus it comes about that, although we are practical and commercial by nature, we too have our stories.

The summons. One morning after a night of shattering dreams the Prince summoned his dwarf to a private chamber and informed the little man that he desired a service of him. Scarbo bowed, noting once again the signs of change in his master, and saying that he desired only to be of service to his Prince. With a show of impatience the Prince said that of late he had been preoccupied with pressing affairs, that he feared the Princess was too much alone, and that he desired his dwarf to spend more time in her company, attending to her needs, listening to her thoughts, and serving her in every way; and he further desired that he should report to the Prince each morning, concerning the state of her happiness. The dwarf understood instantly that he was being asked to spy on the Princess. His pride thrilled at the gravity of the mission, for the Prince was in effect conspiring with his dwarf against his own wife, but Scarbo recognized a danger: the Prince, while desiring evidence against the Princess, would not necessarily welcome the proof he sought, nor be grateful to his spy for easing his way into his wife's confidence and ferreting out her secrets. It would not do to be overzealous in the performance of his duty. Wariness was all.

On vagueness and precision. It is precisely because of our ignorance that we see across the river with such precision. We know the precise carvings on the capital of each stone pillar and the precise history of each soul: they are transparent to our understanding. On our side of the river, even the most familiar lanes bear surprises around well-known bends; we see only a certain distance into the hearts of our wives and friends, before darkness and uncertainty begin. Perhaps, after all, this is the lure of legend: not the dreamy twilight of the luxuriating fancy, in love with all that is misty and half-glimpsed, but the sharp clarity forbidden by our elusive lives.

A walk in the garden. One sunny afternoon the Princess, who had been walking in the courtyard, dismissed her ladies-in-waiting at the garden gate and entered her garden alone. The walls were higher than her head; paths of checkered stone ran between beds of white, red, and yellow flowers; at one end stood a small orchard of pear, apple, quince, and plum trees. In the center of the garden, surrounded by a tall hedge with a wicker gate, stood the Princess's bower, shaped like a pavilion and composed of trelliswork covered with vines. The Princess, in her azure tunic and her heart-shaped headdress, walked with bowed head among the fruit trees of the orchard, raising her eyes at the slightest noise and looking swiftly about. After a time she began to walk along the paths of checkered stone between the flowerbeds, passing two turf-covered benches, an octagon of white and red roses, and a white jasper three-tiered fountain with a column surmounted by a unicorn. At the central hedge she hesitated and seemed to listen; then she pushed open the gate and entered, bending low under a trellised arch. In the green shade of her bower sat two couches covered in crimson silk. Scarbo, seated in the corner of a couch, at once stood up and bowed. The Princess sat down stiffly on the couch opposite and stared as if harshly at the dwarf, who met her gaze and did not turn his eyes aside. "I cannot do what you propose," she began, in a toneless voice. The dwarf, rigid with attention, listened patiently. He was well pleased with his progress.

A lack of something. Although ours is a flourishing town — and we flourish, according to some, precisely to the extent that the inhabitants of the castle have declined in power, and serve a largely symbolic or representative function — we nevertheless feel a lack of something. Our metal artisans are admired far and wide, our sturdy houses with their steep gables and oak window frames fill the eye with delight, beyond the walls our fields and vineyards overflow with ripeness. Our church steeples rise proudly into the sky, and toll out the hours on great bells cast by masters. In fact, it is not too much to say that our lives pass in a harmony and tranquility that are the envy and admiration of the region. Nor is ours a dull tranquility, stifling all that is joyful or dark; for not only are we engaged in vigorous lives, but we are human beings like all human beings, we know the joys and sorrows that come to human hearts. And yet it remains true that, now and then, we feel a lack of something. We do not know what it is, this thing that we lack. We know only that on certain summer afternoons, when the too-blue sky stretches on and on, or on warm twilights when the blackbird cries from the hill, a restlessness comes over us, an inner dissatisfaction. Like children we grow suddenly angry for no reason, we want something. Then we turn to the castle, high on the other shore, and all at once we feel a savage quickening. With a kind of violence our hearts exult. For across the sun-sparkling river, there on the far shore, we feel a heightened sense of things, and we dare for a moment to cry out our forbidden desire: for exaltation, for devastation, for revelation.

The four reasons. Because of his high gifts in the realm of feeling, the dwarf understood something about the Prince that the Prince himself did not fully understand. The dwarf understood that the Prince, despite great wealth, a beautiful and virtuous wife, devoted friends, and a life that inspired the praise of all who knew him, bore within him a secret weakness: a desire for immense suffering. It was as if the experience of so much good fortune had created in the Prince a craving in the opposite direction. He had at last contrived to satisfy this desire by means of his wife, as though wishing to strike at the deepest source of his own happiness; and it was Scarbo's role to confirm the Prince's darkest suspicion and present him with the suffering he craved. The danger lay in the uncertainty of the Prince's gratitude for such a service. Scarbo, radically set apart from the court and indeed from humankind by the accident of his diminutive stature, was a sharp observer of human nature; he understood that the Prince was furious at himself for being suspicious of his wife, and above all for inviting his dwarf to spy on her. The Prince's sense that he had done something unclean might at any moment cause him to strike out violently at the instrument of his uncleanliness, namely, the dwarf. It was therefore essential that Scarbo not bear witness directly against the Princess, even though he crept nightly into the margrave's chamber and listened through the closed bedcurtains in order to learn all he could about their lascivious trysts. To Scarbo's surprise — to his bewilderment and anger — the margrave appeared to be innocent. This the dwarf attributed to a deep and still unfathomable design on the part of the margrave, whom he detested as the Prince's former favorite. The Prince would surely have believed a report of lecherous foul play in the margrave's tangled sheets, but Scarbo feared the force of the Princess's denial, as well as the Prince's rage at a witness of his wife's degradation. There was also something else. Although the Prince desired to suffer, and although the means he had chosen was his wife's infidelity, he also desired to be released from suffering, to return to the time of sunlight before the darkness of suspicion had entered his soul. The abandonment of this second desire, even though that abandonment alone could usher in the fulfillment of the first desire, was sure to be so painful that its agent would appear an enemy. The solution to all these problems and uncertainties had come to Scarbo one night after a week of relentless thought. It was brilliantly simple: the Princess herself must denounce the margrave. The Prince could then have the margrave tortured and killed in good conscience and enter into the life of suffering he craved, without having cause to turn against his dwarf. Now, Scarbo knew that the Princess was steadfast in virtue, and would die rather than yield her body to the margrave; his plan was therefore to persuade her to denounce the margrave untruthfully. For this he urged four reasons. The first was this, that such a denunciation would put an end to the torment of her nightly humiliation, which the Princess had confessed to the dwarf during the first of their bower meetings. The second was this, that the Prince longed for her to denounce the margrave, and that by so doing she would be satisfying the Prince's wish. The third was this, that the margrave in fact desired the Princess, and refused to take advantage of her solely because he feared the Prince; the margrave was therefore a traitor, and deserved to be exposed. And the fourth was this, that to confess the margrave's fall would be to reawaken the Prince's desire for her, and put an end to her nightly banishment from his bed. The Princess had listened to the dwarf's reasons in silence and had promised to give her answer in the bower. Her refusal, on that occasion, had been firm, but it could remain only as firm as her inner strength; and the dwarf knew that under the ravagement of her suffering, her inner strength was weakening.

Of story and history. For the most part we can only imagine the lives of those who live in the castle, lives that may in certain respects depart sharply from the particular shapes we invent as we brood across the river on midsummer afternoons. And yet it has been argued that these imaginary lives are true expressions of the world of the castle, that they constitute not legend but history. They do so, it is said, not simply because here and there an invented episode set in the dim past may accidentally imitate an actual event on the far side of the river; nor because our stories, however remote from literal truth, are images of eternal truths that lie buried beneath the shifting and ephemeral forms of the visible. No, our argument has a different origin. The argument goes that our tales are not unknown among the inhabitants of the castle, and in fact circulate freely among the courtiers, who admire the simplicity of our art or take up our stories and weave them into more refined forms, which we ourselves may sometimes hear recited by traveling minstrels in the courtyards of inns or in our market squares. But if our tales are known among the inhabitants of the castle, may it not come about that they begin to imitate the gestures that give them such pleasure, so that their lives gradually come to resemble the legendary lives we have imagined? To the extent that this is so, our dreams may be said to be our history.

The face in the pool. Day after day the Princess suffered the Prince's displeasure, night after night she lay stony cold beside the margrave; and in her sorrowing and distracted mind the voice of the dwarf grew louder, urging her to put an end to her unhappiness, and restore the pleasure of vanished days. One afternoon when the Princess was out walking in the park with two ladies-in-waiting, she came to a pool, shadowed by overhanging branches. Stooping over, she was startled to see, beneath the water, a wrinkled old woman, who stared at her with grief-stricken eyes. Even as she drew in her breath sharply she knew that it was her own face, changed by sorrow. For a long time the Princess gazed at the face in the water before rising and returning to her chamber, where she dismissed her women and sat down at a table. There she took up her Venetian mirror, with its frame of carved ivory, and looked into eyes that seemed to be asking her a frightening question. After a time she reached for her jars of cosmetic powders and, mixing a small amount of saliva with several compounds, began to apply skin whiteners and rouge to her cheeks. Faster and faster she rubbed the unguents into her skin with her fingertips, before stopping abruptly to stare at her pink-and-white face. With a sudden motion she reached over to a small silver bell that sat on the table beside an openwork pomander containing a ball of musk, and shook it swiftly twice. A moment later Scarbo appeared, with a low bow. Holding up the mirror, the Princess gestured disdainfully toward her pink-and-white image in the glass. At once the dwarf stepped over, climbed onto a stool covered in green velvet, and picked up a cloth. With a headshake and a sigh of disapproval he began wiping the ointments from her face, while he held forth on the art of cosmetics. Had the Princess never been told that a base of white lead was to be avoided, since it was known to produce harmful effects on the skin? Surely she had seen the telltale red spots on the faces of women of the court — spots that had to be treated with ground black mustard or snakeroot. In place of white lead, might he suggest a mixture of wheat flour, egg white, powdered cuttlefish bone, sheep fat, and camphor? When Scarbo had finished cleaning the Princess's face, he carefully selected half a dozen jars of powder from the table, holding each one up and studying it with a frown. In a copper bowl he prepared a whitish paste. Then, still standing on his stool, he leaned forward and began to apply the paste skilfully to the Princess's cheeks with his small, jeweled fingers.

The margrave. What of the margrave? The tales say little of the Prince's friend, save that each night he lay faithfully on his side of the sword. It is true that in one version he becomes the Princess's lover, and they are caught there, in the bed; but this is a version that few of us heed, for we recognize it to be less daring than the versions in which the Princess remains unsullied in the margrave's bed. Let us say, then, that the margrave remains nightly on his side of the sword. What is he thinking? We may imagine that he is troubled by the visits of the Princess, who nightly creeps into his bed and lies beside him without a word. We do not disgrace him if we imagine that he desires the Princess, for he is a man like other men and the Princess is the fairest of all women; but even if we fail to take into account his own sense of honor, the margrave is bound to the Prince by the high law of friendship, and by the debt that every guest owes to his host: he would no more think of possessing the Prince's wife than he would think of stealing a silver spoon. Or, to be more precise: he is forced, by the Princess's offer of herself, to think continually of possessing her, and the thought so inflames and shames him that he must exercise all his vigilance to resist the nightly test, while at the same time he must make certain not to offend the Princess by an unseemly coldness. It is also possible that the margrave senses that the Princess has been sent by the Prince against her will, to test him; if so, the knowledge can only strengthen his resistance, while making him question why he has incurred the Prince's suspicion. The margrave is troubled by the displeasure he senses in the Prince, and by the cooling of their warm friendship; he longs to return to the early days of his visit. It is time for him to return to his distant land, but he cannot make up his mind to leave the castle. Is he perhaps drawn to the nightly test, the nightly overcoming of his desire, by which act alone he can assert the power of his high nature? Or is he perhaps secretly drawn to the possibility of a great fall? Thus do we weave tales within tales, within our minds, when the tales themselves do not speak.

Rats. The rats in our town scuttle along the narrow lanes, crawl from the compost heaps before our houses, scamper freely in the grassy ditch between the double ring of walls. They feed on slops surreptitiously spilled in the streets despite our strict ordinances, on scraps from the dinner table, on carcases brought for burial to the field beyond the gates. The ratcatcher drowns the rats in the river, and it is from the seed of these drowning rats that a darker breed of rat is said to grow. The dark rats swim across the river and burrow in the cliff hollows. Slowly they make their way up to the castle. They penetrate the towers of the outer and inner walls, scamper across the courtyards, invade the larder and the pantry, and gradually make their way down to the underground cells and tunnels. From there they begin their long descent, pushing their sleek bodies through hidden fissures, seeping into the stone like black water, until at last they come to the dungeon. The dungeon rats are longhaired, half blind, and smell of the river. They crouch in the black corners, rub against the damp walls, stumble against an outstretched foot. The prisoner can hear them cracking bits of stale bread, feeding on pools of urine. When he falls asleep the rats approach slowly, scurrying away only when he stirs. If the prisoner sleeps for more than a few minutes, he will feel the rats nibbling at his legs.

The Princess declines. Scorned and distrusted by the Prince, eluded by the margrave, who no longer sought her company by day, thrown always into closer communion with the dwarf, the Princess began to mistrust herself, and to question her own mind. Always she lay awake at night, on her side of the margrave's sword; and she spent her sunlight hours in a melancholy daze. Weary with sorrow, weak with night-wakefulness, she was yet ravaged with restlessness, and could scarcely sit still. Alone she walked in the green shadows of her garden, or wandered alone in the shady paths of the park; and though her gaze was fixed in an unseeing stare, often she would start, as if she had heard a voice at her ear. She ate little and grew thin, so that her chin looked bony and sharp; and in her wasting face her melancholy eyes grew large, and glowed with the dark light of sorrow. One morning she stumbled in her garden, and would have fallen had the dwarf not sprung from behind a privet hedge and helped to steady her; she felt a warmth on her neck and cheeks, and that afternoon she took to bed with a fever. In her fever-bed she had a vision or dream: she saw a girl at a well, holding a golden ball. The girl dropped the ball, which cracked in two, and from the ball a black raven flew forth and circled round her head, trying to peck out her eyes. And though the girl cried out, the bird put out her eyes; and from the drops of blood that fell to the ground, a thornbush grew. And when the wings of the raven brushed the thorns, instantly the bird died, and the girl's sight was restored. Then the Princess woke from her fever-dream and asked the dwarf what it portended. The dwarf replied that the golden ball was her past happiness, and the margrave the raven that had ended her happiness; and the thornbush was her sorrow, from whence would come her cure. For there was a cure, but it must come from her own despair. Thus did the dwarf tend the Princess in her sickbed, bringing her goblets of cool water, and telling her dwarf tales, as though she were a child; and always he watched her closely with his brown, melancholy, slightly moist, very intelligent eyes.

Other tales. The tales of the Princess are part of a larger cycle of castle tales; other tales speak of the Prince's daughter, the contest of archers, the Prince and the Red Knight. These are tales of the castle, but we have other tales as well: the tale of the Black Ship, the tale of the three skeletons under the alder tree, the tale of the raven, the dog, and the piece of gold. As children our heads are full of these tales, which we confuse with real things; as we grow older our minds turn to affairs of this world, and to the promise of the world hereafter. But the old tales of our childhood never leave us entirely; in later years we pass them on to our own children, without knowing why. Sometimes when we grow old, the tales return to us so vividly that we become caught in their wonder, like little children, and forget the cares of the moment in a kind of drowsiness of dreaming; then we look up guiltily, as if we have done something of which we are ashamed.

Outburst. Day after day the Princess lay feverish in her sickbed, attended by the dwarf, who sat beside her on a high stool, held cool water to her lips, and fed her syrups prescribed by the court physician; and bending close to her ear, he urged her to confess to the Prince that the margrave had wronged him. Could she be certain, could she be absolutely certain, that the margrave, who after all possessed a fiery nature, had approached her only in friendship? Had she seen no sign of a more ardent feeling? Could she say, in all truthfulness, that relations between her and the margrave had been entirely innocent? When she looked deep into her heart—and he urged her to look deep, deep into her heart, deeper than ever into that unfathomable darkness where perhaps only a dwarf's eyes could see clearly—when she thus looked into her innermost heart, could she say, in all conscience, that she did not desire the attentions of the margrave? Certainly he was a handsome man, well-knit and hard-muscled, and in all ways deserving of love, so that it must be difficult, for a woman, not to dream of being kissed by those lips, embraced by those graceful, powerful arms. Could she say, in all honesty, that she had not in some small way, if only by a smile or a look, encouraged in the Prince's friend, who was also, as all the court knew, her intimate friend, some slight bending of his mind toward her, some barely perceptible swerve from the straight line of innocent friendship? And was not friendship itself, truly understood, a passion? Could she, when she looked into the darkness of her heart, deny that she had seen her friendship-passion take on a new and unexpected shape, there in the all-transforming and all-revealing dark? Far be it from him to suggest the slightest degree of deviation from the path of wifely duty—although, in such matters, precise lines were difficult, nay, impossible, to draw. And could she say, in all earnestness, that never once, in the margrave's bedchamber, had the tip of his finger grazed her loosened hair, never once, in all those nights, had he looked on her otherwise than in the purity of an unlikely child-friendship? For surely the ardent margrave had been tempted—to deny it would be to insult him, and indeed to insult the Princess herself, whom all women envied. But where there is temptation, there is the first motion toward a fall. Therefore to say that the margrave desired her was but to speak the truth; and for her to say to the Prince that the margrave had acted on his desire was no more than an extension of the truth, as heavy gold is beaten into airy foil. Thus did the dwarf whisper, as the Princess lay on her fever-bed, thus did he teach her to see in the dark; till looking into the darkness of her heart, the Princess saw disturbing shapes, and cried out in anguish. Then she bade the dwarf bring the Prince to her sickbed. And when the Prince appeared before her, the Princess cried out that the margrave had treacherously desired her, and whispered lewdly to her, and lain with her, and touched her lasciviously by day and by night; and for the sake of her lord, she confessed it. Then the Princess fell back shuddering, and cried out that she was being stung by devils, so that she had to be restrained. Then the Prince summoned his guards, who seized the margrave in his chamber; and when he demanded to know what was charged against him, they would not answer him.

Criminals. Our torture chamber and prison cells lie in the cellars beneath the town hall. Some say that a passageway leads down to a dungeon, which lies at the same depth as the dungeon of the castle on the other side of the river, but there is no evidence whatever for such a dungeon, which moreover would be entirely superfluous, since our prisons are used solely for detention during trial. It is impossible to know whether our legendary dungeon gave rise to the tale of the castle dungeon or whether the castle dungeon, in which we both do and do not believe, gave rise to ours. Our torturers are skilled craftsmen and our laws are severe. Murderers, traitors, rapists, thieves, adulterers, sodomites, and wizards are taken in a cart to the executioner's meadow beyond the walls and there hanged, beheaded, burned at the stake, drowned, or broken on the wheel by the public executioner in full view of citizens and nearby villagers who gather to witness the event and to eat sausages sold at butchers' stalls. The peasants say that the seed of criminals buried in the graveyard gives birth to the race of dwarfs. The rigor of our laws, the skill of our torturers, and the threats of our preachers, who paint the torments of hell in lifelike detail worthy of our artists and engravers, are intended to frighten our townsfolk from committing criminal deeds and even from having criminal thoughts, and in this they are largely but not entirely successful. The depravity of human nature is a common explanation for this partial failure, but it is possible to wonder whether our criminals, who are tortured underground and executed outside our walls, are not secretly attracted to all that is beneath and outside the world enclosed by our walls — whether they do not, in some measure, represent a restlessness in the town, a desire for the unknown, a longing to exceed all that hems in and binds down, like the thick walls, the heavy gates, the well-made locks and door panels. It is perhaps for this reason that our laws are severe and our instruments of torture ingenious and well-crafted: we fear our criminals because they reveal to us our desire for something we dare not imagine and cannot name.

* * *

A change of heart. The margrave was tortured on two separate occasions, on the second of which the bones of both arms and legs were broken, but he did not confess his crime, and at length was carried unconscious down to the dungeon and flung onto a bed of straw. Some members of the court were surprised by the leniency of the punishment, for committing adultery with the wife of a prince was considered an act of treachery and was punishable by emasculation, followed by drawing and quartering, but others saw in the margrave's fate a far worse punishment than death: a lingering lifetime of lying in darkness, sustained only by sufficient nourishment to keep one sensible of one's misery, while disease and madness gradually destroyed the body and the soul. The dwarf, who had advised death by beheading, a punishment reserved for rapists and sodomites, saw in the sentence a secret indecisiveness: the Prince did not entirely believe the confession of the Princess. Or, to put it more precisely, the Prince believed the confession of the Princess, but his belief had at its center a germ of doubt, which spread outward through his belief and infected it in every part with a suspicion of itself. The Princess, for her part, soon recovered from her fever, and resumed her former habits; only, there was a marked reserve about her, and sometimes she would break off in the middle of a sentence and grow silent, and seem to gaze inward. She no longer summoned the dwarf, and indeed appeared to avoid his company; but Scarbo well understood the necessity for his banishment, for had he not caused her to fall beneath her high estimate of herself? The Prince, uneasily reconciled with his wife, sensed in her an inner distance that he could not overcome; to his surprise, he discovered that he did not always wish to overcome it. To the extent that he believed her confession, he felt a cold revulsion that she had lain with the margrave, even at his own urging; to the extent that he disbelieved her confession, he blamed her for condemning the margrave to a dungeon death. Meanwhile the Princess withdrew deeper and deeper into her inner castle, where she brooded over the events that had estranged her from the Prince, and made her a stranger even to herself. And as the days passed, a change came over her. For she saw, with ever-increasing clearness, in the long nights when she no longer slept, that the Prince had wronged her, by sending her to the bed of the margrave; and she saw, with equal clearness, that she had horribly wronged the margrave, by her foul lies. Then in the dark the Princess vowed to set right the wrong she had done him. And she who had lain coldly in the bed of the margrave, brooding over the displeasure of the Prince, now looked at the Prince strangely, as at someone she had known long ago; and lying coldly in the bed of the Prince, or lying alone in her private bedchamber high in her tower, she thought of the margrave, in the bowels of the earth, deep down.

Wives. No burgher or artisan can manage the complex affairs of his household without the aid of his capable wife. The wives of our town are practical and industrious; on the way to market in the morning they walk purposefully, with powerful strides. It is true that our husbands, while admiring their wives, expect them to be obedient. A wife who disobeys her husband will be promptly chastised; if she provokes him by continued disobedience, he has the right to strike her with his fist. Once, when a young bride of high beauty and strong temperament argued with her patrician husband in the presence of dinner guests, he rose from the table and in full view of the company struck her in the face, breaking her nose and disfiguring her for life. A wife's conduct is carefully regulated by law; it is illegal for a wife to permit a servant to place a brooch on her bosom, for no one may touch her on the breast except her husband. The wives of our town are strong, efficient, and never idle. They are fully able to manage a husband's affairs if he should depart from town on business, or his trade if he should die. The wives make up the morning fires, shake out rugs and clothes, tend their gardens, direct their servants to prepare dinner. Only sometimes, resting by a window or pausing beside a well, a change comes over them. Then their eyes half-close, a heaviness as of sleep seems to fall on their shoulders, and for a moment they are lost in dream, like children listening to stories by the chimney fire, before they return to their skins with a start.

A meeting. One morning Scarbo received by messenger a summons from the Princess. He had not exchanged a single word with her since her illness, and he appeared promptly at the bower, shutting the wicker gate behind him and entering the shady enclosure with a low bow. The Princess sat on one of the crimson silk couches and motioned for him to sit opposite. Scarbo was struck by something in her manner: she had about her a self-command, as if she were a tensely drawn bow, and she looked at him frankly, without hostility but without friendliness. As soon as he was seated she said that she wished to ask a difficult service of him. The request itself would put her at his mercy, and she had no illusions concerning his good will toward her; but since she no longer valued her life, save as a means to one end, she did not care whether he betrayed her. The dwarf, instantly alert to the danger of the interview, as well as to the possibility of increasing his power in the court, chose not to defend his good will, but remained warily silent, only lowering his eyes for a moment in order to display to the Princess his distress at the harshness and unfairness of her remark. The Princess spoke firmly and without hesitation. She said that because of her weak and evil nature, a nature abetted by dubious councilors in the service of one who no longer wished her well, she had wronged the margrave, who now lay suffering a horrible and unjust fate; and that she was determined to right her wrong, or die. In this quest she had decided, after long thought, to ask the help of the dwarf, knowing full well that by doing so she was placing herself in his power. And yet there was no one else she could turn to. He was intimate with the Prince, adept at hiding and spying, and, as she well knew, at insinuating himself into the confidence of those he served; moreover, it was he alone whom the Prince entrusted with the task of descending the legendary stairway with the prisoner's daily ration of wretched food, which he placed in the hands of the keeper of the dungeon. The service she requested of the dwarf was this: to arrange for the margrave's escape. In making her request, she understood perfectly that she was asking him to put his life at risk by betraying the Prince; and yet she was bold enough to hope that the risk would be outweighed by the gratitude of the Princess, and the advantage of having her in his power. Here she paused, and awaited his answer.

Nightmares. Because of the stories we tell, our children believe that if they listen very carefully, in the dead of night, they will hear a faint scraping sound, coming from the bowels of the earth. It is the sound made by the prisoner as he secretly cuts his way with a pickax through the rock. For the most part our children listen for the sound of the prisoner with shining eyes and swiftly beating hearts. But sometimes they wake screaming in the night, weeping with fear, as the sounds get closer and closer. Then we rock them gently to sleep, telling them that our walls are thick, our moat deep, our towers high and equipped with powerful engines of war, our drop gates fitted with bronze spikes sharp as needles that, once fallen upon an enemy, will pierce his body through. Slowly our children close their eyes, while we, who have comforted them, lie wakeful in the night.

* * *

The answer. To his surprise — and he did not like to be surprised — Scarbo realized at once that he would serve the Princess. The reason was not entirely clear to him, and would require close examination in the privacy of his chamber, but he saw that it was a complex reason consisting of three parts, which under different circumstances might have annulled one another, or at the very least led him to hesitate. The Princess, he clearly saw, considered him morally contemptible, and was appealing to what she assumed to be his cynical lust for power. In this she was quite correct, as far as she went; for indeed he was in part attracted by the vague but thrilling promise of having the Princess in his power, although what precisely she intended to imply by those words was probably unclear to her. She was therefore correct, as far as she went; but she did not go far enough. For her very contempt prevented her from seeing the second part of his complex reason for agreeing to risk his life by serving her. Although Scarbo was ruthless, unscrupulous, and entirely cynical in moral matters, his cynicism did not prevent him from distinguishing modes of behavior one from the other; indeed he would argue that precisely his freedom from moral scruple made him acutely sensitive to the moral scruples of others. Because the Princess was moral by nature, the dwarf trusted her not to betray him; he could therefore count on her in a way he could no longer count on the Prince, whose moral nature had been corroded by jealousy. The third part of the reason was murkier than the other two, but could not be ignored. For the first time since her decline into weakness and confusion, Scarbo admired the Princess. He was helplessly drawn to power; and the Princess, in her proud bearing, in the intensity of her determination, in the absolute and, yes, ruthless quality of her conviction, was the very image of radiant power that he adored, in comparison to which the Prince, gnawed by secret doubt, seemed a weak and diminished being. Yes, Scarbo was drawn to the Princess, looked up to her, felt the full force of her power, in a sense yielded to her, and could deny her nothing, even as he felt the thrill of having her in his power. Such, then, were the three parts of the reason that led to his immediate inward assent. Aloud, the dwarf said to the Princess that there was much to be thought about, in a request that only honored him, and that he would deliver his answer the following day.

Artists. Our tombstone effigies, the carved figures on our altarpieces, the faces of our patricians on medallions, the decorative reliefs and commemorative images in our churches, the stone figures on our fountains, the oil or tempera paintings that show an artisan in a leather cap, or the suffering face of Our Lord on the cross, or St. Jerome bent over a book between a skull and a sleeping lion: all these receive high praise for their remarkably lifelike quality. So skillful are the painters in our workshops that they vie with one another to achieve unprecedented effects of minutely accurate detail, such as the individual hairs in the fur trim of a cloak, the weathered stone blocks of an archway, the shine on the wood of a lute or citole. The story is told how the dog of one of our painters, seeing a self-portrait of his master drying in the sun, ran up to it to lick his master's face, and was startled by the taste of paint. But equally astonishing effects are regularly created by our master artisans. We have all watched our master woodcarvers cut from a small piece of pear wood or linden wood a little perfect cherry, on top of which sits a tiny fly; and our master goldsmiths, coppersmiths, silversmiths, and brass workers all delight us by creating tiny fruits and animals that amaze less by virtue of their smallness than by their precision of lifelike detail. Such mastery of the forms of life may suggest a disdain for the fanciful and fantastic, but this is by no means the case, for our painters and sculptors and master artisans also make dragons, devils, and fantastic creatures never seen before. Indeed it is precisely here, in the realm of the invisible and incredible, that our artists show their deepest devotion to the visible, for they render their monsters in such sharp detail that they come to seem no more fantastic than rats or horses. So strikingly lifelike is our art, so thoroughly has it replaced the older and stiffer forms, that it may seem as if ours is the final and imperishable end toward which the art of former ages has been striving. And yet, in the heart of the thoughtful admirer, a question may sometimes arise. For in such an art, where hardness and clarity are virtues, where the impossible itself is rendered with precision, is there not a risk that something has been lost? Is there not a risk that our art lacks mystery? With their clear eyes, so skilled at catching the look of a piece of velvet rubbed against the grain, with their clear eyes that cannot not see, how can our artists portray fleeting sensations, intuitions, all things that are dim and shadowy and shifting? How can the grasping hand seize the ungraspable? And may it not sometimes seem that our art, in its bold conquest of the visible, is really a form of evasion, even of failure? On restless afternoons, when rain is about to fall but does not fall, when the heart thirsts, and is not satisfied, such are the thoughts that rise unbidden in those who stand apart and are watchful.

* * *

Dwarf in the tower. Scarbo delivered his answer at the appointed time, and now daily he climbed the turning stairway that led to the private chamber at the top of the tower, where the Princess increasingly secluded herself from the cares of the castle to work her loom, brood over her fate, and await news of the margrave in the dungeon. As the dwarf ascended the sunstreaked dark stairway he would rest from time to time at a wedge-shaped recess with an arrow loop, pulling himself up on the ledge and clasping his arms around his raised knees as he stared out at the river winding into the distance or the little city behind its meandering walls. In the long spaces between recesses the air darkened to blackness; sometimes in the dark he heard the rustle of tiny scurrying feet, or felt against his hair the sudden body of a bat. At the top of the stairway he came to a door, illuminated by an oil lamp resting on a corbel set into the wall. He knocked three times, with longish pauses between knocks — the agreed-on signal — and was admitted to a round room filled with sunlight and sky. The light entered through two pairs of tall lancet windows, with trefoil tracery at the top; each pair was set in a wide recess with stone window seats along the sides. On one stretch of wall between the two recesses was a wall-painting that showed Tristan and Isolde lying side by side under a tree; from the branches peered the frowning face of King Mark, circled by leaves. The Princess led Scarbo to the pair of window seats overlooking the walled town across the river, and there, sitting across from her and tucking one leg under him, the little man reported the progress of his plan. The crusty old keeper of the dungeon had at first seemed a stumbling block, but had soon revealed his weakness: a lust for glittering things. In return for a single one of the red and yellow and green jewels with which the Princess had filled the dwarf's pockets — for she had insisted on supplying him with gems instead of buttons or glass — Scarbo had been able to secure the prisoner's release from the heavy chains that had bound his arms and legs to the wall. In return for a second jewel, the dwarf had earned the privilege of visiting the prisoner alone. It was on the first of these occasions that he had provided the margrave with a long-handled iron shovel, which had proved easy to conceal in the pallet of straw, and which was used by the margrave to dig into the hard earthen floor. And here the tales do not say whether much time had passed, during which the margrave's bones had healed, or whether the report of his crushed bones had been exaggerated. Impossible for the dwarf to say how long the prisoner would have to dig away at his tunnel, for the route of escape had to pass beneath the entire castle before beginning its immense, unthinkable ascent. The ground was hard, and filled with stones of many sizes. A straight tunnel was out of the question, since the presence of rocks required continual swerves; already the margrave had been forced to a complete dead end in one direction and had had to strike out in another. The plan, such as it was, called for the margrave to proceed in the direction of the cliff, where a number of fissures in the rockface were known to lead to small cavelike passages; from the face of the cliff he could make his way undetected down to the river, where a skiff would be waiting—not to take him directly across, which would be far too dangerous, but to move him secretly along the rocky shore until he could cross over safely at a bend in the river concealed from the highest of the castle towers. Once in safety, he would raise two mighty armies. One he would lead against the castle, for he had vowed to annihilate it from the face of the earth; the other, across the river, would march up to the walls of the town and demand entry. If refused, the second army would capture the town and use it to control the river, thereby both preventing supplies from reaching the castle by water and threatening a second line of attack along the low riverbank upstream from the rocky cliff. For the margrave, in his fury, would let nothing stand in the way of his vengeance. Moreover, the town still paid homage to the Prince as supreme lord; and although the homage was well-nigh meaningless, since the Council had wrested from the Prince every conceivable power and was entirely autonomous, nevertheless the margrave, in his blind rage, viewed the town as an extension of the Prince and thereby worthy of destruction. The flaw in this grand plan was not simply the daily danger of discovery by the keeper, whose ferocious love of glitter would never permit him to ignore an attempted escape by a prisoner in his charge, but also the immense and uncertain depth of the dungeon, which was believed to lie far below the bed of the river. Scarbo had repeatedly tried to count the steps, but always he had broken off long before the end, when the number had passed into the thousands, for a strange hopelessness overcame him as he made the black descent, an utter erosion of belief in possibility; and in addition the steps themselves became blurred and broken after a while, so that it was impossible to distinguish one from another. If the idea of tunneling in a straight line had had to be abandoned in the short view, though not necessarily in the broad and general view, how much more tricky, indeed fantastic, seemed the idea of tunneling gradually upward to a point below the foundation of the castle but above the surface of the river. It would be far easier to thread a needle in the dark. At some point, moreover, the tunnel would come up against the solid rock of the cliff, at which moment a stonecutter's pickax would have to replace the shovel. But the prisoner was strong, and driven by a fierce thirst for vengeance;

it was possible that in five years, in ten years, in twenty years, the plan might reach fruition. Then woe betide the margrave's enemies, and anyone who tried to stand in his way; for, truth to tell, the margrave was much changed from the elegant, melancholy courtier he had been, and all his force was now concentrated into a fierce and single aim, culminating in a fiery vision of justice. Thus the dwarf, recounting the underground progress of the margrave to the Princess high in her sunny tower, while across from him she sat in silence, now staring at him intently, now turning her head slightly to gaze out the tall windows at a black raven in the blue sky, at the greenish-blue riverbank far below, at the little stone town at the bottom of the wooded hillside.

Invasion. Should an enemy decide to attack us, he must first make his way across the dry moat, one hundred feet deep, that surrounds our outer wall. To do this he must begin by filling with earth, rubble, or bundles of logs that portion or portions of the moat he wishes to pass over. Next he must attempt the crossing itself, under cover of one or more wheeled wooden siege towers supplied with scaling ladders and containing archers, assault soldiers, and perhaps a copper-headed battering ram hung from leather thongs. But while the enemy is still engaged in the laborious task of filling up our moat, we ourselves are by no means idle. From behind our battlements we rain down a storm of flaming arrows and gunshot, while from our towers with their stores of catapult artillery we direct upon the enemy a ceaseless fire of deadly missiles. Should an enemy, against all odds, manage to advance to the outer wall, we are prepared to pour down on him, through openings between the corbels of our projecting parapets, rivers of molten lead and boiling oil, while we continue to shoot at men who are climbing highly exposed ladders that rise against our twenty-foot wall; and since, by design, our towers project from the wall, we are able to direct a murderous fire at the enemy's flank. Should he in all unlikelihood succeed in knocking down or scaling a portion of our outermost wall, he will find himself in a broad trench before a still higher wall, with its higher battlements and towers; and in this trench he will be subject to attack not only from the forty-foot wall looming before him, but from the uncaptured portions of the wall that is now behind him. So inconceivable is it that an enemy in the trench, however numerous, can survive slaughter, that our concern is directed rather at the sappers who, even as we triumph on the battlements, may be digging beneath our walls and towers in an effort to collapse them in one dramatic blow. Therefore we assign soldiers to listen carefully for the sound of underground digging, and we are prepared at any moment to countermine and take possession of an enemy tunnel. Should sappers succeed in toppling a tower or a portion of wall, we are prepared to erect behind it, swiftly, a second wall or palisade, from behind which we can fire upon the invaders as before. Although it is less conceivable that an enemy should penetrate our formidable defenses than that the nine crystalline spheres of the universe should cease to turn, sometimes we dream at night of enemy soldiers scaling our walls. In our dreams they are running through our streets, setting fire to our houses, raping our women and murdering our children, until we can smell the blood flowing among the paving stones, taste the smoke on our tongues, hear the shrieks of the mutilated and dying in a roar of falling and flaming walls and the mad laughter of the margrave as he strides like a giant through the ruins.

A disturbing episode. It was about this time that the dwarf began to lust secretly after the Princess, who lived apart from the rest of the castle, and with whom he spent many hours alone in her tower. Perhaps it would be more exact to say that a desire which had always lurked in the dark corners of his soul now first revealed itself to the dwarf, who had not dared to lust after the wife of his Prince when the Prince was his true master. Nightly in his chamber Scarbo imagined scenes of such melting and devouring bliss that he would sit up in bed with pounding temples and press his hands over his chest to still the violent beating of his heart. But when he climbed the stairs to the Princess's tower, and saw her seated proudly and scorn-fully by the tall windows, he could not recognize in her a single trace of that wild and yielding Princess of the Night, and in his skin he felt an odd confusion, as if he had opened the wrong door and entered a room never seen before. Now the dwarf was above all a courtier, and had drawn deep into his own nature the court's conventions of love, which managed to combine delicacy of feeling, refinement of speech, longing for self-abasement, and relentless lust, all directed toward another man's wife. Therefore his feelings for the Princess, although new to him, were at the same time quite familiar. But in addition to being a courtier, Scarbo was also a dwarf, and herein lay an important difference. As a dwarf he was threatened at every turn with ridicule, with secret laughter; although no one had dared to touch him since he had committed murder in defense of his honor, he was always aware of hostile and secretly mocking eyes. Once, in his early days at court, a lady-in-waiting had sat him on her lap and fondled him laughingly, placing his small hand on her half-bared breast and touching him on the thigh, calling him her little puppy, whispering that he should visit her at night. When he entered her bedchamber that night and groped his way to the curtained bed, she looked at him in surprise and suddenly burst out laughing, so that her naked breasts shook and tears of hilarity streamed along her cheeks. Scarbo drew his sword in order to cut off her breasts, hesitated, sheathed his sword, and left without a word. After that he never permitted himself to be touched by anyone. His sudden desire for the Princess, which grew stronger each night, was therefore frustrated not only by the courtly convention of hopeless love-longing, but by fear — not simply the fear of ridicule, which in itself was intolerable, but the fear that the Princess would look at him in bewilderment, without understanding that she might exist as an object of desire for such a one as he. Secretive and cautious by temperament, Scarbo had trained himself over many years to murder any feeling that might interfere with his advancement at court. Should he not do so now? But the Princess had placed herself in his power. What could that mean except that she was his to do with as he liked? She was entirely dependent on him for the life of the margrave; she could not possibly refuse him the trivial favor of her body, which he longed for so violently that sometimes, as he walked along a corridor, tears of desire sprang into his eyes. But even though he held her in his power, as she herself had repeated more than once, so that he need only exercise that power by a simple act of will in order to take possession of her incomparable body, his pride demanded more — demanded, indeed, that she invite him to take his pleasure with her, that in no vague or uncertain terms she welcome him to her bed. And because he was tormented by ever-increasing desire, and because at the same time he was extremely cautious, Scarbo began to reveal his desire to the Princess, in her tower chamber: at first obliquely, through sly hints that might be taken up or ignored, and then more openly, though not directly. He spoke to her of love affairs at court, describing budding passions, unhappy marriages, and secret trysts, and soliciting her opinion concerning specific questions debated at court, such as whether a wife neglected by her husband had the right to take a lover, or whether a woman should prefer an ugly lover with a noble soul to a handsome lover with an ignoble soul. He contrived whenever possible to pay the Princess intimate compliments, praising the way a sleeve set off the whiteness of her skin, alluding to her fingers and neck, and deploring the threadbare phrases of court poets, who settled for the same old expressions and therefore could not see the precise color, for example, of the Princess's hair, which was not the color of beaten gold but rather of the field of wheat by the bend of the river in the light of early morning, or of a wall of pale stone darkened and made bright by the late afternoon sun. The Princess's failure to acknowledge these compliments, which in one sense might have seemed discouraging, in another sense was almost heartening, for it could at least be said that his words had not awakened her active displeasure; and thus encouraged, the dwarf proceeded, as if by cunning, and yet quite helplessly, to more daring and intimate expressions. One day he spoke disparagingly of the fashion lately taken up by court ladies of binding their breasts with bandeaux, instead of leaving them free to assume their natural shape, as was still, he was pleased to observe, the custom of the Princess herself, who unlike certain of the ladies did not need to wrench into false and misleading forms those gifts of Nature which, as anyone with eyes could see, were of a beauty, indeed a perfection, that made one impatient with the shams of artifice and filled one with a longing to experience the naked truth of things — and as the little man continued to speak, shocked by his boldness, sickened by the sense of having gone too far, but unable to stop, he had the dreamlike sensation that he had entered a forbidden realm of freedom and transgression for which at any moment he would be severely punished. Often he longed to reach out and touch the Princess. She sat across from him on her sunny stone bench, thoughtful, a little tired, with signs of a slight dishevelment; she had grown a trifle slack of late. The subtle laxity in her rigorous deportment, the startling wisp of hair escaping from beneath her headdress, the hint of indifference toward her own body, all this gave her a kind of softness or languor that caused his mouth to become dry, his stomach to tighten, his hands to tremble visibly — but always at the last moment he held back, fearful of waking from his sensual dream. At last, sick with desire, he told the Princess that he often found himself awake at night, thinking of their conversations. He would, at such times, have been pleased to visit her, had he not feared to disturb her rest; and the Princess remaining silent, he added in a low voice, as if not wishing to hear himself speak, that he would like to visit her that very night, in order to discuss certain matters best left to the hours of darkness, unless of course she did not wish to be disturbed. At this the Princess turned her head and looked at him, with a gaze of immense weariness and disdain, and said that he was of course at liberty to visit her when and as he wished. Unsettled by the look of disdain, which he quickly thrust to the back of his mind, but thrilled by the words of assent, the dwarf could not sit still a moment more, and abruptly took his leave. In his chamber he lay down on his small bed, made for him by the court carpenter in accord with precise specifications he had furnished himself, and pressed both small hands against his thudding heart. A moment later he sprang up. He combed his beard in the glass, paced about, lay down on his bed, sprang up. He hadn't expected her to agree so quickly, indeed the details of the scene were unclear in his mind, except for the troubling look that ought to have been accompanied by a refusal, but which perhaps could be explained as a last vestige of loyalty to the husband who had wronged her. She had accepted him, had she not? She hadn't accepted him in the spirit he would have wished, but she had not refused him outright: far from it. In such thoughts he passed the afternoon and evening; and long after it had grown dark he waited in his chamber. At last he looked at himself in the glass, combed his beard with his fingers, slipped a dagger under his mantle, and closed his door softly behind him. The Princess's bedchamber lay in the tower, directly beneath her high room, and as the dwarf climbed the familiar stairs he tried to recall the long history of his relation to the Princess, but his mind produced only disconnected images: sunlight and leafshade trembling on the red silk of a couch, the face of King Mark peering out of the leaves, the body of a bat brushing against his hair. At the door of her bedchamber he paused, listening, then stood on his toes to place his hand on the iron ring that served as a doorknob. The heavy door, unbolted, gave way to his push. In the dark chamber, shuttered against the moon but lit with a single taper, the Princess lay propped on two pillows in her canopied bed, with the curtain open and the coverlet thrown back across her waist. She had removed her headdress, her wide-sleeved tunic, and her underrobe, but not her snow-white chemise threaded with gold. In the dim light of the taper she seemed a shimmer of snow and gold; and the tops of her breasts and her wheat-colored hair were white and gold. She looked at him coldly and said not a word. Scarbo closed the door behind him and began walking toward the bed, which soared above him; when he reached the side his head barely came up to the coverlet. At the bedfoot stood three steps leading up. Scarbo climbed the steps and began to walk along the coverlet toward the Princess. He was keenly aware of the ludicrous figure he cut as he marched along the trembling bed, and he felt almost grateful to her for not ridiculing him, for not requiring him to cut her throat. As he drew closer he saw in her eyes a weariness so deep that it was deeper than disdain. When he reached the place where the coverlet had been turned back, he stopped beside the Princess and stood looking down at her. He saw with utter clarity that she did not and could not desire him, but that she would permit herself to endure his pleasure. He saw further that this permission was in part a desire to punish herself for the wrong she had done to the margrave, and in part a sign of her growing indifference to herself. He felt constrained, formal, and immensely melancholy. He understood that he was not going to tear the chemise from those longed-for breasts and plunge into a night of bliss that would change his life forever. No, he would spare her the need to endure his undesired desire. For this she would be grateful, and her gratitude would increase his power over her. He understood suddenly that renouncing his dream of bliss would not be difficult for him, for he was skilled at renunciation — had he not spent a lifetime perfecting self-denial? Exhausted by his inrush of understanding, almost forgetful of the actual Princess lying at his feet, he understood one final thing: the Princess, who believed that she was acting solely to right a wrong, had not yet realized that she had fallen in love with the doomed and inaccessible margrave, who alone occupied her thoughts, and for whom she was willing to endure any indignity. Tired now, Scarbo sat down on the bed and crossed his little legs. He reached under his mantle and removed the dagger. "A gift for you, milady," he said, handing it to her hilt-first. "To protect yourself against unwelcome guests." She took the dagger hesitantly; and as he began to speak of the margrave's progress, he saw, in her weary and mistrustful eyes, a first faint shine of gratefulness.

Cellar tales. Each of us has heard innumerable versions of the tales of the Princess. From this multiplicity of versions, varying from single details of wording to entire adventures composed of many episodes, each of us selects particular versions that eclipse or obscure the other versions, without eliminating them entirely. The versions selected by any one of us rarely replicate the versions chosen by others, but gradually, in the course of our town's history, certain versions come to take precedence over other ones, which are relegated to a secondary status. It is here that an interesting development takes place. For these secondary versions, which have not been able to survive in the full light of day, continue to carry on a hidden life, and give rise to growths of a dubious and fantastic kind. Such offspring of rejected, inferior, but never-forgotten versions are known as cellar tales, for they grow in the dark, unseen by anyone, mysterious as elves or potatoes. In one cycle of cellar tales, the Princess and the dwarf have a child, whose face is of a beauty unsurpassed, but whose body is hideously deformed. In another series of tales the margrave in his dungeon begins to change: a pair of black wings grows on his back, and one day he appears in the sky above the river as a black angel of death. Although the cellar tales are never admitted to the main cycle of castle tales, they nevertheless do not wither away, but multiply inexhaustibly, staining the other tales with their hidden colors, exerting a secret influence. Some say that a day will come when the daylight tales will weaken from lack of nourishment; then the cellar tales will rise from their dark places and take over the earth.

The Prince. As the Princess withdrew to the solitude of her tower, the Prince retired to the privacy of his oriel chamber, with its great hearth, its hunting tapestries in which the yellows were woven with gold thread, and its many-paned window that overlooked the chapel roof. Here he kept his favorite falcon in a cage, his library of rhymed romances inked on parchment and bound in ivory covers mounted on wood, and a locked chest containing the horn of a unicorn. Alone on his window seat, the Prince brooded over the Princess, the margrave, and his own unhappy fate. Had his suspicions perhaps been ill-founded? Had he acted unwisely in sending the Princess to the margrave's bedchamber? Should he perhaps pardon the margrave and release himself from the worm of doubt that gnawed at his entrails? But such a step was impossible, for at the heart of his doubt was a still deeper doubt, a doubt that questioned his doubt. The Prince remembered reading of a cunning Moorish labyrinth in which a Christian knight had wandered for so many years that when he caught sight of himself in a puddle he saw the face of an old man, and it seemed to the Prince that he was that knight. Sometimes the castle, the margrave, the Princess, his own hand, seemed images in an evil dream. He no longer called for his dwarf, who alone might have been able to soothe him, for he sensed that the little man detected in him a secret weakness, an indecisiveness, a softening of the will to rule. Should he perhaps have the dwarf killed? In the late-afternoon shadows of his oriel chamber, the Prince half-closed his eyes and dreamed of another life: surely he would have been happier as a shepherd, tending his flock, playing his oaten pipes, leaning on an elbow beside a babbling brook.

Dwarf descending. The tales say only that the dwarf passed back and forth between the Princess and the prisoner, but in the hillside vineyards beyond the upper gates, or along the well-laid paving stones of a winding lane, we imagine the details: the walls of damp stone, the crumbling edges of the steps, the sudden softness of a scuttling rat. Always, as he descended, Scarbo had the sensation that he knew the moment when the stairway passed beneath the surface of the river: the air became cooler, water trickled along the walls, the stone steps grew slick with moisture and erupted with soft black growths. Later, much later, the darkness changed, became blacker and more palpable: he had the sensation that he could feel it brushing against his face, as if he were passing through the wing of an enormous raven. It was at this point that the castle far above him began to waver in his mind, like vapor over a pool; somewhere a dream-Princess sat in a dream-tower; but for him there was only the long going down in darkness, as if he were a stone plunging into a well. Later still, he heard or thought he heard a faint tapping sound. This was the sound of the margrave's pick, slowly cutting its way through rock. No longer did Scarbo expect to find the prisoner in the dungeon, but rather in one or another branch of a complex tunnel that veered off in many directions as the margrave evaded obstacles, gave way to discouragement, or followed sudden inspirations. So elaborate had the tunnel become, so crisscrossed with intersecting passageways, that it seemed less a tunnel than an ever-widening labyrinth; the dwarf no longer thought of it as a route of escape, but as a fantastic extension of the dungeon, a dungeon caught in the throes of delirium. Scarbo encouraged the margrave, brought him additional tools and measuring devices (a mason's level, a measuring cord), helped estimate his progress, and discussed with him the most promising direction along which to proceed, but his secret plan was the precise opposite of the margrave's: it was to confuse the path of escape, to delay it indefinitely, to prevent the prisoner from breaking free and throwing the world into chaos. But to confuse the path of escape was a difficult task, for Scarbo himself was unsure of the way out, and it was always possible that he would unwittingly direct the margrave toward the correct route. Therefore he contrived plans, made careful measurements, and brooded over sketches as passionately as the margrave himself, but solely with the intention of misleading him and thwarting his escape. For although Scarbo's allegiance to the Princess was profound, it ceased at the point at which he could imagine a change of any kind in the world of the castle; and as he descended through the always darkening dark, it seemed to him that what he most desired was for the Princess to remain forever in her airy tower and for the margrave to dig forever toward an always elusive freedom, while he himself passed ceaselessly between them, in a darkness that never ended.

The universe. The universe, created out of nothing in an instant by a single act of God's will, is finite and is composed of ten parts: the central globe of Earth and, surrounding it, nine concentric crystalline spheres, which increase in circumference as they increase in distance from the Earth. Each of the seven planets lies embedded in its own sphere; if we move outward from Earth, the first sphere is the sphere of the Moon, followed by the sphere of Mercury, the sphere of Venus, the sphere of the Sun, the sphere of Mars, the sphere of Jupiter, and the sphere of Saturn. The eighth sphere is the sphere of the fixed stars, which remain unchanging in relation to one another. The ninth or outermost sphere is the *primum mobile,* turning all the rest. Beyond the ninth sphere, which marks the boundary of the created universe, lies the *coelum empyraeum,* or empyrean heaven, which is the infinite abode of God. Some churchmen say that on the Last Day, when Christ, robed in glory, comes to judge the living and the risen dead, the entire universe will be consumed in fire; others argue that only that part of the universe will perish which lies beneath the sphere of the Moon; but all agree that a great fire will come, and Time will end, and generations will cease forever. Although we admire the architecture of the universe, which seems to have been created by one of our own master artisans, and although we fear its fiery destruction, we are rarely moved by its immense and intricate structure to the condition of wonder. Rather, our wonder is aroused by the tiny silver insects of our silversmiths, by the minuscule steel wheels of our watchmakers, by the maze of fine lines cut by the burin on a soft copper plate to represent the folds in a cloak, the petals of a dandelion, the eyes and nostrils of a hare or roebuck.

Endings. Just as we are familiar with many versions of the tales of the Princess, so are we familiar with a profusion of endings. Sometimes we no longer know whether we have heard an ending long ago, remembering it carelessly, with changes of our own, or whether we have dreamed it ourselves from hints in earlier episodes. Thus it is told how the margrave, suspicious of the dwarf, binds him in irons and climbs to the tower, where he lies down with the Princess and is tended by her for thirty nights and thirty days; on the thirty-first night they are discovered by a servant, and a great battle takes place, in which the Prince is slain. It is told how the Prince, longing for expiation, one day goes down to the margrave in the dungeon, and insists on changing places with him, so that the margrave reigns in the castle while the Prince languishes in darkness. It is told how the margrave escapes from the dungeon after twenty-four years, and returns to defeat the Prince and marry the Princess, who in other versions dies in her tower after hearing a false report of the margrave's death. Far from deploring the multiplicity of endings, we admire each for the virtues it possesses, and even imagine other endings that have never been told. For a story with a single ending seems to us a bare and diminished thing, like a tree with a single branch; and each ending seems to us an expression of something that is buried deep within the tale and can be brought to light in that way and no other. Nor does one ending prevent the existence of another, contradictory, ending, but rather encourages other endings, which aspire to be drawn out of the tale and take their place in our memory. Sometimes, to be sure, it happens that endings arise that do not seize us like dreams, and so they pass lightly by and are quickly forgotten. And it is true that among those that remain, however numerous and diverse, we recognize a secret kinship. For we understand that the endings are all differing instances of a single ending, in which injustice resolves in justice, and discord in concord. This is true even of the popular prophetic version, which changes suddenly to the future tense while the prisoner is digging through the rock. A day will come, says the tale, when the margrave will break free. A day will come when he will exact a terrible vengeance on all who have wronged him. A day will come . . . Thus we are able to imagine that long ago, in a past so distant that it blurs into legend, a great battle took place, in which the castle and the town were destroyed, while at the same time we imagine that now, at this very moment, the Princess is waiting in her tower, the dwarf is descending the lower stairway, the margrave is digging his way through the rock, the day is steadily approaching when he will burst forth to visit the world with fire and ruin.

A day will come. A day will come when the margrave's pick will suddenly break through the rock. Through cracks of stone he will see a burst of blue sky, brighter than fire. For a day and a night he will cover his eyes with his hands. On the morning of the second day he will widen the hole and peer down at the sun-bright river far below. Unseen by the castle watch he will lower himself on a rope to the river and swim to a waiting skiff. He will row downstream, hugging the cliff wall, for eighteen miles and disembark at the edge of a forest. In a hermit's hut he will sleep for seven days and seven nights. After a long journey he will reach his domain and raise a mighty host, which will exact a terrible vengeance on all those who have wronged him or who attempt to stand in his way. One army will advance against the castle and one army will cross the river and advance against the town; and as both banks of the river burst into towers of fire, the margrave, grown gigantic with avenging fury, will stand astride the river with his face in the heavens and his arms raining destruction.

An afternoon stroll. Far from the river, beyond the upper wall on the slope of the hill, lies the executioner's meadow, where criminals are put to death and buried. Beyond the field, higher up the hillside, the vineyards begin. At the top of the vineyards runs a long path of beaten earth, which divides the vineyards from the forest above. Here one can walk undisturbed in the sun-broken shade of overhanging branches, passing an occasional vintner in a cart, or another wanderer from the town below. We recognize each other at once, we solitary ones who seek the heights above the town, and pass each other with a sense of fraternal sympathy not unmixed with irritation, for it is not society we seek on the upper path where the wood begins. From the path we can see a pleasing view of the town below, with its red tiled roofs, its church steeples, the twin towers of the guild hall, the merchants' fountain in the market square, the garden of the Carthusian monastery, the courtyards of the patrician houses with their wooden galleries, the draw wells in the stone-paved streets. From the town rises a rich interweaving of sounds: the ringing of hammers in the blacksmiths' street, the honking of geese hanging by their feet from the poulterers' stalls, the clatter of cart wheels, the shouts of children, the bang of bells. They are the sounds of an industrious, prosperous, and peaceful town, prepared to defend itself against disturbance from within or without, honoring work and order above all, proud of its wealth, stern in its punishments, suspicious of extremes. The divisions of its day are well accounted for, with no room for idling or dreaming. But now and then, unbidden, a shadow passes across the mind of an artisan in his shop or a merchant in his counting house, and turning his head he looks up to see, across the river, the high castle shining in the sun. Then an image returns, perhaps from a tale heard in childhood, of a dark stairway, a princess with golden hair, a dungeon buried deep in the earth. Long ago these tales unfolded, long ago the prisoner escaped, the dwarf faded into darkness, the Princess closed her eyes. And yet even now we can sometimes see, in the high tower, a flash of yellow hair, we can sometimes hear, in the clear air, the sound of the prisoner cutting through rock. Ships pass on the river, bearing away copper bowls, armor plate, and toothed wheels for sawmills, bringing us spices, velvet, and silk, but under the river live trolls and mermaids. For these are the images that linger, of the river, of the castle, these are the town in dream. Then we smile to ourselves, we solitary ones, we who are of the town but bear toward it a certain reserve, for we see that the town reaches toward higher and lower places than those it honors. But the sun is halfway along the arc of the western sky, it's time to go down to the town, which after all is our home, even ours. Grapes swell on our slopes, deer graze in the grassy trench between our walls, and in the winding streets, bordered by houses of whitewashed wood and clean stone, sunlight and shadow fall equally.

GUSTAW HERLING

TRANSLATED FROM THE POLISH BY RONALD STROM

The Tower

I

It was the summer of 1945, the Italian campaign had just ended, and I had been transferred from headquarters between Bologna and Ravenna to the Polish military mission in Milan. A few weeks after my transfer I applied for leave. I had decided to spend it somewhere in the quiet and solitude of the Piedmont countryside. By a stroke of luck, an Italian assigned to our mission had offered me the keys to a little house in the foothills of the Alps. A distant relative of his, a retired *ginnasio* teacher from Turin, had died there all alone just before the end of the war. The house had been unoccupied since the death of the old recluse.

The house stood on a slope that seemed to form the pedestal of the highest peak of the Mucrone in the vicinity, far above the highway from the central industrial town of the entire upland region. Although the house was on the slope, a wide dirt road, whose sharp curves were guarded by a low stone wall, linked it to the highway three kilometers away, on the outskirts of the nearby village.

The gravel-strewn drive in front of the house, shaded by several maples along an iron fence, led through a gate on one side into a small garden. At the end the old recluse had apparently only taken pains to see that the paths were not overgrown. On both sides of the driveway the wall altogether disappeared under a growth of ivy and wild grape. There were several rooms, all dark, that looked out on the slope, half overgrown with withered blackberry and bushes scorched by the sun. The easy access from the slope may have led the builder to put gratings in the windows, but even without these fixtures there was something of voluntary isolation about the slope that cut off the road from observation.

I took one of the front rooms on the ground floor for myself. The only traces of life in the whole house indicated the former owner's preference for that room too. Through a clearing between two maple trees there was a view of the Elvo valley, with its dark-green clumps of trees, bright patches of meadow, red splotches of roof tops clustered around church turrets, and the faded hoods of hillside castles far away on the horizon.

Although it was large and comfortable, the room had only one window, and it failed to dispel the gloom that hung there from daybreak till dusk or to dry up the open sores of dampness in the corners. The woodworm-eaten furniture, chairs, and a sofa from which the leather was peeling in long strips, a thicket of spiderwebs in the fireplace and on the shelves, and over a chest of drawers a mirror in a once-gilt frame that reflected one's face through a film of soot — it all seemed to harmonize perfectly with the four Piranesi etchings on the wall. Anyone who has seen his engravings knows that Piranesi had a keen predilection for ruins and that he managed to render them with a hint of flesh falling away from bones. In a scholarly essay about Piranesi's "Prisons," Aldous Huxley writes that they express "the perfect pointlessness . . . the staircases lead nowhere, the vaults support nothing."

Above a table in the corner by the window hung a much smaller etching by an unknown artist: against a background of mountains stood a rectangular tower girdled by a high wall and surmounted by a solid block construction broken only by a few small window openings. It was not the artist's burin but an expression of desperation and silent grief in the stone crown of the tower, raised like a weakly clenched fist against the black clumps of cloud, that made the landscape of the drawing so morbid that, in comparison, Piranesi seemed a bucolic poet of the ruins of antiquity.

On the table between two silver candlesticks lay a small volume, so dirty and crumpled and greasy with tallow that it was easy enough to guess it had provided the last occupant's favorite reading for many years. It was an Italian translation of François-Xavier de Maistre's *Le Lépreux de la cité d' Aoste* printed in Naples in 1828 in a limited edition of fifty numbered copies. The translator left the book's motto, from Thomson's *The Seasons:* "Winter," in the original English:

> Ah little think the gay licentious proud,
> Whom pleasure, power, and affluence surround . . .
> Ah little think they while they dance along . . .
> How many pine . . . How many drink the cup
> Of baleful grief . . . How many shake
> With all their fiercer tortures of the mind.

II

The south side of the city of Aosta, De Maistre recounts, was never densely populated. It presented, instead, a view of pastures and cultivated fields reaching right up to the remains of a Roman wall and low stone fences that enclosed small kitchen gardens. Nevertheless, travelers often came by, drawn by two singular attractions. Near the southern gate of the city were the ruins of an ancient castle with a round tower, where, according to popular tradition, the jealous Count Renato of Challant imprisoned his wife, Duchess Maria of Braganza, and starved her to death; the tower is called *Bramafan*, the Cry of Hunger. Several hundred meters farther along the stone rubble of the Roman wall was a second tower, this one rectangular and constructed in part of marble; legend had christened it the Tower of Fright, *Torre dello Spavento*. It was believed to be haunted, and it was said that on dark nights a white lady appeared in the doorway holding a lamp in her hands.

The Tower of Fright was restored about 1782, and a wall over six feet high was built around it, because it was to be the refuge of a leper and his isolation from the world. The unfortunate man came from Oneglia, a small duchy on the Ligurian coast acquired by the House of Savoy in the fifteenth century. No one knows exactly how old the leper was when he was taken to the tower in which he was to die, but he was certainly not yet twenty. The Maurist hospital in Aosta assumed the responsibility of supplying him with food, and the local authorities provided him with a few pieces of furniture and garden tools. He saw no one except the man who brought him supplies from the hospital every week and the priest who occasionally brought the consolation of religion to the *Torre dello Spavento*.

During the Alpine campaign of 1797, fifteen years after the leper's arrival at the Tower of Fright, De Maistre came to Aosta as an officer in the Sabaudian army. One day he was walking by the wall that girdled the tower and noticed a wicket gate standing open. His curiosity got the better of him and he walked in. He saw a modestly dressed man deep in thought leaning against a tree. Without turning his head at the sound of the creaking gate and the steps, the hermit called out in a sad voice, "Who are you, traveler, and what do you want?"

De Maistre explained that he was a foreigner and apologized for his intrusion; he had been attracted by the beauty of the garden. "Don't come near me, sir," the resident of the tower replied, stopping him with a wave of his hand. "Don't come near me. I am a leper."

De Maistre was quick to assure him, and with great warmth, that he had never in his life shunned the unfortunate. Turning his face toward his visitor, the leper replied: "Stay then, if, after seeing how I look, you can still find enough courage in your heart."

For a moment De Maistre was struck dumb by the sight of a face altogether disfigured by leprosy. "I'll stay gladly," he replied at last. "Perhaps my visit, begun in curiosity, may bring some relief to this house."

"Curiosity!" cried the leper. "I've never aroused any sentiment but pity. Relief! It's a great consolation just to see another human being and to hear a human voice. I had almost forgotten the sound."

The visitor was eager to know all about the man's dwelling. The leper put on a large hat, and the broad low brim almost entirely covered his face. He led his guest to a part of the sunlit garden where he bred rare flowers from the seeds of wild plants that grew on the Alpine slopes, trying with the secrets of the gardener's art to enhance their excellence and beauty. He encouraged his visitor to pick some of the most beautiful and quickly added that there was no danger. "I planted them," he explained, "I take pleasure in watering them and in admiring them, but I never touch them."

In this way he kept the flowers uncontaminated; otherwise he could never offer them to anyone. Occasionally the messenger from the hospital would pick some, sometimes children ran in from the streets for them. The children would rap on the gate; the leper would draw the bolt and run to the top of the tower in order not to frighten them or inadvertently harm them. From the window of the tower he would watch as they frolicked a while about the walks and then threw themselves on the flower beds. As they left they would turn at the gate, look up at him, and, making faces at each other, would break out laughing and call: *Buon giorno, Lebbroso!* "Good day, Leper." Those childish shouts were a source of strange delight to him.

He grew several varieties of fruit trees as well, and grape vines climbed to the top of the only fragment of Roman wall that remained in the precinct of the hermitage after the Tower of Fright had been sealed in its stone ring. The remains of that antique wall were so wide that steps had been carved in it and one could stroll along the top and see, beyond the enclosure, the far country, the plains, and the men in the fields, without being seen. This corner of the garden was the leper's favorite retreat. From here the town seemed like a desert. "You don't always find solitude in the heart of the forest or on the cliffs. The unhappy man is alone anywhere."

Now the leper seemed more inclined to talk about himself. He had never known his parents; they had died when he was a child. He was left with only a sister, and she had died two years before. He had never had a friend. That was how God would have it. De Maistre asked him his name. "Ah," exclaimed the tenant of the tower, "my name is awful. It is *Lebbroso!* No one knows the surname I had at birth, nor the name I was given by christening. I am the Leper. That is my only claim on the attention of men. And may they never know that this earth bore me; may every memory of my existence perish forever."

His sister had lived with him in the Tower of Fright for five years. She was a leper too and shared his pain. He had tried to ease her suffering.

"What do you do with yourself in such absolute solitude?" asked De Maistre. "I must confess that the idea of eternal solitude frightens me; I can't even imagine it."

"He who loves his cell," replied the leper, "will find his peace there. *The Imitation of Christ* teaches us that. And I am beginning to understand the truth of those words of comfort."

In the summer the leper worked in his garden. In the winter he wove baskets and mats. He sewed his own clothes and prepared his own meals. The hours left after work he dedicated to prayer. Thus his years passed and when they had passed, they almost seemed short.

It is true that pain and discomfort make the days and nights seem long, but the years pass with the same speed. And in the lowest depths of misfortune there exists a satisfaction that the greater part of mankind never experiences, the simple pleasure of living and breathing. Sometimes the leper spent long summer hours without moving, delighting in the air around him and in the charms of nature. Then all his thoughts became vague and almost hazy. His sadness stiffened and fell to the bottom of his heart, but it caused no pain. His glance wandering over fields and cliffs brought him ever closer to inanimate objects. The leper loved them. Those things he saw day after day became the only companions of his existence.

Every night before going back into the tower he saluted the glaciers of Ruitorts, the dark forests on the slope of the St. Bernard, and the marvelous peaks that dominate the valley of the Rhème. Although the power of God may be as evident in the creation of an ant as in the creation of the universe, it was the magnificent view of the mountains that overpowered him. He could not look at those enormous masses covered with eternal snow without a sensation of religious stupefaction. But even in this expansive panorama he had his favorite spots: most of all the hermitage of Charvensod, where the last rays of the setting sun fell through groves and empty fields. At twilight he would glut his eyes on that scene, and it would set his mind at peace.

That hermitage had almost come to belong to him. Sometimes it seemed that he vaguely remembered having lived there in happier days and that the passage of time had merely dimmed his memory. What particularly moved him was the sight of the distant mountains fading at their peaks into the horizon. The thought of distance, like that of the future, awakened hope in him. His oppressed heart longed to believe that there existed an unknown land where he could finally taste all that happiness which he had only imagined in his nocturnal reveries. A secret instinct accomplished the rest: it transformed hope into possibility.

Had it not cost the leper a great effort of will, once having accepted his fate, not to let himself be overcome by despair, De Maistre wondered. No, the leper would be lying if he said he never felt anything other than resignation. He had not attained that utter self-abnegation which some anchorites achieve. He had not yet accomplished that supreme annihilation of all human feelings. He passed his life in constant battle, and even the help of religion was not always enough to check the course of his fantasies. Often his imagination dragged him, against his will, into an ocean of chimerical desires that spread before him a fantastic picture of an unknown world.

In vain had books taught him of human perversity and the disasters that cling like shadows to man's fate; his heart refused to believe what his eyes read. The lot of free men was that much more to be envied, the more miserable his own was. When the first spring wind blew through the Aosta valley, he felt its reviving warmth penetrate the marrow of his bones, and a lust for life violently overflowed in him, breaking all the dams that stood in its way. He would slip out secretly from his prison then and, drunk with space, wander about the neighboring fields. He avoided those same people that his heart so passionately yearned to meet. Hidden among the bushes on the hilltop like a wild beast, he embraced the entire town with his glance. From afar he would watch the inhabitants of Aosta, who barely knew he existed. He would stretch out his arms to them, crying out for his share of happiness. In his outpourings of rapture (he confessed it with shame) he sometimes embraced the trunks of trees in the woods, begging God to animate them and give him at least one friend. But the trees repulsed him with their cool bark and remained silent. Overcome with fatigue, almost at the end of his strength, he would return in the end to the tower and seek consolation in prayer.

Unhappy man, he suffered all the torments of body and soul together. And those of the body were not the worst. True, they became more painful every month, but then they gradually diminished. When the moon first cut the sky with its thin sickle, the illness asserted itself with increased force. As the moon rounded into a disk, the malady lessened and seemed to change its nature: the skin on his body dried and turned white, and he felt almost no pain at all. The worst was not the pain in itself, but its eternal echo — insomnia.

"Ah! sleeplessness! sleeplessness!" the leper sighed. Unless you have known it yourself you cannot imagine how long and terrible the night is when you cannot close your eyes and when all there is before them is a future entirely barren of hope. No, no one could imagine it. The approach of dawn would find the leper so distraught that his thoughts were all confused, he no longer knew what was happening to him, and he fell victim to extraordinary hallucinations. He would imagine that some irresistible power was dragging him down to a bottomless pit. At other times black spots would weave back and forth before his eyes, increasing in size as they came toward him, and turn into mountains that finally crushed him. Sometimes clouds would emerge from the earth around him, and like swelling waves they threatened to swallow him up. When he tried to rise and free himself from these incubi, invisible chains seemed to bind him to his bed. No, they were not dreams. He always saw the same things, and the dread of these impressions exceeded the anguish of his body. But could not these horrible phantasms have been caused by a fever resulting from insomnia? The leper glanced hopefully at De Maistre. Ah, would that it were only fever! Would it please God that it were only fever! Till then the leper had always trembled at the thought that these were the first signs of madness.

De Maistre unconsciously moved nearer to the leper. "Aren't you afraid," the tenant of the tower warned him, "to come so close to me? Sit on that stone. I'll go around the other side of this bush, and we can talk without seeing each other. Be careful. Your fingers almost brushed against my hand!"

"I wanted to shake it," said De Maistre.

"It would have been the first time in my life," the leper replied, "that I had had that pleasure. No one has ever taken my hand.

"The unfortunate love to talk about their misfortunes." With these words the leper of the tower resumed his story. His sister had been his only link to the rest of humankind. When that link was broken by the will of the Almighty, he was condemned to eternal solitude. The nature of their illness, however, had forbidden them even that normal intimacy which, in the world outside, unites friends in sorrow. Even when he and his sister prayed together they did not look at each other, for fear that terrible sight would disturb their holy meditations. Their glances met only in heaven. After prayers the companion of his solitude usually returned to her own cell, or disappeared behind the hedge of hazel that bordered the garden.

There was a reason for the austere rule of their life together. When leprosy (to which his whole family had fallen victim) finally struck his sister and brought her to the tower in Aosta, they had never before seen each other. Her eyes widened in awful terror at the sight of her brother. For fear that the sight of him would plunge her into despair and, a hundred times worse, that too-near communion might aggravate her illness, he adopted this pitiful regimen. Leprosy had infected only her breasts, and the last spark of hope was not spent that one day she might recover and leave this habitation of the living dead. There was still some of the trelliswork where, after her arrival, he had erected a partition of hop to divide the garden in two. Narrow paths ran down both sides of the green hedge. The brother and sister could walk along together without seeing one another and without approaching each other too closely.

In spite of everything, he had not been absolutely alone then. In his solitude he heard the sound of her footsteps. When he went out under the trees for his morning prayers, the door of the tower would open silently and her voice would join his. In the afternoon when he tended his flowers, she would sometimes stroll up and down in the setting sun, and her shadow would swing back and forth like a pendulum over the flower beds. And when he did not see her, he found signs of her presence everywhere. One night he was pacing up and down his cell in an attempt to stifle some particularly sharp pains. Tired, he sat down on the bed for a while. In the deathly silence of the night he suddenly heard a slight rustle outside the door. He went to the door, put his ear to it, and understood at once. She was kneeling outside the door and in a barely perceptible whisper was reciting the Miserere. Tears flooded his eyes, he fell to his knees and followed her words with his lips. "Go to bed now," he told her at last. "I feel a little better. God bless you for your compassion." She departed in silence. Indeed, her prayer had been answered, and he had a few hours of peaceful sleep. But now? Now he was all alone again.

After her death he fell into a stupor that deprived him of the power to measure the depth of his loss. When he had recovered sufficiently to understand his new situation, he came near to losing his mind. He remembered this period as doubly painful. For it marked the greatest misfortune he had suffered and it recalled a temptation to crime, conquered only at the last moment.

During other periods of depression the idea of ending his life had occurred to him, but he had always known how to suppress it, at least for a while. And now a poor thing that should not have melted his heart nearly drove him to the verge of suicide.

A little mongrel dog had wandered into the tower a few years before. The leper and his sister had lavished the tenderest care on the poor animal, and after his sister's death the dog was all that was left to him. It must have been the dog's ugliness that led it to the haven of the Tower of Fright. Driven out by the living, it was a veritable treasure in the house of the dead. The leper and his sister called the dog *Miracolo* because its perpetual gaiety sometimes gave them a fleeting moment of forgetfulness. Although the dog would run off for long periods, it never occurred to its new master that these adventures might alarm the citizens of Aosta. One day two soldiers knocked at the gate of the tower with orders to drown the four-legged vagabond at once in the Dora River. They tied a rope around the dog's neck and dragged it to the gate. But the crowd assembled outside begrudged the mongrel that end in the clean billows of the Dora and stoned it to death just outside the gate.

At the sound of the howling crowd, the leper ran to his cell more dead than alive. His legs gave out beneath him, and he threw himself on the bed. All the old wounds of his heart seemed to open afresh.

In that state of mind he waited until sunset before going to his favorite corner of the garden. The friendly landscape was calming him when he suddenly spied a pair of lovers on the path near the wall. They walked along immersed in their happiness, stopping every few feet to embrace in peaceful security, never suspecting that an envious glance was tracking them and almost devouring them. Yes, envious! Never before had a picture of human felicity presented itself so vividly to the tenant of the tower, and for the first time envy crept into his heart. He immediately returned to his cell. Oh God, how desolate and bleak, how terrible it seemed now! "Then it is here," he exclaimed, "that I am doomed to live forever. Dragging my miserable life behind me, it is here that I must await the end of my days! The Almighty floods every living creature with torrents of felicity and only I . . . I am the only creature that must live alone. What an atrocious fate!"

Overwhelmed by these sad thoughts, he forgot the one comforter that still remained to him — himself. "Why," he continued his blasphemous monologue, "did I ever see the light of day? Why should I be nature's only stepchild? Like a disinherited son I look on the rich heritage of all mankind, and heaven in its niggardliness denies only me my share. No, no," his wrath overflowed, "there is no happiness for you on this earth. Die, you miserable wretch, die! You have befouled the earth with your presence too long. Let the earth swallow you alive. Let every trace of your being disappear behind you." His unrestrained fury increased every minute. His only thought was self-destruction.

He decided to burn the tower and entrust the immolation of the last traces of his existence to the flames. In his despair he went outside the gate of the tower and wandered around the foot of the wall. Shouts burst from his breast against his will and terrified him in the silence of the night. On the verge of madness, he withdrew toward the gate and screamed, "Woe to you, Leper, woe to you!" And as if everything conspired to his ruin, suddenly from the direction of the fortress of Bramafan an echo repeated clearly, "Woe to you!" He stopped at the gate and looked behind him. The faint echo of the mountains picked it up for a long while, "Woe to you!"

He took a lamp, gathered some dry wood and twigs for kindling, and went to the lowest room of the tower, the room that had been his sister's when she was alive. He had not been in there since her death. Everything looked as if she had died only the day before. He set the lamp on the table and noticed the crucifix she had always worn around her neck. The ribbon of the crucifix was folded between the leaves of the Bible on the table. He froze at the sight and suddenly realized the profundity of the crime he was about to commit. Mechanically he opened the Bible. A sealed letter fell out. "I will soon leave you alone," she had written, "but I will never forsake you. I will watch over you from heaven. And I will beseech God that He give you courage to bear this life with resignation until it pleases Him to reunite us in a better world. I leave you this cross, which I wore all my life. It brought me consolation in pain and was the only witness to my tears. Remember, when you see it, that my last wish was that you could live and die as a good Christian." A cloud seemed to pass before his eyes after reading these last words, and he fainted. It was the middle of the night when he regained consciousness, and everything that had happened to him during the day seemed like a dream. He turned a thankful glance toward heaven. The sky was calm and clear, and a single star glistened outside the window. Was there not some sign of hope in this, that one of the rays was intended for the leper's cell? He returned to his own room and spent the rest of the night reading the Book of Job, feeling with a kind of joy that the dark fog of madness that had driven him to the verge of mortal sin was finally dispersed.

"Oh, merciful stranger!" the leper suddenly sighed. "May God bless you and may you never have to live alone!"

He thought for a moment and added: "She was only twenty-five when she died, but her sufferings made her much older. In spite of the illness that distorted her features, she still would have been beautiful had it not been for that terrible pallor . . . She was the living effigy of death. I couldn't look at her without trembling . . . She suffered so terribly that I watched the end approach with a desperate joy . . ."

When he had finished, the leper buried his face in his hands. After a moment of silence, he got up and said to De Maistre, "If you are ever caught in the snares of pain and grief, good sir, remember the lonely man of Aosta. Then your visit will not have been in vain."

They walked to the gate together. Before going out into the street, De Maistre put on his right glove and again offered to shake his host's hand. The leper jumped back in fright. He raised his hands to heaven and cried out: "Merciful God, lavish all good things on this compassionate traveler."

De Maistre asked if they might write to each other every now and then, taking the necessary precautions, of course. For the twinkling of an eye the leper hesitated. "Why," he replied then, "seek refuge in illusions? I can have no other companion than myself and no other friend than God. Goodbye, kind stranger, goodbye. And may God be with you . . . Goodbye forever!"

The visitor went out. The leper closed the gate and locked it.

III

The nearby Alps temper the heat of summer in these parts, but at the same time they smother the visitor from the lowlands in a kind of dreamlike numbness. The quiet is absolute. Occasionally a bird may fall from somewhere and, rebounding hard from the ground, disappear among the green treetops like a loose stone from the mountain slope that for a moment breaks the dark and motionless surface of a lake. Or the ear may catch the faint tinkle of a bell in a distant pasture, like the echo from the bottom of a well. Only at twilight, when the sun beyond the mountains reddens briefly with a cool luster and disappears, does the first gentle breeze penetrate the dense, sticky air that covers the valley all day with an opaline film.

Anyone looking for solitude will not be disappointed among these hills. The Italians call them *colline;* the word is as fluent and melodious as the shape and golden green color of the melancholy hills themselves. During my leave here, I never saw a human face during the day. In the evening I would go to the village and sit for several hours in the tavern, where the Piedmontese peasants in their big hats drank the local, almost black wine and sang their guttural songs to the crescent moon that shone through the leaves.

In the first days of September it rained. Torrents of water beat against the walls of the house and against the trembling window panes, and hammered an arpeggio across the loose tiles of the roof. The afternoons were dark, and the sky hung low over the Elvo valley like a gray rag wrung out in an enormous washtub by a pair of hands hidden in the clouds. Sometimes the sky cleared for a while in the morning. Even then the rain did not always stop, but turned into a sunny spray of silver drops. Clouds formed a frayed woolen collar halfway up the Mucrone; the peak itself towered above them, fresh and clean in contrast with the ashen steppes below. The dark-green leaves on the trees glittered like bottle glass, and the valley looked like the bottom of a drained pool covered with pondweed.

Sometimes out of boredom and sometimes as if I owed it to the intangible genius of the house, I read again and again the little book by De Maistre I had found on the table. Often, particularly at night, after having read the last words, I would turn away from the dirty walls hung with etchings and broken by the shadows of the furniture, and with relief I would look at the moths gathered on the ceiling over the pale circle of the lampshade. After a while my habitual reading of that book began to call up the same reminiscences. Near the town in Poland where I was born, there is a high mountain dear to the hearts of tourists. It is called the Holy Cross for the relics apparently preserved in the old Bernardine abbey at the peak. At the base of the mountain, by the side of the road leading to the nearest human settlement, there is a stone statue facing toward the abbey. It is the kneeling figure of the "Pilgrim of the Holy Cross," believed by authorities on the region to be an ex-voto set there centuries ago by some pious pilgrim.

Folklore, however, has enveloped the stone pilgrim in legend: every year the kneeling figure advances the space of a poppy seed, and when he finally reaches the summit of the Holy Cross, the world will end. Evidently the contemplation of ultimate things was not foreign to the creators of this legend. Nor—far more surprising—were they strangers to the subtler relationships between hope and hopelessness, faith and despair. Because it is equally legitimate to conclude that—in his endless suffering, cutting his knees on the stones at every step—the Pilgrim of the Holy Cross will one day reach and yet never reach the end of his journey. If he reaches the summit, the only reward for his perseverance will be a momentary vision of the light of salvation before the last fire consumes him along with the whole world.

The stone pilgrim has no face, just a small rough head set directly on the torso. The forehead and nose form a continuous vertical line with the beard. There are two holes for eyes: like those of a blind man, they stare ahead without seeing. His hair hangs down over his arms, which are set unnaturally low on the torso, and his hands are crossed in a pious gesture on his breast. The broad base of the kneeling figure is overgrown with moss. Corroded by wind and rain, chunks of stone chipped away, he is a monument of infinite patience. But only when one sees people who pass by every day, indifferent to the stone figure as if it were a piece of the landscape long unnoticed, does one realize that the pilgrim must also be infinitely lonely.

It was precisely this, aside from his physical appearance, that led my imagination to connect him with the leper of the tower in Aosta.

IV

In the beginning I thought that the former occupant of the house in which I was staying had been attracted by the peculiar solace contained in De Maistre's little book.

The preface to the Neapolitan edition of 1828 suggested that view. The translator had written it in the then-fashionable form of a dedication. The Princess of Torella, Duchess of Lavello, etc., to whom the translation was dedicated, was implored by her humble servant to accept the Italian version of the book that had given so much pleasure to Count Flemming, the Prussian ambassador to the Kingdom of Naples, when he was alive. "It is fitting that the ambassador's untimely death," the translator wrote, "painful to everyone, but most painful to you, Madame, be commemorated in this manner." For Count Flemming had often said that there was no man on earth, no matter how terrible his misery, who would not consider himself fortunate in comparison with that leper. The count called this book the comforter of the afflicted, and since the count himself was victim to pain and affliction he kept that book with him as if it were a vial of ever-soothing balm. The Princess of Torella shared the ambassador's enthusiasm for the book, and it was from her that the translator had come to know of the existence of De Maistre's account.

What touched the translator most deeply when he read the book was the gesture of renunciation with which the tenant of the tower in Aosta declined to shake hands or establish a correspondence with De Maistre. With courage and resignation the leper had accepted his dual cross of patience and solitude — a challenge to our whining epoch, and a magnificent example to those who consider that the nobler answer to misfortune is not complaint and lamentation, but silence—the silence that is nourished by the strength of the soul and looks only to God for its reward.

Could there have been any doubt that the lonesome recluse in his little tower on the steppes of the Mucrone nourished himself day after day on a few drops of this ever-soothing balm?

To be sure, I soon discovered that I was mistaken. I found a notebook in the drawer of the table that indicated the *ginnasio* teacher's concern with the matter went far deeper. To this day I cannot say what end that notebook was intended for—literary, historical, or philosophical—because it included only summaries and extracts of various kinds and not a word concerning the writer.

What I supposed to be the title of the intended work was printed in Latin on the first page: VITA DUM SUPEREST, BENE EST. The succeeding pages—sometimes bearing only a single line at the top, sometimes covered halfway down by his almost illegible script—gave no clue to whether the title was written in bitter mockery, or whether it represented the old man's confession of faith. Actually, the former occupant's notes gave no clear notion of anything at all. Their very randomness rather suggested the chaotic nature of his reflections and study. In one place he had copied down the real name and date of death of the leper of Aosta: Pier Bernardo Guasco, who died in 1803, six years after De Maistre's visit. In another place he had transcribed Octave Mirbeau's observation that leprosy is a disease from which a man neither recovers nor dies. Just under this observation, which belongs to the tradition of leprosy as a "mystical disease," was a quotation from Kierkegaard:

> It is indeed very far from being true that, literally understood, one dies of this sickness, or that this sickness ends with bodily death. On the contrary, the torment of despair is precisely this, not to be able to die. So it has much in common with the situation of the moribund when he lies and struggles with death, and cannot die. So to be sick unto death is, not to be able to die—yet not as though there were hope of life; no, the hopelessness in this case is that even the last hope, death, is not available. When death is the greatest danger, one hopes for life; but when one becomes acquainted with an even more dreadful danger, one hopes for death. So when the danger is so great that death has become one's hope, despair is the disconsolateness of not being able to die.

Further on, there were a few verses from the Book of Leviticus, 13: 45–46:

And the leper in whom the plague is, his clothes shall be rent, and his head bare, and he shall put a covering upon his upper lip, and shall cry, Unclean, unclean. All the days wherein the plague shall be in him he shall be defiled; he is unclean: he shall dwell alone; without the camp shall his habitation be.

I was most interested by two long extracts from the seventeenth-century documents, describing the condition of lepers in the Middle Ages, that Ambroise Paré found in the Hôtel Dieu archives in Paris. One was the medieval *Decalog of the Leper,* which forbade the leper, by order of the king, everything that might even indirectly bring him in contact with his fellow men, in other words, everything except living and breathing. One of the provisions, however, allowed the leper to answer questions if he turned his face in the direction of the wind. The other document was a description of the leper's "investiture," or rather his temporal interment. Wearing the stole and surplice, the priest would await him on the threshold of the church. Then the priest would read to him publicly the medical certificate that declared him, on the basis of the prescribed symptoms, a leper before the law. Later the same priest would sprinkle the leper with holy water and clear a path for him through the crowd into the House of God. The church would be hung with shrouds, and a catafalque would be erected by the main altar for the occasion. After the funeral mass for the peace of his soul, the leper would be wrapped in a white sheet, laid on a litter, and accompanied by the whole congregation to the cemetery. By a freshly dug grave the priest would sprinkle a handful of dirt on the leper's head and recite the sacramental formula: "With this sign you are dead to the world. You will be born again in God. Therefore have patience, the patience of Christ and His Saints, until the day you enter into Paradise, where there is no affliction, where all are pure and beautiful, without blemish or stain, more brilliant in splendor than the sun." At the end the priest would carefully hand the leper a hooded cloak, a basket, a pail, and a stick with three sliding discs, pronouncing the following sacramental formula: "Take this attire and wear it in humility. The basket and pail for food and water. And the rattle that you may warn passersby in time of your presence."

There was one word in the private notes of the house below the Mucrone that might have unveiled something of the sentiments or thoughts of the lonely teacher, but unfortunately that word was too ambiguous. The faithful reader of De Maistre's account had circled the passage on the last page that described the leper's hesitation (for the twinkling of an eye) before declining the offer to exchange letters. And in the margin he had written *Perchè?*, "Why?" It only caught my attention after I had read the notebook I found on the table. Did the word express surprise that the leper of Aosta did not jump at the offer, and did it allude to the Latin phrase on the title page of the notebook? Or did it express disapproval that the leper had hesitated at all, albeit for an instant, instead of bearing bravely and with resignation his "dual cross of patience and solitude," without betraying a shade of fear at the prospect of that eternal silence which "is nourished by the strength of the soul and looks only to God for its reward"? To this day, in spite of everything I learned in the nearby village about my dead host, I cannot answer these questions. But neither can I answer other questions, questions concerning De Maistre's interlocutor himself. Did the pulse of hope, however faint, beat again in that brief flash of hesitation? Did Pier Bernardo Guasco come to life for the last time, if only for an instant, in the creature who as the *Lebbroso* had died to the world years before?

The rains stopped as unexpectedly as they had begun. The end of summer in the sub-Alpine region of Italy is barely distinguishable from the hot and protracted beginning of autumn, which often lasts to the end of October and subsides slowly in the lazy ripeness of the mountain sun. Only in November do the chilly mornings announce a cooler season.

The rustling ribbons of the falling streams, silver in the bright sun, seemed to wash away the dark reflections of my reading. But they only seemed to do so, because a few days after the weather cleared I gave in to the temptation to make a trip, the only point of which could be to touch a tombstone that was sinking into the earth.

V

The town of Ivrea is nominally the entry into the Val d'Aosta but the true valley only begins farther on, at the Chateau d'Issogne, a fifteenth-century example of Late Gothic architecture built by the Counts of Challant — the same family that, according to popular legend, produced the assassin of the Duchess of Braganza in the tower of Bramafan.

The entrance to the Val d'Aosta must seem to every traveler to be the jumping-off place from a realm of light into a domain of darkness, guarded on both sides by the heavy shadow of the cliffs. There are valleys where the light of day only creeps in through mountain passes, but in the Val d'Aosta it emerges as if from underground. One cannot guess the age of a passerby wading through the darkness only a few feet away. Italians call the Aosta valley *la valle tetra*. And it is gloomy, indeed, although such a commonplace word does scant justice to the sullen beauty of that narrow streak of shadow dividing two worlds. As one goes on, his eyes gradually become accustomed to the dark, and he fixes his gaze on the dim strip of fog suspended above the waters of the mountain stream, which smash against the unyielding rock wall with a thunderous roar.

At Saint-Vincent the valley brightens and assumes a more cheerful tone. But along the road that winds monotonously through the chestnut woods and deserted pastures on the slopes, and on to the bridge over the Dora, *la valle tetra* again justifies its name. Beyond the river the deep basin of the actual valley of Aosta springs open. Saturated with the green of vineyards and flatlands, splotched here and there by small settlements and isolated houses, the valley resembles a painter's palette. And for a moment the traveler forgets that nature has imprisoned this colored bowl in a dead fist of naked peaks and glaciers. But the town with its severe air will remind him.

Aosta — the ancient Augusta Praetoria — owes its severity not only to the Roman and medieval ruins that stand like old stumps in the new city. The streets are narrow, but they lack the theatrical bustle of the back streets of southern Italian cities, and the houses have a stiff and repelling cleanliness about them. The people have hard, cloudy faces, and even in moments of animation maintain a heavy dignity that one associates with Protestant rather than Catholic countries. One senses some particular harmony between this human climate and the rocky and ascetic peace of the collegiate church of St. Orso. The city of Aosta is closed on all sides. Beyond the tollgates of most of the roads leading out of the city is a massive and formidable wall of Alps. The road leading to the Great St. Bernard Pass, for example, is simply a prolongation of Xavier de Maistre Street.

Time does all, it erases even the memory of human sufferings. In spite of De Maistre Street, in spite of the Via Torre del Lebbroso, in spite of the fact that Aosta is still essentially a small town, no one I asked could point out exactly the road to the tower where the leper Pier Bernardo Guasco spent twenty-one years of his life. A century and a half had passed since his ceaseless silent agony had received its ultimate reward from God — a century and a half of life, death, birth, and again life and death. A century and a half had passed since the solitary inhabitant of that unreal world isolated beyond the borders of existence had disappeared — a century and a half in which the real world bestirred itself, day after day, month after month, year after year, about its griefs and joys. Is it any wonder, then, that the crest of time's eternal tide had obliterated the memory of the tower, or that the deafening roar of that sea had smothered its silent voice?

It turned out that the other tower, Bramafan, was better known in Aosta. But night had fallen, and the street leading from the railway station to Bramafan was poorly lighted and deserted. In this still sparsely settled quarter of the city (as it had been in De Maistre's day), looking like the outskirts of any provincial town — crooked fences, neglected gardens, houses scarcely rising above the ground, and black coal smoke near the tower — the Cry of Hunger had never abated in the course of centuries. The round tower rose dramatically from the darkness against a background of low floating clouds, which every now and then uncovered a glimpse of the moon, like the flashing glow of a distant blaze.

The pavement suddenly ended and a footpath led off at an angle between the houses that bordered the open fields. Fifty yards farther on, the path entered a small empty square, and disappeared in a narrow alley on the other side. It was even darker here, but at the far end of the alley I could see the pale glow of the lights of the center of town. I stopped halfway down the alley at the sight of a wall more than six feet high.

I had no difficulty in recognizing the sharp rectangularity of the tower and the mute eminence — so well rendered by the anonymous author of the etching — of the stone crown on top. Standing on tiptoe I could see, through the only breach in the wall, part of a yard grown wild with weeds that had once been the leper's garden.

Even in old and long-abandoned cemeteries one does not see such an accumulation of dead mold. The foot of the building was smothered with thick, overgrown stalks and enormous leaves. The walls exhaled the dust that powders tombstones sinking slowly into the ground. The highest window, just under the crest of the tower, was boarded up; the others were black, like hollowed-out eye sockets. But the silence of the place was not altogether dead, and it was this that was disturbing. There was something of the suspended, unfinished, unreconciled about it. It was hard not to fancy that there was someone walled up in there, someone with his ear pressed against a fissure in the stones, listening for sounds of life. The handle of the gate was rusted in its fixture; it had been a long time since anyone had turned it.

The Allied uniform opened all doors in Italy after the war: the next morning the municipal usher from the Ufficio delle Antichità e Belle Arti accompanied me to the tower. The day was sunny and almost hot. If one knows the way, it is only five minutes from Chanoux Square in the center of town to the corner of the alley marked Via Torre del Lebbroso.

It must always have been the street of shoemakers and small craftsmen, for all along the way low, arched entries curved over the artisans' bent backs. Our steps could not be heard over the din of hammers and the whistle of planes, and not a single head peeked out at us from the shops. But several children attached themselves to us, kicking a ball back and forth behind us. Years before, another group of children had fallen on the flower beds in the garden beyond the wall, and had run off at once shouting, *Buon giorno, Lebbroso!* What was it in those laughing shouts that had given the leper such peculiar satisfaction?

The tower lost much of its strangeness by day, but it still mournfully suggested a corner of a cemetery overgrown with weeds and nettles. Stones have an inexplicable quality of their own: they age in one way when they patiently serve man, and in another way when they are ignored by the stream of life.

Abandoned by man the stones seem to dry and crack like a crust of earth untouched for years by a drop of water. Visited by man they thicken and harden like the bark of an eternally green tree — even when man's presence is only his memory and not his solicitous hand.

I approached the tower with the same emotion I had felt on my visit the night before. But now the tower seemed to imprison not so much the forgotten hermit as his whole, vast, inhuman desert without horizons. The only human sign there, the only thing that somehow bound this shred of earth to the world around and acknowledged an interrupted life — rather than a mere void that had existed since time immemorial — was something about the broken, moldering steps that had been cut out of the remains of Roman wall to the left of the hedge.

Inside the tower I could not immediately distinguish the staircase from the rubbish heaped against the wall. It was like being at the bottom of a deep rocky pit, and it took a long while before I could formulate an idea of the place from the play of patches of light, the shadows, and the black recesses. The air was hung with the musty and pungent odor of dampness and decomposition.

Fortunately the stairs turned out to be more stable than I had supposed. Without touching the railing, and bracing my back against the damp wall, I climbed slowly until at last I was able to grasp the ledge of a small window. From there I saw a part of the courtyard and my guide, who had unbuttoned his jacket and was stretched out on the grass with his face to the sun. The stairs cut through the floor above and gave onto a landing illuminated by a sliver of light that came through a half-open door. I opened the door but did not enter: it was the lowest room of the tower, the room in which the leper's sister had lived.

A ray of light fell directly on another flight of stairs at the opposite end of the vestibule. The first steps creaked so menacingly that I wanted to turn back. And again the darkness thickened. But as I stood undecided, I heard a rapid beating of wings just over my head, and a narrow opening appeared above me as if cut by a knife. A fissure of light came through the door a bird had thrust open in its flight. There remained one sign of its presence in the room on the highest landing of the tower — a loose board in the window was still swinging on its upper nails from the violent blow. I pushed the board to one side and saw the gentle landscape of meadows beyond the railroad, strewn here and there with the remains of the morning fog and ribbons of smoke from burned leaves.

The small cell was rectangular, and only now I saw that there was a second window, covered with a piece of cloth. It opened onto the town and the garland of hills under the Great St. Bernard Pass, and the white peaks beyond. The campanile of the collegiate church and the octagonal turret of the cloister of St. Orso seemed to leap forward from the Alpine background of light, clear crystal. What the former inhabitant of the tower probably never knew was that the pride of that church was a centuries-old painting hanging on the left wall of the apse, *La miracolosa guarigione di una storpia nella chiesa e processione*, "The Miraculous Healing of a Lame Woman in the Church, and Procession"; and that three phases of the plagues of Job were carved on the capital of one of the columns of the Romanesque portico in the cloister.

A low, bare cot, almost fallen to the ground, stood in the corner between the windows. Against the wall on the other side of the cell, behind a massive table and a leather-covered stool, stood a long carved chest, the kind the Piedmont peasants use as a cupboard, as a bench, and, if necessary, as a cot for the night. The ceiling turned down obliquely over an earthenware stove. The whole cell suggested a narrow cage — movement within the cell was limited to an absolute minimum.

The central point of the cell, however, was a large crucifix. It did not hang above the head of the bed but at the side, so that one could kneel on the floor to pray and prop one's elbows on the bed. A magnificent wrought-iron figure of Christ, though out of all proportion, hung on a wide-armed cross painted ebony. At first glance, the coarseness of the iron, the distorted swelling of the ribs, and the blotches of rust and encrusted dirt, all seemed to be ulcers covering the entire body of Christ. Instead of a crown of thorns, what seemed like a large black wedding ring was pressed on the exaggeratedly bent head of the Christ.

VI

The Italian assigned to our military mission in Milan did not tell the whole truth about his distant relative in the little house under the Mucrone; but perhaps no one knows the whole truth. Nevertheless, it was decidedly too little to say only that the old pensioner had died there all alone toward the end of the war. After having heard the accounts given in the nearby village, after my return from Aosta, I began to take the word "died" with a grain of salt; the word was correct insofar as the physical fact was concerned. Only the qualification, "all alone," was absolutely right — dreadfully right.

Not much was known of the *ginnasio* teacher's past. He was Sicilian by birth, and before he was sent to Turin he had taught in Sicily, where he lost his entire family — his wife and three children — in the famous Messina earthquake of 1908. It was rumored that he had been retired prematurely because of the scandal arising from an attempt at suicide. He had bought this house in 1938 from the village doctor (a widower who went to live with his sons in Turin) and had moved in at once.

In the last six years of his life he was seen in the village only a few times in all. He spoke to no one except his regular provisioners, and he never acknowledged the greetings that are directed even to strangers in these parts. Although he was entirely gray he was still vigorous, and his not overly tall, lean figure commanded a certain irresistible respect. Perhaps there had been a trace of fear in this respect, for his eyes sometimes glittered with a hidden madness. Sicilians are known for their natural inclination to the tragic. It is said that Sicilians "carry the thought of death with them always, like a thorn in the flesh." The old man's house came to be known as *La bara siciliana*, the Sicilian coffin. Later the name was shortened to *La bara*, and this name stuck. Once a month the local postman brought a pension check from the post office to *La bara*. Every Saturday morning the innkeeper's daughter took the bus to *La bara* with a basket of provisions and laundry; *il padrone della bara* waited for her even in the worst weather at the crossing of the road and the path up the slope to the house, and helped her carry up the basket.

Once the young priest from the village visited him. The interview in the garden was brief, and the priest remained standing. He asked the old man why he never went to mass on Sundays. Without lifting his head from the clipped hedges, the old man replied that he did not feel the need to go; what he was waiting for did not require faith — only patience. Asked how he could live that way, he replied with a shrug: "Because I cannot die."

In August 1944 the remains of a shattered S.S. division poured through the countryside seizing men wherever they could to be sent to labor camps in Germany. There already existed something on the order of a partisan information network in the region, and the village on the Mucrone highlands was warned in time. On a Wednesday night all of the men, even the aged, were evacuated to the hills; only the women and children remained behind, and the young priest. Friday morning a large truck escorted by four motorcycles appeared in the little square in front of the church. As soon as the S.S. sergeant saw the women and children being herded into the square, he understood the situation. He decided to teach the women and children, at least, a lesson they would not forget; and he did not lack imagination. Through his driver who knew some Italian, he announced that if they did not produce at least one male inhabitant within two hours, the priest would pay with his life for the men's flight.

No one knows exactly how the lonely house three kilometers from the village came to play a part in this drama of the war: whether one of the women whispered something to the German driver, or whether one of the soldiers had noticed the house from the end of the road. In any case, a motorcycle with a sidecar leapt for the prey and brought it back to the square fifteen minutes later.

Il padrone della bara seemed mystified by what was going on around him. A soldier shoved him forward toward the sergeant, who was sitting on the running board of the truck. The crowd thronged the steps of the church. The old man was calm and, as usual, silent, but at the same time he seemed pale and bewildered. The soldier left him alone in the middle of the square and took several paces off to one side. At the sergeant's command, the soldier lightly raised the barrel protruding from under his right armpit. The crowd of women and children began to sway back and forth with a mournful lament, and the priest began to recite the prayer for the dead. Only then did the old man waver. He threw his arms across his heart, and his trembling face turned whiter than his hair. The plaintive singing stopped, and the sergeant and the soldier aiming his rifle turned to each other without a word. "No, no, no," the old man wailed in a cracking voice. The priest broke off the prayer, looked at him for a moment, and turned to the driver: "He is not to blame. He's not from here. He's not from our village." The old man repeated in a monotone: "I am not to blame. I'm not from here. I'm not from this village." The sergeant asked the interpreter something. "He's from Turin," the priest anticipated his answer. "I'm from Turin," the old man repeated like an echo. No one had ever heard so many words cross his lips.

The rest happened in a flash. The truck and its escort of four motor-cycles disappeared around the bend of the road leading toward the city. In the middle of the square — dazzlingly white from the sun and the pastel façades of the church and the little town hall — lay an enormous black bird in a pool of blood, the wings of its cassock spread out like a cross. The crowd of women and children huddled around the church door stood motionless. The old man was standing alone on the other side of the square. He stared at the body of the priest for a long time. Finally he covered his face with his hands and turned toward home.

The crowd of women and children followed him at a distance the whole three kilometers in the scorching August heat and the dust of the winding road that led up to his house. The old man halted often, a few times he stumbled, and once he even fell: he crawled over to the little stone wall and pulled himself up again. The crowd stopped then and waited in silence. The whole affair lasted perhaps an hour. The sun was directly overhead when with an effort the old man pushed open the gate and disappeared behind the trees along the iron fence.

The next day was Saturday, and the innkeeper's daughter did not take him the basket of provisions. But there was no reason to do so. The bus driver did not see him that morning at his usual station at the crossing of the road and the path. Curious, he stopped the bus and walked up to *La bara*. *Il padrone della bara* lay dead on the sofa in his room. His body was already cold.

VII

Several times I have tried to write a story about the last six years of the life of the resident of the tower in Aosta, but I have helplessly laid down my pen halfway through each attempt. Like De Maistre, I could not conceive of eternal solitude. And the idea frightened me, as it had De Maistre.

"Often when we dream," a poet writes, "what we see and experience strikes us as something unreal and at the same time as something more than real. Paralyzed, we hover uncertainly on the border between night and day; when we finally open our eyes, for a fraction of a second we are unsure which of two impressions is the true one: the one that actually disappeared or the one that took its place. I try to think of this immeasurably brief moment of suspense whenever I want to imagine the hour of my death."

Perhaps this is a key to the idea of eternal solitude — that moment of suspension between night and day, between dreaming and waking, drawn out endlessly. Or is it a dream of death, in a tower surrounded by the sea, from which one is awakened by an unfathomable spasm of fright only at the approach of actual death? De Maistre took the motto of his story from *The Seasons:* "Winter," by the eighteenth-century English poet James Thomson. I wanted to use a pair of lines from the "City of Dreadful Night," by his nineteenth-century namesake:

> For life is but a dream whose shapes return
> Some frequently, some seldom, some by night . . .

I never managed to establish the circumstances in which Pier Bernardo Guasco died, although I passed through Aosta many times again after the war. But I happened on two traditions concerning him. One had it that shortly before his death the leper stopped accepting provisions, and by starving himself hastened the end of his days. According to the other, one cloudy March night he went out into the deserted street carrying a lamp in his hand, and some late passerby chased him back to his tower with stones and curses, and he died soon after. I was both touched and amused to detect that unequalled ability of simple people constantly to rework old legends: thus two ancient legends of Aosta were kept alive — the starved Duchess of Braganza in Bramafan, and the white lady of the *Torre dello Spavento.*

I do not regret being unable to write a story about the tenant of the tower. If there were not things in human life that man's imagination refused to comprehend, he would end by cursing the despair that penetrates literature, instead of seeking hope in its productions. But I often think of the leper of Aosta when I close my eyes. I like to imagine him finally dragging himself on his knees to the top of the Holy Cross Mountain, infinitely exhausted and worn out by time, and collapsing with a shout of triumph on the naked rock. The shout will die at once in the deafening roar of the end of the world.

MELANIE RAE THON

Duty

The next time Willy Hamilton found himself in the Tylers' house, he and Delores sat in the kitchen. It was late October. He accepted the drink she offered, a short one just like hers, vodka on the rocks with a squeeze of lime. He was still in uniform and knew what his father would say. *You're on duty until the minute you step out of those pants.* But Horton Hamilton wasn't there. He called Mrs. Tyler *Delores,* lightly, as if he had called her that his whole life. *Thank you, Delores.*

"You're so tall, Willy."

"It's the boots."

Those were their first words, and they almost deflated him before he was even inside the house. He was seven years old again, putting his feet in Horton's big shoes, drowning in his father's clothes.

"You look very handsome."

The boots fit. His boots. He tipped the hat. "Thank you, Delores."

Now he was sipping his vodka, sitting across the table from a pretty woman who just happened to be his best friend's mother. "How's Jay?" Willy said.

"The same."

She didn't make excuses this time, didn't pretend he was asleep, didn't say he had the flu. *The same.* Willy had never understood how awful those words could be. They were the soothing words the doctor used at the hospital when his grandmother was dying. *The same.*

Delores Tyler cupped both hands around her drink and stared at the ice splitting in the warm vodka. It was only five o'clock but almost dark. The air turned murky and Delores blurred. Willy wondered if one of them might be drunk.

"I'm afraid I haven't been much of a mother."

"It's not your fault." His words came too fast and sounded false.

"Lousy wife, lousy mother — I made a mess of things." Even in the fading light, Willy could see that her hands were unsteady. He almost reached for her, but she blinked hard, gripped her glass and drained it. "I'm afraid I've had a few too many." She laughed. "So you can't hold me responsible for anything I say." He had never seen her with her hair down, curling around her shoulders. "Or do," she added.

She filled her glass again. "You don't mind, do you?"

"Why should I?" But he did mind. The boy who was Jay Tyler's friend and his own mother's son wanted to take the glass from her and toss the vodka and ice into the sink. This boy wanted to dump his own drink too, but there was someone else here, someone who thought of himself as a young man. He was reckless and scorned the other Willy for his prudish rules. So he drank fast and poured himself another.

"I tried in the beginning," she said. "The good wife part, I mean."

"It's getting dark," Willy said.

"Yes, he'll be home soon."

Willy heard footsteps above his head, then a thud, the dull sound of a body dropping to the floor.

"Jay," Delores said. "He must know you're here."

"Did he fall?"

"Maybe."

"Shouldn't we see if he's all right?"

"He does it all the time." She raised her glass. "Like mother, like son—much to his father's dismay."

Willy thought of the Jay he knew. The Jay who said drinking destroyed the body, who wouldn't touch a drop when he was in training.

"Because of the pain, you know," Delores said. "It started because of the pain."

Willy imagined Jay's legs, the shattered bones, the months in bed. He realized he had no idea how much it hurt, no knowledge of pain beyond scraped knees and a bruised forehead, a cut on his foot that took a month to heal and left a scar an inch and a half long.

"That's how it started with me too," Delores said, "because of the pain."

Willy didn't want to know, didn't want to hear anything about the pain of a woman.

Never talk about sorrow in the dark, his mother said, flicking on lights all through the house before she sat down to tell them their grandmother was dead.

"I was pregnant with Jay. I found a handkerchief in Andrew's drawer. A brand-new handkerchief with his initials embroidered in one corner, the kind of thing he'd never buy for himself, a gift—do you see what I mean?"

Willy nodded. He wondered why she was telling him this. He heard more steps above him, the awkward three-legged gait of a man with a cane.

"I moved it to the back of his drawer, so he'd know that I'd found it, that I knew he had a girl."

She poured her third drink and topped Willy's too.

"I thought he'd see what a fool he was, that he'd look at me some night, pregnant with his child, and realize he loved me. The handkerchief would disappear.

"But that didn't happen. The next time I put his clothes away it was in the front of the drawer again, right on top. He wanted me to know that he wasn't going to stop seeing her. This was our life now, our *vow*.

"I imagined crying myself sick. I thought he'd come home and find me that way, on my bed, in the dark. That he'd see he'd been a fool. But Andrew wasn't like that. It's not in him to be sorry. He would have said, 'Pull yourself together, darling.' So I didn't cry. I made myself a drink and cooked dinner. I got drunk, Willy, and I discovered I didn't give a damn if he was sorry or not."

Willy heard a door open and close.

"I figured out who she was. The next time I stopped by his office, I knew. His receptionist was wearing red shoes. What kind of girl wears red shoes? As soon as I saw them, I knew."

Willy would never understand women. He was sure Delores was right about the girl but couldn't imagine how a pair of shoes could reveal the truth.

"I hated those shoes. I wanted to spit on them. I wanted to tear them off her pretty little feet and jump up and down on them till the polish cracked and the heels snapped off."

Andrew Johnson Tyler stood in the kitchen doorway and cleared his throat. "Fine thing," he said, "for a man to find his wife alone in the dark with a policeman."

Dr. Tyler put on his southern drawl; *policeman* was a joke in his mouth, one more thing in which a medical man didn't believe. He hit the light switch, and Delores covered her eyes. "I'm sorry," he said. "Is that too bright for you?" *It's not in him to be sorry.* "What's for dinner, darling?" He bent down to kiss her cheek. "No, don't tell me — let me guess: chicken pot pies?" He massaged her shoulders so hard she flinched. "My wife's a wonderful cook," he told Willy. "We'd ask you to stay for supper, but I'm sure she doesn't have an extra pie. Am I right, sweetheart?" He squeezed her shoulder again, and Delores gazed at Willy, a silent plea he couldn't comprehend.

When Willy stood, he felt the floor tilt and remembered Coach Brubaker circling him, poking him between the shoulder blades, smacking his butt, thumping his chest. *You are one sorry sack of shit.*

"I hope I'm not driving you out," Dr. Tyler said. "I hate to be the spoiler." He still had one hand on his wife's shoulder.

"No, sir. Time for me to get home for supper anyway." He saw his mother's table: fried chicken, potatoes, vegetables — something green and something yellow: *For my hardworking boy,* Flo would say, and he would want to cry. A boy, yes, as long as he ate dinner in his mother's house.

Delores Tyler had no intention of cooking dinner for her husband. She wasn't even going to slide a chicken pot pie into the oven. He knew where the freezer was, could turn on the damn stove. "You made a fool of yourself," she said.

"Did I? I thought I was quite congenial. Not as congenial as you, of course."

"I'm tired."

"You had an *exhausting* afternoon."

"I'm going to lie down."

"Why don't you, darling?"

Delores lay on her bed and wished she was still talking to Willy. She kicked off her shoes. He was a nice boy. She wished she'd explained that she hadn't always been this way. *I could have forgiven him,* she imagined herself saying, *for the handkerchief, for the girl, for the red shoes. But he wouldn't let me.*

She thought of the day her marriage ended, a hot Saturday in July. Jay was only three. They all drove down to the river, to a bend where the water eddied into a calm pool. Andrew waded in the shallows with Jay. He didn't like to swim; he sank, heavy bones and no fat. Delores was a good swimmer, light and strong — buoyant.

She let the current pull her downstream. When she was a hundred yards away, Andrew called to her to come back. *I pretended not to hear.*

At first she thought she would work her way back to shore, but the thought passed. The cool water numbed her limbs. Even now, lying on her bed all these years later, she remembered how good it felt just to drift, to stop fighting. *I knew I could get back to the bank.* She saw the rushes sweep past her. *Anytime.*

Andrew ran along the river with Jay in his arms. She heard her name bouncing on the water and saw herself as he did, a head bobbing in the distance.

The flow grew swifter; the riverbed was strewn with boulders. Sometimes a whirlpool sucked her under and she thought she'd be smashed against a rock. She pictured her own body popping up hundreds of yards downstream, nothing but a bruise on her forehead, like a boy she'd known as a child, a boy whose brother had killed him with a stone, an accident. There was no blood, no open wound, just the swollen place above the brow, the pale violet bloom on his white face. *Angel,* she whispered, *taken that fast.*

Slowly she worked her way toward the bank, swimming at an angle, not fighting the current, letting the river do the work, being swept farther and farther downstream.

Soon she sat among the rushes along the shore. *I didn't mean to hide.* Andrew was barely fifty feet away. *But I was hidden.* Jay clung to his chest. *I let them pass.*

Andrew knew he had to turn around. If he waited too long there would be no hope. *I knew what he was thinking.* He was imagining the long ride to town, his own muddled explanation, the shame of it all, the way other men look at you when you admit you've lost your wife, when you say: *She swam away from me.* He envisioned the men in boats, dragging the river till dusk drove them to shore. He'd worked with such men before, peering into cloudy water. He knew how terrible it was, how every clump of weeds looked like a woman's hair, how the nets and hooks dredged up all that should stay at the bottom of a river: a rusty fan, a child's shoe, a punctured inner tube.

She was sitting on her towel when he came into the clearing. She saw him before he saw her, his chest streaked with the white trails of salt sweat, as if his whole body had been weeping. Jay toddled beside him, rubbing his eyes.

"There you are," Andrew said, fear already turned to fury.

"Yes, here I am."

"I was looking for you."

There was still time, Willy. I thought he might say the right words, that he might drop to his knees beside me.

Jay rushed to her open arms and she hugged him tightly, too tightly, until he squirmed and fussed and tried to get away.

"Time to go," Andrew said, the words hard and precise, three pellets spit on the ground.

Why couldn't he tell me he was afraid? Then I could have said I was afraid too. Every time I opened his drawer I was afraid. She thought that the great sorrows of life were all the things you imagined saying but didn't, all the fears you carried alone, the words unspoken that day at the river, this story untold even now.

Delores Tyler drifted on her white bedspread and saw herself through all the long evenings of that hot summer. She imagined standing in the kitchen after supper, listening to the moths as they fluttered against the screen door. They hung on the mesh, their bodies fat and gray, their pale wings tattered.

Willy Hamilton got the news on Halloween. He was on his way home, wondering if his mother had bought enough Tootsie Rolls and M & M's to last the night. He'd already stopped at the store once today—for a Dracula mask with fangs. Now Fred Pierce's voice cracked over the radio with the word that Matt Fry had busted out of the hospital in South Bend. "He's bound to head this way—sooner or later. If he's got two brain cells left to rub together. Keep your eyes open, Willy."

Willy. He'd tried to be Bill, but what good did it do if everyone he knew still called him Willy? A light snow had begun to fall. It was going to be a cold night for the kids. Damn Pierce. Why tell him at the end of his shift? *A policeman never goes off duty.* That's what Horton would say. Did they think Matt Fry might put a sheet over his head, stand on the stoop of the Hamiltons' house and ring the bell? Maybe a boy who was already a ghost wouldn't bother with a costume. *He's one of our own, Willy.* His mother was always reminding him. Better to be a policeman in Spokane or Seattle—even Boise. Here in White Falls everyone was one of your own: your neighbor, your cousin, a bad girl you knew in high school, your best friend—everything happened to you.

Willy slipped in the back door of his house, wearing the mask. Flo sat at the kitchen table. He bent down, nibbled at her neck with his plastic fangs. She neither yelped nor giggled. Her cheeks were red, her eyes brimming. Horton had called, so she already knew that Matt Fry was out there alone, wandering in the dark.

By nine o'clock the doorbell had stopped ringing. All the little goblins and witches had gone home. Snow fell in wet clumps, and the streets were slick and white. Flo fretted. She worried about Horton cruising the side streets. She worried about children darting in front of cars, ghosts in the snow, invisible until it was too late. She couldn't help seeing her own hands on their sweet, cool faces. Willy remembered how she'd wept the day she washed and dressed ten-day-old Miranda Arnoux and laid her in her tiny baby coffin. He had been eight. Horton said, "maybe this work doesn't suit you, Flo." But that only made her cry harder. "You don't understand," she said. "You've never understood what's important to me." Hands deep in pockets, forehead creased, Horton turned and walked out the back door to stand in the yard, looking at the sky before he drove away in the dark.

Willy knew he had the right to leave just as his father had, without explanation or goodbye. He could drive away through the snow—leave his joyless mother—if only he could figure out where to go.

Flo would fuss about him, out on these icy streets, and he was glad for that. He took the Chevy. He was Willy Hamilton, citizen, definitely off duty, no matter what Horton said.

He didn't realize that the Dracula mask was still on the top of his head till he looked in the rearview mirror to back out of the drive. He tossed it on the seat, stupid thing—he hated it now. Flocks of children fluttered along the sidewalks, scurrying home, clutching bags full of goodies. He saw a horse head with a boy's body, a sheet that walked, a troll with hair down to her knees. On Main Street, a group of teenage girls clustered on a corner, smoking cigarettes. Snowflakes melted in their long hair. They were in costume, too: leather jackets and cowboy boots, thin white faces, black lips.

He crossed the river to circle the trailer park. There was plenty of space: an irregular border of pines on one side, an endless stretch of field on the other. But the two dozen trailers were packed close together, fifteen feet apart, three perfect rows. Some had pink awnings over the windows or a screened porch built onto the door. But these additions did not disguise the tin boxes, quite the opposite—decoration made them all the more pitiful.

A stuffed man with a pumpkin head sat in a lawn chair at the edge of the park. He looked human at first but too still, sitting outside in the cold, wearing jeans and a flannel shirt, not flinching as snow piled on his shoulders and bare head, as snow fell into his eyes and into the hole of his mouth.

Willy Hamilton had choices: south to the reservation, north to the wilderness; he could drag Main like the high school boys or head out to the Roadstop and drink like a man. A couple of beers might settle his nerves, but by the time he got to the bar he remembered the last drink he'd had, the vodka with Delores Tyler. That hadn't calmed him down at all, so he turned around in the parking lot and drove back downtown. Tricksters had vanished but left signs: graffiti soaped on windows, tires slashed, pumpkins crushed against concrete.

He took a side street and found himself on Willow Glen. Not habit or coincidence, he knew — the thought of Delores Tyler had led him here. He wanted to see her, and for once he knew why: Delores understood failure. He needed to see her weary face and feel her soft hand on his arm. *You're not the only one.* Who would say it first?

He was glad for the mask — a friend after all. There wasn't quite enough time to feel like a fool before Delores opened the door. "Willy," she said.

"Trick or treat."

"We're out."

"Then it's trick," he said.

"I never bought anything."

"I just wanted to say hello." He started to lift his mask.

"No," she said. "I like it." He wondered why she didn't ask him inside. "Dr. Tyler's out for the evening, overnight in fact. Boise — on *business.*" Good, he thought, it was good to be out here, breathing clear, cold air. "I'd offer you a drink," she whispered, "but I'd rather go for a drive." She reached for his hand and squeezed his fingers. He'd forgotten his gloves. Her hand was small and warm. "You're freezing," she said.

"I'm all right."

"Let me get my coat."

He waited in the entryway. They were going for a drive, but he couldn't remember if he'd agreed to it or not. Puddles formed around his feet as the snow melted off his boots. His hair was damp. He took off the mask and rubbed his chilled hands together.

"Where do you want to go?" he said when they sat beside each other in the car.

"Away from the lights."

He drove toward the river. She slid across the seat and sat close. "To keep warm," she said.

He parked in the clearing overlooking the Snake, the same place where he'd parked with Jay and Belinda and Iona, the same place where he'd come with Darryl and Luke and Kevin the weekend before graduation. He wanted to laugh at his former priggish self. *Boot the sucker out of his car and let's have some fun, boys.* Darryl had been the one to threaten that night, but now Willy agreed: he'd give himself a kick in the butt if he had the chance. Delores pulled a flask from her purse, and he drank greedily, grateful for the way the thick sweet liquid burned all the way down his throat and warmed his stomach. "Cognac," she said, "for winter nights."

She had her hand on his thigh and her head on his shoulder. He wanted to tell her about Matt Fry and his own mother, about his friends who got Matthew drunk and dragged him along the tracks before Matt torched the shed. He knew Delores already and could almost hear her say: *It's not your fault, baby.* He thought of driftwood washed up on the bank of the river, how it heaped on the shore like piles of bone.

Snow fell on the hood of the car and melted from the heat of the engine. Snow fell on the river and disappeared without a sound in the black water. Willy felt a weight against his chest, as if he lay at the bottom of the river. He handed the flask to Delores; she didn't drink — she screwed the cap back on and kissed him instead, lightly, near his mouth.

He gasped, but the weight pressed on all sides, the air dense as water, too thick to breathe, so he grabbed her and held her tight, kissed chin, neck, nose, opening his mouth wide to feel her whole mouth inside of his, forcing his tongue between her lips. He tugged at the buttons on her coat, frantic lover, impatient child. He had never kissed anyone like this. He thought of Belinda pushing his hands away each time he strayed. *No, Willy.* A voice from his past told him to stop, warned him about adultery, reminded him of the wages of sin. But Delores wasn't fighting — she was helping him undo the buttons. The voice muttered but no longer made words. Delores whispered: *Yes, baby.* Now his hands were inside her coat where it was warm, so warm. He remembered Iona Moon's torn shirt and small breasts that night by the tracks; he remembered the day he discovered Belinda Beller's bra was stuffed with tissue. Delores Tyler's breasts were real, heavy when he cupped them in his hands. He clutched the front of her dress, wanting to rip it open.

"Slow down," she said, taking off her coat, guiding his hands to the long zipper down the back. He tugged. No zipper had ever seemed so stubborn. His fingers felt numb, as if his hands had fallen asleep.

It was impossible to kiss Delores and get the zipper down at the same time, so he focused all his attention on her clothes. Now that her mouth was free, she laughed, and Willy knew the whole thing was a mistake. The zipper gave. She pulled her arms from the sleeves, unhooked her bra, let her breasts spring loose. She lay down on the seat with her dress bunched around her waist. Willy pressed his whole face against her chest. He thought he might smother but didn't care. He moved hard and fast. There was no time to wrestle with panty hose, no time to unfasten his belt or wriggle out of his pants. She gripped his balls through his jeans, and he exploded, biting down on her nipple to keep from screaming. She had to swat the side of his head to make him stop.

Lying on top of the woman in the cold car, Willy Hamilton was already sorry. He covered her breasts with his hands. "I'm half frozen," she said, so he helped her hook her bra and zip her dress. She pulled her coat around her shoulders. He remembered Iona's tires spinning in the mud and knew things could still get worse.

But he wasn't stuck. Delores had found her flask again. She didn't sit so close to him on the way home, but she touched his arm and said, "Don't worry, it's always like that the first time."

The first time. He couldn't look at her. He was a virgin and a fool. *The first time.* Surely she didn't think there would be a second time.

He meant to just drop her off, but she said, "Please — walk me to the door. I'm a little tight."

Whose fault is that, he thought. And his father's voice answered: *Every woman deserves to be treated like a lady.* How could Horton believe that? Because he had never done what Willy had done, had never found himself with a woman like Delores Tyler.

Willy left the car running. He walked around the back to open Mrs. Tyler's door for her, offered his arm as she climbed out and held her steady up the long walk. "Will you be all right?" he said.

"My husband's not home."

"I know."

"My son's asleep."

He felt sick to his stomach and blamed it on the cognac.

"I know it's silly," Delores said, "but I'm afraid to go in alone. This old house is so big at night."

It's a man's duty to protect a lady. Willy hated the ring of Horton's words and wanted to ask: Who will protect the man? But he knew his father could never understand that question. *What kind of man needs protection?*

So, he was going to see her inside, flick on a few lights, blow the ghosts out of the corners. It was past midnight. Halloween was over. He thought of the Dracula mask. He couldn't remember where it was — in the car or still on the table. Jay might have already discovered it. Perhaps he knew everything and was sitting on his bed in the dark, wearing the rubber face, waiting to scare his mother.

The mask was on the table. Delores was safe, moving down the hallway, hitting every switch she passed. "Let me make you some tea," she said.

"I left the car running."

"Just a quick cup."

He looked at her smeared lipstick, her wrinkled dress. He had done this. He had bitten her nipple, much too hard.

"Please, Willy, sit with me for a minute or two."

He nodded. He owed her this.

They didn't make it to the kitchen. Jay wobbled down the stairs. Willy stared at his friend, and thought he might not have recognized him on the street. Jay's dirty blond hair was pulled into a scraggly ponytail. He clenched the banister with one hand and his cane with the other. Willy wanted to embrace him so that he wouldn't have to see Jay's squinting eyes and furrowed brow, so he wouldn't know how much each step hurt him.

"Has my mother been filling you up with her sad stories, Willy Boy?" Even his voice had changed, had turned thin and cruel. Did the pain in his legs cause that too? Jay looked from Delores to Willy. He knew where they'd been and what they'd done. He probably even guessed that Willy hadn't managed to get his pants off. "How the mighty have fallen," he said.

Delores Tyler's face crumpled; every line deepened.

Jay limped down the last steps, into the light of the hallway. He had aged too, in a sudden, brutal way. He was red-eyed but not drunk.

Delores covered her face with her hands. Her shoulders heaved, but there was no sound. "We've upset my poor mother," Jay said.

Willy touched Delores's arm, and she batted him away with one hand, revealing half her face. Mascara ran down her cheek in gray streaks. "Go," she said, "just go."

He drove too fast, slammed the brakes too hard, skidded at every stop sign. He was halfway home when he saw one of those damn kids sprint across the street, a stolen jack-o'-lantern tucked under his arm. He longed to hit the siren and scream out after him, but of course the Chevy had no siren. The kid was fast, climbing fences, cutting through backyards, but Willy kept catching him, a narrow shadow moving through the long beams of his headlights. He spun into a curb and leaped from the car to chase the boy down an alley. One block nearly finished him. He was stiff, out of breath, no match for the lithe child. But he had luck on his side, his father's just god. The boy stumbled and the jack-o'-lantern flew from his arms. He sprawled; the pumpkin burst, an explosion of orange shards and splattered seeds. Willy was on the kid in a second, straddling his backside. "What the fuck do you think you're doing?" Willy said. He gripped the boy's neck and pushed his nose into the snow.

"I didn't do nothin'."

"Goddamn thief."

"It was mine."

"Then why you running?"

"I'm late," he said, "my pa's gonna whup me for sure."

Willy wondered if this might be true. The child was younger than he'd thought, ten — twelve at most. Halloween was over and it was just a jack-o'-lantern, after all. "Come on, kid, I'll give you a ride." Willy stood and the boy scrambled to his feet.

"No fucking way," the kid said. He looked older again, mean, a thief for sure. "You're a crazy motherfucker."

Willy wanted to choke him for that, but the kid was off; Willy didn't have a chance. The car door had swung open. From a distance, the yellow light of the dome made the Chevy look submerged in murky water.

He sat on the cold seat rubbing his knee. *How the mighty have fallen.* He must have bashed it when he jumped the boy. Now he remembered the mask lying on the table in the Tylers' entryway. *Motherfucker.* He'd forgotten it a second time, left it for everyone to see: Delores, Jay, Andrew Johnson Tyler. His frightening disguise was false and harmless, his own face ridiculous.

Willy stood on the steps stamping snow off his boots, watching Flo and Horton through the window. As soon as he was inside, Flo said, "Your father found him; he's okay. No gloves or hat, just a thin jacket — who knows how he got here — but he's all right. He was walking back and forth across the bridge, as if he couldn't decide whether to come to town or head out to the Flats." Willy wished he'd seen Matt Fry. There would have been no visit to Delores Tyler, no vision of Jay hobbling down the stairs, no skinny kid sprawled on his belly.

"And do you know what your father did?" She waited for Willy to shake his head. "He drove Matthew straight out to his parents' house." Her throat tightened. She couldn't finish the story.

"They said they'd give him another chance," Horton said. He was both humble and proud, too shy to look at his own son.

Alone in his room, Willy gazed out the window, at the snow falling on the street and on the lawn, on all the lawns as far as he could see. Would Matthew learn to talk again, get a job, make his parents glad — or would he set the drapes ablaze — one more time — light the whole goddamn house some night while his mother and father slept, forever safe in their beds upstairs. Sometimes the object itself forces you to act. A knife demands to cut: to whittle a stick or open a fish, to stab the dirt or draw blood from your own thumb. Perhaps that's how it was with Matt Fry. The match said: *Strike me,* and the curtains said: *I want to burn.*

The next morning, Willy took a drive out to the Frys' place. He remembered how Clifford Fry had boarded up the basement windows years ago to keep the boy from breaking into his own house. Now the boards were gone. The Frys had put Matthew's brother Everett in the attic. This time they took the opposite approach. *The dark is merciful.* Willy wondered about the room downstairs. If a child cried out in his sleep, would his parents hear?

He drove slowly but didn't stop. The snow was melting, and it had started to rain. Ruts of the road ran with muddy water.

The dark is merciful. A lie. The dark leaves its own memories, more powerful because you cannot see: flowers crushed in a sweaty palm, a woman's perfume, the taste of cognac in his own mouth, the taste of it in hers.

And the dark made its own claims. That night, hours after he was off duty, Willy Hamilton found himself turning down Willow Glen Road. If he'd known what he wanted, he might have had the courage to stop. But he wasn't even sure who he wanted to see. He imagined himself burying his face between Delores Tyler's soft breasts, begging her for another chance. He saw himself running up the stairs, pounding on Jay's door, telling him to get up off the goddamn bed and start living his life. He knew he couldn't do both, so he did nothing at all.

Hunched under the covers of his bed, Willy thought of Delores, how surprised he had been when she lay down and her breasts flattened, turning loose and flabby, not at all as he had pictured them. Her body scared him; he didn't know why.

None of Willy's imaginings could bring him close to the thoughts of a woman. How could he guess that she waited for him to come again. How could he know her shame, how it hurt her to think of taking off her clothes in front of him, how the difference between them was a cruelty he did not mean to inflict, how his lean body reminded her of all the things she could never be and never have. She touched her own scarred belly, her fat thighs, her white dimpled buttocks. How could she ever bear to let him see.

No, if it happened again it would be exactly as it was the first time. They would be in a car by the river. She would hike up her skirt and pull down her panty hose. No man would ever gaze at her, full of longing, while they made love in a rose-lit room.

One day passed and then another. He drove by her house. She stood at the window. She saw him, but he did not stop. It snowed again. His headlights carved a pair of yellow tunnels in the street.

The calls started a week later. At first he only breathed while she said, "Hello. *Hello?*" The third time he called, she said, "Willy, is that you?"

He hung up and thought about the kind of girlfriend he wanted, one with smooth skin and silky hair, a girl with a nice smell who would sit beside him at the movies and hold his hand, a girl who would be afraid of men on the screen but not of him. He wanted this girl to kiss him passionately in his car by the river, her tongue exploring his mouth, her body arching against his until he grew hard and she said: *That's enough.*

The girl he dreamed had round cheeks and big eyes, a small nose and pretty little mouth. Her eyebrows were high and light. She was fair, not necessarily blond, but pale. She didn't look like anyone in particular, and Willy realized that the face was childlike, unformed. As soon as it began to take on more definite lines the fantasy dissipated and the girl said things he didn't want to hear: *Don't worry, baby. It's always like this the first time.* She kept a flask in her purse and drank too much. She moved from shadow to light, and he saw that her face was lined and the skin beneath her eyes was so dark it looked bruised. She unbuttoned her own blouse. No one said: *That's enough.*

He didn't call for two days. On the third day, he rang. She said, "Hello," and he said, "Are you alone?" Just like that, an obscene caller without a name. She knew him, knew what he wanted, not like the little girl in his fantasy who didn't know anything, who could always say *no.* "Do you want to come over?" He was nodding. "Willy?" He realized she couldn't see him. *"Yes,"* he said. "Then come."

She'd fixed herself up, lipstick and blush, yellow hair pulled back and pinned in a French knot. It had been a long time since he'd seen her in daylight. "You look nice," he said, and it was true.

In the car he asked her where she wanted to go. She answered quickly; everything had been decided. He wondered how this had happened and if he should be afraid, but he drove west, toward South Bend, just as she said.

He said, "Shall we have lunch?" And she said, "I know why you called." He waited. "It's only fifteen dollars." For a moment he thought she meant he'd have to pay. "For a room," she said.

His first silent call had set this in motion, and now he couldn't stop — they were here, climbing three flights of stairs at the South Bend Hotel, putting the key in the lock, opening the door. He knew what Flo said, that God heard only silence and hushed words. It was too late to pray nothing would happen, so he prayed to be kind.

The day was overcast, already dark, but Delores pulled the blinds. She'd brought a candle. Stains on the bedspread, dirt on the rug, in this flickering light almost invisible. *Merciful.* She pulled the pins from her knotted hair and shook it loose. When he sat beside her on the bed, they kissed, lightly — there was time now. She took off her coat and he reached under her sweater. Her camisole was satiny, smooth as skin over skin.

She touched his shoulders and his arms. Beautiful boy, she said, and the words shocked him. She told him to take off his clothes, and he stood before her, completely naked, unashamed for the first time — because he was beautiful; in her eyes, he was. She guided him to parts of his body he'd barely known, arch of the foot and inner thigh, the delicate space between each finger, the hollow between each rib. He came too fast but grew hard again and was amazed when he moved inside of her, so warm there, so different from his own hand; nothing had ever felt like this. And he was surprised by his own tenderness, his longing — a desperation to make her feel what he felt.

She still wore the red camisole, afraid her belly would frighten him, ashamed to think her breasts might remind him of the vast gulf of age between them. He felt too good to her, a sting, flesh on flesh, the long muscles of his legs, tongue in her mouth, fingers in her hair, the bones of his hips pressing into her, an imprint she would feel for days. She didn't want to scream, didn't want her face to contort or turn a brilliant red, so she held herself back and still she came, a ripple of small shocks that racked her body. It had been so long since anyone had made her come — she wanted to weep with gratefulness.

He came a moment after her, thrusting hard. Her eyes teared but she didn't sob.

The second orgasm left him limp, exhausted. He curled around her, one leg over hers, soft cock nuzzling her thigh, face pressed to her neck under her damp hair.

The candle flickered out while they slept. They woke in darkness and made love again, but the afternoon was wearing on and they were both thinking of the night. He strained to come quickly, to be done with it. He heard his Sunday school teacher say: *An animal act,* and thought of the old woman's dry hands, the ropes of blue veins, how her hot blood seemed to leap into his body where she touched him. His hands pressed the sheet as he moved against the woman in this bed. He did not kiss her or look at her. He thought only of himself, of his own breath, the way that sound filled the room.

Delores showered alone, and Willy lay on the bed, listening to the water. He smelled her now, on him, and wished he had been the first to wash.

While Willy was in the bathroom, Delores turned on the light to gather up her clothes. He found her that way, on her knees, white rump in the air, looking under the bed. They dressed quickly and slipped out the back entrance of the hotel, their hair still wet.

In the car on the way back to White Falls, they had nothing to say. He parked in front of her house, hoping she would climb out quickly. "Call me," she said.

Willy drummed the steering wheel with his fingers. "Sure," he said, "of course."

Willy saw the dark Chrysler careening across the bridge around midnight. Horton had been on his case all week: *You haven't written a ticket in ten days.* Now it was sixteen days. He couldn't believe his luck. Bad, that is. How could he arrest Delores? He couldn't just write a ticket and let her drive home. Not in her condition. She'd do a U-turn and jump the rail, go flying into the frigid Snake. How could he explain? He hadn't seen her since that day in South Bend. Sixteen days. A coincidence. And hadn't called, either. He hoped she understood but knew she didn't. In a way he was relieved to catch her this way. It restored order: she was drunk; he was a policeman.

He hit the siren and set the blue light flashing. She punched the gas and surged ahead of him, speeding toward the Flats. He hadn't expected this, had imagined instead that Delores Tyler would pull over carefully, sorry and contrite, that she'd climb in the back of his cruiser without any trouble.

The road was slick, puddles frozen in the ruts. He chased her for a mile or more until they were alone on a black road.

She stopped. So this was the point of it all, to be alone. The door opened — not Delores. He'd never considered this. Jay headed toward the cruiser, limping but powerful.

Willy got out too. "You crazy sonuvabitch—you could have gotten us both killed."

Jay didn't answer and kept coming. Willy thought he might have to take a swing to make him stop, but he couldn't imagine hitting a man with a cane. What would Horton do? No words of wisdom came to mind.

"Motherfucker," Jay said.

Willy's face felt hot despite the cold. *Motherfucker*. He heard the kid in the alley, saw the crushed jack-o'-lantern, knew the simple truth. *Motherfucker*.

Jay leaped before Willy had a chance to brace himself. Both of them went down, and Jay pinned Willy to the road. Willy remembered wrestling in the grass, how good it felt, nothing like this, a hot summer day, their bodies slippery with sweat, wearing cutoffs and nothing else, moving against each other like fish. Jay wasn't playing now. His elbow hit the center of Willy's chest, a soft spot that took Willy's breath and left him stunned.

Jay kept pressing. He leaned close and Willy saw his face, every muscle tensed, jaw clenched tight forever, tendons popping in his neck. He smelled Jay, bitter, not just his breath but his skin, a burned smell that made Willy taste hot metal. He thought of Horton: *When you catch a whiff of that you better have your hand on your gun.* But Jay's knees dug into Willy's arms, held them to the ground. He wanted to tell his father: *If you're close enough to smell a man it's already too late.*

"Buddy," he whispered, "it's me."

"Goddamn right," Jay said. "I fucking know it's you."

Willy twisted, arched his back. Jay smacked his chin and rolled off him, grabbing the cane he'd dropped in the snow. Willy took one breath. He thought it was over now but the quick pain blinded him and a brilliant yellow pool spread in front of his eyes like blood. If he'd had any air he would have screamed, and the cry would have carried across the fields to a girl's house on the Kila Flats, up the tracks to a burned shed, across the river to his mother's house, along the tree-lined streets to Delores. She would see them, clearly and without doubt, her lover lying in the snow clutching his balls, her son crumpled to his knees beside him.

The yellow pool bled thin enough for Willy to see sky, but the clouds looked yellow too. Snow melted beneath his back. Snow melted under Jay's knees.

* * *

"Fucking cop," Jay muttered. "Whatever happened to your goddamn sense of duty?"

Those were his last words on the road, and he remembered them now, just a week later, when he realized he needed Willy Hamilton. Willy was a policeman, after all. This was his job. Jay didn't want to make it official by filing a report with Fred Pierce or Horton Hamilton. He didn't want half the town out looking for his mother, waving their flashlights in the woods, shouting her name in the dark. Besides, she'd left the house at noon and it was only eight. She wasn't a missing person for another sixteen hours — just an absent mother. *A woman needs some privacy once in a while*, that's what Pierce would say, implying Delores was shacked up with her lover for the night and Jay Tyler was a fool.

Jay didn't have to explain much to Willy. He told him his father was in Boise again and that Delores had been out all day. He said some pills were missing, and Willy said he'd be right over.

Jay was waiting at the curb when Willy came by the house. Willy thought of Delores waiting for him three weeks ago, just this way. "What kind of pills?" Willy said as Jay got in the car.

"I don't know. Sleeping pills."

"How many?"

"How could I count them if they're gone?"

They headed out the River Road, toward the bridge. "I know how you are," Jay said. "You'll want to blame yourself. But you're an arrogant bastard if you think one roll with you could make a woman miserable enough to do this."

Willy nodded. Jay was right. He did want to blame himself. He was an arrogant bastard.

The Chrysler wasn't parked on the bridge. Jay told Willy to stop and got out of the car to look at the water. Snow on the bridge had frozen to a hard crust. The moon was bright, three-quarters full, and the crescent left in shadow cupped the fuller part, a dark hand holding the yellow head in the sky. Jay peered down at the black water and stony bank.

He called her name, and it bounced off the water: *Delores*. Jay used the loud voice of a man, but inside a child cried: *Where are you?* This child was lost in his own house. There were so many rooms. He went from one to another, opening closets, peeking under beds, as if this was a game. But he wasn't having fun. He felt that frustration now, the panic in his chest as he ran up and down the stairs. His legs were short and tired. He was four years old.

"Where to?" Willy said when Jay got back in the car.

"To that place where we always parked."

As much as Willy wanted to find Delores, he hoped she'd gone somewhere else. Maybe he was an arrogant bastard to imagine he had anything to do with her unhappiness, but it would be hard not to blame himself if this was the place she'd chosen.

Jay and Willy both thought of the woman who'd jumped from the bridge and was saved. They saw her red coat billow around her, a small parachute slowing her fall, a preserver that kept her afloat when she hit the water. They saw her blue lips when the men pulled her from the river. They saw her breathless body and knew that she was dead in this moment. But the man struck her chest. Water spurted from her mouth. He pressed again with both hands until she sputtered and gagged. He breathed into her, covered her nose and mouth with his mouth, called her back with his own breath, gave her his own life. *Damn you.* Her words of gratitude, the only ones the curious boys heard. She moved away a month later, left her husband and five kids in their trailer. Jay wondered if she was thankful in the end, if leaving her troubles was better than leaving her life, or if her problems followed her to every little room, if one night she leaped from a window instead of a bridge, to cement instead of water. He wondered if Lazarus lived long and joyfully, or if he grew sick and bitter, if he cursed the Lord and wished there had been no miracle.

There was one car parked by the river. Willy thought the Pinto with the fogged windows belonged to Twyla Catts. He hit the car with his high beams but no heads appeared. They were down on the seat for sure, eyes screwed shut, bodies locked. If a flood swept their car into the river the divers would find them this way: arms clutching, legs entwined, hair tangled together. Willy laid on his horn, and Jay grabbed his wrist. "Save it," he said.

"Any other ideas?" Willy said when they were back on the road.

"Just drive west for a while."

Every time they rounded a curve, Willy expected to see the Chrysler hunkered on the shoulder. Maybe she'd slid into the ditch and had been out cold for hours. She might wake at any moment, confused and afraid. He imagined her running on the road, her blond hair blowing. He drove slowly so he could stop in time.

Jay said, "I'm sorry about the other night."

And Willy said, "Forget it."

"Lost my head."

"I deserved it."

"Maybe," said Jay, "but not from me."

"She's your mother."

"I haven't treated her so well myself."

They were halfway to South Bend and had only seen two cars coming toward them on the narrow road. Each time they thought it must be her, heading home. But the cars were unfamiliar, driven by strangers who didn't know how cruel they were to drive this road, to give boys hope and snatch it back.

"This is stupid," Jay said. "We won't find her this way. Maybe the pills rolled under the bed — why should she off herself when she can just leave?"

But they both knew she didn't have the courage for that: running away meant making a new life. "Let's check the bars," Willy said.

"Yeah, why not."

They stopped at the White Bull and River's End on Main, but no one had seen her. As they veered east, Willy suddenly felt certain they'd find her at the Roadstop, drunken Delores about to fall off her barstool, leaning up against any guy who happened to sit beside her. They'd scold her and take her home. They'd laugh in the car, pretending they weren't that scared.

But the Chrysler wasn't in the lot. "She's not here," Jay said.

They drove to the bridge again but crossed it this time and headed toward the Flats. Willy slowed as they passed the cluster of trailers. The stuffed man with the pumpkin head still sat guard, but the head had rotted and begun to shrivel, sinking into the shoulders.

Jay said, "Take me home. I think she's at home." Willy saw that Jay's cheeks were wet.

"It's not your fault," Willy said. He thought it was important to say this now, before they found her. Jay nodded. "If she's not there, I'm going to call my father."

"She is," Jay whispered. "She is." He saw her, curled in the basement. That's where he'd found her the other time, wedged in a dark corner under the cellar stairs; he poked at her with his small hands, but she didn't wake.

The memory of the sirens was so close he had to cover his ears. He was sure he'd find her in exactly the same place. Maybe she'd been there all along. Maybe she'd driven the car away to fool him and had sneaked back later, like a thief in her husband's house, tiptoeing down the stairs to steal her own life. Her name welled in his chest; the sound of it filled his whole body.

The Chrysler was in the drive. Someone had turned on the porch light. Willy followed Jay, up the walk and into the entryway. At the end of the hall, light burst from the kitchen.

She sat at the table, hair loose at her shoulders, just as Willy had imagined, hours before on the River Road. She wore an oversized cardigan and hugged herself to hold it wrapped around her.

Jay stood in the doorway, eyes filling with shame and gratitude. Willy peered over his shoulder.

"I'm drunk," she said.

"I was afraid," Jay whispered.

Delores heard those words at last, the ones Andrew could not say at the river. "I didn't have the guts," she said.

"We've been looking for you all night." He gestured toward the doorway with his head. Willy backed into the shadows of the hall. He saw mother and son through a haze, as if a veil had fallen in front of him, and he couldn't find the place where it parted to let him in. He realized she had spared three lives tonight, that he and Jay had been saved, pulled from the freezing river at the last moment.

He hurried toward the door, his own footsteps so loud they frightened him. He glanced back as he stepped outside. The house was quiet, but the light burned in the kitchen, fierce and steady.

JUDY TROY

Prisoners of Love

Last year, when I was twelve years old, my mother married her pen pal, Bennett Jensen, who was in the Wyoming State Penitentiary for holding up a gas station. She had gotten Bennett's name from an ad in the newspaper. He and my mother got married in the warden's office on a Friday morning, while I was in school, and on Saturday afternoon I went with her to the prison, which was almost two hours away, in Rawlins. The three of us ate lunch in the visitors' room. My mother had brought sandwiches wrapped in heart-shaped napkins.

"With a little luck, Scott," Bennett said, "I'll be out in four years." He was small and stocky, and had blue eyes and black glasses.

"Four years goes by like nothing," my mother said. "Think of how often we have a new president."

"It will seem faster now that I have a family to come home to," he told her.

We were living in the Medicine Bow Mobile Home Park, next to the Chevrolet dealership where my mother worked as a secretary. I went to the middle school across the highway. I was on the soccer team, and we played schools from all around Laramie and usually won. My father, who was also remarried, sometimes came to the games with his stepson, Gerald, who was eight. We had a game the week after my mother married Bennett. "Tell me what he's like," my father said. He already knew that Bennett was in prison. It was the end of September, and we were walking to the car, after the game, through fallen leaves.

"He's nice," I told him. "I don't know him too well."

"I guess he doesn't come over to the trailer much," my father said. He laughed, and Gerald imitated him.

We got in the car and drove to Ted's Pizzeria, near the University of Wyoming, where our team went to celebrate after we played. The sun was going down, and the sky was red in front of us and dark behind us. Gerald was sitting in the front seat, between my father and me, pushing buttons on the radio. "Quit," my father told him.

"Yes, sir," Gerald said. My father was 6′4″ and weighed two hundred and fifty pounds. He was the assistant principal at Gerald's school.

At Ted's Pizzeria, my friends on the team—Curtis Whaler and Joe Kemp—were sitting at a booth next to the jukebox. They already had their pizza and Cokes. My father and Gerald and I sat at the booth behind them and my father ordered a pepperoni pizza, Cokes for Gerald and me, and a beer for himself. Most of the parents didn't drink beer after the games, in order to set an example for us, and I was embarrassed that my father didn't know that. He didn't come to the games as often as they did, and he had never volunteered to referee.

"I'm going to play on a Little League softball team next year, Scott," Gerald said. "Dad said I have to." He had a crewcut and was overweight. Until my father married his mother, a year and a half earlier, he had lived in an apartment with his grandmother. My father said Gerald had never done anything there except watch TV and eat cookies.

"Softball's fun," I said. "I used to play, too." As I was listening to Gerald, I was also trying to listen to Joe and Curtis's conversation about a girl I knew, describing the things she was supposed to have done with a ninth grader. They were talking quietly, but I heard, "took her bra off," and "on her knees," along with some things I had done with her myself. What they were saying bothered me more than I thought it would.

"You can get to be just as good an athlete as Scott," my father told Gerald. "It's just practice. There's no talent involved, as far as I can see."

"I don't agree with that," I told him. But he had turned away from us, to watch Joe Kemp's mother's backside as she leaned over a table to clean up a spilled drink.

After we ate our pizza, we drove to my father's house—he wanted me to say hello to my stepmother. They lived in a ranch house off the highway, at the foot of the Laramie Range. They had five acres of land and a corral, where they kept two horses. Their dogs, Cody and Belle—two white German shepherds—ran out to greet us. It was dark now, and the moon was rising over the hill in back of their property.

Inside, my stepmother, Linda, took some cookies out of a package and put them on a plate, and we ate these in the kitchen. "So who won?" she asked.

"We did," I told her.

"Isn't that nice," she said.

"Why don't you stay overnight?" Gerald asked me.

"I can't," I told him. "My mother doesn't like to be alone, unless she knows in advance, so she can make other plans." I noticed my stepmother's eyebrows raise. "What she does," I explained, "is make plans to stay with a girlfriend, or have the girlfriend stay at our trailer."

Gerald took me into his room to see his hamsters, and then we went outside to visit the horses. He was supposed to start riding lessons soon. My father taught me, when I was four or five, but Linda was nervous about letting my father put Gerald on a horse. She was afraid he would be too reckless.

Their horses were sorrel mares that looked pale in the moonlight. I climbed the fence and mounted the smaller one bareback. "I'll help you up, if you want," I told Gerald.

"I'm not sure I should," he said.

"Just climb the fence and get on in back of me," I told him. I helped him on and walked the mare around the corral. Gerald had his hands pressed against my back. "She can tell how you feel," I said. "She'll be easier to handle if you can get her confidence."

"I am trying to get her confidence," Gerald said.

"I can tell," I told him. "I'm just trying to tell you about horses in general." We got off and walked back to the house, toward a square of light that was shining through the sliding glass door in their family room. Cody and Belle were playing with us, running in circles around our feet and nipping at our jeans.

"You won't tell my mom I rode the horse, will you?" Gerald asked me.

"Why would I?" I said.

My father took me home at ten o'clock. My mother was waiting for me outside, sitting on the steps of our mobile home. "I was worried about you," she said, when I got out of the car. "You usually don't stay at Ted's that long."

"Dad took me to his house afterward," I told her.

"I bet that was fun for you," she said. "I know you like those dogs." We went inside and took off our jackets. It had gotten cool out.

"I'd still like to get one of my own," I told her.

"I know you would, honey," she said, "but all anyone has here, in the mobile home park, are chihuahuas and miniature poodles. And they're locked up all day in these little trailers." She brushed some dirt off my jeans. "When Bennett gets out," she told me, "we'll move into a house like Dad's and get a German shepherd. Bennett mentioned in his last letter that he'd also like to have a swimming pool."

"What kind of job will Bennett have, when he gets out?" I asked.

"I don't know exactly," she said, "but I think he has some automotive skills. He might work in a service station, fixing cars." She sat on the floor and unlaced her tennis shoes. "Well, maybe not in a service station. Maybe at the dealership where I work. The swimming pool may be a little unrealistic," she added.

On Saturday, while my mother was visiting Bennett, I walked to the mall to meet Curtis, and we each spent fifteen dollars on a video game called Rancho Deluxe. The object was to make the little cowboys rope horses that galloped in from both sides of the screen, while helicopters tried to shoot them down with lasers.

Afterward, we walked through the stores, looking for girls we knew. Curtis's girlfriend had broken up with him a few days earlier. "You're not looking for anyone in particular, either, are you?" he asked me.

"Not at all," I told him. "Just anyone good-looking."

"I know what you mean," he said. We stopped in front of a shoe store, to look at a pair of black cowboy boots with silver trim along the sides and outlining the tops. "There aren't many girls worth really liking," Curtis said. "Mostly, they're a lot of trouble."

"I know that," I told him.

"That's why it's better to see more than one at a time," he said. "If you start to like someone too much, you can switch to the other girl, and go back and forth like that."

"It might even be safer to have three," I told him.

We walked on past the shoe store and into McDonald's, and ordered Cokes. "I guess that at some time," Curtis said, when we sat down, "like when you want to get married, you have to narrow down your choices to one. Or else just get someone pregnant."

"That's probably the easiest way to decide," I told him.

It was six o'clock when I got home, and I cleared off the table and got out the plates and silverware. My mother came home a few minutes later. "How was your day, honey?" she asked me.

"OK," I told her. "How was yours?"

Without answering, she took a dish of meatloaf and mashed potatoes out of the refrigerator and put it into the cabinet that held our pots and pans. Then she realized her mistake and put it in the microwave. "My mind is on Bennett," she said. "I was thinking about him, in his cell, being unhappy, and how he could be here with us. I was thinking about what a long time four years is." We sat down to eat dinner. I had been invited to a party that night, which I wanted to go to, but when I mentioned it to my mother, she said, "I had planned on an evening with just the two of us, Scott. I thought we could make popcorn and watch TV."

"I can't stay home with you all the time," I told her.

"I know," she said. "But it would mean a lot to me tonight." We washed the dishes and went into the living room. My mother put on her glasses and turned on a movie about a serial killer.

"What's wrong?" I asked her, halfway through. I had noticed she had tears on her face.

"Look at how they portray criminals on television," she said. "Like they're not even human beings."

"But this man killed a lot of people," I told her.

"That doesn't mean he's not a person," my mother said, "or that he doesn't have feelings." She stood up and went into her bedroom to change into her nightgown and robe. While she was gone, I called the house where the party was taking place and asked to speak with the girl Joe and Curtis had talked about.

"I haven't seen you in a while," I said. "I just wondered how you were."

"Why don't you come over and find out?" she asked me.

"I can't," I told her. "I'd like to, though." My mother came back into the room, and we watched the rest of the movie. I had a hard time paying attention. I was worrying about who else might be at the party, and daydreaming about what I might be doing if I were there.

My father called the next morning, to say that he wanted to take me to a livestock auction. He didn't want any livestock, himself, but he liked to guess the animals' weights and what they sold for. He said that Gerald was staying home, this time.

After the auction, we went to a steakhouse on the road to Horse Creek. My father took off his cowboy hat and set it on an empty chair. "Order anything on the menu," he told me.

"Why?" I asked.

"Because I said so." When I couldn't make up my mind right away, he ordered for me — the largest steak and an extra order of onion rings. We spoke about cattle until the food came, and then he said, "I thought you might want to talk about Bennett Jensen, Scott. It would be good for you to get it off your chest."

"I don't have anything to say about Bennett," I told him.

"Aren't your friends giving you a hard time about the thing prisons have now," he asked me, "where the married convicts can spend time alone with their wives?"

"My friends don't know yet about Bennett," I told him. "And anyway, I don't know what you're talking about."

"I'm asking you if your mother had a honeymoon night with Bennett Jensen," he said.

"No," I told him. "At least not that I know of."

"Is that right," my father said. He ate the last bite of his steak, and, without asking, cut off a small piece of mine and put it on his plate. "The reason I wanted to know, Scott, is I was worried about your mother being alone with Mr. Jensen. I'm sure you are, too."

"Not really," I said. "If you met him on the street, you wouldn't guess he was a criminal."

"What do you mean, 'If you met him on the street'?" my father said. "Is he getting out early?"

"No," I told him. "I meant, if you saw him in prison, you'd know he'd done something wrong, but only because he was in jail."

"I see," my father said. "OK, then." He whistled for the waitress and paid the bill, and we walked outside and got in the car.

"Are we going to your house, to see Linda and Gerald?" I asked.

"Who?" my father said. "Oh. No, not today." He drove in the direction of the mobile home park and stopped at a bar a few blocks before it. I waited for him outside, on the sidewalk. It was almost hot out, and I stood in the shade of the neon sign. He came out carrying a paper sack. "I bought a wedding present for your mother," he told me.

She was cleaning the trailer, wearing old clothes, and when my father walked in behind me, she went into her bedroom and changed into a blouse and skirt. "Do you know what I was thinking about the other day?" he said, when she came out of her room. He was opening her present, which was a bottle of his favorite whiskey, Black Velvet. "That trip we took to Deadwood, South Dakota." We had gone there when I was seven, to see the graves of Calamity Jane and Wild Bill Hickok.

"What made you think of that?" my mother asked him.

"A book I was reading," he told her, "called *Outlaws and the Women Who Loved Them.*"

"Was the book about particular couples," my mother asked, "or was it making general statements? Because I don't believe you can put women in categories like that."

"Of course you can't," my father said. "That goes without saying." He suggested that I go outside to ride my dirt bike, since the weather was so nice. "Take your time and get some exercise," he told me. "I'll take care of your mother."

I stayed out all afternoon, and when I came home, it was almost dark. My mother was in the living room, waiting to talk to me. She hadn't started to make dinner yet. "Sit down and listen to me," she said. "Dad is thinking about coming back to us. We talked for a long time, and he made me see some things. For example, he helped me understand why Bennett wanted to marry me. What did he have going for him before he met me? Absolutely nothing. Besides that, he's a criminal."

"Well, you already knew that," I told her.

"I know I did," she said. "But I didn't think of it as such a bad thing." She closed the curtains and heated up soup for dinner, which we ate without talking. I was thinking about where we would live, if my father came back, and who would end up with his dogs and horses, and what would happen to Gerald. My mother was crumbling crackers into her soup. She had already taken off her wedding ring, and it was on the table, next to the bottle of Black Velvet my father had bought. "I think Dad loved me all along," she said. "I think he was just waiting for the right time to tell me."

"Like right after you married somebody else?" I asked.

"That was just bad timing," she told me. "It was an unfortunate coincidence."

"Are you going to come in with me?" I asked her on Saturday, as she was driving me to Rawlins so that Bennett and I could say goodbye. He had written me two letters, before my mother decided to get a divorce, and he had sent me a football he had ordered from a catalogue. My mother and I had just passed the STATE PENITENTIARY. DO NOT PICK UP HITCH-HIKERS sign.

"I don't think that would be a good idea," she said.

I went in by myself, and Bennett and I sat at a table in a corner, under the clock. He kept looking at the door, expecting my mother to walk in. "I'm sorry we didn't get to know each other very well, Scott," he said. "I wanted you to have a dog someday, and all the other things you want."

"I know that," I told him.

"Now I don't care if I live or die," he said.

"Maybe you can find another woman to write letters to," I told him.

"I don't think I'll ever care for anyone else the way I care for your mother." He was looking down at the table. His hair was ruffled up from the way he had been running his fingers through it, and he stood up and shook my hand and disappeared through the steel door. I went outside and got in the car.

"How did it go?" my mother asked me. "How upset was he?"

"He was sad," I said. "He was almost crying."

She looked out the window at the prison. There was a cyclone fence all the way around the parking lot, and the way the sun was slanting made the top of it look shiny and sharp, like a knife blade. On the other side of the fence, there was a cemetery with probably a hundred rows of gravestones. "Well, I don't think he'll be much lonelier than he was before he met me," she said. "Do you?"

"Sure," I told her. "But probably not too much," I said, when I saw the look on her face.

We drove back to Laramie, and my father came over soon after we got home. He was wearing a black Western shirt and a new pair of jeans. He sat down on the couch and refused the glass of iced tea my mother offered him. "Linda and I have decided to see a marriage counselor," he told us. "You can't let something as important as a marriage just fall apart. You should be able to work out your problems."

"You're joking," my mother said.

My father was looking at me. "I'm sorry, Scott," he said. "I guess I was confused about my feelings." My mother stood up and went into her bedroom.

After he left, I knocked at her door and went in. She was sitting on her bed, looking out the window and watching my father drive out of our mobile home park. I sat down next to her and she put her arm around me. It was thundering outside, from a long distance away, but it hadn't rained. You could still see a few stars, and the moonlight was shining down through the trees. "Your father shouldn't go around talking about love when he doesn't mean it," she said. "It's not fair. It's like he doesn't realize how serious it is."

We went into the living room to watch TV. My mother chose *Gnaw: Food of the Gods II*. "A horror movie about giant rats," she read out loud from the *TV Guide*. It was still clear outside at midnight, when the movie was over, and we took a walk through the trailer park. No one else was awake, except people's dogs, and by the time we got back to our trailer, they were all barking and trying to get out through the screens.

T. CORAGHESSAN BOYLE

The 100 Faces of Death,
Volume IV

He knew he'd really screwed up. Screwed up in a major and unforgiving way. You could see the perception solidifying in his eyes, eyes that seemed to swell out of his head like hard-cooked eggs extruded through the sockets, and the camera held steady. He was on a stage, faultlessly lit, and a banner proclaimed him RENALDO THE GREAT ESCAPE ARTIST. He was running sweat. Oozing it. His pores were huge, saturated craters trenching his face like running sores. Suspended six feet above his head, held aloft by block and tackle, was a fused meteorite of junkyard metal the size of a truck engine, its lower surface bristling with the gleaming jagged teeth of a hundred kitchen knives annealed in the forges of Guadalajara. Renaldo's hands were cuffed to his ankles, and what looked like a tugboat anchor chain was wound round his body six or eight times and bolted to the concrete floor. His lovely assistant, a heavily made-up woman whose thighs ballooned from her lacy tutu like great coppery slabs of meat, looked as if her every tremor and waking nightmare had been distilled in the bitter secretions of that moment. This was definitely not part of the act.

"Watch this," Jamie said. "Watch this."

Janine tightened her grip on my hand. The room shrank in on us. The beer in my free hand had gone warm, and when I lifted it to my lips it tasted of yeast and aluminum. And what did I feel? I felt the way the lovely assistant looked, felt the cold charge of revulsion and exhilaration that had come over me when I'd seen my first porno movie at the age of fourteen, felt a hairy-knuckled hand slide up my throat and jerk at a little lever there.

When the video opened, over the credits, Renaldo was clenching a straw between his teeth—a straw, a single straw, yellow and stiff, the smallest part of a broom. He was leaning forward, working the straw in the tiny aperture that controlled the release mechanism of the handcuffs. But now, because he'd begun to appreciate that this wasn't his day, and that the consequences of that fact were irrevocable, his lips began to tremble and he lost his grip on the straw. The lovely assistant gave the camera a wild strained look and then made as if to dash forward and restore that essential wisp of vegetation to the artist's mouth, but it was too late. With a thick slushing sound, the sound of tires moving through wet snow, the timer released the mechanism that restrained the iron monolith, and Renaldo was no more.

Jamie said something like, "Dude really bought it," and then, "Anybody ready for a beer?"

I sat through another ninety-nine permutations of the final moment, variously lit and passionately or indifferently performed, watched the ski-masked bank robber pop his hostage's head like a grape with the aid of a .44 magnum and then pop his own, saw the fire eater immolate herself and the lumberjack make his final cut. Jamie, who'd seen the video half a dozen times, couldn't stop laughing. Janine said nothing, but her grip on my hand was unyielding. For my part, I remember going numb after the third or fourth death, but I sat there all the same, though there were ninety-six to go.

But then, who was counting?

The following weekend, my Aunt Marion died. Or "passed on," as my mother put it, a delicate euphemistic phrase that conjured up ethereal realms rather than the stark black and white image of damp soil and burrowing insects. My mother was in New York, I was in Los Angeles. And no, I wasn't flying in for the funeral. She cried briefly, dryly, and then hung up.

I was twenty-five at the time, a graduate of an indifferent university, a young man who went to work and made money, sought the company of young women and was, perhaps, too attached to the friends of his youth, Jamie in particular. I listened to the silence a moment, then phoned Janine and asked her to dinner. She was busy. What about tomorrow? I said. She planned to be busy then too.

I hadn't laid eyes on my Aunt Marion in ten years. I remembered her as a sticklike woman in a wheelchair with an unsteady lip and a nose that overhung it like a cutbank, a nose that wasn't qualitatively different from my mother's, and, in the fullness of generation, my own. Her death was the result of an accident — negligence, my mother insisted — and already, less than twenty-four hours after the fact, there was an attorney involved.

It seemed that Aunt Marion had been on an outing to the art museum with several other inmates of the nursing home where she'd been in residence since Nixon's presidency, and the attendant, in placing her at the head of the ramp out back of the museum dining hall, had failed to properly set the brake on the back wheels of her chair. Aunt Marion suffered from some progressive nervous disorder that had rendered her limbs useless — she was able to control her motorized chair only through the use of a joystick which she gripped between her teeth, and even then only at the best of times. Left alone at the summit of the ramp while the attendant went off to fetch another patient, Aunt Marion felt her chair begin to slip inexorably forward. The chair picked up speed, and one of the two witnesses to the accident claimed that she'd bent her face to the controls to arrest it, while the other insisted she'd done nothing at all to save herself, but had simply glided on down the ramp and into eternity with a tight little smile frozen to her face. In any case, there was blame to be assigned, very specific and undeniable blame, and a cause-and-effect reaction to explain Aunt Marion's removal from this sphere of being, and in the end, it seemed to give my mother some measure of comfort.

Try as I might, though, I couldn't picture the face of Aunt Marion's death. My own blood was involved, my own nose. And yet it was all somehow remote, distant, and the death of Renaldo the Great stayed with me in a way Aunt Marion's could never have begun to. I don't know what I wound up doing that weekend, but in retrospect I picture the Coast Highway, an open convertible, Jamie, and a series of bars with irradiated decks and patios, and women who were very much alive.

Janine passed into oblivion, as did Carmen, Eugenie and Katrinka, and Jamie went off to explore the wide bleeding world. He spent the next eight months dredging the dark corners of countries whose names changed in the interim, the sort of places where people died in the streets as regularly as flowers sprang through the soil and pigeons fouled the monuments to the generalissimo of the month. I worked. I turned over money. Somebody gave me a cat. It shat in a box under the sink and filled the house with a graveyard stink.

Jamie had been back two months before he called to invite me to a party in the vast necropolis of the San Fernando Valley. He'd found a job inculcating moral awareness in the minds of six- and seven-year-olds at the Thomas Jefferson Elementary School in Pacoima five days a week, reserving the weekends for puerile thrills. I didn't realize how much I'd missed him until I saw him standing there on the landing outside my apartment. He looked the same — rangy, bug-eyed, a plucked chicken dressed in surfer's clothes—but for his nose. It was inflamed, punished, a dollop of meat grafted to his face by some crazed body snatcher. "What's with the nose?" I said, dispensing with the preliminaries.

He hesitated, working up to a slow grin under the porchlight. "Got in a fight in this bar," he said. "Some dude bit it off."

They'd sewed the tip of his nose back in place—or almost in place; it would forever be canted ever so slightly to the left—but that wasn't what excited him. He moved past me into the living room and fumbled around in his pocket for a minute, then handed me a series of snapshots, close-ups of his face shortly after the operation. I saw the starched white sheets, the nest of pillows, Jamie's triumphant leer, and an odd glistening black line drawn across the bridge of his nose where the bandage should have been. The photos caught it from above, beneath, head-on and in profile. Jamie was looking over my shoulder. He didn't say a word, but his breathing was quick and shallow. "So what is it?" I said, swinging round on him. "What's the deal?"

One word, succulent as a flavored ice: "Leeches."

"Leeches?"

He held it a moment, center stage. "That's right, dude, latest thing. They use them to bring back the tiny blood vessels, capillaries and what-not, the ones they can't tie up themselves. It's the sucking action," and he made a kissing noise. "Suck, suck, suck. I wore them around for three days, grossing the shit out of everybody in the hospital." He was looking into my eyes. Then he shrugged and turned away. "They wouldn't let me take them home, though—that was the pisser."

The party consisted of seven people—three women, four men, including us—sitting around a formal dining room table eating carnitas and listening to inflammatory rap at a barely audible volume. The hosts were Hilary and Stefan, who had a house within hearing distance of the Ventura Freeway and taught with Jamie in Pacoima. Hilary's sister, Judy, was there, the end product of psychosomatic dieting and the tanning salon, along with her friend, Marsha, and a man in his forties with sprayed-up hair and a goatee whose name I never did catch. We drank Carta Blanca and shots of Cuervo Gold and ate flan for dessert. The general conversation ran to Jamie's nose, leeches, bowel movements and death. I don't know how we got into it exactly, but after dinner we gravitated toward a pair of mallowy couches the color of a Hass avocado and began our own anthology of final moments. I came back from the bathroom by way of the kitchen with a fresh beer, and Judy, sunk into her tan like something out of a sarcophagus at Karnak, was narrating the story of the two UCLA students, lovers of nature and of each other, who went kayaking off Point Dume.

It was winter, and the water was cold. There'd been a series of storms bred in the Gulf of Alaska and the hills were bleeding mud. There was frost in the Valley, and Judy's mother lost a bougainvillea she'd had for twenty years. That was the fatal ingredient, the cold. The big sharks — the great whites — generally stayed well north of the Southern California coast, up near the Bay Area, the Farallons and beyond, where the seals were. That was what they ate: seals.

In Judy's version, the couple had lashed their kayaks together and they were resting, sharing a sandwich, maybe getting romantic — kissing, fondling each other through their wetsuits. The shark wasn't supposed to be there. It wasn't supposed to mistake the hulls of their kayaks for the silhouettes of two fat rich hot-blooded basking seals either, but it did. The girl drowned after going faint from blood loss and the chill of the water. They never found her lover.

"Jesus," the older guy said, throwing up his hands. "It's bad enough to have to go, but to wind up as sharkshit — "

Jamie, who'd been blowing softly into the aperture of his beer bottle, looked perturbed. "But how do you know?" he demanded, settling his eyes on Judy. "I mean, were you there? Did you see it, like maybe from another boat?"

She hadn't seen it. She wasn't there. She'd read about it in the paper.

"Uh-uh," Jamie scolded, wagging his finger. "No fair. You have to have seen it, actually been there."

The older guy leaned forward, lit a cigarette and told about an accident he'd witnessed on the freeway. He was coming back from the desert on a Monday night, the end of a three-day weekend, and there was a lot of traffic, but it was moving fast. Four guys in a pickup passed him — three in the cab, the fourth outside in the bed of the truck. A motorcycle stood beside him, lashed upright in the center of the bed. They passed on the right, and they were going at a pretty good clip. Just then, feeling a little bored and left out, the guy in the back of the truck mounted the motorcycle, as a joke. He got up on the seat, leaned into the wind raking over the top of the cab, and pretended he was heading into the final lap of the motocross. Unfortunately — and this was the morbid thrill of the exercise; there was always a pathetic adverb attached to the narrative, a "sadly" or "tragically" or "unfortunately" to quicken the audience's blood — unfortunately, traffic was stalled ahead, the driver hit the brakes, and the erstwhile motocross champion careened into the cab and went sailing out over the side like an acrobat. And like an acrobat, miraculously, he picked himself up unhurt. The older guy paused, flicked the ash from his cigarette. But unfortunately — and there it was again — the next car hit him in the hips at sixty and flung him under the wheels of a big rig one lane over. Eight more cars hit him before the traffic stopped, and by then there wasn't much left but hair and grease.

Hilary told the story of the "Tiger Man," who stood outside the tiger exhibit at the L. A. Zoo eight hours a day, seven days a week, for an entire year, and then was discovered one morning on the limb of a eucalyptus that hung thirty feet over the open enclosure, in the instant before he lost his balance. She was working the concession stand at the time, a summer job while she was in college, and she heard the people round the tiger pit screaming and the tigers roaring and snarling and thought at first they were fighting. By the time she got there the tiger man was in two pieces and his insides were spread out on the grass like blue strings of sausage. They had to shoot one of the tigers, and that was a shame, a real shame.

Jamie was next. He started in on the story of Renaldo the Great as if it were an eyewitness account. "I was like at this circus in Guadalajara," he said, and my mind began to drift.

It was my turn next, and the only death I could relate, the only one I'd witnessed face-to-face and not in some voyeuristic video or the pages of *Newsweek* or *Soldier of Fortune,* a true death, the dulling of the eyes, the grip gone lax, the passing from animacy to quietus, I'd never spoken of, not to anyone. The face of it came back to me at odd moments, on waking, starting the car, sitting still in the impersonal dark of the theater before the trailers begin to roll. I didn't want to tell it. I wasn't going to. When Jamie was done, I was going to excuse myself, lock the bathroom door behind me, lean over the toilet and flush it and flush it again till they forgot all about me.

I was sixteen. I was on the swim team at school, bulking up, pushing myself till there was no breath left in my body, and I entertained visions of strutting around the community pool in the summer with a whistle round my neck. I took the Coast Guard-approved lifesaving course and passed with flying colors. It was May, an early searing day, and I wheeled my mother's tubercular Ford out along the ocean to a relatively secluded beach I knew, thinking to do some wind sprints in the sand and pit my hammered shoulders and iron legs against the elemental chop and roll of the Pacific. I never got the chance. Unfortunately. I came down off the hill from the highway and there was a Mexican kid there, nine or ten years old, frantic, in full blind headlong flight, running up the path toward me. His limbs were sticks, his eyes inflamed, and the urgency rode him like a jockey. *"Socorro!"* he cried, the syllables catching in his throat, choking him. *"Socorro!"* he repeated, springing up off his toes, and he had me by the arm in a fierce wet grip, and we were running.

The sand flared with reflected light, the surf broke away to the horizon beneath the blinding ache of the sky, I felt my legs under me, and there it was, the moment, the face of it, lying there in the wash like some elaborate offering to the gulls. A man, big-bellied and dark, his skin slick with the wet, lay facedown in the sand as if he'd been dropped from the clouds. The boy choked and pleaded, too wrought up even for tears, the story I didn't want to hear spewing out of him in a language I couldn't comprehend, and I bent to the man and turned him over.

He wasn't sleeping. No sleep ever looked like that. The eyes were rolled back in his head, white flecks of vomit clung to his lips and stained the dead drooping mustache, and his face was huge, bloated, as if it had been pumped up with gas, as if in a minute's time a week had elapsed and all the rot inside him was straining to get out. There was no one else in sight. I straddled that monstrous head, cleared the dark slab of the tongue, pressed the side of my face to the sand-studded chest. I might have heard something there, faint and deep, the whisper of the sea in a smooth scalloped shell, but I couldn't be sure.

"Mi padre," the boy cried, *"mi padre."* I was a lifesaver. I knew what to do. I knew the moment had come to pinch shut those gaping nostrils, bend my lips to the dark hole beneath the vomit-flecked mustache and breathe life into the inert form beneath me, mouth to mouth.

Mouth to mouth. I was sixteen years old. Five and a half billion of us on the planet, and here was this man, this one, this strange dark individual with the unseeing eyes and lips slick with phlegm, and I couldn't do it. I gave the boy a look, and it was just as if I'd pulled out a handgun and shot him between the eyes, and then I got to my feet in a desperate scramble — think of a kitten plucked from the sleeping nest of its siblings, all four paws lashing blindly at the air — got to my feet, and ran.

My own father died when I was an infant, killed in a plane crash, and though I studied photos of him when I was older, I always pictured him as some faceless, mangled corpse risen from the grave like the son in "The Monkey's Paw." It wasn't a healthy image, but there it was.

My mother was different. I remember her as being in constant motion, chopping things on the drainboard while the washer chugged round, taking business calls—she was an accountant—and at the same time reaching for the sponge to scrub imaginary fingerprints off the white kitchen phone, all in a simultaneous and never-ceasing whirl. She died when I was thirty-two—or "passed on," as she would have had it. I wasn't there. I don't know. But as I've heard it told, digging round the crust of politesse and euphemism like an archaeologist unearthing a bone, there was no passing to it at all, no gentle progress, no easeful journey.

She died in public, of a heart attack. An attack. A seizure. A stroke. Violent and quick, a savage rending in the chest, no passing on, no surcease, no privacy, no dignity, no hope. She was shopping. At Safeway. Five-thirty in the afternoon, the place packed to the walls, the gleaming carts, this item and that, the little choices, seventeen-point-five cents an ounce as opposed to twenty-two-point-one. She writhed on the floor. Bit her tongue in two. Died. And all those faces, every one of them alive and condemned, gazing down on her in horror, all those dinners ruined, all that time wasted at the checkout counter.

We all knew Jamie would be the first of us to go. No one doubted it, least of all Jamie himself. He courted it, flaunted it, rented his videos and tried, in his own obsessive, relentless way, to talk it to death. Every time he got in his car, even to drive to the corner for a pack of cigarettes, it was like the start of the Indianapolis 500. He picked fights, though he was thirty years old and should have known better, dove out of airplanes, wrecked a pair of hang gliders. When he took up rock climbing, he insisted on free climbs only—no gear, no ropes, no pitons, only the thin tenuous grip of fingers and toes. I hadn't seen him in two years. He'd long since left L. A., teaching, any sort of steady job, steady income, steady life. He was in Aspen, Dakar, Bangkok. Once in a while I got a dirt-smeared postcard from out of the amazing pipeline, exotic stamps, a mad trembling hasty scrawl of which the only legible term was "dude."

This was the face of Jamie's death: Studio City, a golden winter afternoon, Jamie on a bench, waiting for the bus. It had rained the week before—the whole week—and the big twisting branches of the eucalyptus trees were sodden and heavy. They have a tendency to shear off, those branches, that's why the city keeps them trimmed back. Or used to, when there were funds for such things. A wind came up, a glorious dry-to-the-bone featherbed wind off the desert; the trees threw out their leaves and danced. And a single branch, wide around as any ordinary tree, parted company with the trunk and obliterated my friend Jamie, crushed him, made dogmeat of him.

Am I too graphic? Should I soften it? Euphemize it? Pray to God in His Heaven?

When the phone rang and I heard the long-forgotten but unmistakable tones of an old high school sometime acquaintance — Victor, Victor Cashaw — I knew what he was going to say before he knew it himself. I set down the phone and gazed through the kitchen to the patio, where Linda, my wife, lay stretched out on a rattan sofa, absorbed in a magazine that revealed all the little secrets of nail acrylics and blusher and which towel to use when you wake up at his house. For all I knew, she could have been pregnant. I walked straight out the door, climbed into the car and drove down the block to Video Giant.

In a way, it was perversely gratifying to see that the *100 Faces of Death* series had grown to twenty volumes, but it was Volume IV that I wanted, only that. At home, I slipped quietly into the den — Linda was still there, still on the patio sofa, still motionless but for the beat of her eyes across the page — and inserted the cassette into the slot in the machine. It had been nine years, but I recognized Renaldo as if I'd seen him yesterday, his dilemma eternal, his sweat inexhaustible, his eyes forever glossy. I watched the lovely assistant slide toward panic, focused on the sliver of straw clenched between Renaldo's gleaming teeth. When did he realize? I wondered. Was it now? Now?

I waited till the moment came for him to drop the straw. Poor Renaldo. I froze it right there.

XIAODA XIAO

TRANSLATED FROM THE CHINESE BY THE AUTHOR

AND KURT WILDERMUTH

The Visiting Suit

The first sunny day after the rainy season happened to be our day off. From very early in the morning the cement yard in front of the barracks was flooded with noise and an atmosphere reminiscent of the market street of my hometown. The sounds, filling the space enclosed by brick walls as high as a two-story building, caught the attention of two guards perched on top of the watchtower beyond the barracks. Prisoners who had taken their damp quilts and mattresses outside at sunrise were walking busily to and fro. They were now feeling impatient to lie on their bunk beds, hoping to find good spots to air their quilts in the sunshine during the morning ahead.

My groupmate, Cockeye, had wakened me with a shove. He leaned from the bunk below me. "Wake up," he shouted in my right ear. "I saved a place for you." He had no doubt just finished placing his quilts.

I felt angry with him. In what was left of that morning's dream time, I'd been trying to keep the smile of my girlfriend from fading. She appeared in my dreams only when I was in good spirits, and her image could keep me in good psychological health for several days. I opened my eyes and was about to tell him off, when I remembered that the night before I had asked him to wake me in the morning.

I lifted myself on my elbows, and after sighing for the lost dream I said, "OK, I'm awake." I rolled up my quilts and mattresses as quickly as I could, and took them to the spot that Cockeye pointed out to me. I had just finished placing them on the iron rack when the cement yard came alive with prisoners dashing from other doors, quilts and mattresses in their arms. What an unpleasant swarm they were! Terrible quarrels broke out as prisoners arrived at the same place simultaneously, trying to occupy the sunniest iron racks. Cockeye gave me a knowing look and said, "We were lucky we got here first."

We squeezed between some of the quilts and squatted, resting for a bit until the bell for breakfast was sounded.

After breakfast, Cockeye returned to our spot between the quilts, to repair his plastic shoes. I prepared a basin of hot water, wrapped a towel around my head, and got ready for a haircut. None of the razors in the prison camp had been sharpened for months, and I knew the only way to alleviate the horrible rough ache the razor would leave behind was to make the hair softer than usual with a hot wet towel.

On one side of the big iron gate, a queue of prisoners held basins and towels. Old Wang, the trustee of the General Service Group, was patiently shaving one head after another. He seemed quite unaware of the cracking noise his razor made. I asked someone ahead of me to watch my basin and, wearing my towel around my head, began to walk around the cement yard.

On the other side of the iron gate a crowd of newcomers formed a circle and listened to Zhang, who was considered an elite member of the prison community and was now giving a lecture on the three worldwide enigmas in math. He declared that he would now solve "The third equal division of an arbitrary angle." After working intensely on a thick piece of wrapping paper with his homemade compass and ruler, he loudly requested that someone pass him a pair of scissors. He cut off three angular pieces of paper and fitted them together to demonstrate his solution. "Look at this, everyone!" he cried triumphantly.

"But how can you show this is a valid proof?" someone asked.

Zhang paused for a while, and then said, "Well, I'm afraid that I can't just yet, but I'm sure that I will before I finish my term here." He continued to wave his wrapping paper in the air, as eager as a quack trying to peddle cure-all herbs. The crowd rewarded him with a burst of laughter, then dispersed. I walked to the toilet, which stood at the opposite end of the cement yard. The toilet had no door, but everyone was used to the lack of privacy.

About twenty prisoners were busily occupied nearby. Their number was gradually increased by those who had been part of Zhang's audience. Zhang himself soon arrived and pushed his way into the crowd, which caused many complaints. The prison's barter market was in session.

"Hey, get out of here! This is no place for display," Yu Fuchai, the broker, bawled, cradling his homemade scale in his arms to protect it from damage. This market was usually held in the front hall of the barracks, but today it had been moved outside, along with the shabby quilts and mattresses.

Yu Fuchai, a nimble salesman, stood on a small soapbox in the center of the circle, waving a shirt in the air. Two prisoners who were to be released in a few days stood on either side of him.

"Have a good look first," Yu Fuchai said seriously to the prisoner on his right. He then turned to the one on his left while squinting at another prisoner, the owner of the shirt who was standing beside me and watching them. The man on Yu Fuchai's right came to a decision after a moment's hesitation, and he bought the shirt for four jins of rice powder. When released, he would need some decent clothes to put on so he could pass for an ordinary person. It was said that those who were released wearing shabby clothes would have troubles outside. Big Yang, for example, who, when released last fall, had put on his old shirt and a pair of numbered pants before going to a restaurant for his first dinner out, had waited for more than an hour to get his food.

I joined the group in time to see the man pour rice powder from his cloth sack onto Yu Fuchai's scale. He then took the shirt and departed.

"Who's next?" said Yu Fuchai in a soft voice. No one answered.

At that moment, as I turned to leave, remembering that I had to have my head shaved, I suddenly caught sight of Ji, his wide, bony face half hidden among the others. He seemed unaware of me. His attention was fixed on Yu Fuchai. He then turned to watch the former owner of the shirt pick up his rice powder from the scale and move away. As I watched Ji, I sensed that he was struggling to make a difficult decision. He was on the brink of surrendering to the constant pangs of hunger that troubled most of us. Perhaps he would make a decision now; I knew he had frequently attended the barter market as a quiet onlooker. Today he was standing on the edge of the crowd instead of in his usual front-row spot. He no doubt wished to avoid being singled out by Yu Fuchai, as he had been on the last market day.

"You can't get anything unless you give up your suit," Yu Fuchai had chastised him. "You'd better stop coming here. It's no place for timid types. Understand what I mean?"

Trade at today's market had certainly set a record, with the biggest deal ever having been transacted. I had never imagined that one shirt could be exchanged for four jins of rice powder. An excellent opportunity presented itself to Ji, for there were other prisoners present, holding heavy cloth sacks of rice powder, hoping to acquire clothes.

Ji owned a well-tailored blue suit of very good quality, though its style was slightly outdated. He did not put it on for festivals or holidays, but only when his wife came to visit him. Therefore, to tease him, we had named it the "Visiting Suit."

Ji kept his Visiting Suit wrapped in paper in a wooden crate under his iron bunk. On sunny days off, like this one, he would air the suit on the iron rack in the cement yard and sit quietly next to it. Sometimes we saw him cleaning soiled spots with a wet brush. After brushing the suit for a while, we noticed that he would step back to look at it with half-closed eyes, like an artist admiring his work.

But this day we didn't see Ji airing his Visiting Suit; we didn't even see him in the barracks early in the morning. He must have been the first one of our group to enter the cement yard and wait.

Ji was not at all talkative, and he often looked altogether sluggish. I knew that his prison term had begun when he was forty years old, and that he had lived in a small town on the Grand Canal. He had owned a small photography studio there, which he ran with his wife — his only assistant. He had told me that his business was sometimes very good, especially during festival periods, though nearly all his customers were from the neighboring countryside. "In holiday seasons," he said once, "I would be so busy, I couldn't speak to my wife all day."

I imagined that Ji's household was a small but prosperous one, similar to those in small towns I had seen in my travels as a high school student. All that was missing was a child, and Ji seemed sorry about that. He remarked to me that he would have had a son or daughter by now if he had not been accused of listening to foreign broadcasts and imprisoned as a counter-revolutionary.

Most of the other prisoners disliked working with Ji, because he was so slow, and his taciturn manner distanced him from them even more. We few who did chat with Ji were, in fact, curious about his exceptional style of dress, his peculiar way of walking, and the formality of his appearance on the occasions of his wife's visits. There was a certain amount of respect behind this curiosity, but we behaved among ourselves as though Ji was just someone good to joke about. It was our way of entertaining ourselves after exhausting days at hard labor, and we mocked him cruelly when he returned from visiting with his wife.

"Hey, Ji, how goes the ceremony today?" we would ask him.

Not only was Ji's Visiting Suit the finest piece of clothing in the prison, but those who had seen his wife knew how beautiful and courteous she was.

* * *

On a hot afternoon in the middle of summer, three days after Ji was sent to the prison, I first saw his wife. While moving stones in the quarry, stripped to only shorts, Ji and I were interrupted by a prison officer who had come to inform us that relatives were waiting to see us in the reform office. Realizing that my mother had come to visit, I was happy at the thought of the bag of rice powder she would soon give me. Nearly half of the prisoners in our barracks had received rice powder, which was the only foodstuff allowed in. Some received parcels; others got rice powder when their relatives came to visit. You simply mixed it with hot water and ate it. I had been in the prison for eight months, and so far my mother had visited four times, each time bringing a bag of rice powder weighing about twenty jins. I felt confident that I could survive the rest of my five-year term if she continued to visit as frequently. I was so excited about seeing her that I completely forgot my aching muscles and the sweat streaming down my forehead and into my eyes.

Ji and I climbed out of the quarry along a narrow path.

"So who's here to see you?" I asked Ji as we walked along a dirt road leading to the reform office. He seemed reluctant to answer. The news of a visitor had apparently not lifted his spirits at all. "It's my wife," he said. Unlike most of the husbands hurrying to see their wives for the first visit, he displayed no sign that his wife was waiting for him, neither in his bearded face nor from the way he walked.

"You just got here, didn't you?" I asked.

He nodded absently. I felt annoyed by his silence. The walk would have seemed much shorter if he had been a bit more talkative. Instead we walked along as though we were headed for a cell.

I considered for a moment that Ji's behavior was not actually so strange. I had experienced similar feelings during my first days in prison. Remembering how miserable I had been then, I knew that he had still not accepted the fact that his old life was gone forever. I myself had experienced great difficulty in letting go of my former life. I was thankful that I was now at least mentally accustomed to prison life, that I could firmly resist any feelings about the past, and that I was aware of the lack of connection between myself and the ordinary teenager I had been. I had let go of all my teenage fantasies and ambitions, and sometimes even doubted that once I had shared wonderful times with my girlfriend. Such pleasures seemed as remote as life on another planet.

So it seemed that Ji, suffering in the same way I had during my first days, and as yet unawakened from the dream of his previous peaceful life, was feeling too much pain to understand that I had once felt the same.

When we reached the big iron gate of our barracks, Ji stopped and said, "I must change my clothes," and hurried inside.

The officer, who had followed us, caught up to me and said, "What is he doing in there?"

"Changing his clothes."

We waited uncomfortably at the gate. There was no shade at all, and the scorching sun was shining on my bare head and back. Sweat was pouring down my face. I felt ready to voice my annoyance, when Ji came out again. He walked over to us without a word. I was so surprised that I forgot my irritation, for he had put on his suit. When he'd said he was going to change his clothes, I hadn't expected to see him wearing a formal wool suit in the hot sun. The officer was surprised, too. After staring at Ji for a while, he said, "You don't think you are going to a party, do you?"

True, Ji looked as serious as an important guest on his way to a party, walking along with calm and purposeful steps. Yet the front of his suit was already soaked through with sweat.

Watching the man for a moment, I shrugged. My back too was soaked with sweat. I decided Ji must have had a few loose screws in his head to wear such a heavy suit on a hot summer day.

"What's going on?" the officer asked him again, as though Ji were a madman.

Without replying, Ji walked calmly toward the red brick building where the reform office was located.

When we arrived at the reform office, my mother was sitting at one corner of a long table and a slim, beautiful young woman was sitting at the other. I realized that this young woman, in a patterned blouse and skirt, was Ji's wife.

She was as serious and calm as he was. Unlike most wives who came to visit, she seemed neither frightened, nor tearful. Instead, as Ji entered the room the corners of her mouth lifted with a shy half-smile. Watching them, I had the impression that the prisoner and his wife were both making efforts to present themselves well, and preparing their minds like performers about to appear on stage.

While my mother was talking to me, I could hardly take my eyes off the Jis. Having put my hand on the sack of rice powder my mother had brought, I once more felt safe from hunger. This sense of security was much more important than my mother's words.

Chief Chai, the head of our prison, who sat between my mother and myself, ordered me to listen to my mother. I nodded. I wished that he would leave us alone, so that I could tell my mother that as a growing young man I needed more to eat, and that she should bring more rice powder with her next time.

When Chief Chai turned to look at the Jis, I got my chance. I made a few gestures. I pointed to my mouth with my fingers, and my mother understood immediately what I meant.

When Chief Chai turned back, I had nothing else to say, so I took the sack and was about to leave. But as I turned to go, I was again struck by the Jis' meeting. Ji sat stiffly before his wife. She was speaking in a soft voice, talking about her relatives who had come to visit her since Ji left home. Controller Dong sat between them, but they ignored him entirely as if he were merely a stone.

Then Ji's wife lifted her bag onto the table and, in a way that reminded me of how my girlfriend showed me her birthday gifts, began to show Ji what she had brought for him. When I glanced at their sack of rice powder, I saw it was only about half as full as mine.

It seemed to me that Ji wore an invisible smile while listening to his wife, and that she smiled in the same manner when he began to speak. He maintained his formal pose and was unaware that he was soaked through with sweat, his suit sticking to his body like a wet towel.

Ji's wife reached out her hands, calmly, the way she talked, to where Ji's hands were. Now came the time for visiting wives to cry. It was the end of the visiting time and the wives still had a lot to say. With so much left to say, their words escaped them — leaving nothing but sobs. There were, however, no tears in Ji's wife's eyes. Nor had she held Ji's hands tightly as most of the other wives did during their visits. And Controller Dong, who was used to such scenes during the prisoners' visits, looked awkward.

"She is so lovely," my mother whispered, half to herself and half to me. Certainly, I thought; but what was just as striking was the transformation of Ji. This was not the Ji who moved stones with me in the quarry, scraped porridge out of his bowl with his index finger, or remained indifferently silent when I'd spoken to him. He was not a prisoner now. He looked like a man who was going to receive honor from the government.

I watched the couple without missing what my mother said. She told me she had met the wife on the boat. They had rented a room together at the inn. "The manager seemed to do more for us than she had ever done for prisoners' relatives before. She allowed us the room on the second floor, which has windows facing south."

According to my mother, though, Ji's wife didn't seem grateful for such special treatment. "I guess she's kind of inexperienced, for it was the first time she has traveled so far and spent the night away from home by herself. But I like the fact that she didn't feel inferior. We two will have a lot to talk about this evening."

Perhaps my mother and Ji's wife will become good friends, I thought. I hoped so.

The couple's talk ended. I saw Ji smile gently at his wife. Her eyes responded, but Ji's wife was so shy that her face displayed only that mysterious half-smile.

All of a sudden, my girlfriend's shy smile surfaced in my memory, so clearly that I wanted her more at that moment than I ever had. There had been no letters from my girlfriend, and I was not allowed to write to her, because Regulation 6 said prisoners were not allowed to write to anyone other than their direct relatives. I felt as though I could put up with the endless hunger, years longer than my term, if my girlfriend were to visit me wearing such a smile.

Ji went in through the big iron gate before me. When I entered the barracks, I saw that he was carefully taking off his suit. He then took a piece of old newspaper and wrapped it inside. After this was done, he took his bowl out of his wooden case. Running a hand inside the sack that his wife brought him, he put a handful of rice powder into the bowl and mixed this with hot water. He blew on his bowl while mixing so that he was able to eat without stopping. I saw his neck move with each gulp he took, and noticed that he still seemed troubled. Sweat streamed down his face as he choked down the food. Once, with the same hand that held the spoon, he rubbed the sweat from his face briefly with the back of his hand.

I moved to face him, thinking that I might see in his expression some trace of the meeting with his wife. Had he sunk into his past again? Maybe he would like to talk to me about his wife. No, he looked as indifferent as he had been before his wife's visit. From the manner in which he choked down his food, he appeared as resigned as an old-timer to prison life. He most likely had known at the time of his arrest that he would be separated from his wife for quite a long period, and would have to meet her in some other place. He must have prepared himself for this before coming to the prison.

After that first visit Ji's wife visited him every two months. Other prisoners, whose relatives happened to visit them at the same time, also got the chance to see the Jis meeting. All who witnessed their meeting would talk about it after supper. This was how we came to rank Ji in the list of important men among our group of prisoners. There were five on the list. Our group leader was certainly the most important man of all, and was highly appreciated for his skill in distributing dishes impartially. Shen

Chenshing, who was held in high esteem for his creative humor at bed-time, was second to him. Next were Chen Jei and me. We were both praised for our hard labor and for assisting weaker prisoners. The fifth was Ji, but his importance was different. Our regard for him was based solely on those occasions when he wore the suit that he left wrapped in old newspapers and stepped out solemnly to meet his wife. At that moment, he far surpassed the rest of us in importance.

In our group, Chen Jei and I were most interested in Ji's unique manner, and so we always tried to talk with him, especially when we saw him standing by himself in the cement yard after our thought-reform class at night. We were patient and restrained when talking with him, usually beginning with polite questions. Sometimes we asked him about his career, sometimes his photo studio or his customers, but every time received nothing more than a simple yes or no. I would exchange looks with Chen Jei, hoping that he would ask about what really interested us, but he wasn't bold enough to do so either.

Eventually, we did learn a little about Ji. He told us that the suit he wore, when his wife came to visit, was his wedding suit. But that was all he would reveal to us.

We told the others the history of Ji's suit before going to bed that night. Everyone agreed that Ji still looked like a newly married man when he was wearing his suit. But as Shen Chenshing remarked, "Ji's wedding suit has now become a Visiting Suit."

Ji served the first two years of his four-year prison term in this way. He would air his suit on holidays and would wear it when his wife came to visit. If we happened to see him come back from a visit with his suit on, we would say, "Hey, Ji, time flew fast for you. . . . Let's count how many times you should wear your suit before you go free. Eleven, twelve?"

As time passed, Ji wore his Visiting Suit less frequently. We only saw him airing it out during fine holidays because his wife stopped visiting as frequently as she had done at first. The periods between her visits stretched to six months or more. Ji stood by himself in the cement yard every night as always. We saw under the moonlight that his wide, bone-framed face was filled with sadness. Sometimes we heard him sighing from deep in his chest: It sounded like the groan of a dying man.

Then came a night when Ji seemed at last unable to bear his loneli-ness and hunger any longer. Too desperate to control himself, he began a conversation with Chen Jei and me. "Do you think my wife would change her mind?" he asked. We were shocked by his words, for we didn't expect him to ask us such a question. More so perhaps than the other prisoners, we tended to regard the relationship between Ji and his wife as the most private to be seen in the camp.

Chen Jei stammered, "No, no, I don't believe your wife would . . ."

With a deep sigh, Ji said, "But many women do change their minds during their husbands' imprisonments."

There was a heavy silence, broken when Ji asked us whether we could help him out with some rice powder. "If my wife comes to visit, I'll pay you back," he added, as though he were unsure whether his request would be met. It occurred to me that Ji's real reason for speaking to us might have been just to get some rice powder. Afraid that we would turn him down, he said again, "I'll pay you back when my wife comes."

We, of course, gave him the rice powder he needed, and found him quite grateful. He said that he wouldn't forget our help.

After Ji left us, Chen Jei and I stood together for a while in the cement yard. Neither of us looked at each other, or said anything.

Gradually we became estranged from Ji. We felt uneasy with him and made excuses to leave whenever he met us on the cement yard and stood beside us. The man we had looked up to with such respect had become an ordinary prisoner. We almost hated him, seeing that he had taken advantage of our naiveté. We were sure that if we had asked him about his relationship with his wife, we would have been disappointed with his answers. In short, we decided that Ji was no match for his wife at all.

It was midday and the sun was scorching my bare head. All the prisoners' activities were over, and those few who remained in the yard were new-comers. I must go back to the barracks, I thought, and dragged myself to the door. It was silent inside, and I saw that everyone, except for Cockeye, was there resting. Chen Jei was lying on his bunk, humming a folk song from his homeland while staring into space and rocking his legs. As I passed by him he glanced at me as if I were a stranger.

"I've got something to tell you," I whispered.

"What?" he grunted.

I gestured for him to follow, and we went out. I saw Ji, who was relaxing on his lower bunk, watching me, anxiously moving his hands from his sides to his chest.

Chen Jei caught up to me as I stepped over a whitewashed cement bench, and we walked partway across the cement yard. The sun's bright glare seemed blunted only by a narrow strip of shadow cast by the high dark brick wall.

"So what's up?" said Chen Jei, leaning on the wall without looking at me.

"I think Ji has sold his Visiting Suit," I said.

"That's why you dragged me out here! All can I say is, it's none of my business. I already knew about it. Cockeye witnessed the sale of that suit to Tong Shanyuan, and Yu Fuchai got one jin of rice powder from the trade," he said loudly and looked at me.

"Don't talk in such a loud voice. Ji might hear us."

"You're afraid of him. But you drag me out here! Why aren't you afraid of me?"

We stood facing each other, our eyes dazzled by the sunlight burning off the oily cement surface of the empty yard. Except for the rustling sounds the prisoners made while resting in the stale and hopeless atmosphere of the barracks the yard was silent.

Chen Jei looked at me angrily. We were on the verge of lunging at each other. But the moment passed; I stepped aside to hide the anger in my eyes.

That night, after the thought-reform class, Ji told me what had happened that morning. Then he began to beg for my assistance.

"Do you think I'm soft," I asked him, "and easier to cheat than Chen Jei?"

Ji opened his mouth, but no words came out. And then with an effort, he said, "No, I don't mean that. I want you and Chen Jei to help me once more. No one else can help me."

"Sorry," I said, "we've helped you through enough."

"Even as I was selling my suit to Tong Shanyuang for the nine jin of rice powder, I knew I shouldn't. Now I'm afraid that my wife will feel deeply hurt. I've decided that I've got to get it back, but I can't handle it all by myself." Ji spoke urgently, as though I were the only person he could rely on.

I decided in a few seconds. I called Chen Jei out to the yard. We stood in a dark corner and discussed what we would do. We both forgot our earlier disagreement as we constructed a plan for the redemption of the Visiting Suit. Ji stood shamefully in the darkness close by.

Chen Jei finally turned to him and said, "OK, bring the rice powder and we'll go find them."

We found Yu Fuchai in the toilet. I strode over and put my right hand heavily on his shoulder. Yu turned with a start and said, "What's the matter?" But when he saw Chen Jei, who stood behind me, looking at him and Ji, he seemed to understand, and followed us out without another word.

We found Tong Shanyuang in the cement yard. He was talking to a group of prisoners about his big plans for eating in a restaurant after his release in a couple of days. It took us only a few minutes to take Tong Shanyuang aside and order him to get the Visiting Suit, give it to Chen Jei, and accept the return of his sack of rice powder.

Later, back in the dark corner, where we had held our earlier discussion, I saw a smile appear on Ji's face. He tried to hide it when Chen Jei looked at him. But Chen Jei continued to behave so magnanimously that he suggested we bestow some rice powder on Ji. I agreed, though I was almost out of rice powder myself.

We remained in the moonlit yard after Ji left. It was very quiet. The moonlight seemed to emphasize the emptiness of the space between the big iron gate and the high walls. I thought of my mother, who was probably falling asleep now. She always wrote to me, "I get up early and go to bed early, too. I fall asleep as soon as I go to bed. I've been used to that schedule since you left home . . ."

Chen Jei, who stood beside me, suddenly broke into my thoughts by slapping me on my bare head. "You look stronger and more threatening than before, because of your newly shaved head. Yu Fuchai and Tong Shanyuang must have been scared by the green light that reflects off it under the moon!"

I answered by slapping him back, and we fought playfully in the empty yard.

Ji did not return to the barter market after that. He continued to wander around the cement yard at night as before. He grew thinner, his face more angular. He became more taciturn than ever, and seemed to ride out the rest of his term by means of his silence, which we read as a sort of self-confidence. Maybe he would get through it yet, we thought.

Ji would put his Visiting Suit on the iron rack every sunny holiday, and brushed the soiled spots as carefully as before. The Visiting Suit, however, became so full of holes that as Yu Fuchai remarked mockingly, "It is no longer worth even one jin of rice powder."

During the last year of his term his wife came to visit him more frequently. And Ji wore his suit each time his wife came, except for her final visit, two months before he was set free. Ji did not wear his Visiting

Suit when he was called to the reform office. Instead, he wore an old black wadded coat, a prison uniform for winter.

That evening, after the thought-reform class, Controller Dong entered our group and asked Ji, "Today was your wife's last visit. Why didn't you wear your suit?" Dong actually seemed angry at Ji. Rising up from his bunk slowly, Ji said, "I couldn't wear my suit today because a rat has eaten a big hole in it." He took the Visiting Suit out of his wooden box and spread it out on his bunk. The suit was completely worn out. The soft wool was so worn away that its color had greatly faded. And in the front of it was a gaping hole shaped like a new moon.

Dong, the controller, told Ji to give the suit to him. "I'll tell the sewing group to mend it."

The day on which Ji's prison term came to an end happened to be a fine holiday. He put on his Visiting Suit early in the morning. The front chest of the suit had been replaced with a piece of cloth of similar color, in a way that looked as though Ji had put a handkerchief halfway into his top pocket. I looked at him for a while, then walked to Ji's side, because it seemed that he had something to say. I found he was clenching his large hands together, as though to control himself when he began a speech. But when he spoke, it was only one sentence: "My wife will come to meet me this afternoon."

Sure enough, his wife appeared in the afternoon. I was taken aback by her appearance, however. The woman had changed so much that I doubted whether she was really Ji's wife, the woman I had first seen four years past. She looked thin, tired, and old. All her former vitality and beauty was gone. The only thing remaining to identify her as Ji's wife was her shy smile.

While his wife waited outside the big iron gate, Ji shook hands with me. I turned my eyes on Ji's Visiting Suit and then to his wife, both worn out since I had first seen and admired them four years ago. I recalled the first time that Ji's wife visited him, the occasion when Ji exchanged his Visiting Suit for rice powder, the way he moved his mouth when he was watching the barter market, and his desperate sighs in the cement yard late at night. When I moved my eyes from Ji's Visiting Suit to his wife's face, I wondered what had happened to her during the period in which she had failed to visit her husband. Had she had some experience similar to Ji's with his suit?

As I stood watching the Jis, I felt tears rolling down my cheeks. I thought of my groupmate Chen Jei, who had died in the quarry, crushed by huge stones, the year before. He had also witnessed the couple's meeting and helped Ji as much as I had. Had he been standing next to me to witness the Jis' reunion, he would have tapped me on the head and said the parting words that I was unable to get out of my mouth.

Ji walked out the big iron gate and joined his wife. Those of us who had lived with him for years followed him with our eyes. We began to walk with him. And then for the first time we too walked out of the big iron gate. Turning back, we saw that Controller Dong and a few other officers had also stepped out of the reform office to watch until the couple had disappeared from sight.

JOSIP NOVAKOVICH

Bread and Blood

Prolonged cries of cricket wings came astride frogs' voices on damp winds from a distant pond and drowned in the grease of Ivan's ear, scratched the eardrum, bounced around in the cochlea, and entered through the Eustachian tube into his throat, where the cries were hard to swallow, thick with the blood of the prisoners slain in the pond the night before. That his army, Croatian Home Guards, protected Ustasha execution squads sickened him. As he paced around the storage barracks, his sweat glued his shirt and socks to his skin; he shivered now and then despite the heat as though he could shake off the clothes, the sweat, and even his skin, and emerge into a cleansed world of his imagination, except that he could not imagine anything clean and cool.

"Tomo!" Ivan startled his sleepy fellow guard. "It's going to rain." He laughed although it was hard to laugh through the heavy phlegm of his throat. "Your nerves are thin! Don't worry, so are mine."

Tomo lit a cigarette.

"Put it out. You mustn't smoke at night."

"This is my last cigarette. That Ustasha guy last night gave it to me."

"I wouldn't take anything from him. Man, he boasted of smashing the heads of Serb peasants and Croat communists with a sledgehammer!"

"I know."

"So how can you . . . ?"

"A cigarette is a cigarette."

Ivan snatched the cigarette from Tomo's lips and squashed it under his boot into the sandy cement.

"Jerk!" Tomo said. "If I wasn't so sleepy, I'd trash the crap out of you for this!"

"I doubt it." Ivan remembered that when they had been boys and Tomo hit him he would not fight back because he'd followed his father's Christian teachings. But once, the last time they would fight, he had grabbed Tomo by the throat, knocked his head against the road gravel, and knuckled his nose out of bent. Analyzing now the curve on Tomo's broken nose, Ivan said: "You have no courage. If you had any—and if I had any—would we stay on in this ridiculous army?"

A blue lightning spread silently through the humid air.

"The Germans are beginning to lose in the East. They'll drag us down to hell with them. You are right, we should split, save our asses. But how? Where? Partisans shoot Croat Home Guard deserters."

"That's what they tell us here so we won't run over."

Far away a steam engine whistled, sounding like an owl without a mate. Then, a succession of explosions came so strongly that pots in the storage room rattled.

Ivan packed smoked ham in his leather bag. His hands trembled as he wrapped a kilo of salt in a newspaper. A loud rain fell and for the time being washed away the cricketing, the bloated voices of frogs, the train whistles.

When the rain turned into a broad waterfall, as though a sea was sifted through a perforated sky, Ivan and Tomo ran across the soccer field outside the barracks. German shepherds neither smelled nor heard them. The deserters walked through a torrential ditch, through muddy corn-fields, over the train tracks, into the sylvan mountains, as comfortable in the water as a pair of frogs.

They walked all night. The morning was so lucid that they squinted at the mountain peaks near Zagreb eighty miles east, which resembled a flat hunter's cap without a feather. They sat on the outskirts of a white-washed village, on the smooth bark of a thick beech which had apparently fallen that night—not because the winds had been powerful but because the waters had loosened the ground so much that the tree fell like a tooth pushed by the tongue out of an old abscess. The rain had washed the soil from the roots so that the blind, naked limbs silently groped in the air, black against the translucent turquoise of the emptied sky. The deserters squeezed water out of their shirts and socks and lined them up on the bark. Ivan took out the wrapped salt, which had become a stone in the wet newspapers. He rubbed smoked ham against the salty stone and chewed the meat, and so did Tomo. They gazed at old women in their black skirts and wooden shoes herding geese with sticks down the main—and only—road of the village. When the women saw them, they shrieked. Soldiers, no matter from what army, meant a good likelihood of pillage, rape, drunkenness, house burning. Tomo and Ivan picked up their rifles, clicked them ready, and said, "Calm down, we aren't going to shoot you." The women cried even louder.

Tomo went into the nearest house while Ivan stood guard outside. They went through several houses in this fashion, picking up two Sunday-best suits and two sheepskin jackets. Then they poured gasoline over their military uniforms and burned them, and ran into the woods.

After wandering for two days they found a band of partisans. They buried their guns in the leaves, stuck out their white shirts atop two twigs, and walked into the camp. The guards kept them at gunpoint and called the captain. The captain walked out of a tilting tent, picking his teeth with a thin branch, which he kept thinning with his thumbnail before having another go at his molar. His small narrowly set hazel eyes, made green by the forest, scrutinized Tomo's and Ivan's lips and teeth as he interrogated them, as though the truthfulness of their words could be mirrored in their teeth. Ivan became self-conscious of his two silver incisors since the captain focused on them especially keenly. Perhaps all would not have gone well if there hadn't been a partisan from Byelovar, who knew the two men and said so to the captain. "They are all right. Ivan Toplak is the town baker and Tomo Starchevich, the basket weaver. I know them from the time when we pissed together making mud out of dust."

"What else do you know about them?" the captain asked.

"Ivan is some kind of new believer, a Methodist, I guess, and Tomo is a gambler and whoremonger."

"Eh, that's no good," said the captain. "You need no God in this war. If there is one he's hiding now, and then in peace he'll come around and ask us for money? No, boys, that won't do. We have a new religion, us and freedom. Brotherhood and unity."

Ivan frowned. Tomo yawned.

"What else?" asked the captain.

"After the German invasion, when Ustashas burned down Serb Orthodox churches outside Byelovar, Ivan Toplak went around collecting protest signatures."

"You are a Serb?" The captain turned to Ivan. "That's good—almost everybody here's Croatian and we should be international."

"No, not a Serb, a mixture of Croat and Hungarian, but since I am a god-fearing man, I did not want to see any churches burn."

"All the churches should burn. And what else?"

"Ustashas looked for Ivan, but he fled into the woods, and that's the last I heard of him." Either the man did not know that Home Guards captured Ivan one night at home and conscripted him, or he did not want to make it harder for Ivan to be accepted. Probably the latter, for he winked at Ivan after he'd done telling.

The captain swallowed a shot of plum brandy and passed the yellow bottle on to Ivan and Tomo, who accepted because they were not sure how the captain would take it if they declined, and because they genuinely liked it.

"And you, what was your name?" the captain asked. "Tomo the Whoremonger? That's all right with me, but remember, no rape, not while I am in charge. Hmm, Ivan the Baker, you say. Why not a smith, or something more vigorous?"

"Why not?" Ivan said. "During the Depression, blacksmiths had more apprentices than they needed. I really wanted to become a doctor, but I had to quit school after the fourth grade to help support my younger siblings. My mother convinced me that being a barber would be almost like being a doctor—so at first, before becoming a baker, I was a barber. I learned the trade in a couple of months so that when my boss went binging in the taverns he'd let me run the shop. It was all right until one day when my neighbor Ishtvan comes along for a shave. I set him up in the chair, place a white apron around his neck, sharpen the switchblade on leather, and lather him up nicely."

"All right, all right, speed up the story, we all know what barbers do—so what?" the captain grumbled.

"Foam touches Ishtvan's hairs, which stick half an inch out of his nose, and he sneezes.

" 'Do you want your nose hairs cut or plucked?' I ask. He does not answer but sneezes again, blowing the foam down all over the shop.

" *'Gesundheit!'* I say."

"No German words allowed here," the captain interrupted. "Don't do it again!"

"All right. 'God bless you!' I say."

"No, that won't do," the captain said. "No God around here, isn't that clear once and for all?"

"But," Ivan was losing his temper, "I am trying to tell you how it was. So, Ishtvan sneezes again, for the third time, and let's say that I said, 'To your health, neighbor Ishtvan! May you outlive many wives!' But Ishtvan does not say 'Thank you!' though he is a famously polite man. Instead he keeps his hand in front of his nose. He waits for the sneeze to come up and out. After he hasn't sneezed a minute later, I say, 'Should I hit your back?' As I raise my hand, his hand drops in his lap. His head nods to one side. I take a look at him and shake him, until I realize that he's dead. I fetch his wife. She runs in and says, 'He's going to get rid of his moustache? Is that what the fuss is about?'

" 'Just look at him,' I say. 'Don't you see? He's dead!'

"The woman gasps, and shouts 'Oh my God! *Wie schrecklich!*' "

"I warned you!" the captain said.

"I am just telling it like it was. So, I ask the lady, 'What should we do? Should we carry him back?'

" 'Wait, what should I do, what should I do? Tell you what, why don't you finish the shave?'

" 'But what good will that do?'

" 'A lot of good,' she says. 'He'll need a clean shave for his wake.'

" 'You've got a point there. But look, I'll have to throw away the blade and the brush after I shave the corpse. Nobody will want a shave here otherwise.'

" 'That's all right, I'll pay for all that.'

"She liked the shave so much she made me promise that during the wake I'd give him two or three more shaves because the hairs of the dead grow fast. As soon as we carried him back home I closed the shop and ran off. Not that I was horrified or anything—actually, I was so surprised by how calmly I took it that a man died while I worked on him that I thought I should become a doctor. But I did not want to be a barber."

"So, in other words, you deserted," the captain said. "A bad sign, a very bad sign." But the partisans, welcoming the story with laughter, overshadowed the captain's comment.

The mood was festive. An untended herd of pigs ran down the mountain slope, as mad as the pigs possessed by demons that ran into the Galilee lake and drowned. Partisans shot several. They found it hard to start a fire because all the wood was wet. Tomo came up with the idea to strip the fat off the pigs because the fat would burn like gasoline. After they put the fat and a sheepskin jacket among the branches, the fire caught on and sent up a cloud of smoke and steam so that the meat was both burned and steamed. The soldiers ate heavily, soaking bread in the grease that dripped into pots, and drank plum brandy, sang, told jokes. There was so much grease dripping that all the soldiers polished their shoes and greased their guns with it.

They feasted for four days. Ivan was scandalized by the disarray of the army—clearly they had seen no battle in weeks, perhaps months. They avoided the enemy but talked about imaginary battles, which grew greater and greater day by day.

One morning the captain asked, "How's your family, Ivan?"

"I have no idea. My old woman, a son and a daughter, they are stuck in a small apartment, two-thirds under the ground, with small windows to the streets, so that all day long they watch shoes pass by."

"Give me your address."

A week later, when several soldiers came back to the camp, one told that he'd visited Ivan Toplak's family.

"We walked in, and when the comrade saw us, she turned pale. 'What's the matter?' she asked.

" 'Well, comrade, we wonder how you are managing in this small apartment.'

" 'Fine,' she says.

" 'How about if we give you a sunny, three-room apartment? How would that be?'

" 'What for?'

" 'Well, since now you are one of us.'

" 'And how's that?'

" 'Don't you know? Your husband's with us, he's a partisan.'

" 'Good heavens. He a partisan!' And she laughs at us and says, 'No, my husband's no soldier. You can't make him one.'

" 'He is. So, take up the new apartment, you'll like it.'

" 'No way,' she says. 'I don't want it. We are fine here.'

"And can you believe it, she would not go along? What kind of soldier are you when not even your wife trusts your gun?" The soldier tapped Ivan on the shoulder and laughed.

The captain dug his fingers through his shirt, plucked the hairs on his chest, and eyeballed Ivan's military boots.

Ivan sat one morning on a rock in the sun and read his Bible. The captain snatched it. "Why were you so stingy? We could have started the fire with your book! My, what silky pages!" The captain fingered a page between his forefinger and thumb. "Fine English paper, isn't it? Good, I'll use it to roll my cigarettes." And he tore a hundred leaves, and tossed the rest into the glowing coals beneath a piglet. The paper burned blue and, as the fat dripped over it, changed to red, hissing. Ivan gripped a stone in his fist. When the Bible had burnt, the ashes retained its shape; Ivan could see between the fine pages into the pink middle. A slight breeze shifted the ashen leaves of the book, almost turning them, as though it wanted to open to the right page to find its golden verse, the guide for the day, which would tell it where and how to blow next. And then one large drop of fat fell on the silhouette of the Bible, piercing a hole in the middle. The ghost of the book collapsed into flimsy ashes. Above the camp the fine, transparent gray paper hovered and floated, the millennial letters falling apart in midair.

Just as the biblical words had all scattered around the camp and fallen softly on the trampled ground, the partying mood came to a close. Two couriers informed the captain that a detachment of Germans had taken the Raven's Peak and built a bunker there. The invaders intended to set up a line of bunkers over the Papuk-Psunj mountains, to divide western Slavonia.

The captain said, "We have to take the bunker, that's all there is to it."

At night the partisans marched through beech, pine, and oak forests, crackling branches and sliding over last year's leaves that had rotted but hadn't turned to soil yet. After they set up their position in a cave, the captain selected three soldiers—Ivan and two other novices who had come over from the Home Guard—to creep up to the bunker and take the machine gun nest. "Go up and prove yourself. If you bring back the machine guns, I'll know you aren't bullshitting." Tomo was not chosen for the perilous task because he had already proven himself as a soldier of integrity, demonstrating his arsenal of bawdy jokes every night after gulping down half a liter of brandy. On a misty morning, as low clouds drifted beneath the peak, and the forest steamed under a fresh sun, the three soldiers crawled up the mountain.

Ivan was enraged that he should be given the horrendous task. If he succeeded, the captain would get the credit. If he failed, the captain would continue to party, as though nothing had happened, while Ivan would be left dead to rot like the last year's leaves. As they crawled up the slopes, they caught glimpses of a machine-gun barrel sticking out, like the damning finger of a sinister god above the clouds. The finger pointed far above them, to the horizon. Ivan led the way. When he was a hundred yards away from the bunker, the machine-gun barrel turned downward toward him. He fired at it. A series of bullets came from the bunker, in smoke and steam. Ivan rolled down the slope, like a child over a meadow, except that there were stones sticking out of the grass here, but that did not matter. Death was after him, casting lead and fire. A bullet struck him on his left side. He rolled on, wondering whether he was still conscious. The sensation that he was losing it, that he was hit, comforted him. No more of this. Bullets roared down the slopes, swishing the brush and tall grass, cracking stones, sinking into tree bark. A verse resounded in Ivan's head: *The earth is utterly broken down, the earth is clean dissolved . . . The earth shall reel to and fro like a drunkard.* One of Ivan's comrades rolled past him, red, missing his face. Ivan stood up and ran, feeling no ground—flew. He realized that he was not running back to the partisan positions, but away from both the bunker and the cave.

That was all right. The captain would find a way to get him killed, sooner or later. He stopped to examine his wet wound; the bullet had blasted away his skin, a layer of fat, and his muscles above his left hip. He tore a sleeve off his jacket and held it tight over the wound, but the jacket kept drinking his blood the way an inkblotter draws ink out of a fountain pen.

His gun had disappeared though he did not remember dropping it. Did he need a gun? For what?

Should he run back to Byelovar to his wife? That would not do. He had deserted two armies, and the soldiers of both might soon be looking for him. Should he look for another army? No, he'd had it with armies. But could he make it alone? He wished he had his Bible, because the Bible—like an amulet—made him feel secure. Without it he felt absolutely desolate. But then again, what good did religion do him? It taught him to be a pacifist and yet abandoned him to serve in the army for two years before the war, and left him even more forsaken in the war, in the bands of murderers. He stumbled, pessimistic, skeptical, wondering if his religion had merely misled him in these dark woods, and just then he chanced upon a pine forest, with a magnificent calm in its cool darkness. Treading softly, he stepped over a carpet of pine needles half a foot deep and inhaled the aromatic air, light-headed.

Beyond the woods, he staggered into a deserted, burned village. He crawled into a house and collapsed in ashes. He slept for days perhaps, until a wet sensation on his forehead and eyebrows awakened him. A purring cat was licking him. Weak from loss of blood, he was not sure if he was awake—or if it mattered whether he was awake—and he did not resist the raspy tongue, which now covered his eyelids and pushed them open. That seemed to please the cat, so that she ceased to lick him and rolled against the side of his face, warmly purring, instilling the rhythm of life into his neck. He tried to move, but a thick pain in his left kidney dissuaded him. He felt the side—a rough crust covered his wound. There was no wet blood there anymore, no great swelling, apparently no abscess. Lying in a burned-out house helped because there weren't many bacteria around, and so there was no danger of gangrene, he thought, though he was not sure what exactly caused gangrene. Was the cat dangerous for his wound? Did she lick it, too? Now the cat licked and tickled his ear as though to tell him, You'll never know.

When he got up, the cat walked into the yard toward an unusually large brick oven, which the owners must have used to bake bread for most of the village. She walked proudly and significantly, lifting her tail straight up and letting the very tip of it wiggle out a code of satisfaction. She invited him to a nook where she must have spent her days. He gathered hay in a meadow to make the small abode comfortable; that he did not have much space was good because space was not to be trusted. Armies that might pass through would not bother to look in here.

In the woods Ivan gathered wild strawberries, mulberries, cherries, wild onions, and mushrooms of all kinds. He wished he had salt to rub on the mushrooms to draw out their moisture before frying them. In the bushes he found a nest of lark eggs and made a sweet mushroom omelette.

Food was his only preoccupation. From an old linden he scraped fungi, which he burned to smoke a nest of wild bees from the hollow of an old mulberry. He chewed cool honey out of the oval balls of wax honeycombs, the acacia aroma pleasing his tongue and scratching his throat.

When the tabby cat vanished at night, he missed her purr. He woke up to a choir of nightingales that flooded the forest with a brilliant melody. The cat appeared after sunrise, dragging a young rabbit nearly her size over a brick pathway to the oven. He started a fire with two stones and hay, and roasted the rabbit. He felt a little selfish doing it, until the cat caught a nightingale and ate it ostentatiously, as though to tell him he should not worry about her going hungry. The following morning, the cat caught another rabbit for him, and then, to pay her back, Ivan sharpened several twigs, and went down, below the village, to the creek, which was so quiet and slow that it formed a pond. The cat loved the carp he gave her.

The summer, the blessed season when it was easy to hide, went quickly. Leaves began to turn red and cold winds blew from Hungary. What chilled Ivan most was the image of leafless and bare mountains. Food would escape his reach unless he figured out a way to store it, like a squirrel.

He would have perhaps managed to spend the winter in the burned-out village, had the sounds of gun battles not come close. Detonations, explosions, machine-gun fire, and air-strikes seared the ground several miles away and drifted in dry biting smoke to him. From a crack in his oven one day he saw partisans walking through the village, and a day later, Germans, and on the third day, Serb Royalists, Chetniks. Alone, he would be a sitting duck for all of the armies in the winter — but despite that, he might have stayed, had his cat not vanished. He wondered whether soldiers had killed her to eat or to exercise their cruelty.

Walking westward, outside a village his grandmothers came from, he found a Golgotha monument. The statues of Christ and the two robbers were torn off and thrown onto thick heathers on the side of the road, and in their place three corpses were pierced to the crosses with large rusted nails. Two were circumcised Muslims, and the third, occupying the place of the talkative thief, was a Catholic, with a tattoo of the Virgin Mary on his forearm. Now and then their blood, still only turning brown, emitted a sparkle of ruby red in the sun. Every head had a hole in the pate — a Chetnik signature — with a thick trail of blood curling around the neck onto the chest.

Near another village, in a pit of dried mortar, Ivan saw corpses of ten young men, stomachs slashed. Their murderers had thrown them with open wounds into the wet mortar to be eaten by it. They turned into white sculptures of the betrayed and desperate will to live, their fists sticking up, groping for the bank, for roots of trees, for anything to lift them.

Ivan avoided people and stayed in haystacks — and when he couldn't find any haystacks, in ditches — even in late November, when a terrible winter gripped the continent with excessive ferocity as though God had tried to freeze out the destructive race for the sake of the rest of creation. He had tried fire, brimstone, and water before, and none had worked. And now, He tried ice — water with fire taken out of it — and Ivan, who shivered and plucked ice out of his beard, felt that this new cataclysm might work.

Gaunt, with bulging eyes, driven out of his mind by solitude, he shivered in a haystack, near Chazma, and daydreamingly recollected glimmers of his childhood: every Sunday after church when he was thirteen he would walk in a field, where a shepherdess waved him to sit by her and lean his cheek against her neck. She bared her breasts and let him squeeze them. With his tremulous hands upon the smooth venous warmth of her skin, he floated in the green clouds wavering in the playful winds. He caressed the shepherdess's breasts every Sunday, for a year — and that was all, but now it came back to him as the modicum of warmth in a universe of ice.

That night he was caught by Home Guard soldiers. They wrapped him in a rough woolen blanket as though he were a corpse and drove him to their barracks in Zagreb. They gave him hot tea with aspirin, which dissolved in his throat before he could swallow it, and there it spread its dusty bitterness of bleached charcoal, a mock Eucharist, which recalled the ten slain men metamorphosed into mortar sculptures.

That winter, pneumonia filled Ivan with fevers and nightmares, and he replied to no questions and no answers, until he saw the sun in the spring and recovered.

By that time, several Home Guard soldiers had recognized him. The Guards kept him in jail for three months, and after that, employed him in their bakery.

In 1945, as the Red Army advanced from the East and the partisans from the South and the North, many Home Guards deserted to join the partisans or to hide, but Ivan stayed. He had done it all, and none had worked for him.

A colonel pardoned his desertion and gave him a rifle to be a regular soldier once again, and Ivan could not decline. And so when thousands of partisans surrounded his garrison, and his regiment surrendered because of a promise of amnesty, Ivan became a captive of the army he had once served.

Under gunpoint, he climbed into a cargo train among many soldiers. The train went through Sisak, around Zagreb, and on to Slovenia, Maribor, toward Austria. A partisan told them that Croatian armies would be handed over to the British and French troops, who would treat them well according to the fancy international conventions on POWs.

But as the prisoners exited from the trains into a field, fire from a hundred machine guns strafed them down. Partisan officers on tractors ploughed the twitching corpses into the soil, disking it over and over again. Thousands and thousands of Home Guards perished there. When it was Ivan's turn to step out, the machine-gun fire quit — perhaps partisans had run low on ammunition — and Ivan's detachment was held at bayonet point. Partisans pushed bayonets into the captives' ribs, and said, "You want to go home? Fine, we'll show you your home, croaking Croat pigs." A partisan pumped a machine-gun round into the group of captives, as if to punctuate the speech, but nobody fell to the ground, because the captives were so squashed that those who were killed or bleeding to death remained standing in the crowd.

"The rules are simple," the main speaker went on, with a megaphone. "If you make it on foot to Osijek, you are free, if not, you are dead. You aren't going to get any breaks, food or water."

For two hundred miles — from Maribor, through Krizevci, Virovitica — they marched. Whoever among the captives leaned on a fence along the way was bayoneted and left in a ditch, his eyes spooned out or ears cut off as trophies.

The second day was scorchingly hot as though God had changed His mind and turned away from ice; He again contemplated burning the sons of men off the earth. Ivan stumbled, his feet blistery and bloody, eyeing the tilted gray wood fences along the road the way a drowning man a stroke away from a rock arising out of the sea stares at the rock. He gazed at spindle-wells in the village yards even more wistfully.

The partisans sang. Many disappeared in the villages they passed, to chase girls into the woods, wink at them, court them, and if that did not work, to rape them.

By the time the captors and the captives reached Vocin, one-half of the captives had perished. The old partisans left, and new ones joined. Ivan had seen some of the partisan faces before, in the burned-out village, except that they were Chetniks then.

At dusk, a partisan poked his bayonet into Ivan's kidneys, on the healed side. "Long time no see!" Tomo, his old comrade, laughed. "How in the hell did you get stuck here? I thought you were dead and gone. I bet you wish you were!"

Ivan did not say anything. Tomo had a gulp of Slivovitz; he passed the open bottle under Ivan's nostrils, asking whether he'd like a sip. This style of torment was the usual — a cheerful soldier tantalizing a POW of his choice — so that nobody paid any attention to Tomo's pushing, jostling, and nudging Ivan: not even Ivan did until Tomo slid a flask of water into Ivan's pocket. When clouds covered the moon, Ivan gulped all the water and tossed the flask away during a thunder.

The clouds grumbled, cleared their throats, but did not spit out a drop of rain. They gathered low, furrowed, like Stalin's eyebrows, trapping heat and moisture, making the air musty. In the morning Ivan sweated profusely. Salt from his forehead slid into his eyes and stung them as though they were open wounds, and that they were, with dust specks, gnats, and sand grating them almost as much as did the sight of his colleagues collapsing, partisans crushing their heads with the wood stocks of rifles, brains flowing out like borscht.

By noon of the new day his lips were cracked dry and swollen. The villages they passed seemed deserted, for if there were survivors they hid as though witnessing the horrendous procession would be too awful a burden to carry into peace — peace that was upon the land, blown from Russia, as a putrid stench, and from America and Britain, as the smell of a deodorant — and beyond peace, to the grave, and beyond, to hell.

As the partisans grew more and more drunk on plum brandy another thick night, some POWs managed to sneak out of this Trail of Crosses, though most were stabbed as soon as they jumped to the ditches. Ivan did not try. He trudged on, stumbling over stones. Ivan was sure he would have collapsed had it not been for Tomo's flask of water, but now Tomo was gone. The insides of Ivan's thighs bled from the constant friction and sweat, but that may not be right, for by now there was no sweat because he was so dehydrated. He could barely swallow what was in his throat, for it was not spittle but dust.

At night, he tried to urinate, stealthily taking out his penis. Nothing came except scorching pains, burning from his kidneys down his penis, into his fingers. He put his penis back and remembered how, as a young boy, six years old, he had loved to piss in public, even in the church yard, until his mother taught him how to be modest. He had just pulled out his winnie, proudly, when she said: "Put it right back. A cat will snatch it and eat it like a fish." After that, he pissed in bathrooms, terrified of cats. That memory made him smile—it amused him that his memories had regressed to early childhood—and his smile widened the cracks in his lips so that blood oozed down his stubbly chin, obliterating memory.

The captives made it to Osijek, where they were allowed a pot of beans. The partisans waited for a two-day storm—a tremendous outpouring—to end, and then pursued their captives for a hundred fifty miles more, to Popovacha, in the same cruel manner.

Past a burned-out and gutted steel mill, the decimated regiment of Home Guards stumbled through a field of craters that bombs had dug. Water filled the craters, out of which rough-skinned gray frogs leaped as beating hearts that had deserted the bodies of warring men and now roamed the doomed landscape. Ivan found the sudden leaps of so many hearts out of the gray earth unsettling. He could not see any of them, until they were in the air, so that it seemed to him that the earth was spitting up useless hearts and swallowing them back into the mud.

In Popovacha, having made the whole stretch, Ivan swooned and collapsed. After he recovered in a Zagreb hospital as much as was in the power of his damaged kidneys, he was drafted into the Yugoslav People's Army for a correctional service of two years, as a baker, for even this army loved bread.

Jorge Luis Borges, 1982 (Photograph by Larry Murphy).

JULIO ORTEGA

TRANSLATED FROM THE SPANISH BY MARK SCHAFER

The Art of Reading

I

Borges is notified that the son of a friend of his has died. He asks his assistant to compose a message of condolence for him to sign, but the girl cannot find the right words. Borges dictates two lines, but rejects them at once. They don't seem right, he says. I offer to write something less obvious: a Borgesian poem of condolence. True, Borges has never written such a poem, but it is also true that his poetry (like a dictionary) contains all the necessary elements. He likes the idea and, curious, asks me to press on. I write the first stanza: it is direct, clear; it mentions the moon, the father watching the moon, and the night that surrounds him. Later, the poem speaks of the dead son who lies under the trees on the hill, asleep. The lines are nine syllables long. I read and reread the poem and find it to be restrained and enumerative: the tragedy is not stated; the world says it better. But at the end the poem changes: I read it again, memorizing the play of words: mouth, mute, music . . . The mute music of the mouth, or even better: of this world we keep the music of the words.

It is no longer a Borgesian poem. I repeat it with my eyes closed before it disappears.

II

That morning in February of '82, as we were dining in his hotel in Austin, an urgent phone call tracked him from the reception desk to the restaurant. By the cashier, he took the phone, faltering a bit, from the hand of María Kodama. Borges stammered, nodding, but passed the phone to María, who listened dumbfounded: a woman from Texas was demanding that Borges meet her son and read his poems. There was no room for another appointment, but María agreed to a meeting in the airport just before their departure in two days.

III

I went with Borges and María to his old office on the second floor of Batts Hall. The window faced the center of the campus. Borges wished to recognize the places he had been twenty years ago, which in his case was an exercise in remembering. He sat down in the desk chair and tested its comfort, enjoying himself. He ran his right hand, a large and timid hand, over the wood, trying to remember its texture. "It is light," he said, and asked, "What color is it?" María answered sandy gold; I, bright sepia. It is a Platonic object, I said. "An archetype," Borges agreed. The office now belonged to a professor of Germanic literature and voluminous tomes of philology filled the shelves. I alerted Borges to this: the books are unquestionably German, I said. "It would be worse if they were irreparably German," he joked, and corrected himself right away, "I owe much to German," and he began to recite a poem by Goethe.

"Light" was a word he found at the time to be just right: almost everything good was light. Later, he handed me his cane: "See how light it is," he said. But lightness was not just the weight or ease of the object but how adequate its idea or name was. I concluded that lightness is that which words rescue from the indistinct and dramatic density of the world. We were waiting for the photographer from some newspaper and, seeing that the knot of his tie was crooked, I told him and straightened it. The tie was not something light; it was a convention. In the slim Borgesian dictionary, lightness designates the internal texture of things; names are the stuff won from the world. That is why the name in this dictionary of languages is the intelligence of its object.

IV

That nostalgia of the name itself, of the name as the transparent structure of the entire object, like a classical ear of wheat;

that differentiation of the lightest fruits of speech, like flowers alight with their lymphatic tincture;

that theory of the weight of things in the balance of language, where values don't come from economy or precision but from identification; they feed the dictionary of the poetry of things, from which springs the thread of memory, the net knotted by speech.

V

The motif of the dead son is absent from Borges' poetry. Perhaps he thought that sons belong to life, not to death, and that a son — as in his own case — is a son forever. As a boy, Borges experienced the extraordinary friendship of his father, who was a sort of theoretical anarchist — or at least Borges preferred to remember him as such. His father's death left him disconcerted, alone in the street of men where the *compadritos*, the fellows of the poor neighborhood, were already characters from a heroic epic of his first stories. That small subworld, patriarchal and oral, was soon replaced by the riddles of time, the arbitrariness of love, the rewritten books. His mother watched over the house and his life almost forever. Soon blindness freed him from the world and honed his language.

On the other hand, Borges was certainly disturbed by the idea of the Golem, whose father, rather than begetting the Golem (copulation, like mirrors, is repugnant because it multiplies men, Borges wrote), thinks it up in an alchemical laboratory, on the hidden page, in Jewish metaphysics. This creature is less than a son and more than a monster: made without speech, it contradicts the natural order of language and is thus a blasphemous act against law.

Later, Borges dreamed that he was his own son or, rather, the father of himself. Finally, old and repetitive, he met in his dream the young Borges. It seems he was never blind in his dreams, he could see everything again. And he saw himself young again; and the young man saw himself elderly and vaguely unreal. The young man wished to be Borges and Borges wished to be the young man so as to cease being himself. In that instant, on that page, they speak on a bench in a wintry park and know that time is a miracle.

VI

The first thing Whitman did that summer morning in Texas was to kill his mother. He left at once, crazed and armed, and no one suspected a thing when he climbed the thirty floors of the tower at the University of Texas at Austin to the small clock room at the top. Perched there, he overlooked the width and breadth of the campus and a good part of Guadalupe Avenue. He started firing.

Borges, I've been told, asked to be taken to the tower and took the elevator up to the highest floor. He wanted to feel the time of the assassin heading to his lair. The clock room had been shut by university authorities to prevent any new local cult, but the tower clock continued musically ringing out the time of day. The pealing of the bells, just like the music, was a recording played through loudspeakers. Before going down, Borges touched the doors and walls of the room with both hands and said: "To think his name was Whitman."

VII

Luis Loayza, in Geneva, took me to visit Calvino High School where Borges had studied during the first years of the First World War. Borges had said that in Geneva no two corners look alike, and that hyperbole was perhaps based on the walk (usually a veritable journey) to the school which stands at an intersection of hills, and might give the impression of one of those baroque streets from German silent movies.

When I told him of taking this walk, Borges came alive and started giving an inventory of Geneva, one of his favorite cities, where he chose to die. He was living in memory, which was not the past but rather the space of a dilated present, he was living in the simultaneous presence of his whole life. I did not, however, tell him that on another visit, I found the Genevan plaza of bordellos where his father brought him one night to initiate him into adult life. His father paid for the services of a prostitute and waited outside the doors. The timid young man was initiated instead into the anguish of sexuality. He lived his entire life in love and there was always a woman close to him. But near the end of his life he came to a stoical conclusion—I haven't been happy, he said.

VIII

Concerning the campus lampposts: These are the only moons Lugones couldn't grasp.

Concerning *One Hundred Years of Solitude:* They tell me it is a novel one hundred years long.

Concerning Professor Merlin, who forgot the keys to an office: How strange, a Merlin who needs a key.

The worst metaphor in Argentine poetry?: "Vase with feathers" was what one poet called a canary.

Favorite Buenos Aires street name: Calle de los Hermanos Jiménez.

Concerning Whitman: He believed that being happy was his obligation as an American.

The best poet?: Emily Dickinson.

Concerning the success of the Latin American novel: It is incomprehensible, for we have nothing comparable to the Russian novel.

Concerning María Kodama: Her stories of the fantastic are better than mine.

Concerning Joyce: He was a magnificent poet, because of his musicality.

Concerning love: Yes.

Concerning Borges and I: There are too many Borgeses. Perhaps you are speaking with a third or fourth Borges.

IX

The father of *Don Quixote* is not Cervantes, but Pierre Menard, the somewhat extravagant reader who makes his reading into a work of art. The art of reading would thus be that of ascribed paternity: I read this page, I am its maker. Reading, then, doesn't multiply men but books. There are more books than men, more words than objects, more libraries than readers; that is, the world is badly made. It is made in inverse relation to the logic of developments. It forms a redundant figure, an ellipsis in which the I and the you end up finding each in the other.

Pierre Menard is a French "Symbolist," himself a symbol of reading as trans-transcription: to recopy *Don Quixote* is to re-edit it, to discern it, to unread it at random. In that way, *Don Quixote* is inexhaustible No one has ever read *Don Quixote;* we have read the part of our inscription, that perfect page that bears our name. We are the children of our reading.

Don Quixote, in short, is a book multiplied by all its readers, a Babelic library where mere Spanish is transformed into the tongue of tongues, the spring at which drink the survivors of the desert of the blank page. That is why *Don Quixote* can only be a guide to *Don Quixote,* an abridged edition for children at the quixotic age.

Mother of truth was what Cervantes called history, using a commonplace phrase. Mother of truth was what Menard called it, implying the tragic force of history that reveals us. It is the same text. The mothers are not the same because the sons, the line of La Mancha, are not the same: we are history, its true handwriting.

To Cervantes, his Quixote was "a gaunt, parched, fanciful son, full of a variety of thoughts never imagined by anyone else." Gaunt, full, unique.

"To be Alonso Quixano and not dare to be Don Quixote," wrote Borges in 1979.

X

In "Pierre Menard, Author of *Don Quixote*" one reads that a "philological fragment of Novalis — the one bearing the number 2005 in the Dresden edition — that sketches out the theme of the *total* identification with a specific author" is one of the texts that inspired his undertaking. I bumped into it in Ernesto Volkening's translation of the "Pollen" series published by *Eco* (Bogotá, No. 147, July 1972):

"I show I understand a writer only when I know how to act according to his own understanding, when, without reducing his individuality, I might know how to translate and change him around in a multiplicity of ways."

Novalis literally proposes translation as an activity that substitutes the reader for the author: becoming the author is the only way of understanding him, and that is demonstrated in the free rewriting of the work of the other, now one's own.

I had another version, which my friend Wolfgang A. Luchting did for me, not without warning me that German is untranslatable into Spanish:

"I show that I have understood an author only if I am capable of acting in his spirit; if I can translate him and transform him in many ways without diminishing his individuality."

Here, Novalis is, I believe, closer to Borges. In Volkening's text, the conditional and the future (when I know), the symmetry (understand, understanding) and the single phrase belabor the meaning (when I know, I might know.) In my friend's, however, the second phrase illustrates and amplifies the first.

To act in someone's spirit without diminishing his individuality means: without losing myself in those translations of boundless variations. Translation, evidently, is not just reading. It is reformulation, remaking the text, pursuing it from where its author left it to our (other, own) discourse.

Borges prefers to call this phenomenon of intra-writing *"total* identification with an author," but it's clear that he is stretching the meaning, inasmuch as the individualities don't mingle. The identification is complete but textual.

Menard, in this poetics of the felicitous collaboration with the literary work, rewrites *Don Quixote* without copying it but literally appropriating its words to actualize its meaning. The total reading would thus be the most textual: the de-explication of texts. Reading capable of the greatest faithfulness, that of being other and the same in the other yet same act of reading another page.

XI

Mario Usabiaga passed through Austin shortly after Borges' visit. He had been living in Mexico since he was released from the Argentine military prison where he was held for several years. His life was saved thanks to international protest, and also by a crude fluke of the killing. Torture marked him profoundly: he had glimpsed a horror that few men have managed to speak of. Mario's face was etched with anguish and he spoke with a calm, painful intensity. After the torture sessions, the jailer decided who would die that night. The prisoners knew it, and waited in silence, unreal. They would fall asleep in the exhaustion of waiting. Suddenly the footfalls, the trembling doors, the light in one of the cells. And voices and shouting. Twice they opened the doors to his cell and took away his two cellmates. They had anticipated this: the three of them had memorized messages, papers, goodbyes. That solidarity of death made them less mortal. "Tomorrow we will come for you," they told him each of those nights. Finally he was set free, but he was desolated by the horror and fear. He would remember all the days and nights of his imprisonment one by one and in his dreams he was still in prison: he would wake up as if he had glimpsed the exit. As a semiologist, he was obsessed with the discourses of violence, by its technology. What type of sin was torture if the torturer is Catholic? What penance would the Church assign him in the confession? Less systematic, no less atrocious, would be the inability of justice to do justice. Did it all begin with the old dichotomy of civilization and barbarism? Based on what ancient negations of the other could this killing have begun?

There weren't answers to so many questions. And his life was running out as he tried to understand it. He died soon after. He left me a few essays he had translated of Umberto Eco and the letter in which Eco asked the Argentine military to guarantee the life of the young, imprisoned professor.

He also left me an unpublished article on Borges which he signed as Mario García. It was in reality a secret letter to Borges in which he complained of the disagreeable nationalistic praise certain writers (of substance, as Bustos Domecq would say) dedicated to him on the occasion of his having lost, once again, the Nobel prize for literature. That utilitarian nationalism ("thanks to the recognition of Borges, the Europeans know that the Argentines are not the bunch of savages we are made out to be by the international campaign") legitimated the dictatorship, denounced Mario García, and reduced Borges to a name manipulated by the military.

This letter protested to Borges on behalf of Borges, and ended up as another chapter in the periodic dialogue between "Borges and I."

But the article ended with something unusual: a poem written in slang by an imprisoned *compadrito*. While in prison, Mario translated it into another poem in common Spanish, parallel yet understandable. The *compadrito* had written a refutation of Borges: he reproached him for talking of his fellows without knowing them, and in the only verbal maneuver that Borges could not have made his own, he wrote the poem in pure slang, in a secret argot that rejected literature to preserve the language of his survival.

"What we have [my friend wrote] is a poem written about twenty years ago [around 1959] in a prison of Córdoba, Argentina, by someone in prison for murder. One of his friends who would visit him in the pen collected these verses by memory, which never had any propagation other than an occasional wine-soaked delivery, very infrequent, by this friend late at night in some bar. The language of the poem, similar to that of the underworld of Buenos Aires in the early part of this century, remains current today in the jails and on those vague borders between bohemians and marginal people."

As we see here, Mario rewrites both the slang (he poses as a *compadrito*) and Borges' style (through his use of metaphor and adjectives).

The poem is entitled "Pa' Borges" [For Borges]:

Te bato de butaca la ganzúa
de mirarte chamuyar pulentería,
de chorros, mecheras, taquería
y el buzonear de giles y de púas.

Te furqueo sobrador chapando el vuelo
pa' escrachar de tu tálamo de rosas.
Yo en mi fule lunfardear engomo un cielo
bien debute del batir de tantas cosas.

Tu verso rebuscado no es la yeca
donde rula la mersa del estaño.
Vos amás al salame sin zabeca
que no manya el rebusque de los caños.

Por: el gomía de la reja

It is, we shall add, a total rewriting of Borges starting with its use of words: the words tell of reality and of our place in it. This argument for language, for the street and its speech, doesn't ignore the work of Borges; to the contrary, it wishes to, so to speak, deborgesize Borges.

Mario Usabiaga (Mario García, on translating his transcription) offers this "more universal" version:

> I want to tell you how strange it is
> to hear you speak of serious things:
> of thieves, pickpockets, the hateful cops,
> and all that goes on between the dumb and the quick.
>
> I find you vain, recording jumbled particulars
> to concoct false tales from your bed of roses.
> I, in my poor slang, embrace a sky
> made beautiful by the voice of so many things.
>
> Your obscure verses are not the street
> where the night and the real suburbs walk.
> You love the hollow men who don't understand
> the laws of rogues and the wit
> by which so many wretches survive.
>
> By: The friend behind bars

It is certainly a very loose rendering but at the same time a fair one. The tension and edge of the original is lost but it takes on conversation and fable. Rewriting a rewrite of Borges: this manner of reading is already included in the Borgesian hypothesis that we are all a single text, variable, fluid, and perpetual.

Mario understood with lucidity that the poem he held in his hands (it is known that the prisoners stay sane, at times, thanks to a few verses which they cling to as to the edge of language) possessed its own strength far beyond the reading of irony: that power had to do with politics, with what he called "the use of Borges." Not knowing what else to do with the poem, he included it in a note of protest against the nationalism of the hypocritical bourgeoisie. But his note was exceeded by the poem at the end. For if there were many Borgeses, it was because there were many readers. What the poem demonstrates is that if the bourgeoisie was attempting to possess Borges, the people, in order to claim him, began by rejecting him. This reading demanded his rewriting and was, therefore, more radical.

Carlos Fuentes is right: when someone tells us his life, he is entrusting us with a tale that burns our hands, and all we can do is immediately pass it on.

XII

And what if Mario was in fact the author of that poem written in slang? I would prefer that not to be the case, but literature is infinite, in contrast to reality.

The story of that poor prisoner who composes the poem in code, of the friend who visits him in jail and memorizes the text and later repeats it to friends over wine, and, much later, of someone who copies and translates it is — to say the least — the universal history of literature.

It is believable that Mario might have written the poem during his prison years and translated it as an intellectual game to pass the time with his companions. Mario was a semiotician and was interested in the image of Borges then being circulated with antagonistic values; he was a politician and saw in the improper use of that image a cultural loss which he proposed to correct; and he was, above all, a translator (I've lost Umberto Eco's letter but I believe Mario was his student in medieval religious rhetoric in his seminar in Milan). It wouldn't surprise me at all if what he calls the translation is the original which he actually retranslated into slang. I suspect that few poets write in slang but I can believe that someone might rewrite a text in that demotic code. Author, translator, critic: Mario multiplied himself to make the voices that speak behind the texts of Borges more genuine. He made Borges father of his creature so that this *compadrito,* upon faithfully contradicting him would release him into unconstrained speech, into the heart of history.

From prison, Mario proposed the freedom of Borges.

XIII

In that slightly sarcastic tone of voice by which Borges subverted his own comments, he had said to me: this world is excessively written. But there are some pages, a few, that have the texture of time. In the printed jungle, time turns on these pages, on itself, and watches us.

Alfonso Reyes, I said, affirms that "the other *Quixote* must still be written: the *History of the Ingenious Hidalgo Who from So Much Reading Devised Writing.*"

This other *Quixote*, he laughed, devoured books which are, as Gracián says, "grass of the soul."

Someone asserts, I asserted, that reading is an "escape from time" and that the reader must be suspected of "the secret desire of removing himself from the implacable succession of time that leads to death."

That would be the equivalent then, he said, to dreaming. And I don't know anyone who reads while asleep; although one can't put anything past Lugones. I now remember that I myself have said, as a young man, that one nods through *Ulysses*.

If life is a dream, who reads in the book of life? Someone who dreams he is awake? I asked.

I'm going to tell you a sentence that came to me as I woke, not long ago: Imagine an executioner who was able to create a phrase out of strange words which, when uttered, would produce the immediate death of the condemned person.

I recorded the sentence and said, with excessive enthusiasm: There would be a different and unique phrase for each condemned person and his death.

We are all condemned, he smiled, and one word would be enough.

Wallace Stevens, I continued, asked the wind what syllable it was looking for in the distance of the dream.

"Vocalissimus. Say it." The wind is the word of the dream that doesn't speak, he commented.

After a long pause, he added: Attempt, nevertheless, to tell us something. Stammer. Vocalize, try the possible vowels. The wind will say one thing instead of another, right?

You, as a young man, said that writing is doing one thing instead of another, I said, unable to follow him.

I don't remember, he replied. You see, all that awaits us is stuttering, forgetfulness.

I remained silent.

Reading is risky, isn't that true? There is a page I'm still composing in my head; I no longer write and scarcely dictate. Would you like to hear it?

I opened my notebook to a blank page and prepared to copy it. Dictate it to me, I told him. Improve it, he said, and dictated:

To choose a book in the profusion of books. I stop at any one whatsoever and read a page I seem to remember. The last word continues with the first: when I reread the first word, time has already passed. I understand that this page multiplies a single phrase, that I continue as if I had recovered the time when I began. The whole book is made of that solitary phrase: its unity is the same as its infinity. So nothing is perverted by memory. But soon the phrase that turns back on itself becomes a single word that proliferates on the page. The leaves of the book try to say the word in a rush. Time is bisyllabic and it affirms and denies. The word that fulfills the book, in the end, surpasses it. Now I am reading a single letter. I repeat it, resisting the expanding vertigo. Now its form abandons the book, opening my eyes. There is no one in the circle of that astonishment.

I reread what I'd written and made, more or less, the following comments: If the circle of ink of a letter takes up the page and expands to where it exceeds the page, swallowing the reader, there would be no way to finish the fable. There would be nowhere to put a final period.

That's the point, he agreed, amused. The end must be thrown out. Now I will tell you the beginning. This fable, as you call it, was dictated to me by a dream. When I woke I knew I would record it later and I spoke, outside the dream: "Father, why have you forsaken me?" To abruptly recite a famous quote, it doesn't make sense, does it?

Perhaps that was the phrase you were reading on the page in the dream, I exclaimed, not without renewed enthusiasm. I mean, the phrase that opened until it was a word, a letter, the void.

We are rushing headlong into allegory, he laughed, because we lack the words.

In the dream, you were the son, I continued, unperturbable; when you woke, you were then the father.

In that case, I would be an orphan, he said. One of those little heroes of Kipling who are adopted by the English language.

The father has died, I added, not the son. The dream speaks with inverted imagery. With anachronistic attributions, remember? It is the art of reading . . .

I've dreamt it, he reminded me, but you've written it down.

I'm not very sure of that, I joked. I don't have any other memorable quotation.

We're left with the wind, he remembered ironically. It passes right by and has no name.

It asks for the father, I responded, allegorically. It rereads the world, that Chinese encyclopedia.

In dreams, he sighed, the father is alive and he walks hand in hand with the son . . .

I was trying to call forward a quotation when a robust Texan lady and her adolescent son, weighed down with lyric and epic poetry, rushed toward our table with a triumphal cry.

JOHN BARTH

Borges & I: a mini-memoir

We learn from our students, perhaps in order to teach our teachers. It was two students of mine, their names now lost to me, on two different university campuses, who serendipitously introduced me to the work of Latino writers profoundly consequential to the way I myself think about the art of fiction and the way or ways that I have attempted to practice that art. The second of those writers happens to have been the late great Argentine Jorge Luis Borges; I was pleased recently to drive up from Johns Hopkins to the Pennsylvania State University to join in honoring him once again,* as I have numerous times gratefully paid homage to him else-where.

My story begins with a leisurely digression:

In 1953, when I *first* came up from Johns Hopkins to Penn State — to begin my professional academic career in the English Composition Department of what was then still the Pennsylvania State College — I had not yet found my voice as a writer of fiction. The shortest way to put it is that the muses would not sing for me until I found some way to book Scheherazade, James Joyce, and William Faulkner on the same tidewater Maryland showboat, with myself at both the helm and the steam calliope. To put it another way, I needed to discover, or to be discovered by, Postmodernism — but I had not yet grasped that truth (much less that aesthetic concept, not to mention its label) when I arrived in State College, PA, with my young and ever-increasing family and confronted the gloomy prospect of perishing academically for want of publishing, and the gloomier yet of putting aside what I had come to feel deeply was my true calling, however inadequately I was responding to the call.

But then, mirabile dictu, it came to pass that one of my Penn State students — I wish I could recall which one, for I owe him or her much thanks for a great unintended service — indirectly showed me the way, by introducing me to a turn-of-the-century Brazilian writer named Joaquim

At the conference "Borges Revisited," held in University Park, Pennsylvania, April 12 and 13, 1991. This memoir is adapted from my address to that conference.

Machado de Assis, several of whose novels were just then appearing in English translation from the Noonday Press. I checked Machado out of the Pattee Library—first his *Braz Cubas* (retitled *Epitaph of a Small Winner* in its English translation) and then *Dom Casmurro* and *Quinças Borba* (retitled *Philosopher or Dog?* in its English version)—and those novels supplied me with model resolutions of a problem whose terms I could not have articulated before it was well behind me. Never mind the particulars; never mind as well that various happenings in my lived life, as well as happenstances in my reading, turned me around corners necessary for writing my first published novel *(The Floating Opera)* and all the books since; this is not about those, though it may seem for a while yet to be. Paul Cézanne is said to have said, vis-à-vis painting, that "the road to nature leads through the Louvre, and the road to the Louvre leads through nature." Similarly, for a writer of fiction the road to "life" may well lead through the library, and the road to the library—to the shelf with one's own books on it—will no doubt lead through life. Life teaches the storyteller his themes and subject matter; literature teaches him how to get a handle on them: what has been done already, what might be redone differently, what's a *story* anyway, and what is to be found in the existing inventory of situations, attitudes, characters, tonalities, forms, and effects accumulated over 4,000 years of written literature. If that writer happens also to be a teacher, his students and colleagues may occasionally point him toward something important that he was ignorant of in the vast corpus of the already said, just when he was ripe for the revelation. My thanks to the forgotten Penn Stater who, nearly forty years ago and unwittingly to both of us, did me this favor. Joaquim Machado de Assis (1839–1908) happens *not* to be a writer of ongoing importance to me; in a recent conversation about him on the BBC, I realized (in midst of praising him as a proto-Postmodernist) that I haven't reread him since the Penn State 1950s and scarcely remember now what his novels are "about." But once upon a time he showed me how to become the novelist I was trying to be, and for better or worse I up and became that novelist.

Twenty years subsequently, in conversation in East Lansing, Michigan, with Señor Jorge Luis Borges—who by that time had become as important to my thinking about the art of fiction as Machado de Assis had briefly been—I asked the eminent Argentine what he thought of his eminent Brazilian predecessor. I am sorry to have to report that although I remember quite a number of things from my three personal path-crossings with Borges, I cannot remember his response to that question. I happened at the time to have recently sat in on the Ph.D. dissertation defense at Johns Hopkins of an Argentinian young woman whose thesis topic was the fiction of Borges's Buenos Aires crony and sometime collaborator Adolfo Bioy-Casares; I had interrogated the candidate about Machado de Assis as a feasible precursor of "el Boom"—the explosion of Latino fictive talent in recent decades—and I had discovered that although her background knowledge of that phenomenon was extensive, she had scarcely heard of my man Machado. I believe, but cannot swear to it, that Borges and I shook our heads together in East Lansing over the prevailing indifference to Portuguese-Latino writers among Spanish-Latino writers and their readers.

Borges himself, needless to report, was quite familiar with the writings of Joaquim Machado de Assis and with the salutary influence on Machado of Lawrence Sterne's *Tristram Shandy*, which in my earlier Penn State innocence I had not yet encountered either. The consequence for me, I remarked to Borges, had been Borgesian: When I'd gotten around to reading *Tristram Shandy*, I'd been delighted by the extent to which the eighteenth-century Englishman had been influenced by the late-nineteenth-century Brazilian. As Borges observes in his essay on Franz Kafka, great writers create their own precursors.

Among those of us less than great but never less than serious about the art of literature, it is a matter not so much either of creating our precursors on the one hand or, once we've found and established our characteristic voice, of being unduly precursed by them on the other, as it is of finding in them some validation of this or that aspect of what we take ourselves to be up to, musewise. That is how it was with Borges and I (regardless of grammar, I want always to say "Borges and I": *Borges y yo*, the title of one of his loveliest meditations) at another consequential turn in my professional road, when another student, at another university, serendipitously introduced me to the *ficciones* of Jorge Luis Borges, just when, without knowing it, I most needed them.

Borges y yo, Borges and I—him the precursor, me the precursed (in this case, preblessed): Herewith the sum and substance of our relation, and selected trivia of our personal encounters. Needless to say, the relation is absolutely a one-way street: Nobody is likely to read Borges differently for having read Barth, the way I read *Tristram Shandy* differently for having read Machado's *Epitaph of a Small Winner*. Furthermore, the Borges street—*Calle Borges*—is only one street among others in my personal city of words. But it turns a meaningful corner, and a quarter century after first discovering it, I'm still working out its ramifications in my own practice of fiction.

In 1965 I left Penn State after twelve agreeable and productive years: three children nurtured, three novels published and a fourth nearly completed, much innocence lost but an invincible remnant preserved, the warmest academic and personal friendships of my life before or since, and the commonplace tribulations and delights of living through one's twenties into one's mid-thirties—ups and downs echoed and amplified in this case by our culture's moving from what we think of as the American 1950s into the tempestuous, counterculturalist 1960s. I moved to the former University of Buffalo, which had just joined the New York state university system and was enjoying a virtual carte blanche from Governor Nelson Rockefeller; the governor wanted a major university center at each end of the Thomas E. Dewey Thruway as well as one in the middle, at Albany. Eighty percent of my bustling and distinguished new department had been recruited within the previous two years, all as additions to the existing faculty. It was the bloody Fat Sixties; almost anything went. I began my new professorship with a free semester to finish up the novel *Giles Goat-Boy*, begun at Penn State and extended in Spain, and after so many bucolic years in rural Pennsylvania I relished the pleasures of living again in a sizeable city. It must be acknowledged that Buffalo is not Paris or Berlin or Madrid or New York; but just then, at least, there was a remarkable amount of new art going on in town, and the ambitious expansion of the university, coincident with the flowering of the counterculture, effervesced the whole scene. Even its marginality, geographical and otherwise, seemed positive: "art on the edge" at the edge of our troubled republic; John F. Kennedy's "New Frontier" on the old Niagara Frontier of the War of 1812; a sometimes volatile mix of avant-garde aesthetics, protest politics, and hippie culture, with Niagara Falls thundering and crumbling in the background and great Canada just across the river.

I myself was and remain, politically, just another more or less passive, off-the-shelf liberal, but I inhaled that radical air deeply except when the campus was being teargassed. I spent time in the contemporary wing of the Albright-Knox Art Gallery, catching up on what had been happening since Abstract Expressionism. I was befriended by iconoclasts like Leslie Fiedler and front-edgers like the composer-conductor Lukas Foss, who was then directing the Buffalo Philharmonic and encouraging all sorts of far-out new music both downtown and on the campus. I heard my new colleagues lecturing on the likes of Marshal McLuhan and Claude Levi-Strauss, Lacan and Derrida. And—thanks again to some savvy student in my graduate-level fiction-writing seminar—in 1966, as *Giles* was going through the press and I was waiting to see what my muse would do for an encore, I "discovered" the fiction of Jorge Luis Borges.

The experience of being stopped cold in one's tracks is not unusual among younger artists. Indeed, I have written somewhere or other that I take it to be the responsibility of alert apprentice artists—alert apprentice *anythings*—to be swept off their feet with some frequency in the face of passionate virtuosity: great power under great control, as encountered in their predecessors both distant and immediate. So *I* had been upon first discovering James Joyce and Franz Kafka, for example, back in undergraduate days. It is another matter when one is half through one's thirties and for better or worse has pretty much become who one is. But upon first encountering such astonishing stories as "The Secret Miracle," "The Zahir," "Pierre Menard," "Funes the Memorious," "Tlön, Uqbar, Orbis Tertius," and the rest, I felt again that urgent, disquieting imperative from apprentice days: that everything must halt in my shop until I came to terms with this extraordinary artist.

Whatever their aesthetic merits, the record of my efforts in the way of this assimilation comprises two chief items: an essay called "The Literature of Exhaustion," written in 1966 and first published the following year, and a short-story series called *Lost in the Funhouse*, written over the same period and published in 1968. The essay (with its much-misunderstood title) was my attempt to articulate, with Sr. Borges's assistance, what I saw going on round about me and felt in my aesthetic bones in the American High Sixties. With the clarity of hindsight I see it to have been groping toward a definition of the spirit of postmodernism, as I understand that slippery term: an aesthetic for the making of new and valid work that is yet responsible to the exhaustive, even apocalyptic vastness of what has been done before. The *Funhouse* stories, I readily acknowledge, have not the delicacy and depth of their inspirer: the short story has never been my long suit, and my muse's agenda is not coterminous with Borges's. But his example taught me, among other things, not merely what art critics call "significant form," but what I call the principle of metaphoric means: the investiture of every possible aspect of the fiction (let's say) with emblematic significance, until not just the conceit, the images, the mise-en-scène, the narrative choreography and point of view and all that, but even the phenomenon of the text itself, the fact of the artifact, becomes a sign of its sense. That is very high-tech taletelling; the wonderful thing is that Borges can bring it off with such apparent ease and unassuming grace, his consummate virtuosity kept *up* his sleeve rather than worn on it; so much so that only after the initial charm of his best stories has led us to ponder and reread them (their brevity makes light work of rereading) — only then are we likely to appreciate just how profoundly their imagination is wedded to their rendition. (Italo Calvino told me, years later, that his collection of stories called *T-Zero* was a similar response to the impact of Borges on his imagination.)

I was, in a word, wowed — and delighted to learn that my new literary hero was scheduled to be the 1967 Charles Eliot Norton Lecturer at Harvard. Armed with my department's Nelson Rockefeller budget for distinguished visitors, I telephoned Borges in Cambridge the day after his arrival there, introduced myself, and eagerly invited him to come speak at the State University of New York at Buffalo. At that time, I believe, despite the Norton lectureship, he didn't yet appreciate the size of his reputation in the literature departments of North America and the number of such invitations that were about to shower upon him. Before we had even got to the matter of honorarium, Borges said at once that he would be delighted to come: His bride had never seen New York.

Through the literary grapevine I had heard already that Sr. Borges — then 68 years old and all but sightless, and theretofore customarily escorted on his travels by his mother — had indeed married, for the first time, just a couple of days before leaving Buenos Aires for Harvard, and that among the efficient causes of this late large step was precisely that the quite elder Señora Borges felt herself not up to a New England winter and all the associated junketing. The marriage, alas, turned out to last not much longer than the Norton lectureship, but at the time I called it was brand new, and Borges was touchingly fond of invoking the epithet: *mi esposa* this, *mi esposa* that; *mi esposa* has never seen New York. . . .

I gently explained that we were not exactly New York City; that we were, in point of fact, Buffalo. Quite all right, the great man came back graciously: "My wife has never seen snow, either." He then asked me what I would like him to lecture on, and offered his belief that he could lecture on any great American writer of our classical period, if I preferred him to lecture on an American writer. What impressed and depressed me in this was my recognition not only that *I* couldn't do that, even in American on Americans, but that Borges could as easily do it in English on the English (*Beowulf* was a professional passion of his), in French on the French, German German, god knows how many more. Anything at all, I assured him, would be just fine.

They arrived in Buffalo — the courtly, amiable, somewhat fragile-appearing multilingual groom and his vigorous, fiftyish, previously widowed, non-English-speaking bride — and when we had settled down to chatting, I pressed Borges a bit on that "any great American writer" business. He acknowledged that while he was indeed fond of Poe and Whitman and Hawthorne and company, he had all but ceased to lecture on individual writers of whatever nationality because of the difficulty of reviewing their works and checking references since his eyesight had failed; he preferred to address some more general topic — Metaphor, say, or the Literature of the Fantastic (his Buffalo subject) and then from his remarkable memory summon whatever examples suited his theme.

This he did, that evening, to an overflow audience of Buffalonians. I had asked advice from friends at Harvard and elsewhere about the choreography of the presentation, as it was my first go at introducing an all-but-sightless Latino genius (that "all but" was important to Borges; he liked to insist on the point himself, remarking that to be totally blind would put him in the company of Homer and John Milton, for which he felt unready). Excellent instructions came back to me from Cambridge: There should be both a stand-up microphone and a table mike; I should guide the guest of honor onstage and then, as we both stood, give him an introduction like a presidential nomination speech, a catalogue of all the compliments I saw fit to lay on. I was even told that if I glanced overshoulder while delivering this homage, I might see the great writer nod a slight acknowledgment of each tribute, as if ticking off the list. Then I should seat him in his chair at the table mike, whence he would lecture from memory.

All this came to pass, with but one small glitch. It was no chore at all for me to write the introduction, fulsome but sincere (which I was assured was traditional Latino literary courtesy, though I cannot vouch for that bit of cultural anthropology); I truly believed the man to be a living literary treasure, as I currently believe him to be, alas, a dead one: among the all-time great masters of his art. I said this, and more, and sneaked a peek overshoulder as I did so, and, sure enough, saw him register each superlative with a courteous little nod. I then turned to lead him to his chair, and there came the glitch, for my otherwise detailed instructions had not advised me of the ritual *abrazo* at this juncture, which I ought to have known about but did not. Borges moved his arms. In my own blindness I supposed he wanted to shake hands; I thrust forth mine, gringo-style, which Borges couldn't see, and there ensued a few marvelous moments-worth of slapstick crosscultural dumbshow until we got things sorted out. Then he sat, looked up as if at the ceiling of the auditorium or the abode of the muses, and transfixed us for 55 minutes.

I say *transfixed* because his notelessness, his sweetly accented English, his dignified but unintimidating mien, and his unwavering sightless gaze above our heads did indeed have some of the effect of a benign Homer or Milton live. But with the *what* he said, apart from the how of its saying, I confess to being disappointed. For the first several minutes, Borges declared in effect that in the literature of the fantastic there may be found a variety of patterns. For example, he then said, there is a story by Henry James called "The Jolly Corner," which goes like this. . . . He summarized it in circumstantial detail, at the end asserting, "There is one pattern." Next he invited us to consider the old Norse saga about So-and-So, who valiantly fared forth to do such-and-such, et cetera, for quite a few minutes: "Another pattern." And on he went for three-quarters of an hour from his prodigious memory of his prodigious reading: this tale from the *Thousand and One Nights,* this from here, that from there, each summarized in considerable particular and identified as exemplary of yet another pattern, without a clue to what those patterns were or how they related. Through my transfixion I began to fidget, waiting for him to floor us with some brilliant synthesis at the close. But at the hour's end, what he declared in effect was, "and so you see, there are many patterns of fantastic literature" — adding, dutifully, "yet none of them is as fantastic as what we call Reality."

Oh well. In the subsequent Q & A, on the other hand, he was quite wonderful (and indeed, in his later American tours he spent less time on his "prepared" lectures and more on his exchanges with the audience). On science fiction, for example: He did not much care for it, he allowed, and to make his point he brilliantly contrasted H. G. Wells's "The Invisible Man" with Plato's myth of the Ring of Gyges. To imagine a ring that makes its wearer invisible, said Borges, requires one simple impossibility from which all else plausibly follows; but to imagine a *chemical* that makes a man invisible requires continual buttressing with plausibilities. The ring is easier to swallow, as it were, than the chemical. *Olé:* a splendid quarter-hour of such graceful obiter dicta.

By the time of our second path-crossing, eight years later, I had returned to Johns Hopkins, the Peronistas had returned to power in Argentina, and Borges, despite his fame, had acknowledged to a *New York Times* interviewer some misgivings about his position under the regime he had outspokenly opposed. We immediately telephoned Buenos Aires to offer him permanent political asylum in Baltimore, sweetening the pot with Johns Hopkins's excellent geriatric-medical facilities for his now quite ancient but still-living mother (the short story of his marriage had long since reached its quiet denouement). Borges politely declined our invitation. His political apprehensions fortunately proved groundless; unfortunately, they led him more or less to accept the junta that displaced the Peronistas and to accept as well an award from General Pinochet himself in Chile, and that got him into regrettable hot water with fellow writers of the Latino "boom," quite a number of whom were political expatriates. Anon the ancient mother died. Friends feared for the physical and emotional welfare of her aging son in his bereavement — Borges was in his mid-70s then. But after registering that bereavement in a delicate elegy or two, in 1975 he accepted Anthony Kerrigan's invitation to a residency at Michigan State, where along with numerous others I went to rewelcome him to the USA and again to pay him public homage.

For me it was a memorable reencounter, in several ways. Borges himself appeared in excellent fettle, as if drawing new breath from what his friends feared might devastate him. Even his eyesight was said to have very slightly improved. In my essay "The Literature of Exhaustion," I had made the remarkably fatuous assertion that for my "postmodern" literary generation the question was how to succeed "not Joyce and Kafka, but those who *succeeded* Joyce and Kafka and are now in the evenings of their own careers." I was referring, grandly, to Nabokov, Beckett, and Borges. Now in East Lansing, as if by way of exquisite retribution for that presumptuous remark, the several days of public homaging built to the main event, Borges's own presentation — not in the evening of anything, but in the bright Michigan afternoon — whereas the act with the impossible job of succeeding him that evening and wrapping up the proceedings was Yours Truly. After Borges . . . *yo*.

The rationale for this painful piece of programming was the guest of honor's age. I took what comfort I could in the reflection that if he was too old and frail to do his number in the evening, at least he wouldn't be there to audit mine. For an engaging hour that afternoon he chatted easily with his audience about his poetry and fiction and essays and about literature in general, making along the way some surprising responses to predictably routine questions. E.g., to the unexciting query, "What do you regard as the writer's chief responsibility?" he did *not* reply, "The artful contamination of reality with irreality" or "The investiture of every aspect of the fiction with emblematic significance, including even the fact of the artifact." What he said, unhesitatingly, was "The creation of character." Imagine: the creation of character — this from a writer of unforgettable stories whose least memorable aspect is their characters! (Indeed, I can scarcely recall any Borges characters except Funes the Memorious, that poor fellow cursed with the inability to forget, and even he is not so much a character as an extraordinary, pathological characteristic.) I must conclude that it is precisely the relative unimportance of *character* in Borges's fiction that prompted his reply—though the tone of it was not wistful.

From this entirely satisfying climactic event, the guest of honor and we other invitees withdrew to a testimonial dinner, where—while Anthony Kerrigan read handsomely in Spanish and in English what he called the great writer's "essential page," *"Borges y yo,"* and while Borges (I noted) made his polite little nod of registration at each of its graceful periods—I fiddled with my chicken tetrazzini and wondered what in the mothering *world* one does for the evening show after such a matinee. The problem was compounded by the circumstance that I had been invited not to deliver one more critical appreciation, as the scholars at the conference had done, but to read from my own fiction then in progress—a most unBorgesian long novel called *LETTERS.* Ah well, I thought: the old hombre will go to bed; the others will hit the East Lansing hotspots; I'll pay my dues to a chasteningly empty hall, go back to Baltimore, and never again speak metaphorically of afternoons and evenings.

Alas: The entire company moved en bloc from banquet hall to auditorium—a well-filled auditorium, I was for the only time in my career sorry to see, the same auditorium as that afternoon's—where front-row seats had been reserved for the conference participants, and the center front seat, directly before my lectern, for Borges himself, who was escorted thither to general ovation from the house. What ensued I would happily pass over, except that it culminates in two memorable remarks by Sr. Borges. I spoke, of course, of "afternoons," "evenings," and ironies, and then duly read two letters from the novel *LETTERS:* one by my imaginary English gentlewoman, Lady Amherst, the novel's main character, who resents being cast in the belletristic role of Literature personified; the other a manic bit by a literal maniac who may be a very large insect mimicking an avant-garde writer (somewhat the way *I* felt that evening). I was not so transported by my own words that I failed to notice Borges at one point turn to murmur something into the ear of Professor Kerrigan, beside him. At the post-reading party (which Borges also attended, still going strong in the evening of the evening), I took Kerrigan aside and urged him to give it to me straight. He smiled and reported that what Borges had said was, "In John Barth I hear the voice of Macedonio Fernández."

For us nonspecialists, that remark needs a footnote. Macedonio Fernández, Kerrigan explained to me, a near-contemporary of Borges, had evidently been something of a literary eccentric, an "original," perhaps even something of a trickster, of whom nonetheless Borges had been fond. In Borges's wonderful one-pager called in English "The Witness," there occurs this passage (I came upon it en route home from East Lansing; in the quotation that follows I have rearranged the closing members for present effect):

> There was a day in time when the last eyes to have seen Christ were closed forever. The battle of Junín and the love of Helen died with the death of some one man. What will die with me when I die? What pathetic or frail form will the world lose? Perhaps the image of a horse in the vacant lot at Serrano and Charcas, a bar of sulfur in the drawer of a mahogany desk, the voice of Macedonio Fernández?

We ended that evening quite late around a small table in the host's kitchen: my wife, Borges, y yo. I was tired, and no wonder; Borges seemed tireless. He and I spoke briefly of Machado de Assis and of Gershon Scholem and the Kabbalah (I had been in the habit of calling it Kab-*ba*-lah; Borges gently offered the preferred pronunciation). My wife had been teaching a number of Borges stories to her high-school students; she and he spoke at some length of those texts and of the students' responses to them. At the long evening's end, I remember, she thanked him for having given her — and by extension her students and for that matter all of us — so much. Replied Borges with a twinkle (echoing one of the works they'd been discussing): "I have given you *todo y nada:* everything and nothing."

Our final path-crossing was in Baltimore, another eight years later, by which time Borges was eighty-four and I in my fifties. Although I still venerated him as a writer, my own muse had long since wound up her visit to the neighborhood of the short story and had lit out for the expansive territory of the novels *LETTERS, Sabbatical,* and *The Tidewater Tales,* where she felt more at home. Among my living literary idols, Jorge Luis Borges had been edged out by one more Latino, of whose masterpiece I once heard Borges say, "Maybe *ninety* years of solitude would have been sufficient." Gabriel García Márquez is a writer whose genius is no doubt less refined than Borges's but more wholly human; what's more, he is congenitally a novelist, broadcasting on a wider range of my personal frequencies. Anyhow, I had by 1983 delivered so many encomiums to Borges that they bade to become a subgenre of my own writing; for that reason I had passed up a couple of opportunities to salute him publicly once again on his several lecture tours between 1975 and 1983 (Borges was by then under the admirable care of his young Japanese-Argentinian factotum, María Kodama, and his capacity for being a portable public figure was astonishing in a person his age). I was happy to leave the arrangements for his Johns Hopkins visit in the hands of my chairman, John Irwin, a high-tech critic at work on a study of Borges and Poe. My contribution was simply to ghostwrite an introduction to be delivered by Johns Hopkins's president at Borges's main public presentation—which, by the way, took place not in the afternoon but in the evening; JLB's new companionship really did seem to have replenished his spirit.

In that introduction I spoke—rather, I wrote and President Steven Muller spoke, while Borges nodded acknowledgment—of what it means for a writer to turn into an adjective—Homeric, Rabelaisian, Dickensian, Kafkaesque—and I attempted to itemize some of the field-identification marks of a *Borgesian* situation or phenomenon. E.g. (though I didn't bother President Muller with these particular examples), when I follow my old teacher Pedro Salinas's advice and reread *Don Quixote* every ten years or so, I find it quite Borgesian the way the text keeps changing from decade to decade. Or consider the more elegant example cited in "The Literature of Exhaustion": the actual history of a text called *The Three Impostors:*

> a nonexistent blasphemous treatise against Moses, Christ and Mohammed, which in the seventeenth century was widely held to exist, or to have once existed. Commentators attributed it variously to Boccaccio, Pietro Aretino, Giordano Bruno, and Tommaso Campanella, and though no one . . . had ever seen a copy of it, it was frequently cited, refuted, railed against, and generally discussed as if everyone had read it—until, sure enough, in the *eighteenth* century a spurious work appeared with a forged date of 1598 and the title *De Tribus Impostoribus.*

That's Borgesian, no?

On the evening prior to this public event, Borges y yo had what turned out to be our final hello and good-bye, in the company of colleagues at a dinner hosted by Professor and Mrs. Irwin—a dinner fraught, as I recall, with Borgesian allusions. All these I have alas forgotten, except for rhomboid canapés evocative of the pattern of murders in the story "Death and the Compass" and something quincunxial about the dessert, having to do I believe with Borges's influence on Sir Thomas Browne's "The Garden of Cyrus." The whole excellent dinner, I suppose, might have been regarded as a *hrön:* one of those Borgesian phenomena called into literal material existence by their intensely imagined possibility, like that treatise on the Three Impostors. (This memoir is another. And the *hrön* of *hröns*, of course, is Borges's story "Tlön, Uqbar, Orbis Tertius," in which the phenomenon occurs: the fact of the artifact is a sign of its sense.)

Surrounded by deconstructionists, semioticians, and members of the Spanish Department, Borges y yo did not speak much directly to each other. I'm not sure that we would have had a great deal to say if we had had the chance. I would have liked, I guess, to teach my teacher: to make clear to Borges that I've never thought literature to be exhausted or exhaustible (as, evidently, he thought I thought); only that felt ultimacies in an artistic or cultural generation can become a considerable cultural-historical datum in themselves, turnable against themselves by a virtuoso to generate lively new work. That is what I had had in mind in "The Literature of Exhaustion"; indeed, it is what I had said there—but I let it go. I was more interested in observing how graciously the old monument enjoyed his late monumentality. He was himself as inexhaustible as old Robert Frost had been, with whom I once spent a memorable long evening at Penn State very late in the poet's life. María Kodama kept murmuring, "He's tired, you know; he really should get to bed." But to me it seemed that it was she who was ready to pack it in, and I sympathized; she must have heard all those excellent anecdotes and remarks time after time.

I close with three anecdotes of my own from that final encounter. I managed to ask Borges what might seem a dumbheaded question, but I meant it as one writer to another: What do you think of the language you write in? What is your opinion of Spanish as an instrument of literary composition? Borges replied (and I have learned since that I was not the first to whom he made the remark), "Spanish is my fate." He went on to say that Goethe had felt the same ambivalence about German—indeed, it may be that Borges was paraphrasing some remark of Goethe's to Eckermann—and then he politely added, "All writers feel that way about their working language, no?"

Well, no. But a) his question was put rhetorically, not (as mine had been) from one writer to another; and b) had it *not* been rhetorical, it would have been hypothetical in my case, for the monolingual cannot speak, so to speak, to that point. If it still appears to me, after forty years of fiction-writing and circa 5,000 published pages, that the English language is an inexhaustible instrument the range of whose possibilities I have scarcely reconnoitered, that sentiment *machts nicht,* inasmuch as I know no other instrument.

Some other low-tech dinner guest asked him whether in his elder decades he found it harder or easier to write than earlier in his career. That question interested me, as I was not getting younger book by book. Borges's prompt reply had nothing to do with his loss of eyesight, which of course obliged him to compose and revise in memory (like the Czech-Jewish playwright Hladik before the firing squad in "The Secret Miracle") and dictate to Ms. Kodama. What he said was, "It is much easier than it used to be, because I have learned what I cannot do." I suppose I envy him that, inasmuch as my own, rougher muse has yet fully to learn that energy-saving lesson, and I suspect will never.

The final anecdote I report as a mortified auditor from the rear of the auditorium the following evening. At the time of his Hopkins visit (April 1983), Borges had once again been passed over by the Swedish Academy for the Nobel Prize in Literature. For many of us, this dereliction of theirs with respect to Borges had become an ongoing annual embarrassment. One knows how it is with literary prizes: I once defined a worthwhile literary prize as one that from time to time will be awarded to a writer *despite* the fact that he or she deserves it, and by that rigorous standard the Nobel remains a worthwhile prize. It is true and deplorable that James Joyce, Franz Kafka, D. H. Lawrence, Virginia Woolf, Vladimir Nabokov, and others who would have done honor to the Nobel never received it; on the other hand, aside from the abundant second- and third-raters to whom the prize did honor, we find after all among its winners Thomas Mann, W. B. Yeats, Ernest Hemingway, William Faulkner, T. S. Eliot, Samuel Beckett, Gabriel García Márquez. So: it's an okay accolade. But year after year Borges had been passed over (that particular year it had gone to William Golding). And I am obliged to report that our man really *wanted* the thing. I believe it was as embarrassing to him as to us that he hadn't got it; we were all, let's say, embarrassed for the Swedish Academy, for our literary culture. The subject kept popping into Borges's conversation: Even sixteen years earlier, in Buffalo, when I had arranged for the newly-weds to tour Niagara Falls as newlyweds should, he had thanked me afterward by saying, "I would rather have had this afternoon than the Nobel prize." Et cetera. And now here he was, eighty-four years old, damn it, and passed over sixteen more times since that Buffalo afternoon, and you may be certain that none of us had brought up the subject at dinner with him the night before — but in the public Q & A that last evening in

Baltimore, a student went to one of the aisle microphones and said, "Señor Borges: Once again you have been passed over for the Nobel prize. Would you share with us your feelings about that?" Some of us, at least, were stunned. But Borges, unblushing and unruffled, smiled his twinkliest smile and declared to that space above our heads: "You know, I have been on their short list for so long, I believe they think they already *gave* me the prize years ago."

That is a world-class reply, from a world-class writer and gentleman. Ah, Swedish Academy: Be it on your heads that you passed over Jorge Luis Borges yet three times more after that before his death in Geneva in June 1986.

Well. Borges's great contemporary and fellow Nobel-prize-nonwinner Vladimir Nabokov once said mischievously that when he and Vera first discovered Borges's writings, they felt as if they were standing on a wondrous portico—and then they discovered that there was no house. For most of us—certainly for *yo*—that "portico" is a marvelous freestanding specimen of postmodern literary architecture, rich in what Umberto Eco calls "responsibility to the already-said," consummately civilized, virtuosically crafted, beautiful even in translation. Its author remains among my principal navigation stars, even though he never attempted a novel and I rarely attempt anything else, and despite my understanding that in my whole literary production he would, at best, "hear again the voice of Macedonio Fernández." So be it.

In his own product I admire least certain of the stories that some of my higher-tech academic colleagues seem to admire most: such tales as the afore-mentioned "Death and the Compass," which seem to me to have little or no human interest, only a cerebral ingenuity. Even "Pierre Menard, Author of the *Quixote*" I put in that category, inspired as is its conceit and graceful its rendition. I quite love his short essay-meditations (such as *"Borges y yo"*), as rereadable as good poetry, but I am not floored by the poetry proper, no doubt because my Spanish is inadequate to the originals. Such stories as "Funes the Memorious," however, and "Tlön, Uqbar, Orbis Tertius" are unforgettable (even though "Funes" has in my opinion a serious architectural flaw that I intend to discuss with the author if there turns out to be a heaven for postmodernists, or at least a postmortem Q & A). And his very best stories—such *Meisterstücken* as "The Secret Miracle," "The Zahir" (which I read as an exquisitely oblique love story), "Averroes's Search," and "The Aleph" (another love story)—are in my judgment perfect works of literature, perfect fusions of Borgesian algebra and fire. They can be reread a hundred times with delight. They rise from the printed page directly into the empyrean of transcendent art, and make me grateful that while their author's body was (in Borges's phrase) "living out its life," and mine mine, the separate patterns of our footsteps intersected at three points. Borges speculates (in a footnote to "The Mirror of Enigmas") that all the literal footsteps a person takes in his or her lifetime may trace out a figure as readily apprehensible to the mind of god as is a circle or a triangle to our human minds. To *my* human mind, these three pathcrossings of *Borges y yo* are triangulations, privileged celestial position-fixes, even though I have learned better than to confuse my navigation stars with my destination.

JORGE LUIS BORGES

TRANSLATED FROM THE SPANISH BY ALASTAIR REID

Borges and I

It is to my other self, to Borges, that things happen. I walk about Buenos Aires and I pause, almost mechanically, to contemplate the arch of an entry or the portal of a church: news of Borges comes to me in the mail, and I see his name on a short list of professors or in a biographical dictionary. I am fond of hourglasses, maps, eighteenth-century typography, the etymology of words, the tang of coffee, and the prose of Stevenson: the other one shares these enthusiasms, but in a rather vain, theatrical way. It would be an exaggeration to call our relationship hostile. I live, I agree to go on living, so that Borges may fashion his literature; that literature justifies me. I do not mind admitting that he has managed to write a few worthwhile pages, but these pages cannot save me, perhaps because good writing belongs to nobody, not even to my other, but rather to language itself, to the tradition. Beyond that, I am doomed to oblivion, utterly doomed, and no more than certain flashes of my existence can survive in the work of my other. Little by little I am surrendering everything to him, although I am well aware of his perverse habit of falsifying and exaggerating. Spinoza understood that everything wishes to continue in its own being: a stone wishes to be a stone, eternally, a tiger a tiger. I must go on in Borges, not in myself (if I am anyone at all). But I recognize myself much less in the books he writes than in many others or in the clumsy plucking of a guitar. Years ago I tried to cut free from him and I went from myths of suburban life to games with time and infinity; but those games belong to Borges now and I will have to come up with something else. And so my life leaks away and I lose everything, and everything passes into oblivion, or to my other.

I cannot tell which one of us is writing this page.

CONTRIBUTORS

JOHN BARTH is the author of eight novels, two collections of shorter fiction, and a collection of essays. His latest novel is *The Last Voyage of Somebody the Sailor* (Little, Brown). He is Professor Emeritus in the Writing Seminars at Johns Hopkins University.

AMY BLOOM's stories appeared in *Best American Short Stories 1991* and *1992*. Her book of stories, *Come To Me,* will be published by HarperCollins in May 1993. She is currently working on a novel.

T. CORAGHESSAN BOYLE lives in Los Angeles and is the author of three volumes of short stories and several novels. His most recent novel is *East is East* (Viking Penguin).

ROBERT COHEN is the author of a novel, *The Organ Builder.* His stories have appeared in *Harper's, GQ, Paris Review,* and many other magazines. He teaches at Harvard University.

EVAN S. CONNELL is the author of fifteen books, including *Mr. Bridge, Mrs. Bridge, Son of the Morning Star,* and most recently, *The Alchymist's Journal* (Penguin).

STUART DYBEK is the author of two books of short stories, *Childhood and Other Neighborhoods* (Ecco) and *The Coast of Chicago* (Knopf), as well as a volume of poetry. His work has appeared in several O. Henry Prize story collections.

GUSTAW HERLING was a founding member of Instytut Literacki, the celebrated Polish émigré publishing house. His works include *A World Apart* and *Diary Written by Night.*

STEVEN MILLHAUSER'S most recent book is *The Barnum Museum* (Poseidon), a collection of stories. He lives in Saratoga Springs, New York, where he teaches at Skidmore College.

R. K. NARAYAN'S work includes numerous short story collections, several works of nonfiction, and more than a dozen novels. He lives in Madras, India.

JOSIP NOVAKOVICH was born in Daruvar, Croatia. His stories have appeared in *New Directions, Boulevard, Threepenny Review,* and *Columbia: A Magazine of Poetry and Prose.* He teaches at Moorhead State University.

JOYCE CAROL OATES lives in Princeton, New Jersey, where she is on the faculty of Princeton University. Her recent books include the novel *Black Water* (NAL/ Dutton) and a collection of short stories, *Where Is Here?* (Ecco).

JULIO ORTEGA was born in Peru in 1942. He is the author of *Poetics of Change: The New Spanish-American Narrative* (University of Texas Press) and several other works of criticism and fiction. He is a professor of Latin American literature at Brown University.

ALASTAIR REID writes for *The New Yorker* and has published over twenty books, including translations, poetry, prose, and children's books.

MARK SCHAFER is a translator of Cuban and Mexican modern fiction. He lives in the Boston area.

RONALD STROM lives in Rome.

MELANIE RAE THON is the author of *Meteors in August,* a novel, and *Girls in the Grass,* a collection of stories. In 1992 she received a grant from the NEA. Her new novel, *Iona Moon,* will be published later this year by Poseidon.

JUDY TROY lives in Alabama and teaches at Auburn University. Her book of stories, *Mourning Doves,* was just published by Scribners.

KURT WILDERMUTH is a student in the MFA program in creative writing at the University of Massachusetts at Amherst. He is currently working on a collection of short stories.

XIAODA XIAO was born in 1950 in Shanghai and served five years in a prison camp for tearing a poster of Mao Tse-tung. He now teaches at the University of Massachusetts at Amherst, where he lives with his wife and son.

"HIS WORK IS ART, AT HIS BEST, BOWLES HAS NO PEER." — TIME

"Let's hope this Bowles

reader will further the cause

of Bowles' widespread

appreciation, for no one

who imagines himself or

herself to be well read

should be unaware

of his vivid work."

— Booklist

$29.95   ISBN 0-88001-295-1   720 pages

Available at your local bookstore

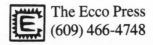 The Ecco Press
(609) 466-4748

AN ANNUAL SMALL PRESS READER

THE 1992/1993 PUSHCART PRIZE XVII

BEST OF THE SMALL PRESSES

"The single best measure of the state of affairs in American literature today."

New York Times Book Review

EDITED BY
BILL HENDERSON
WITH THE
PUSHCART PRIZE
EDITORS

"This annual anthology of the best stories, essays, and poetry published by small presses continues to illustrate that high literary standards can survive despite the power wielded by profit-hungry publishing behemoths."

Publishers Weekly

JUST PUBLISHED
570 PAGES
$29.50 cloth

"This book is essential." *Library Journal*

"A national literary treasure." *Kirkus Reviews*

PUSHCART PRESS
P.O. BOX 380
WAINSCOTT, N.Y. 11975

"Those who despair of finding good writing in mass media America need look no further than the Pushcart Prize."

Booklist

COMING UP DOWN HOME

A Memoir of a Southern Childhood

by

CECIL BROWN

"*Coming Up Down Home* has echoes of Wright, Twain, and Richard
Pryor; but it's Cecil Brown's unique voice that you hear rising
out of his juicy, searching, questioning coming of age memoir.
It's an anguishing and entertaining portrait of the artist
as sharecropper's son." — Philip Kaufman

"With his latest work, *Coming Up Down Home,* Cecil Brown has
firmly established himself as my favorite American author. This book
is definitely a milestone in the body of Afro-American literature."
— Claude Brown, author of *Manchild in the Promised Land*

From the author of
The Lives and Loves of Mr. Jiveass Nigger

$22.95   ISBN 0-88001-293-5   256 pages

The Ecco Press

Where

you can

still

hear

people

thinking

for

them-

selves

Personal Voices on Cultural Issues

Stanley Cavell   "Macbeth Appalled"

Nancy Huston   "Erotic Literature in Postwar France"

Leo Bersani, Ulysse Dutoit   "Beckett's Sociability"

Linda Dowling   "Esthetes and Effeminati"

Edward W. Said on Schlesinger and Fukuyama

Harriet Zwerling   "Alfred Chester, a Memoir"

Claude Rawson on Political Correctness

Arts • Literature • Philosophy • Politics

RARITAN
Edited by Richard Poirier

$16/one year $26/two years
Make check payable to RARITAN, 31 Mine St., New Brunswick NJ 08903
Sorry, we cannot bill.

DANTE'S INFERNO

TRANSLATIONS BY
TWENTY CONTEMPORARY POETS

EDITED BY DANIEL HALPERN
INTRODUCED BY JAMES MERRILL
WITH AN AFTERWORD BY GIUSEPPE MAZZOTTA

——————————— TRANSLATIONS BY ———————————

AMY CLAMPITT	CYNTHIA MACDONALD
ALFRED CORN	W. S. MERWIN
DEBORAH DIGGES	SUSAN MITCHELL
CAROLYN FORCHÉ	SHARON OLDS
JORIE GRAHAM	ROBERT PINSKY
DANIEL HALPERN	STANLEY PLUMLY
ROBERT HASS	MARK STRAND
SEAMUS HEANEY	RICHARD WILBUR
RICHARD HOWARD	C. K. WILLIAMS
GALWAY KINNELL	CHARLES WRIGHT

——————————— AT BOOKSTORES NOW ———————————

 The Ecco Press

$24.95   ISBN 0-88001-291-9   216 pages

SAN FRANCISCO
REVIEW *of* BOOKS

*"Of all the needs a book has,
the chief need is that it be readable."*
— Anthony Trollope

Subscribe to the *San Francisco Review of Books*,
the chief read on readable books.

Name:_____

Address:_____

_____

State:_____ Zip:_____

Visa/Mastercard No:

_____

Exp. date:_____

OR

❑ Payment enclosed

for:

❑ 4 issues for $9.95

❑ 8 issues for $19.95

Mail to:
555 De Haro Street
Suite 220
San Francisco, CA 94107
Tel 415-252-7708
Fax 415-252-8908

■ **A BRILLIANT DEBUT NOVEL** ■

STEPHEN AMIDON

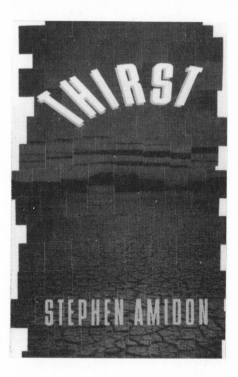

"*Thirst* is a brilliant novel, and true to its title, it leaves
you crying more." —Times Literary Supplement

"Dreams of drowning, cactus rustling, Guns N' Roses, dusty lust
—they're all here, the unlikely mixture served up by a master
chef and finger-lickin' good to the last surprising bite."
—Time Out

■ THE ECCO PRESS ■
AVAILABLE AT YOUR LOCAL BOOKSTORE

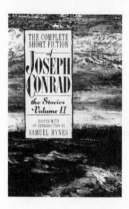

THE COMPLETE SHORT FICTION

of

JOSEPH CONRAD

Volumes 1 & 2 • *The Stories*

Volumes 3 & 4 • *The Tales*

EDITED WITH AN INTRODUCTION BY
SAMUEL HYNES

A definitive collection of Conrad's short fiction that highlights a genre too often overlooked among the author's considerable body of work. These stories, with their clear, powerful narratives and thrilling adventures, confirm Conrad not only as one of our most important writers, but also one of our most engaging.

Vol. 1 $24.95 cloth 320 pages ISBN: 0-88001-307-9
Vol. 2 $24.95 cloth 320 pages ISBN: 0-88001-308-7

Vol. 3 $24.95 cloth 320 pages ISBN: 0-88001-287-0
Vol. 4 $24.95 cloth 320 pages ISBN: 0-88001-288-9

 The Ecco Press
(609) 466-4748

Antæus   *"The most distinguished literary magazine in the English language."* — *Tennessee Williams*

4 issues (2 years) $36.00 includes postage in U.S.
                outside U.S. add $1.50 per issue for surface
                add $4.50 per issue for air

☐ New   ☐ Renewal
  if new, begin with
☐ current
☐ upcoming issue

☐ Check enclosed
☐ Money Order
☐ Please charge my American Express
☐ Please charge my MasterCard/VISA

Card No. _____ Expires _____

Signature (as on card) _____

Ship to: Please send an Ecco Press Catalog to:

Name_____   Name_____

Address _____   Address _____

City _____ State_____ Zip_____   City _____ State_____ Zip_____

Detach this form and mail to: The Ecco Press, 100 W. Broad Street, Hopewell, NJ 08525

SPECIAL OFFER TO ANTÆUS SUBSCRIBERS: 10% OFF ALL ECCO PRESS BOOKS